This Time Love

By

Elizabeth Castle

Name: Castle, Elizabeth, author

Title: This Time Love

Description: Series: Bennett Family Series

Publisher: In The Air Publishing

Identifiers: ISBN 9781967731282 (ebook) | ISBN 9781967731299 (paperback) | ISBN 9798304729734 (amazon hardcover)

Cover Design by thebookcoverdesigner.com. Designer: betibup33

Chapter One

The bedroom was done in soothing sage greens with accents of bright orchid pink. When the sun came up in the morning, light filtered through the gauzy cream-colored curtains, easing her into wakefulness. The sanctuary feel of the room had been purposefully created with the help of her family. It was supposed to be relaxing and calming. The fresh flowers decorating the low table and dresser were supposed to appeal to her senses.

Nothing in the room could calm her today.

Evelyn Bennett refused to humiliate herself again. Her grandfather had called it "her cussed stubbornness," but Evelyn called it something else. Self-preservation. Evelyn stood in nothing but her plain, functional white underwear while she struggled into her back brace. The thing was harder to fasten than a bridle and harness. She prayed that for today it would be enough. By the end of the day, her back would hurt. Her hip would hurt. Her knees would hurt. She only hoped that her pride remained intact. When it was all one had, one defended it fiercely.

"Evie, hurry up. We're going to be late." Anne Bennett hollered up the stairs. Evelyn would have laughed at the unladylike display, but she was too upset. She was also too tired to remember to correct Anne for calling her Evie. It had been a childhood nickname, and she'd never broken her grandfather of it. The woman he'd married seven years earlier had picked it up as a result. Since the rest of the family used it as well, Anne wasn't letting it go without a fight.

"I'm coming. I can't imagine what your rush is." Neither of them wanted to go to the lawyer's office today. Of course, neither of them had wanted to go to the hospital the month before when Howard Bennett slipped quietly into death, either.

Tears stung Evelyn's eyes, and she pushed them ruthlessly away. She refused to cry, and crying publicly would be the ultimate humiliation. Her grandfather hadn't been the type of man who was comfortable with tears. If he thought his granddaughter and his wife were weeping uncontrollably over his death, it would have made him cringe.

"What are you doing?" Anne watched in disbelief as Evelyn fought with the brace. "You hardly ever wear that thing anymore, though heaven knows we keep trying to get you to. Take it off, get your dress on, grab your cane, and let's go."

"I am not bringing the cane." Evelyn's tone was final, but it never got through to Anne. She took her role as a grandmother quite seriously. Never mind that she wasn't old enough to be her grandmother. Anne was old enough to be her mother, perhaps, but not her grandmother. Evelyn was twenty-five, and Anne was forty-four.

"I am not using the cane," she reiterated as she saw Anne's temper start to build. Evelyn managed to completely fasten the stupid contraption and went for her dress. She looked bigger than she was in the baggy dress, but it hid the brace and was comfortable. All of Evelyn's clothes were comfortable and easy to put on, and in soothing colors much like her bedroom. The clothes had functional lines and were easily managed.

She turned her head side to side, then grabbed a couple of hairpins. She pulled her hair back into a strict bun. Wouldn't the wavy reddish-brown hair that now hung to the middle of her back surprise Sebastian? He'd called her short hair boyish and unfeminine. It was probably the most flattering thing he'd said to her that day, no matter that it was an insult. He'd insulted her in much more hurtful ways than calling her unfeminine.

"Everyone knows you use a cane, Evie." She gave the younger woman an exasperated look when it became apparent that Evelyn wasn't going to listen. "Your cousin David and your cousin Leslie have never made fun of it. They care about you too much to feel anything but sympathy for what you've been through. I've seen it, your sister has seen it, and her husband has seen it when he's at work with you and when you visit. Even the lawyer has seen it. Stop being so sensitive. You had an accident, and you need it."

Evelyn felt the unreasonable panic rise. It always did when she thought about the crippling "accident." She couldn't tell her family she was sure it wasn't an accident. They'd think she was crazy. She thought she was crazy. She had no real memory of what happened. She had been horseback riding alone. Though the trail was a public one, she had been fairly isolated that day. In her more rational moments, she knew it had to have been an accident. Her dreams were her only proof, and she kept them to herself. The ominous dreams threatened her peace of mind, and she refused to discuss them. It would just be another excuse her family would use to try to get her back into therapy.

She took a deep breath and practiced the techniques the therapist had taught her to help her stop the panic attacks. Her heart rate slowed, and the blind panic faded. She knew Anne was watching her and feeling helpless. It was a response she was used to. She hated the sympathy almost as much as she hated the constant supervision.

Evelyn got a better grip on her emotions and concentrated on finishing getting ready. She dabbed a bit of powder on her face and wondered if she should add a bit more makeup. She hadn't seen Sebastian in five years, not since he'd witnessed her most public humiliation. Today Sebastian was the person she didn't want to face. He hadn't seen the cane, and she didn't want him to. She needed to project all the strength she could, although she was sure he knew about the accident. Funny how pride worked. But he'd been there to see almost every humiliating moment of her life, and she'd had enough of looking like a fool.

Sebastian had been there during her awkward teenage years when she'd been having a hard time dealing with her thin, bony body and lack of development. He'd been there when her mother had embarrassed the entire family before running her car off a cliff road because she'd been high and drunk. He'd been her boss and had watched as she'd struggled to do her job while she failed time and again. He'd been there when she'd made a fool of herself by accusing her sister's soon-to-be husband, Sebastian's nephew John, of cheating with her cousin Leslie. Leslie had been dating Sebastian at the time, and he hadn't appreciated the accusation one bit. And he'd been there when she'd been left standing at the altar, her wedding gown swamping her thin body, her limbs visibly trembling. He'd capped it when he quit his job with her grandfather's company earlier that same day, saying he wouldn't take orders from her. Her grandfather was putting her in charge of the company, and Sebastian predicted that she and her cousin David would ruin the business in less than five years. The final humiliation was that he'd been right. He'd find that out today.

Evelyn did a final check in the mirror. Anne had been seeing to it that Evelyn ate right. Her body had filled in a bit, and she looked pretty good, if you covered up the scars. Her breasts had finally made a late appearance. They might only fill out a B cup, but on her thin, short frame, they looked much bigger. Her hair had lost a lot of the brassy red color and was a more attractive shade of brown with red highlights. Her eyes were still an odd gray color, but with the right makeup and contacts instead of her old glasses, they stood out nicely on her rather plain face. With her small nose, square chin, and high forehead, she wasn't a great beauty, and she knew it. She tried to make up for it with a strong attitude and willpower.

"I'm ready." It was a big fat lie, but Evelyn grabbed her purse anyway. The drive was going to be long, and already she could feel her muscles tensing. The doctor had warned her time and again to lessen her stress levels. If her body relaxed, her muscles wouldn't tighten, and her back and leg wouldn't hurt so much. It was easier said than done.

The minivan Anne had bought five years ago allowed her to stretch out, and she had been so grateful for the legroom that she hadn't reprimanded Anne for buying something that had been solely for her benefit. Evelyn could drive herself now, but in the early days after her accident, driving had hurt more than it was worth. Five years ago, Evelyn had an impractical but cute sports car. With her busted left hip, she just couldn't get herself in and out of the low-slung car. She'd sold it, along with her most prized possession, four years earlier.

Anne helped Evelyn into the van. She drove slower than usual when Evelyn was in the van and tried not to make any sharp turns. Evelyn had assured her time and again that she was much better, but ever since she'd refused to have the last surgery, Anne had been overbearingly protective. At least she was overprotective when she wasn't nagging.

"I'm looking forward to seeing Sebastian. It's been a long time. He called after the funeral. He was sorry he missed it." Anne took another corner and watched Evelyn from the corner of her eye. She didn't know if Sebastian was the sole reason for Evelyn's sudden nerves, but Anne was certain he was at least a small part of the tension that was clear in Evelyn today.

"I wasn't aware that he called." Evelyn wasn't surprised he had, but she hadn't known. He'd kept in touch with Howard and Anne Bennett, but he'd been in Europe the last five years, supposedly learning about the overseas markets.

He couldn't have made it any plainer how much he wanted to get away from her.

Evelyn glanced over at Anne. Sebastian had introduced Anne to Howard eight years before, and they'd married a year later. Anne and Sebastian had been friends for a long time. Evelyn knew Anne had been best friends with Sebastian's older sister, and the friendship had been passed along. Anne was closer to Sebastian's age than she was to Howard. Sebastian was thirty-eight this year. His birthday had been last month, Evelyn knew. She knew just about everything about the man. It was funny how you could dislike someone so much and still be fascinated by them.

"He did. I called him, but he was on a business trip and couldn't fly out for the funeral. When he got back, he offered to come so I wouldn't be alone, but I told him I had you. When he received word from the lawyer that he was mentioned in the will, he called again to say he'd be here."

Evelyn imagined what he had to say about her being the one to console Anne, but she refrained from making any comment. Anne knew that the two of them didn't get along. There was no point in dragging up an old feud.

"Has he visited with John, do you know?" John was not only Evelyn's executive assistant; he was also her sister Kimberly's husband and Sebastian's nephew. John had started with the company shortly before Sebastian had quit. Evelyn had given John a promotion to be her assistant right before her accident, right after Sebastian had left. John thought she did it so she could keep an eye on him. He married her younger sister almost four years ago, just after Evelyn had recovered from the majority of her injuries and had gone back to work. John had been acting as an executive assistant to her grandfather, who had taken back the reins while she recovered from her accident.

On her first day back at work, John told her he was marrying Kimberly; it was just too bad if she didn't like it, and that she could fire him if she liked. Evelyn had shrugged, ignoring the hurt she'd felt at the verbal attack. But she knew she'd earned it when she'd accused him of having an affair with Leslie. The real question was why he had decided to stay on with her? She knew he was happy with his position in the company and with the large paychecks he received, but that explanation didn't completely satisfy her.

"Sebastian has been out to visit his parents and sister, but I don't think he's seen John. I know they chat from time to time. And of course, Sebastian has been back to see his kids a few times."

Evelyn dropped the subject of Sebastian and closed her eyes for a while. The drive took an hour, and by the time they got there, Evelyn was ready to get out of the van. When she had to sit for long periods, she always took a break and stretched. She managed to get out of the van with the brace on by herself. She could maneuver much more easily with the cane, but she gritted her teeth and headed for the office. Anne trailed slightly behind her, ready to give her a hand should she need it. Evelyn had been trying to exercise her independence, but it was hard when people were always doing things for her without asking if she needed them to.

"Do you need to stop at the bathroom?" Anne held the

door open for Evelyn and made it a point to look like it wasn't a calculated move. Anne hated it when Evelyn refused to take her cane. It was a rare occurrence, but this wasn't the first time. Anne had a spare in the back of the van, and she would drag it out if it looked like Evelyn needed it, no matter what Evelyn had to say about it. She understood Evelyn's pride. She also understood her embarrassment. Evelyn had a habit of not letting things go. Her embarrassment over what had happened five years ago was still as prominent today as it had been then. Evelyn put on a good act, but it was only that, an act.

Evelyn shook her head in response to Anne's question. She didn't want to fight with the brace. The sooner they got over with whatever the lawyer had to say, the better. Evelyn knew the company was to be divided equally between Howard's four grandchildren. Evelyn and Kimberly were on one side; David and Leslie were on the other. Neither Kimberly nor Leslie cared about the chemical company that Howard owned, and each would vote with their respective sibling. The votes always ran two to two. Howard had been the deciding factor in the decision-making at Brown Chemical Labs. David had one idea of how things should run. Evelyn had another. Howard chose between the two. In the last few years, the decisions had swung equally between the two of them. Without Howard, Evelyn knew the company didn't have a chance. She and David would never agree on how to run the company. Howard liked to say that the competition made both of them work harder. Now it would destroy the company Howard had bought out years ago and rebuilt.

Evelyn carefully measured her steps and kept her body rigidly straight. Anne's lips pursed, but she didn't say anything. As the secretary led them into the conference room that was being used for the will reading, Evelyn wasn't worried about upsetting Anne. She was concentrating on the upcoming confrontation. Howard's long-standing attorney, Bruce Bickerstaff, gestured for them to enter the room.

"Come in and have a seat." He took Evelyn's arm and seated her.

Evelyn gave him a slight smile in thanks while internally gritting her teeth. "Thank you, Mr. Bickerstaff."

"No problem." He held a chair for Anne.

Evelyn knew Sebastian was in the room. She refused to look his way, although she could feel he was watching her. He was sitting next to David, who had Leslie, John, and Kimberly between him and her. Evelyn turned her attention to Kimberly. Kimberly was bottle-feeding six-month-old Patrick. John was on the other side talking quietly to Leslie. John was the peacekeeper in the family.

"How is he doing?" Evelyn turned carefully in her seat. Kimberly was frowning at her, and she knew the reason why. Kimberly nagged her just as much as Anne. They thought that between the two of them, they could bully her into having another surgery to fix her back and hip. Evelyn wanted nothing to do with another surgery.

"He's fine. I see you're feeling spry today. Where's your cane, Evie?"

Evelyn was going to correct her sister but dropped it. Every member of the family called her Evie, even though it annoyed her. Because she was annoyed, she forgot to watch her temper. "I threw it in the trash."

"You didn't!" Kimberly ignored all the turned heads their way.

"Of course, I didn't," she whispered. "Would you please be quiet? You're embarrassing yourself." Evelyn prayed that they weren't overheard.

"I'm not in the least embarrassed. You should be, though. Your behavior lately has been getting out of hand. Perhaps your therapist would have something to say about your outrageous behavior."

Evelyn wanted to tell her that she hadn't been to her therapist lately just to see how she'd react, but John interrupted. He turned and patted Kimberly's shoulder. "Your sister is a big girl. She knows what she's doing. Don't you, Evelyn?"

When Evelyn shifted her eyes, they clashed with Sebastian's instead of John's. That cool reserve was still there, she noted. His piercing green eyes were glued to hers. His hair was still that almost black shade. The light spattering of silver in his hair had barely grown in the last five years. He was still tall and lean. His body was still wrapped in the trappings of sophistication, and they still only barely masked his true personality. He could be cruel when he felt like it. He could be openly passionate when he cared about something. She knew few dared cross him. He'd grown up in rough neighborhoods, and that fact was a permanent part of him. He might look like a businessman, but his rough background was always only partially hidden.

He swamped her five foot four by seven inches. He

wasn't the tallest man in the room, but he was the hardest, both in looks and personality. To her, he was a massive presence. It had always been that way. The thirteen years he had on her didn't help alter the impression of power. His age only increased it.

"Hello, Evelyn." Sebastian watched as she shrank into herself.

"Sebastian." Evelyn pulled her eyes from his. That dark, deep, gritty voice made her quiver. It had been too long since she'd seen him last. It had taken years to get used to her reactions to his powerful presence.

"If we're all ready, I'll begin." Bruce interrupted. Evelyn knew he was feeling the increased tension in the room.

Anne took over. As the oldest in the room and Howard's widow, she held the authority. "Please begin." She didn't bother to glance around to see how they all took the decree. Howard had been the driving force behind the family. As his wife, she had wielded the same power.

For the first few minutes, it was Howard's personal effects that were divided up. Anne would keep the house. Everyone expected it. Howard had openly adored his much younger bride. Anne, in turn, loved Howard. The years that separated them had meant nothing. Howard's money meant nothing to Anne. No one doubted either one of their motives for the hasty marriage.

By the time the business was brought up, everyone was satisfied. Nothing in the will had been a surprise. All the various members of the family, except for Evelyn, had their own homes, and they all had their own money. The business was what everyone had come to hear about. So far,

Sebastian hadn't been mentioned, and it made Evelyn nervous.

If Howard hadn't left any of his personal effects to Sebastian, then that meant he'd left something of his business. Evelyn felt ill as trepidation gripped her. She didn't want to hear what came next but knew she had to sit through it.

The room was silent as they all waited for what came next.

Chapter Two

"As you all know, Howard had planned to divide his company into four parts. He wanted each of his grandchildren to inherit an equal piece of the company. Over the last few years, he left the day-to-day running of the company to Evelyn and the daily decisions between her and David. But Howard approved all major decisions. He knew that if he left the complete running of the company to either Evelyn or David, the company didn't stand a chance." Bruce broke off, turning back to the will.

"So who did he leave the company to?" It was David. He was tired of sitting around wasting time. The will hadn't said anything he didn't already know. But like Evelyn, he feared what was coming. With Sebastian's presence, things were taking an unexpected turn.

"The company has been divided into five equal shares." Bruce looked pointedly at Sebastian. "Howard left you a fifth of the company, Mr. O'Connor. He knew that out of all of his acquaintances, friends, and business associates, you were the only one who could take on the task."

The room was completely silent. Sebastian simply folded his hands in his lap. When he finally spoke, it was like a gun going off. "And if I refuse?"

Bruce Bickerstaff handed him a folded sheet of paper. "Howard wanted you to read this before you make your decision."

The paper slowly unfolded in Sebastian's large hands. He read the single sheet slowly. A flicker of amusement lit his somber face, but only for a moment. "I accept."

Bruce nodded. Everyone was glancing curiously between Bruce and Sebastian. Evelyn, however, kept her gaze in her lap. Howard had done it. He'd threatened her he would. They'd had a conversation, more of an argument really, shortly before he died. Howard had told her if she didn't have the last surgery, he wouldn't leave the company in her hands. She hadn't thought he'd meant it. Between David, Leslie, and Sebastian, she would lose her position as president. Sebastian would take her place. She and Kimberly would be outvoted, and she would be out of a job. She didn't know if she could handle taking orders from Sebastian again. It had been hard enough at twenty when she'd graduated from her two-year business program. It seemed almost impossible now.

"Hold on just a minute. Grandfather shouldn't have left the company to the five of us. Sebastian isn't even family. He should have just left a fifth to John." David knew Sebastian would most likely side with him over Evelyn, but like her, he didn't want Sebastian owning a piece. Sebastian wouldn't be easily manipulated. In fact, the task would be impossible. John was much more malleable, even if he was Evelyn's personal assistant.

"I refused." It was John who spoke up. "Howard offered me a piece, but I knew better than to get between you and

Evelyn. That job needed to go to someone stronger than me. Besides, I'm happy with my job. I get to work during the week and spend my free time with Kimberly and now Patrick. I don't relish the idea of spending the next few years trying to salvage the company."

"Salvage it?" It was Sebastian's angry, temper-filled voice that interrupted.

Evelyn sat forward. "You were right when you left. David and I almost managed to destroy the company."

"Figures," Sebastian said, disgusted with both of them, but mostly Evelyn. "I knew you couldn't set aside your squabbles to do what was right. You argued with me at every turn, and you weren't in charge then. David and Howard could have run the company without your interference."

Evelyn rose, her unimposing height rigid. She knew he hated her queen-to-peasant tone the most. "If you hadn't turned tail and run off like a coward, the transition within the company wouldn't have caused so much upset. Several deals fell through when you walked out."

Sebastian rose and faced her. "If you were a man, Evelyn, I would—"

Evelyn immediately interrupted the expected tirade. "You wouldn't have taken off in the first place. You would have stuck around. But you couldn't face the fact that you'd have to take orders from a woman."

"More like a little girl. And from what I can see, you haven't grown up much. And I'd refrain from calling me a coward if I were you." Sebastian had tolerated a lot from Evelyn over the years, but she still managed to make him lose his temper on occasion.

In this case, it might just have been a slightly twisted form of cowardice that made him quit, and he hated that she knew it. The thought of having to take orders from that smarmy-mouthed little brat had been more than Sebastian could take. He valued his friendship with Howard too much to allow Evelyn to ruin it. He had come close more than once to shaking her. Instead, he quit. Right after he told her he quit, he told her she was an unfeminine, spoiled brat who would one day make some man's life miserable.

It had been a petty shot, and he knew it, though the description had been accurate. With her thin body and her hair cut into a short cap that looked masculine, he hadn't been able to help himself. She'd looked like a little boy in her stupid black and gray suits. He knew she played down her femininity as a foil to her overtly feminine mother. What had truly bothered him was that he'd found her attractive in an odd way, despite her efforts. He also admired the fact that she wasn't afraid of him, and she didn't cower. She always gave back as good as she got.

She hadn't looked or acted like the women he knew, and that was another thing about her that had attracted him. She'd been twenty, and he had been thirty-three and recently divorced. He'd felt like a dirty old man, and he hadn't liked it. Besides, he couldn't stand her. It was a nasty trick life liked to play on a man. He hated being attracted to a woman he despised but couldn't help himself.

For the first time, he took a good look at her. He'd been studying her face when she'd arrived. She'd filled out a bit, and it suited her. She wasn't thin and bony anymore. She had walked into the room with a feminine grace that had surprised him. She was still too short, not that he'd expected her to grow taller, but her body was curved where it was supposed to. Her face had more color, and he could tell despite the severe hairstyle that her chestnut hair was longer than it had been. What surprised him the most was the loose-fitting knee-length dress. He'd never seen her in a dress. She'd worn slacks all the time. Her legs were in stockings, but they were shapely. Her hips had a swing to them that hadn't been there before. The dress didn't mold her body, but it hinted at the curves beneath.

But her personality hadn't changed. Perversely, it pleased him. Arguing with her had been invigorating in a way he hadn't known with any other woman. Other women seemed tame in comparison. Telling himself he didn't like her and that she wasn't his type, not to mention way too young, didn't stop him from enjoying their fights.

Evelyn saw his perusal and stood under his gaze. She knew what he saw. She didn't lie to herself. But there was still that glimmer of what she thought might be masculine interest in his eyes, and it always made her heart beat faster. She pulled herself back to what he'd said and gripped the back of the chair for support. "Don't bother threatening me."

Anne knew that the two would argue anytime, anywhere. "Please sit down, Evie."

It was the worried strain in Anne's tone that had her obeying. Anne had been through a lot over the last five years. She'd accepted her husband's semi-retirement happily. Then she'd had to help take care of her step-granddaughter, taking on the burden of having a disabled person living in the house while her husband went back to work. Shortly after that, Howard had had a stroke. It hadn't been so bad, but he'd had to slow down. Then his body had started to deteriorate. The cancer that had been discovered after the stroke had begun eating at him, and it had been that which ultimately took him from them. The last two years had been hard on Anne. She'd stayed beside her husband, taking care of him. Evelyn had tried to help, but some things she simply couldn't do.

"I'm sorry for the outburst." She addressed the group and then faced Sebastian. She'd been wrong, and she knew it, but some habits apparently did die hard. "I apologize. I had no call to insult you."

Evelyn offered no explanation for her behavior. Sebastian just stared for a moment. Evelyn was always defending her decisions. She could be fierce when provoked. This sudden capitulation was unlike her. But he only nodded at her, accepting the unexpected and unwelcome apology.

Bruce cleared his throat. "That is all that's in the will. Howard knew all of you would be a little upset, but he knew this was the best decision under the circumstances. What the five of you choose to do with the company is now up to you."

The group broke up, and low voices permeated the room.

"I can't believe Grandfather did that." Kimberly handed Patrick to John and helped Evelyn back to her feet. She was beginning to struggle in the chair. Kimberly figured Evelyn hadn't wanted Sebastian to see the cane. Her sister's pride had become an awesome force over the last four years. Once her awful depression had passed after the accident, Evelyn had become a different person than she'd been before. Seeing her argue with Sebastian was the closest thing to the old Evelyn she'd seen in a long time. Perhaps Sebastian would be the one to get through to her. So far, she and Anne had failed.

Evelyn accepted the help. "I can. I should have known this was coming. Grandfather was always unpredictable."

Evelyn and Kimberly watched as Sebastian and Anne embraced and began talking. Kimberly watched the pair closely. "I often wondered why they hadn't gotten together."

Evelyn had wondered the same thing, and she'd asked. "Anne says they're too much like brother and sister. Plus, she says Sebastian had never been interested in her years before. Sebastian married at twenty-three."

"Yes. And divorced with two children eleven years later. I know Sebastian's past. He brought his children to Anne and Grandfather's wedding." Kimberly just shook her head. "I just can't help wondering. They're so close."

Evelyn remembered the odd feeling of resentment she'd felt when he'd attended her grandfather's wedding. But she'd only been eighteen, and Sebastian had still been married, although his wife hadn't attended the wedding. The divorce had taken place shortly after. She'd been an emotionally confused eighteen-year-old then. It wasn't a surprise she fell for Andrew a year and a half later without any effort on Andrew's part and had planned to marry him.

His jilting her had been the best thing that had ever happened to her, though she hadn't thought so until she found out what he'd done to her.

Evelyn forced her mind to focus on the present. She had to make a dignified exit before she collapsed. And she needed to start working out again. Her physical therapist had warned her time and again to keep up with her exercises. Her muscles relied on the cane too much. It looked like she'd have plenty of time to get in her workouts now that Sebastian would be in charge.

Surprisingly, it was David who helped her out to the van. Despite their dislike of each other when it came to matters of business, they were family. "Surprised by what Grandfather did?"

Evelyn took a tighter grip on him. "Now that I've had a chance to think about it, no. I suppose I'm not surprised by having a fifth. I am shocked; however, that he chose Sebastian. He hasn't stayed with any company longer than a few years. I don't know why Grandfather thought he'd stick around to babysit us."

David chuckled. "I suppose we need a sitter. More like a referee, I think."

He always had to contradict her, but Evelyn let it go. These peaceful moments between them were rare. "I wonder what that letter said."

"Whoever gets a hold of it first has to share it with the other. Agreed?" David opened the minivan door and helped Evelyn into the seat.

"Deal. But my guess is neither of us is going to be able to pry it out of him." She pulled her seat belt into place. She saw Sebastian holding the door for Anne at the entrance of the building. "But I'd bet you'd have a better shot."

"I'm not sure about that. He might not like your business practices, but he's fascinated with you. As fascinated as you are with him." David slammed the door before Evelyn could reply. He waved at the pair and headed for his car.

Leslie had come with John and Kimberly. They were getting Patrick into his seat, but Evelyn found herself watching Sebastian as he led Anne to the driver's side door. They were deep in discussion and didn't notice Evelyn's scrutiny. She thought about what David had said and knew he was right. The fascination was mutual. But Sebastian would never act on it. He disliked her, maybe even hated her, and she didn't fool herself into thinking otherwise. His fascination with her was probably like other people's fascination with deadly snakes. You kept your eye on them, and you kept a wide distance between you and them.

"I'll think about it." Sebastian opened the door for Anne.

"Please do. I'm looking forward to having you over tomorrow. It will be good for me to start socializing again. I get lonely sometimes, and I have to admit boredom is starting to become a major problem. Howard never minded when I had my friends over. It was a lot less frequent when he was feeling at his worst, but he always joined us for a meal when he felt up to it. Evelyn is at work a lot, so I'm by myself quite a bit." Anne was ignoring Evelyn's glare.

Evelyn wasn't going to be silent. "What are you talking about?"

Sebastian had the great pleasure of not telling her all that they had talked about. "Anne has invited me over. I haven't been to the house in five years."

Evelyn wasn't feeling up to sparring any longer, but she wished she did. She didn't like the glint that made Sebastian's eyes glow like emeralds. That usually meant he was up to something.

But she couldn't resist at least one jab. "Whose fault is that? You didn't have to bury yourself in Europe. Grandfather understood why you had to quit. I enjoyed explaining it to him in great detail."

Sebastian's grip visibly tightened on the open door. "Told him about our last conversation, did you? It would figure you'd go running to him when things got a little rough. You're too soft." He knew that would insult her more than anything else. She tried to be tough, as tough as he was, and she'd always fallen short. It was her attitude that he had known would ruin the business. Instead of acknowledging her weaknesses and compensating for them, she ignored them and pretended they didn't exist.

"Yes, I told him. He had a right to know why you left. Who knows what you did with the knowledge you'd learned in the years you'd worked for him. Who knows what secrets you could sell overseas." Evelyn knew that insult would anger him just as much as his had hurt her.

"That's twice today, Evelyn. It's good to see you're still in top form." Sebastian turned to Anne. "I'll see you tomorrow."

Evelyn flinched at the controlled power with which he shut the door. She sank back into her seat, praying the ride home would go quickly.

"Couldn't leave it alone, could you?" Anne started the

van and backed out of the parking space. She wasn't so much angry as confused. "What did he say to you before he left for Europe?"

"Are you sure you want to know?" Evelyn leaned the seat back and tried to relax.

"Yes, I do. I don't know why the two of you attack each other the way you do." Anne looked as if she wanted to say something else, but she remained silent, waiting for an explanation.

"Who knows? But to be honest, I'm not sure how seriously he takes me. Before he left, he said he refused to take orders from me. Then he said I didn't have what it took to run the business. Said I was too soft. Then he made a few derogatory comments I won't bother repeating, but they were true, nonetheless. Then he said the only thing I cared about was myself and my horse and that I may as well bury myself in the stables and stay there."

Anne heard the pain in Evelyn's voice. What Sebastian had said was mostly true. Howard had bought Evelyn a horse when she turned sixteen. That horse had become Evelyn's life. She'd spent as much time with it as she could. Once college started, Evelyn had come over in the evenings to tend to it. Evelyn treated it more like a child than an animal. No matter what the hour, day, or season, Evelyn could be found at the stables.

Anne knew Howard had never forgiven himself for having bought her the mare for her sweet sixteen. Four years later, the mare had tossed Evelyn over a cliff.

Chapter Three

Sebastian couldn't believe his eyes when he arrived at the house the next afternoon. The property was a mess. The grass needed to be mowed, and there was a lot of it. The trees and hedges were overgrown. The roses ran wild on and over the trellises. The scent of rotting fruit came from somewhere behind the house. There was a lovely fenced-in patio and garden behind the house, and he knew there were a few fruit trees. The apple tree had been his favorite.

This was not the stately home he remembered from five years ago. The house looked all right, which relieved him. It looked like it had been recently painted. The gingerbread trim was white and the house itself was a light blue. If he remembered correctly, it used to be a tan and beige color with a few light green accents. It usually had sparkling windows that gleamed for miles, and the porch always had flower baskets that were well-tended and always seemed in bloom no matter what the season. Now the windows were dulled a bit by a layer of dirt and the flower boxes were empty. He'd known Howard had been ill. He'd spoken to him often enough. Sebastian had no idea that the house and surrounding land had suffered as well. It wasn't as though the house was run down; it was just that it lacked its usual immaculateness.

Sebastian got out of his rented car and took a better look. There was no one about, but that wasn't necessarily strange. Howard liked to hire people to help with the house, but they didn't live there, as a lot of wealthy people were known to do.   Even the housekeeper left at the end of the day. Sebastian saw the minivan parked outside the house but saw no other vehicles. The red sporty little car Evelyn used to drive was nowhere in sight. He knew she lived here. She'd moved out at eighteen, but she hadn't gone far.   She'd moved closer to her school, but she'd spent her weekends here with her horse. After her accident, it had been either move back home or hire a private nurse. Evelyn had chosen to come home. He figured she could have moved out again, but likely she was comfortable living off her grandfather. Now that he was gone, Sebastian idly wondered if she'd continue to live off the estate or finally move back out on her own.

Sebastian saw the stable as he walked around the side of the house. The storm shutters were closed and fastened, and the door had a deadbolt on it. He looked around for any other sign of life. Perhaps Evelyn didn't live here, after all. Evelyn was more attached to her horse than she was to most people. That much he remembered well. It was one of her greatest weaknesses as far as business was concerned. She had always made sure to leave early enough from work to get home to tend her horse. That was fine for the employees but not for the future boss.

But Sebastian also remembered what Anne had said just yesterday. Evelyn did live here. Anne had told him when she'd invited him to stay here until his things were shipped and he had a new place to stay. Something around here wasn't right. It was his nature to find out what that something was.

Anne came down the steps just as he returned to the front. He walked up the steps and kissed Anne's cheek. "I was just taking a look around."

Anne looked a little embarrassed. "I know how bad things must look. We had to lay off the staff, and things have started falling apart."

Sebastian was startled. He shut the front door behind him and faced Anne. "Are you broke?"

Evelyn spoke from a lounging chair. "Yes."

"Evie, please. We aren't broke. We just have had a lot of expenses lately, and things are a little tight."

Evelyn didn't bother trying to sit up. She'd tucked away the novel she was reading under the couch and had shoved the cane out of view when she'd heard his car. She didn't want to be caught reading her newest romance novel, and she didn't want Sebastian to see her cane. At least not yet. "Why try to gloss over the truth? Between my accident and Grandfather's cancer, along with a failing business, we're in more than a little financial trouble."

Sebastian didn't know what to say to that. When Evelyn had said the business was in trouble, he hadn't believed it to be to this extent. In fact, with Howard controlling his two grandchildren, he'd expected the company to be in much better shape, no matter how sick Howard had gotten.

Anne sent a last disapproving look at Evelyn and turned her attention to Sebastian. "I've been meaning to hire some people to take care of the yard. I also have a cleaning team coming in after I leave for my trip. I don't want Evie to try tackling any of the jobs herself."

"As if I would." The sarcastic statement wasn't completely true, but it served Evelyn's purposes. She wanted Sebastian to think she was a lazy slob, and the look he was giving her told her he thought just that. It made her feel better in some perverse way. It was much better than him thinking she couldn't do it. It was that pride of hers again. One of these days it would probably get her in trouble.

Sebastian took the chair Anne gestured to. He took a good look around. Things looked much better inside. He'd bet that Anne had taken to doing the dusting and vacuuming. Evelyn looked as if she had no intention of budging from her seat. She was lounging around like a queen.

Anne left for only a second and came back with a tray she'd prepared for his visit. "Have you thought about what we talked about?"

Anne never changed, Sebastian thought. She always got to her point. "I thought about it. Tell you what, I'll take care of the yard work in exchange for room and board."

Evelyn choked a bit on her coffee. "Room and board?"

Anne chuckled. "You don't have to earn anything. But if you want to try to tackle that mess, I'd appreciate it. I know how bored you get when you have nothing to do."

Evelyn tried again. "What room and board? Is Sebastian staying here?"

Sebastian had the great pleasure of telling her. "Anne invited me to stay here until I settle into a new place. It will take a while to get my things shipped from my flat in London. I need a place to stay, and Anne offered me a room."

"You mean she asked you to babysit me while she's away." She couldn't believe that Anne had asked him to watch over her. "I don't need a keeper."

"Anne disagrees. She says you need someone around just in case." Sebastian didn't understand the look on Evelyn's face. He knew she'd fallen off a cliff a few days after her non-wedding. She'd been out riding at some local horse trails. From what Howard and Anne had told him, she had been in bad shape. She'd had a couple of surgeries to fix the injuries she'd sustained. She still needed another one from what he understood, and she was still not completely better. But she'd walked into the lawyer's office just fine, and she had stood her ground, literally, when she'd confronted him about the business. He figured Anne was just being overprotective.

But staying with Anne was a good idea. He did need a place to stay until he could arrange to have his things shipped from overseas. He hated living in hotels. He hadn't planned on staying in California, but now that he was a partial owner of Brown Chemical Labs, he had changed his plans. Brown was a business he knew well. He'd worked there longer than any of the other places he'd worked over the years. Now that he had gotten used to the idea, it appealed. He was ready to settle down.

He'd enjoyed Europe, but it was good to be home. He'd been toying with the idea of moving back to the States for a while and had quit his job the month before. He'd been tying up loose ends when he'd gotten the call from Howard's lawyer. He wanted to be closer to his children, and once he had a house, he could have them stay with him from time to time. He hadn't had the heart to drag them across the ocean again after their first visit. He'd taken them for a few weeks and shown them England, Scotland, Ireland, and France, but Becky had worried excessively, and he'd brought them back a little early. He came and visited them after that. Now he could buy a house and spend more time with them. But right now, he had to deal with Evelyn.

"Don't worry; the house is big enough for both of us." Sebastian took a sip of his coffee, satisfied to have upset her.

"Don't look at me that way." Anne gave Evelyn a stern look, one that was designed to show that she, too, could be just as stubborn. "I'm leaving in less than two weeks, remember? My friend Diana and I are going on a cruise."

Anne addressed Sebastian. "Everyone in the family has decided I should go. I didn't want to go so soon after Howard died, but then again, it might be good for me. Diana is sure the fresh sea air will do wonders for me."

Sebastian approved. "I think it's a good idea. It's been difficult for you these last few years. Between Evelyn and Howard, you need a break."

Anne thanked him and turned to Evelyn, who was getting ready to argue. "I told you about it when Diana asked me to go three weeks ago. You told me I should go. I want someone with you. It's for your own good."

"Isn't that why everyone does the things they do, because it's good for me? Why don't you try asking me once in a while what I think is good for me? My body may be a mess, but my mind works just fine." Evelyn spoke, briefly forgetting that Sebastian was listening.

"I never meant to imply otherwise. But you're stubborn and you're not always thinking straight when it comes to proving what you can and can't do. I'll feel better if you're not alone. It's either have Sebastian stay with you or I'll sick Kimberly on you." Anne knew the threat hit home.

"It will never work. Sebastian and I won't be able to get along. And just what do you think he'll do for me? I don't see him waiting on me hand and foot. I don't picture him doing the laundry or the cooking and cleaning. Besides that, he wouldn't go out of his way for me."

Anne gave an exasperated sigh and sent Sebastian a quick, apologetic look. "Either Sebastian stays in the house with you, or I won't go."

"You lived with Grandfather too long." It wasn't the most graceful acceptance, but it was all she had. Living with Sebastian wouldn't be that bad. He'd be wrapped up in work. But Evelyn made a fool of herself enough without having Sebastian witness her clumsy awkwardness. She knew it was stupid to try to pretend nothing was wrong with her, but she felt the need to try. Now she might be working with him temporarily, as well as living with him. She couldn't go around without the cane all the time; the back brace was mighty uncomfortable.

Evelyn glanced back over to him. He was sipping his coffee as if she hadn't just insulted him again. He usually didn't let insults go.

Sebastian was pleased with Evelyn's wary look. He knew they probably wouldn't get along while Anne was gone, and most of the time he was sure he almost hated her. But the thought that she thought he'd leave her to fend for herself when she needed him was disturbing. Did she see him as some sort of sadist? That he'd take pleasure in her pain? He decided he didn't want to know the answer to that. With his bright green eyes, nearly black hair, and harsh features, he'd frightened more than one female. Of course, the same looks attracted quite a few females as well.

The room was silent for a minute, then Evelyn took the initiative. "It's your house, Anne, and you're welcome to invite anyone you like." She turned to Sebastian. "I hope you can cook. If not, you'll starve. Megan only comes in once a month to help out with the heavy cleaning."

Megan was the housekeeper, and Sebastian remembered her. She was in her fifties and still a very attractive woman. She had long brown hair that she always had braided down her back, and she had a tall, trim figure she enjoyed showing off. For as long as he'd known Howard, she'd run the house. She took care of organizing the staff, and she'd done the cooking. It was a pity she wouldn't be around; the woman could cook.

"I'm sure I can manage. I've been taking care of myself for years." Sebastian set down his cup and shook his head when Anne would have refilled it. "I don't keep staff. I couldn't afford them even if I wanted to."

Anne cleared her throat. "How are your children?"

Sebastian smiled and pulled out his phone. He knew Anne would be dying to see pictures. He'd made sure he had new ones on his phone to show her. He loved his children, and most people adored them. Lucy looked so much like him. She had dark hair only a little lighter than his own, but it curled adorably around her face. Her eyes were the same deep green. But she had the small features of her mother and the full mouth that Becky had. She even pouted just like her mother. Daniel resembled his mother in coloring. He had blond hair that was straight and shaggy along with his mother's chocolaty brown eyes. But he was getting sharp angles in his face as he grew older. He would look a lot like him in the face.

Sebastian handed over the phone after pulling up the pictures. "They're great. Daniel is getting excited about starting junior high. He says he's done with baby school. Lucy's upset. She wants to start junior high, too. She'd settle for Daniel staying behind."

"My, how they've grown. Daniel is starting to look a lot more like you. Lucy still has the delicate look of her mother." Anne gushed over the pictures. She'd never had children of her own, and it was one of her regrets. "What are they, eleven and eight?"

"Eleven and nine. They're only two years apart." Sebastian took the phone Anne held to him, and he put it back without showing Evelyn. He didn't think she'd want to see them.

"How is Becky?" Anne knew that Sebastian didn't hold a grudge against his ex-wife. They had just wanted different things. Becky didn't try to keep him from his children, and that was all that mattered.

"She's fine. Pregnant again. She called and told me the news just a month ago. She and Dwight are quite happy. This is their third child together." Sebastian mock-shuddered.

"Does the thought of having five children running around scare you?" Anne laughed at him.

"Let's just say that it was hard enough with two babies running around. We've been divorced for six years now. I miss a lot of the bickering that goes on. When I have Daniel and Lucy, they're a handful. Becky's other two are only four and eighteen months old."

"She got remarried quickly after the divorce, didn't she?" Evelyn spoke up and instantly regretted it. She'd only spoken out of pique at having been ignored. Not for anything would she ask to see the pictures, even though she was dying of curiosity.

"A year after. She'd known him from work. They'd been friends. Dwight admitted that he'd been in love with her for a while. Becky felt a little guilty at first. She was newly divorced. But she and I hardly saw each other the last two years of our marriage. It was the last straw, as far as Becky was concerned, and she knew the marriage was over. I wasn't sure how I felt about her remarrying so soon, but I no longer had any say. Dwight is good to Daniel and Lucy. That's all that counts." It was hard to admit that it had been his fault that Becky had given up on him and found someone else who could give her what she needed. But he'd accepted the fact and now, with time, he agreed with her decision. She was much happier with Dwight, and he was happier not having a wife nag him all the time about the amount of time he spent working.

Evelyn nodded. She accepted another cup of coffee from Anne, so she'd have something to stick in her mouth to keep her from making comments.

The room was silent for a moment, then Anne cleared her throat. "I hope you're hungry. I made lunch for us."

Sebastian nodded, relieved that the questions about him and Becky were over. "Starved. I had an early breakfast and then I made a trip over to Brown. I wanted to get some financial statements and ask a few questions. David was there to show me around."

Evelyn shifted uncomfortably in her chair. She had remained here because she didn't want to go into the office. She'd stayed up half the night worrying about the company. Knowing that she wouldn't be in charge anymore was hard to deal with. At the moment, she never wanted to set foot inside the building again. It was stupid and selfish, and she knew it. But she wasn't feeling rational at the moment. What future she had was falling apart before her eyes, and this odd panic was setting in, a panic unlike the panic attacks she could eventually control. She didn't even want to run the company, but it was all she had, and she knew Sebastian was going to take that away from her. She knew he would work wonders for the company, and his leadership was what the company needed. It was a bitter pill to swallow that she hadn't been able to run the company. She'd tried. And she'd failed.

David wasn't doing much better. He hadn't studied business. He worked in product development and was happy to stay there. Evelyn composed herself. "David is always there. It's why he isn't married."

Sebastian heard the neutral tone and wondered at it. "Why weren't you there today?"

"I didn't feel like going in. I've been in and out so much over the last month that I figured today didn't matter. John handles most matters for me, and he lets me know when he needs help."

"So John is running the company?" Sebastian wondered how involved Evelyn was.

Evelyn responded honestly. "Essentially. He's good at his job. He knows his limitations."

Sebastian folded his hands and said what was on his mind. "I was surprised you gave him the job."

Evelyn knew why he said that. "Because he's your nephew? I try not to hold that against him."

Anne rose. "This conversation is deteriorating rapidly. Are you eating with us, Evelyn?"

Evelyn was hungry, but she didn't want to eat with Sebastian. "No, I had a late breakfast."

"Did you?" Anne was sure Evelyn hadn't eaten yet, but she should have expected an argument. "I don't remember seeing you in the kitchen."

Sebastian got to his feet. "I think it's the company. She can't stand the thought of eating with me."

"I'm simply not hungry. The company hardly matters." Evelyn remained seated, hoping they'd go into the kitchen so she could get up. Her leg was starting to protest the position.

"Liar." Sebastian went to where Evelyn sat. He reached down and pulled Evelyn to her feet.

Chapter Four

Evelyn knew her eyes glazed over in pain and the harsh moan echoing in the room was hers. If he had pulled her up from her other arm, it would have hardly hurt at all. But she had been sitting sideways, and her body twisted in the wrong direction. The shaft of pain caused her to sag in his arms.

"Dear heaven." Sebastian grabbed her other arm and turned to Anne. "What's wrong?"

Anne was accustomed to Evelyn's pain and knew what to do. "Lie her down for a second."

Sebastian shifted Evelyn to the couch, but his hands were shaking. Evelyn moaned again, but her eyes flickered open.

"Leave me alone." Evelyn gritted her teeth and tried to sit up.

"Stay still, Evie." Anne laid a hand on her shoulder and pushed her back down. The fact that she went told Anne it hurt badly.

"Does she need a doctor?" Sebastian felt guilt gnawing at him.

"No. This happens when she isn't careful. She's refused to have the surgery to correct it. When you tugged her up, her back or hip must have caught. You have to come around to her front and pull her straight to her feet."

"I am still here, you know." Evelyn loosened her gritted teeth as the waves of pain started to recede. "Help me sit up now."

Anne helped her up and cautiously watched Evelyn's face. She was breathing deeply, but her face wasn't white anymore.

Sebastian breathed a sigh of relief as her color returned and her pained cries stopped. "I didn't mean to hurt you. I had no idea it was this bad."

Evelyn used the arm of the sofa to get to her feet despite Anne's protesting hand. "I'm fine now. This happens from time to time. Just do me a favor, Sebastian."

"What's that?"

Evelyn turned on him, angry and more than a little embarrassed. Her gray eyes were stormy clouds. "Keep your big mitts off me."

As far as insults went, it was a good one. And he'd earned it. "Fine."

Anne reached around the chair and grabbed Evelyn's cane. "For heaven's sake, use it. And come eat."

Evelyn didn't protest. She wished for a shot of whiskey and looked over at the banquet. Anne would refuse. A pain pill would have to do. But Anne would insist she eat first, then take the pill. "Fine."

Sebastian took a seat and kept an eye on Evelyn. "Why are you refusing to have surgery?"

"Because I don't feel like it."

Anne shook her head disapprovingly. "She's as stubborn as her grandfather; that's why. There is no good reason on earth not to have it done."

Evelyn stayed silent. The thought of having to go through the pain of surgery was enough of a deterrent. The physical therapy that would follow was another. She'd had to learn how to walk again after the injuries she'd sustained. It was only a miracle that her spinal cord hadn't snapped. With her back mostly healed and her broken legs completely healed, surgery was the last thing she wanted to go through again. She could walk with a cane instead of a walker, and her body was completely erect. Another back surgery along with a hip replacement was out of the question.

"Could we change the subject?" Evelyn knew it came out more like a plea than a demand. But she was still feeling a lot of pain, and she didn't want to talk about it.

Sebastian didn't know what to say. He wanted to know more about the accident. He could just question Anne about it later.

Sebastian unknowingly picked a worse topic. "What happened to the horse? What was her name?"

Evelyn's eyes darkened, and her voice wavered. "You do have a talent, don't you?"

"For what?"

Evelyn fisted her hands. "For picking the one thing that would upset me the most."

Anne cleared her throat. "Evelyn sold the horse four years ago. Since she couldn't ride her and she couldn't afford her with all of her medical expenses, she decided to get rid of her. Howard took care of the sale."

"He wanted to shoot her." Evelyn knew her grandfather blamed the mare. But Evelyn hadn't been thrown off her horse. She was pretty sure she had been dismounted when she'd gone over. Her recollections were vague, but she remembered tying up the horse while she walked around. A storm had rolled in that night, and Isabel, her horse, had pulled loose from the tree. It had been the horse that had been found first. Getting rid of her four years ago had been the hardest thing she'd ever done. She couldn't ride her, but she would have kept her anyway. But Isabel had been a reminder of what had happened, and it was painful for her grandfather to have her around. Evelyn decided to sell her. She'd needed the money anyway.

Sebastian felt like dragging himself outside and beating himself. He supposed the sadist image was a sure thing now. "I'm sorry. When I saw the stable was shut up, I wondered. I remembered you had her."

"Yes. I bet you do. You told me I cared about the horse more than I did about the people around me. You told me to go bury myself in the stable. I chose a cliff instead."

Anne rose, tears filling her eyes. "Evelyn Bennett, you will apologize for that remark right now."

Evelyn felt immediately guilty. "I apologize."

"If your grandfather had heard that, he'd have taken a horsewhip to you." Anne sniffled.

Evelyn shifted uncomfortably in her seat. It seemed she had a talent for upsetting people, too. "My grandfather never took anything to me. I imagine Sebastian wished he had. I shouldn't have said what I said. Blame it on fatigue and pain."

Anne pushed back her chair. "I'll go get you a pill."

Evelyn didn't bother to ask for the whiskey instead. She

watched Anne's retreating back and then faced Sebastian. "I do apologize. I shouldn't have said that."

"That's the second time you've apologized to me and meant it." Sebastian was still shaking a bit, and it surprised him.

"Yes, well, don't get used to it." Evelyn nervously began biting her nails.

Sebastian took her hand. "Don't do that."

Evelyn looked up into his eyes. There was a warmth there she had never seen before. She stammered a bit. "B-bad habit."

Anne interrupted the moment, and Evelyn felt a loss when Sebastian looked away and let go of her hand. Evelyn felt an unfamiliar warmth flowing through her. She frowned down at her hand, hoping to see an explanation there. There was none.

"Here you go, Evie." Anne handed her a pill and a glass of water.

"Thank you." She took the pill and shuddered at the foul taste. "You'd think they'd coat these things so they wouldn't taste so bad."

Her wry remark set the tone for the rest of the meal. This was the first time she'd sat down and eaten with Sebastian since her grandfather's wedding. He was every inch the gentleman, despite his ungentlemanly looks. It abruptly occurred to Evelyn that she'd missed him these last five years. She'd met him when she was fifteen, right after he'd gone to work for her grandfather. She had been living with her grandfather then, had been since she was twelve and her mother had dropped her and her sister off.

Jeannette had often left her daughters with her father. Jeannette did whatever she pleased. But Evelyn loved her grandfather and was happy that her mother had the sense to leave her with him instead of strangers, as she had been prone to do in the past.

The years that she lived with her grandfather had been the best. Howard hadn't been the most affectionate of parents, but he had loved her, and Evelyn knew that. He had a gruff way about him that had appealed to her neglected emotions. Sebastian was a lot like her grandfather that way. It was probably one of the things about Sebastian that attracted her. But Evelyn had been a child when they'd met, and he'd been a grown man with a family. When she'd gone to work for her grandfather while she attended business school, they'd learned to despise each other. In a way, it saddened Evelyn that their relationship had gone the way it had. On the other hand, it had kept her sanity. Evelyn would rather be in an adversarial relationship with Sebastian than in one where she pined for him. She'd had a crush on him at fifteen. It had developed into the opposite feeling in the short five years before he'd left her grandfather's company.

Perhaps now they could try to get along. Evelyn didn't fool herself into thinking they would be best friends, but perhaps they could meet somewhere in between.

On that note, she addressed Sebastian. "Are you glad to be back in America? Did you miss it?"

Sebastian saw the sincerity in her now clear gray eyes. "I missed it. I did miss living here, too. I love the western states. I missed the mountains. Washington State is beautiful, and I miss my kids. Here in northern California is nice, too. I missed the rolling hills. Being halfway around the world was straining at times. But I love Europe. It has so many places to go and has charms of its own. You can't get the history here that you do there; there isn't a sense of so much past behind us. We are such a young nation that I think we lack a lot of what the Europeans have."

"A sense of history. You're surrounded by it in Europe, I imagine." Evelyn had never been to Europe, but she wanted to go. She wanted to see everything there. She wanted to see the old castles and abbeys. She wanted to see the museums and old works of art. But that seemed like an impossible dream now.

"You'll find plenty to occupy you here. The company could use you right now." Evelyn took another bite of her salmon.

"I'm surprised to hear you admit that." Sebastian was enjoying Evelyn. It was a first.

"I know. But I can't devote myself to the company as I could have if I hadn't had the accident. Grandfather had a hard time running the company while trying to stay retired. David had to carry most of the burden. He wanted to have control of the company, but he didn't want the day-to-day running of it. He likes making decisions and having others carry them out. David is happier running the labs. He's happy letting me run the business so long as I don't make decisions that conflict with his ideas of how it should be run. He could use your leadership."

"Do you want your job?" Sebastian was surprised by what Evelyn was admitting.

"I like being in charge. But even I have to admit that I needed Grandfather's influence and guidance. But don't think for a second that I want to let you boss me around."

"Wouldn't dream of it. You and I aren't going to be able to work side by side."

How well Evelyn knew it. But she needed this job. It was probably a sure bet no one else would want to hire her with her physical disabilities that caused her to miss work now and again, not to mention Brown was the only job she'd ever had, and she hadn't done such a great job with it. Without her position at Brown, she didn't know what she would do. Right now she never wanted to see the place again, but she had to if she was to support herself. She didn't think she could articulate what she felt. She wasn't even sure she wanted to try. Once her resentment faded because of what her grandfather had done, she'd be able to go back to work and put things into perspective.

"So, you want me to get the company back on its feet, then take over the position that Howard held? Pretend I'm retired but keep a hand in it, so things don't fall apart?"

Evelyn had the grace to blush. "Something like that."

Sebastian surprised everyone by chuckling. "Something tells me I wouldn't do such a good job in that role, either. But perhaps after I've been back a few years, I'll be willing to take on that job."

Anne joined in. "I'm glad your back. And I hope everything works out. I've missed you and I bet your children have, too. After you settle down, you could get remarried, maybe have more children. I know how much you miss them."

Sebastian looked up. "I don't know about marrying and having more children. Don't get me wrong, the idea appeals. But I'm thirty-eight. I probably won't find a woman before I'm too old to have more kids."

Evelyn watched Sebastian closely. "Do you want more children?"

Sebastian considered the question. "I guess I do. I do love my kids. I'd like to be there for them. Divorce is hard no matter how much you know it's the right thing. I've missed out on a lot of my kids' lives. I don't want to go through that again. It's hard enough with Daniel and Lucy."

Evelyn stabbed her salmon again. With all she'd been through, marriage and children seemed just as impossible to her as climbing a mountain. She had nothing to offer a man. When she'd become engaged to Andrew, she'd had all sorts of plans, and children had been a part of them. Evelyn felt her eyes sting again. Tears were threatening more and more lately, but she refused to cry.

She took a bite and concentrated on Sebastian. "A lot of men have children later in life. If you get yourself a younger wife, you could have a whole slew of them."

Sebastian saw the bright glimmer in her eyes. "I suppose so. But I don't think at forty I should marry a twenty-year-old."

Anne, too, saw the shimmer in Evelyn's eyes. "I don't imagine marrying a twenty-year-old appeals to most decent forty-year-old men. But you're not forty yet."

Sebastian gave her a wry smile. "Ready to marry me and have my children?"

Anne smiled, not in the least offended. "Be careful, or I

might take you up on it. Those Hollywood women marry younger men and have babies in their forties these days. But to be honest, I'm enjoying being a great-grandmother to Patrick. I love that little guy."

Evelyn glanced up and saw the sincerity in Anne. She loved the family she married into as if they had always been hers. Evelyn knew Anne didn't have a family of her own anymore. She embraced her new family as if they were blood relations. Evelyn accepted Anne the same way. She looked over at Sebastian, her curiosity getting the better of her. "Have you visited with John? You're Patrick's great-uncle, you know?"

Sebastian winced. "I have been over there, and I get a kick out of him. However, I have a hard time with the 'great' part."

Evelyn laughed at him. "Just wait until Daniel or Lucy have kids."

Sebastian's pale face was genuine. "Don't remind me. I feel old enough."

Anne cleared the table after that, and Sebastian took his leave. He promised to return the next day with his things. Evelyn prayed that the camaraderie they experienced at lunch could be maintained. She didn't have very high hopes.

She would be proven right.

Chapter Five

The sparkling water of the pool had been more than she could resist. Evelyn had decided in a moment of inspiration that pretending her scars and her cane didn't exist for Sebastian's sake was just plain stupid. Sitting in the lounge chair, the water drying on her now exhausted body, she knew she'd made the right decision. The water had felt wonderful, and she loved the fluid, buoyant feeling the water always gave her. She felt whole and free in the water.

Kimberly saw the tired but satisfied face of her sister. "Feels good, doesn't it? I can't believe you forgot your bathing suit."

Evelyn had the grace to wince. "I didn't exactly forget it. But you already know that. I had decided I wasn't going to swim today, so I left it at home."

"Yeah, and I know the reason why." Kimberly handed her sister a glass of lemonade and settled beside her. "You could probably afford a pool, you know. Not that I mind you coming here. It's hard enough to pull you out of the office without coming up with a really good excuse. I invited everyone over to celebrate Sebastian's return just to get you here."

Evelyn snickered at that, knowing that there was probably a tiny shred of truth in that statement but not willing to pursue it. "I couldn't maintain it. And Anne certainly has enough on her plate these days without giving her a pool to clean. Sebastian has started tackling the back garden. Quite frankly, Anne and I are grateful."

"John has offered to help more than once. And I've offered to come help clean." Kimberly's eyes went automatically to John. He had Patrick, but the baby wasn't fussy. He was being passed around and enjoying all the attention. Patrick loved people.

Evelyn felt a bit wistful and jealous and let the emotions roll through her. It was perfectly natural, she assured herself time and again, to want what her sister had. "You and John have enough to do without coming over and cleaning up after me. Right now John can't spare much time. He's covering my job and assisting Sebastian. I know he's working tons of hours while trying to spend as much time at home as he can. He sure has taken to being a father."

Kimberly heard the wistfulness in her sister's tone but didn't say anything. She didn't want to upset her. Evelyn was a nurturer. She loved children and animals. The horse had been a substitute for children. Evelyn acted tough, or at least she used to. But she had a soft spot a mile wide. Kimberly was always telling Evelyn she could have children, with or without the last operation. She would probably end up spending most of her pregnancy in bed without the surgery, though. Kimberly doubted Evelyn could carry the additional burden of a baby and still be very mobile. But Evelyn was only twenty-five. The family had hopes that the stubborn streak would eventually lessen and hopefully go away if she met the right man.

Kimberly looked back over to John. "He's been wonderful. He also feels guilty that he's not here more. I keep telling him I'm fine during the day alone with Patrick. Tons of mothers do it every day."

"John adores you and he often wonders how you're coping now that you quit your job. It's kind of sweet. Maybe one of these days he'll forgive me." Evelyn stifled a yawn.

Kimberly hated it when Evelyn said that. "Evie, you thought you were doing the right thing. John might not have cared for or liked your delivery, but I appreciated it. I was touched by your concern."

Evelyn snorted at that. "John was beyond angry that I thought he was sleeping with Leslie behind your back. He thought I was trying to ruin your relationship out of spite. When I saw the two of them alone in that restaurant, I assumed he was cheating on you. Sebastian wasn't advertising his relationship with her. If he had, I wouldn't have thought it because I know Sebastian wouldn't have tolerated infidelity. Besides, you were only eighteen when you got engaged. With my marriage pending, I was under a lot of stress, and I jumped to a lot of stupid conclusions."

Kimberly was silent, but it didn't last. "There have been some rumors floating around."

Evelyn took a deep breath. "I've heard them. Office gossip is something else. I'm well aware that Andrew is back in town. You can be sure people were fighting to be the first in line to tell me the man who jilted me was back. And not only back in town, but also very successful and flaunting his wealth."

Kimberly bit her lip but kept on talking. "I know I don't involve myself much in Brown. But he started his own business and he's been rivaling ours for the last three years. I know that much from John. Andrew started it up fast and he succeeded fast."

Evelyn would only have been surprised if he'd failed. "He's smart. He has an extensive background in chemical companies. He worked for Brown. Then he went to work for a rival. His own company was the next step. Add the necessary capital, and nothing could stop him."

"Yes, but it seems odd he'd choose to open up his headquarters here. You'd think his engagement to you would be an embarrassment since he left you waiting at the altar."

He was incapable of feeling embarrassed, Evelyn thought, but she didn't voice it. She'd never told anyone what Andrew had done to her. Only her grandfather had known. After the accident, it just hadn't seemed important. Besides, he'd left her a note telling her why he'd done what he'd done. He'd had a good reason. It might have been a twisted reason, but it was a good reason, nonetheless. "It was five years ago. The gossip will die down quickly. He changed his mind. People are entitled to do that. In the end, it all turned out for the best."

"What a crock. He had no right to do that to you." Kimberly realized she'd spoken a bit too loudly.

Evelyn saw the embarrassed flush on her sister's cheeks. "I don't want to talk about Andrew. I don't want to talk about my injuries. And I don't want to talk about anything else that happened five years ago."

Sebastian was carrying Patrick when Evelyn noticed he was beside Kimberly. Sebastian nodded at Evelyn. "Dragging up the past usually doesn't do much good."

Kimberly held out her hands and accepted Patrick. "Does he need something?"

Sebastian dragged over a nearby chair. "Not that I know of. But he weighs a ton, and my arms are tired from carrying him around."

"Yeah, he's big. He was eight and a half pounds when he was born, and he's been packing on weight since." Kimberly adjusted her son's hat and shifted him in her lap so he could watch the crowd.

Sebastian watched Evelyn shift uncomfortably. He was surprised to see her in a bathing suit, though she had a towel wrapped around her waist that covered most of her lower half. He'd have bet good money that she wouldn't wear a bathing suit in his presence. The suit didn't quite fit her, so he bet it wasn't hers. The black one-piece suit was a little baggy on her, but she looked good in it. Her legs were stretched out in front of her, and her arms were lying quietly by her side. She had a hat on her head that shaded her face, but her hair hung limply around her shoulders beneath it. He'd been right; her hair was past her shoulders these days.

Evelyn saw his scrutiny, but she was too drained to care. If she had the energy, she'd go find a bed to take a nap in. Just the thought of some cool sheets and a firm bed was heavenly. But she just gave Sebastian a small, tired smile. They'd been living together for a week now. It had been easy since Anne was there to referee, just as David had suggested they needed. She hated it when David was right.

Sebastian didn't like that small smile. She looked like she could drop right off to sleep at any moment. She had that face a lot. By the end of the day, nothing could get a rise out of her, and he'd tried. She'd come out swinging in the morning then lost all her spunk by the evening. "So, when are you coming back to work?"

Evelyn bit back an exasperated sigh. She'd known this was coming, and it figured he'd hit her with it when she was too tired to argue about it. "I suppose I can't stay away forever. I thought maybe at the next meeting. You'll be voted into my job. Until then, I'm on vacation. I've been working my butt off for the last month since Grandfather died. I need a break, and you're there to pick up the slack."

"It'd be easier on everyone if you came in. You know more of what is going on than I do." Sebastian watched her carefully. She was getting her stubborn face again. It wasn't as potent when she was half asleep, but it was still sexy.

"Turnabout is fair play and all that. I needed you to stick around five years ago, and you bailed. Don't bother asking me for any favors." She would have gotten up and stormed off if possible. The leg was such a nuisance. She was forced to brazen out all situations.

"That's really mature, Evelyn. I should have expected it from you. What are you now, twenty-five? Practically still a baby."

Kimberly stifled a laugh. She sobered when her sister glared at her. "Evelyn is right. She's been under a lot of stress and pressure since Grandfather died. She was spending fourteen hours a day at the office. I know because

John didn't want to leave her there alone, and he was hardly ever home."

Evelyn struggled to her feet. The problem with the lounge chairs was that there was no graceful way for her to get out of them. She gripped the towel so she wouldn't lose it and grabbed her cane. The carved wood cane had belonged to her great-grandfather. Her grandfather had given it to her when she refused to use the walker. "I don't need a babysitter. And I won't be talked around."

"Evie, I didn't mean anything by it. We worry." It didn't take much to set Evelyn off, and Kimberly was genuinely sorry.

"You can all stop. Anne invited Sebastian to stay with me and she threatens to sick you on me if I argue. Even David, who usually can't stand to be around me for more than five minutes at a time, assists me. Leslie, thank goodness, still resents me for what I did five years ago. She doesn't talk to me unless she has to, and there aren't very many reasons."

Sebastian watched Evelyn walk away, a bit perplexed by her exit. Evelyn usually faced all problems head-on. She'd never been a quitter. "She do this often?"

Kimberly nodded. "More so than before. We're all worried about her. Even Leslie, although she won't admit it. Anne says she's been drinking too much again. It was hard enough to break her of the habit before. The doctor has been saying she's strong enough for surgery on her hip and back, but she's been adamant about not having it done. We all know how painful her recovery was. None of us want to see her go through it again. But she's in pain now, and the surgery would stop the everyday struggle."

Sebastian saw her struggle with the glass sliding door. She slipped inside and disappeared. "I haven't seen her drinking."

"Give it a few more days. Anyway, she says it's better than the pain pills the doctor gives her. She may have a point." Kimberly started bouncing Patrick. He could sense his mother's tension.

"I broke my leg once. Trust me, a couple of shots of brandy now and again went a lot further than those pills to relax you and ease the pain. They make you tired and they eat holes in your stomach. Alcohol might do the same, but it doesn't make you lose control unless you drink too much." Sebastian got to his feet.

"Where are you going?" Kimberly frowned at Sebastian.

"I'm going to go talk to her. I do need her help. John is doing the best he can, but he's running around so much that he's going to burn out at the pace he's going."

"Good luck. You know, Evelyn never wanted to work at Brown. She only did it to please Grandfather. Now she feels trapped, although she probably would never admit it out loud."

"I know." And he did. He'd tried to push her away the two years she worked under him, but she'd persevered. He admired it as much as it made him angry. He knew the pressure she was under. His own family had pushed him, but fortunately for him, he'd wanted what his father wanted.

Sebastian went up the stairs, figuring that Evelyn was finished getting dressed by now. When he found her, she was sprawled out on a bed. "Evelyn?"

She stirred but didn't get up. Her face was pale, he

noted. She was lying face down on the bed. Her hair was spilled out down her back and her eyes were closed. She had put her dress back on, but in the sunlight, he could see the scars on her calves. She'd been facing him when they were chatting outside, so he hadn't noticed them. He'd been looking at her back, not her legs, when he'd watched her go inside, so he hadn't seen them then. He wanted to talk to her, but he didn't want to move her. The flash of pain the day he'd pulled her to her feet remained strong with him. He'd felt helpless. Her words startled him.

Evelyn knew where he was looking. "I wasn't wearing my chaps that day. Grandfather had given me a pair. He said if I was going to scramble around the cliffs on horseback, then to wear them. I was constantly tearing my jeans. I usually had scratches on my arms and legs by the time I came home after a long ride, so I wore a lot of thick shirts. The day I fell, I had left the chaps at home and was only wearing jeans and a long-sleeve t-shirt. Had I been wearing them, I wouldn't have so many scars from open wounds. The scars on my hip and back are quite a sight. The ones on my calves are nothing in comparison. You should see the rest of them."

Sebastian was staring. Dear heaven, she really could have died that day. She could have smashed her head on a rock, never to regain consciousness. She could have bled to death. California winters might not be what folks in the Midwest would call cold, but it rained a lot in the winter, and rock climbers and hikers were likely to turn up dead if injured as seriously as Evelyn had been. "Who found you?"

Evelyn rolled awkwardly onto her back. She was

groping for the sheet, so Sebastian grabbed it and pulled it up to her waist. "A young couple did. They found Isabel wandering right before a storm rolled in. They called the police. It was dark and storming when they finally arrived. I don't remember it, of course, but the doctor explained what happened. I have no real memories. I hit my head, but I was wearing my riding helmet. The doctors think it was more from the pain that caused me to pass out, not the head injury. Given the nature of my fall, my head injury was pretty mild and didn't do any lasting damage."

He imagined hypothermia was another reason. Lying hurt on a rock ledge would suck the heat right out of you. Add a thunderstorm and the chances of dying were high. "Why don't you take a nap and get some sleep?"

Evelyn gave him a small grin. "The trick is getting me not to take one."

Sebastian left her alone after tugging the sheet higher, his initial plan to talk to her about coming into the office temporarily on hold.

Chapter Six

Sebastian took a deep breath after he closed the bedroom door. He'd heard about the accident, although the details had been vague. Anne and Howard had been out of town. Evelyn should have been on her honeymoon. Sebastian guessed that she had convinced Anne and Howard to go ahead and take the trip they'd been planning. They were taking a second honeymoon. Evelyn always seemed strong and able to take care of herself. He'd noticed that when she was fifteen. She didn't cower, and she didn't whine or cry. Since he'd been married to a woman who tended to do both, Evelyn had been a nice change of pace. But she'd been a kid, and he hadn't seen her much. When she'd turned eighteen and begun working at Brown, that changed. More often than not, she aggravated him, and he wished she were more docile and malleable.

He couldn't say he'd ever liked her, but she had always intrigued him. On some days, that hadn't been a good thing, especially when she'd irritated him just as much as she intrigued. He'd been having trouble with his marriage, and he and Becky had discussed divorce. He'd taken a lot of his frustrations out on Evelyn, and he knew it now. He hadn't been consciously aware of it then. And he wasn't sure when his irritation had become attraction. She might have been of age, but she was way too young for him, even if he'd been thinking of an affair, which at the time he hadn't been.

He'd hooked up with Leslie after his divorce more out of boredom than anything else. It soothed his ego to have a woman hanging on his every word. Leslie's feelings for him were as superficial as his were for her. The relationship had been blessedly brief. After Evelyn had accused Leslie of sleeping with John, he knew he'd either have to make the relationship known or end it. He'd chosen to end it. Leslie still hadn't forgiven him for it. Even now she gave him dirty looks every time he saw her.

Thank heavens he'd ended it before things had gone too far. He had only slept with her once, and it hadn't been memorable. If he remembered correctly, he'd been more than a little tipsy that night. Leslie had probably gotten him drunk on purpose. He'd still felt weird about his divorce, and he hadn't slept with her again. When he'd finally had a real affair, it had been with a woman in Europe. It had lasted only a year, but it had made him feel much better about himself. Since Becky remarried so soon after the divorce, he figured he was getting even more than anything else, but Nadia hadn't seemed to mind. She'd been recently divorced and using him as much as he had been using her. But they'd had a lot in common besides divorce, and they'd had fun together.

Sebastian headed outside. It was good to be home. Despite all the complications moving back was causing, he was excited about it. He wondered if Becky would be surprised that he was ready to settle down into one job and one place. He'd moved his family around once too often.

Becky had had enough. His steady restlessness must have been obvious to her, and he now wondered if she thought he wasn't happy with her. He had been happy with her. At the time he hadn't known what was causing it. Becky thought he was getting ready to quit his job. Moving again was the excuse she used to end their marriage, even though he hadn't asked her to, at least not that time.

The funny part was that Dwight had moved to Washington State shortly after he'd married Becky, and she'd trailed after him. Of course, Becky had loved the three years they'd lived there, and she'd never really forgiven him for moving out of the state. Dwight taking a job there had probably been the only move she would have tolerated. But when Sebastian had been offered a high-paying position at Brown, he'd been eager to take it. Becky hadn't been the same since that move. He should have known that his restless behavior would set her off.

That restlessness still bothered him because, at the time, he hadn't had any thoughts of moving again. He hadn't known what was causing it, and leaving Brown hadn't alleviated it at first. Time had done that for him.

He knew now what had caused it.

Seeing Evelyn again, seeing her half-naked body stretched out on a lounge chair, made a man face the facts. He was attracted to her and had been for a long time. It hadn't been physical before. He would have remembered if he'd been lusting after her. He'd been attracted to her spirit. She'd had a lively presence that his wife lacked. He wondered if Becky had sensed his interest in another woman. He hoped not, since he'd been oblivious to it.

Now, however, he was single and unattached. Evelyn had a body to match her personality, and she was old enough.

Get that right out of your head, he demanded of himself. Lusting after Evelyn was a supreme waste of time. She couldn't stand him. He could hardly stand her. They argued more than they got along. What confused him was the effort she had made to hide the extent of her injuries. He didn't understand why she made the effort, but he could make an educated guess. They were adversaries, and you never let your adversary see your weaknesses. They would exploit them and use them against you.

"Hey, Sebastian." David waved.

Sebastian headed his way, glad for the distraction. He admired and respected David Bennett. He didn't always agree with him, however. David liked to play hardball. Sebastian wasn't one to step back from a challenge, but he generally avoided confrontations when he could. In the end, no one usually won. It surprised most who knew him. Sebastian was well aware of what his physical looks made people think. Thick black hair, a muscular body, and deep green eyes gave him a presence that a lot of people lacked. He stood out in a crowd. Sebastian used it to his advantage. Intimidating people came easily. David lacked some of his cousin's spirit, and it made him easy to manipulate. Evelyn had a presence of her own and was not easily intimidated. David, although attractive in a conservative way, lacked it. But the man relied on his brain, not brawn; Sebastian admired that.

"How are you, David?" He accepted the beer that was

handed to him.

"Fine. I hear you're still hanging around the office. I was surprised you didn't stop by the lab again. I was half-expecting you to show up at least one more time after I showed you around on Monday."

After the first visit with David, Sebastian hadn't made it a point to see him again. He and John had been working around the clock. "Right now I'm trying to familiarize myself with the company's finances. I figured you didn't need me poking around the lab. I've been occupying Evelyn's desk for the last week."

David took a large swallow of his beer. "I hear she's hiding out at home. Not like her."

"No?" That was curious. He figured Evelyn disappeared routinely. After what she'd said about leaving the running of the company to John, he had been thinking she was just a figurehead.

"Nope. She comes in no matter what. Since she stopped going to her therapist and stopped going to physical therapy, she's in the office six days a week. She spends Sundays in bed resting up for the following week." David gestured to Sebastian to have a seat.

Sebastian sat more out of curiosity. "What about before Howard died?"

David spun his bottle between his palms. "She was always there no matter what. Grandfather didn't bother coming into the office once Evie was better. A year after her accident, she started coming in occasionally. Not long after, it was daily. We all figured it was good for her to get out of the house. She'd been depressed, but the doctors assured us it was perfectly normal. Once she snapped out of it, she became pretty restless. Said she needed something to do."

"Is that when she sold her horse?"

David thought about it for a second. "I think so. She did it because of Grandfather, but it was just about the same time she came back to work. She'd had staff working the horse for her. She figured it was time to get rid of her since she couldn't ride her. But I wonder. If the horse threw her off the cliff, it's possible she was just too scared to go near her. She never once went to the stable after the accident."

That was curious. But it made sense, too. He hadn't been joking when he'd said the horse was her life. He figured she'd raise them eventually and get out of the family business. Her job at Brown was a good substitute for what she wanted. Or what she had wanted. He bet if he asked her, she'd deny it. He couldn't help but wonder what it was she wanted out of life now. This curiosity was out of place but was becoming a regular habit. Thinking about Evelyn was a dangerous pastime, but one he wasn't sure he wanted to put an end to.

David let the silence remain for a moment, and then curiosity got the better of him. "Why all the questions? Heaven knows I like the idea of her not being in charge. We never see eye to eye. But I know the business means a lot to her, and she's done her best. Are you going to get rid of her?"

Sebastian didn't demur. "I won't take orders from her. I quit five years ago because she took over. Yes, I want her out of her current position. But I don't necessarily want her out of the company."

"If you take her job, you'll essentially be doing just that. I can't see Evie going back to taking orders when she's gotten so used to giving them. I figure she won't be back in the office so long as you're in charge. Then again, who knows what she'll do. That pride of hers is powerful, but even she has to pay her bills. Brown is the only income she has."

"Where is her inheritance from her mother?" Sebastian knew when Jeannette had died, she'd left behind a large amount of money. No one was sure where it had come from, but it had all been left to her two daughters. Kimberly's share had gone into a trust to be controlled by Evelyn until Kimberly turned twenty-one. Evelyn had gotten immediate control over hers even though she hadn't been that age.

"Gone. I figure the doctor bills ate it up. She didn't have insurance at the time, and heaven help anybody who suggested she look for financial assistance. Grandfather could only help out so much. He had money, but he didn't have that much extra. Evie's bills were excessive, as I'm sure you can imagine. She still makes monthly payments on what her insurance doesn't cover."

"I can imagine." Sebastian could also imagine what she must have been going through at the time. It was hard to feel sympathy for Evelyn, but he did. Her mother had killed herself when she'd gotten behind the wheel of a car while drunk. A year later, Evelyn's engagement ended with her being left at the altar. Then she'd gone over a cliff and endured a painful recovery. Added to her grandfather's ill health, the last six years had been very rough on her.

David interrupted his musings. "You know, I always figured she got what she deserved. Kimberly was always so laid-back and easy to get along with. Evelyn was always arguing and pushing people away. She was a lot like her mother, and no one could quite figure out where Jeannette had come from. My mother was a lot like Grandfather, but Aunt Jeannette was something else entirely. She got pregnant with Evelyn and then had Kimberly two years later. She took off a lot after that. Evelyn copied most of her mother's attitudes, if not her behaviors."

Sebastian had felt much of the same. Evelyn did deserve most of what she got. But what had happened five years ago, no one deserved that. "She didn't deserve the last five years."

David's eyes hardened. "No, maybe not. Andrew did a number on her. She never would have taken off the day she fell off the cliff if it hadn't been for him. Evelyn was nearly destroyed by what happened. Grandfather was never certain, but he often wondered if she hadn't gone over that cliff on purpose."

Sebastian watched as David sucked down the last of his beer. "Howard thought she'd done it on purpose?"

"Her mother drove herself off a cliff. Why not Evelyn tossing herself off one? Like mother, like daughter, and all that. I'm not saying she did it on purpose. But she refuses to talk about what happened. She claims she doesn't remember much, but sometimes when she drifts off and gets that weird look in her eyes, you have to wonder."

Sebastian, too, finished his beer. It had never occurred to him that Evelyn might have done it intentionally. But with one blow after another, she just might have. She'd only been twenty. She was still practically a kid then. He'd been pretty much still a kid at that age. But he'd had the support of his family behind him. It never mattered how much trouble he got himself into; they were always there. Evelyn's family was a close-knit group, but she was definitely on the fringes of the family because of her attitude.

"She seems back to her normal self." It was the only response Sebastian had.

David agreed. "She is, although she's lost her edge. Anne is convinced that you're the reason she's got more of her spunk back. You tick Evie off faster than anyone else, even me. She hardly bothers to argue with me. She caves in more times than not."

"Not exactly a positive trait in a person. But if I can get her back into fighting form, I'm willing to put the effort into it." Sebastian couldn't help the satisfied grin.

David slapped him on the back. "Great. Get her back into the office. As much as I hate to admit it, I could use her right now. This administrative and management stuff is all gibberish to me. She might not be the best person at her job, but she does it, and she has the respect of the staff. It's a lot more than what I have with them. They know I don't care one way or the other about how the business end is run. They go around me and do as they please without Evelyn around."

"I'll see what I can do," Sebastian promised. He was looking forward to working with her. Or more specifically, her working for him.

He'd gone more than one round with her at the office. At the time, he was ultimately the one in charge, so the arguments had ended when he put his foot down. That usually hadn't stopped her completely. She simply regrouped and came back fighting.

"You look like you're looking forward to it," David said.

David looked a bit too cheerful, but Sebastian ignored it. "It's been a long time since I had a good fight with Evelyn. That day at the lawyer's office just whetted my appetite."

Kimberly sauntered over and interrupted. "Whetted your appetite for what? If you're hungry, there's more food."

"We weren't talking about food." David accepted the beer Kimberly handed him. "Thanks."

Kimberly nodded. "What were you talking about?" She looked pointedly at Sebastian while dangling a beer in front of him.

"Evelyn. Who else would we be talking about?" He snatched the beer, figuring another one wouldn't hurt.

Kimberly looked over at Leslie, who was lying on a lounger in a bright red bikini that revealed more than it covered. "There are others that you might be talking about. Leslie has been salivating since you got back."

"Has she? I believe she told me to drop dead when I told her I was moving. Evelyn accusing John of having an affair with her ended our relationship a bit prematurely, but it was on the outs anyway. My ex-wife called it a rebound affair. I wouldn't call it that since it never really got to the affair stage."

"What do you call it? Cheap sex and fast thrills?"

Kimberly didn't particularly care for Leslie's easygoing attitude toward men. It reminded her too much of her mother.

Sebastian glanced at David, but he didn't seem to mind. "It was fast, if nothing else. Not exactly thrilling, though. It was a classic one-night stand based on availability, boredom, and a little too much alcohol. I can count on one hand the number of times we even went out."

Sebastian didn't like to think about the one night he'd spent with Leslie, and this was the second time today. The sex hadn't been thrilling, but it had managed to make him feel cheap. Leslie had moved on quickly once he'd told her he was leaving. He'd been embarrassingly grateful. He'd also been happy to leave the country afterward. Evelyn had been a big motivator for quitting his job, but Leslie had been an even bigger motivator for taking the job overseas when it had presented itself. The affair of the century it hadn't been.

"All that was five years ago. I'm not interested in rekindling my relationship with Leslie. If she's honest with herself, she's not interested in me either." He could see Leslie as she flirted with another man. "My guess is she's bored. She's probably already dated every man in the area and has run out of options."

David shook his head in exasperation. "It's embarrassing but true. I think she's having to make a second round through the same crowd of men. This is a small area, all things considered. I always figured she'd move to a bigger city, but she's stuck it out here. There's this one man, though. Forget his name. He's been hanging around Leslie for a while now. Leslie's never been married, but this guy has been hinting at it. She doesn't seem to be discouraging him."

Since Kimberly quit her job and stayed home, she had the chance to hear a lot of gossip. Some days she felt guilty, but mostly she just enjoyed her new role as a housewife. When she wasn't taking care of or playing with Patrick, gossiping on the phone was becoming her favorite hobby. "His name is Philip Anderson. He's an attorney with Mr. Bickerstaff's firm. He's thirty-five and divorced, no children. Tall, blond hair, blue eyes. He's interested in Leslie, big time. He practically pants when she's in the room. Leslie practically pants, too, but she's in some kind of denial or something because she doesn't talk about him much. Something tells me this might get serious."

David considered it. "You could be right. Leslie is not shy about her men. She's keeping this relationship under the radar, so either she plans to end it or she's in love."

Sebastian didn't care either way. He just wanted her away from him. "For my sake, let's hope he's persistent."

The conversation drifted from there, and Sebastian was content to listen. It was getting better and better being home. He'd missed this place, and he'd missed the family. They might not be his relatives, but he was a part of the group. His own family was close and always would be. But they were a predictable group, though a loving one. These people added spice wherever they went. A one-night stand with Leslie hadn't changed their acceptance of him. Anne and Howard were close friends of his, and he'd been thrilled when they'd gotten married. The twenty-year age difference hadn't mattered one bit. The family had accepted

Anne as a member. Sebastian had been made an honorary one. When John married into the family after Anne, he'd just gotten more involved in their lives.

As the afternoon wore on and Evelyn still hadn't made another appearance, he began to dwell on her again. He never thought of her as family, that was for sure. Their adversarial relationship hadn't produced any soft feelings such as affection. It was disconcerting to have them now. Her accident had fundamentally changed their relationship. She needed protection now, whether she wanted it or not. She needed coddling, whether she was willing to accept it or not. She needed caring and understanding. It was odd, but he was sure he could give her those things.

That gave him plenty to think about. The thoughts weren't as disturbing as they might have been five years ago.

Chapter Seven

Evelyn shot up in bed. Her heart was pounding; her ears were ringing. She had this sudden urge to hide. The dizzy feeling prevented her from moving more than her legs.

Light shot across the curtains, and Evelyn pulled herself further under the blanket she was clutching in a death grip. The thunder rolled over the house, and lightning flashed again. With every boom of thunder, her stomach clenched.

"It's just a storm. It's just a storm." Whispering the words and repeating them out loud helped sometimes. The thunder was further away now, and the lightning wasn't coming so quickly. Her heart was still racing, but her breathing was evening out.

Evelyn didn't know how long she lay there on her bed, the covers up to her nose, her eyes squeezed shut. The storm receded, and the rain became a steady sprinkling. When she finally snapped out of her paralysis, she glanced over at the clock. It was almost five in the morning. Her sister had told her it might storm. When Evelyn had woken up from her nap at her sister's house, Kimberly had warned her that a storm was predicted. Kimberly knew about the panic attacks thunderstorms triggered. Anne had told her a couple of years ago when Evelyn had woken up in the middle of the night screaming. Evelyn had managed to contain her screams, but the cost was high. She knew she wouldn't be sleeping anymore.

Evelyn stayed in her room until six. When the sun started to lighten up the dreary, cloud-filled sky, she got out of bed. She thought she could smell the coffee that had been set to brew the night before. It was Sunday, and everyone would probably sleep in. Normally she would, too.

As Evelyn tugged a bright pink sundress over her head, she heard footsteps in the hall. When they passed her room, she knew it was Sebastian who was awake. Anne's bedroom was at the front of the hall; Sebastian had taken the last room at the end. Evelyn considered staying in her room a while longer but figured that was cowardly. Besides, she was up and dressed, and she desperately wanted a cup of coffee. Caffeine wouldn't do anything to calm her nerves, but perhaps it would help with the pounding headache that the panic attack had caused.

Evelyn took a good look at herself in the mirror. She looked as bad as she felt. But she'd feel stupid going downstairs with all her makeup on at six o'clock in the morning. She settled for the sleepy, tousled look. She brushed the tangles out of her hair but let the reddish mass hang down her back and around her shoulders. Perhaps it would hide some of the paleness in her face. The dark circles were impossible to hide, so there was no point in even trying.

Evelyn slipped on a pair of ballet-style slippers. She never went around the house without rubber treads on her feet. She was deathly afraid of falling. The cane could only provide so much assistance if she took a wrong step.

She took the stairs carefully and headed straight for the kitchen. Sebastian was there. He looked like he'd tossed on a shirt and pulled on a pair of jeans but hadn't bothered washing up. He was standing sideways to her, watching the rain fall while sipping his coffee. His shirt was unbuttoned, and his feet were bare. Evelyn found herself staring at his disheveled appearance. He needed to shave, and his hair needed to be brushed. She was so used to seeing him perfectly groomed. She'd imagined what he looked like getting out of bed in the morning. Her imagining usually ended when she tried to picture him nude. Though her imagination was a good one, it wasn't that good. It also did nothing for her peace of mind.

She tore her gaze away from what she could see of his bare chest and cleared her throat. "Good morning. I'm surprised you didn't sleep in."

Sebastian gave her a look over. She was wearing another one of the floral sundresses she seemed to favor, this one a shocking pink with small purple flowers. It should look ridiculous on her, but it didn't. Since he returned, he hadn't seen her in anything else but dresses like the one she was wearing now. Her hair, once so short and boyish, was loose around her face. Her legs were bare, and he was used to seeing her in a pantsuit. He felt an urge to run his fingers through her mass of hair and then run his hands up those legs. He clenched his coffee cup instead. He was becoming more and more aware of her as a woman, and he wasn't completely happy about it. The cane she was leaning on didn't detract from her feminine appeal.

Sebastian nodded at her and turned to completely face

her. "I usually sleep in, but I'm still getting used to the time change. I'm surprised to see you up though. You usually don't venture from bed until long after I've left for the day."

Evelyn ignored the accusation in favor of finding a coffee mug. She tried to look nonchalant, but she knew she was still trembling in the aftermath of the earlier panic attack. She managed to get the cup down without rattling it and poured herself a cup. She added a bit of sugar and milk to it and wound her way to the breakfast table. It was still drizzling, but there was no sign of another storm. She hoped another one wasn't on its way. She usually handled the ones during the day with nothing more than her nerves being rattled. But when it woke her from a sound sleep, she panicked. Evelyn had gone over it with her therapist, but so far, she hadn't been able to dissociate her fear of storms from the accident.

She'd woken up dazed in the middle of a thunderstorm the night she'd fallen. She'd been half-crazed with pain, and she'd seen shadows coming toward her. In the flashes of lightning, and in her half-conscious state, it looked as if demons had been coming toward her. In reality, it had been the rescue crew. But in their dark clothes, their drenched forms had caused her to freak out. And "freak out" seemed to be the best term. She'd begun screaming hysterically. She remembered that much. The doctor told her the team had sedated her after that, and she'd been rushed to surgery once her body had stabilized. Hypothermia had set in, and her body had lost most of its heat by the time she'd been rescued. The only thing that had saved her life was that the boulders had retained much of the heat from the day, and she'd been warm from being in the sun most of the afternoon until the storm had rolled in.

"Evelyn?" Sebastian watched as her eyes glazed over and her hand began trembling. Her lips were pursed tight, and she hadn't heard him. "Evelyn?"

It was the crash of the coffee cup as it hit the floor that pulled her out of her nightmare. Her eyes flew to Sebastian's as his hands came to rest on her shoulders. She shot to her feet, a great feat because she managed to do it without hurting herself. But she knew whose hands were on her, and she didn't fight him. She knew her eyes were tearing up, and she blinked them away. She instead looked down at the mess she'd made. Thankfully, the cup had not shattered.

"What happened?" Anne came into the room, swiping at the hair that was falling into her face. She saw the coffee puddle spreading and finally noticed that Sebastian was holding Evelyn upright.

Evelyn steadied herself and took a small step back from Sebastian. He let her go. "I dropped my cup."

Sebastian interrupted. "You didn't just drop it. What happened?" He was shaking inside. He didn't know what she had been thinking about, but whatever it was, she had been terrified.

"Nothing happened. I just dropped my cup." Evelyn couldn't easily get down on the floor to clean up the mess, and she looked over at Anne.

Sebastian saw the apology on her face and realized instantly what it was for. "I'll clean it up."

Sebastian grabbed a rag and a towel and cleaned up the

mess. The coffee had splattered all over the underside of the table and on the wall. He knew there was no way that Evelyn was going to be able to clean it up. She was still trembling beside the table. He peeked at her from his position under the table, unsure of what had happened. She'd been staring out the window and just drifted away, as if she had been a child daydreaming.

"I think that's it." Sebastian climbed out from under the table to see Anne watching her worriedly. He watched as Anne took hold of Evelyn and led her from the room. Curiosity made him follow. He watched as Anne poured Evelyn a shot of whiskey. Apparently, Anne's concerns about Evelyn's drinking habits were momentarily brushed aside. Evelyn grabbed the glass, sipped it, and set it back down in her lap. Anne looked over at Sebastian, shook her head, indicating that he should remain silent.

It took maybe fifteen minutes before Evelyn looked like she was back in reality. She looked up at him through her lashes, then back to her drink. She downed the rest of its contents and rose.

"I'm going to go lie down for a while." Evelyn didn't wait for a response but grabbed the cane Sebastian had brought in with him and went straight up the stairs.

"You going to tell me what happened?" Sebastian knew his words sounded harsh but couldn't restrain them. Anne was frowning at the staircase as Evelyn made her way up.

Anne waited to answer until she heard Evelyn's bedroom door close. "She had a flashback. The storm must have triggered it. It's been a while since she's had one. The doctor said it's normal for someone who has suffered a great trauma to relive it. He said it's just like the soldiers from war who come back and relive parts of it. She sometimes relives the accident. She won't tell me what she remembers. She won't tell anyone. When Howard insisted she go to a therapist, she made the woman keep everything confidential. She didn't want anyone in the family to know. We certainly would like to know what she told the therapist, but it was enough for us that she went."

Sebastian watched helplessly as Anne cried. She didn't weep, but tears streamed down her face. He went to her and pulled her to him. She went willingly enough. "It had to be rough on all of you."

Anne squeezed him and pulled away. "Much more for Evie. I wish she weren't so secretive about it. She probably thinks she's doing us all a favor by keeping it to herself, but I wish she wouldn't."

"At least she went to a therapist." Sebastian poured Anne half a shot of the same whiskey and pushed her gently into the chair Evelyn had vacated.

"She went unwillingly at first. Howard kept threatening her. Told her that if she didn't go see one, he wouldn't leave her any shares in the company. Then when she went, he told her if she didn't have the surgery he wouldn't leave her in control of the company. He kept that promise." Anne looked up amused. "He left a fifth to you because she was being stubborn. I can't say I blame her for refusing. She doesn't want to go through it again."

"That's completely understandable."

"Howard disagreed. But then again, when it came to his family, he didn't always think straight. Leaving you a portion surprised all of us."

Sebastian could laugh at that now. "I bet none of you expected I'd accept it either."

"Whatever was in that letter must have been very persuasive. I'd have bet money you'd turn it down. Evelyn and David haven't done a great job with the business, but they are both too young to run it. David doesn't want to run it, and Evelyn only does because she wanted to please her grandfather. She'd never have gotten into business at all if it weren't for him."

Sebastian agreed with Anne, but he had always figured she'd be good at business regardless of what she wanted. Evelyn had been aggressive and hard to please. Both those traits were necessary to run a business, but they weren't the only ones. She had drive and ambition, too. She was also smart enough. But she wasn't as driven as she needed to be. She'd had other ambitions five years before that would have kept her from dedicating her life one hundred percent to the company. He had added to the probable failure when he'd left. But at that point, he hadn't cared one way or the other. The company wasn't his, and Howard was determined that his grandchildren run the company. That left Sebastian out of the running. And it had driven him to seek his fortune elsewhere.

Sebastian spent the rest of the morning reading the newspaper for a break. Then he delved back into the financial papers he'd brought back with him. He'd been looking through everything that pertained to the last five years. The trouble had started immediately. When Evelyn had told him his leaving started the downward spiral, she hadn't necessarily been exaggerating to anger him. Several deals had fallen through when it became public knowledge that he'd left the company. Distributors had been wary of working with Brown when he'd left. They didn't know how the business would fare without his leadership. Howard had already made it public that he was no longer going to run the company but was going to let his two grandchildren run it. Without Sebastian, the company had struggled to keep its contracts.

He felt a small stab of guilt but pushed it away. Howard had made a reappearance at the office during Evelyn's recovery. Whatever doubts the customers and distributors had should have been put to rest when Howard grabbed the reins once again. But soon after, several more problems had arisen. Recently they'd lost a lot of their customer base to competitors. One particular competitor was the biggest threat. Sebastian needed to know more about Crown Chemicals before he could figure out how it had happened. He made a note to look into them. Right now he had other things to worry about. He needed Evelyn to come back to work. In the last four years, she'd gained the trust that she needed to run the company successfully. Between her and David, they'd made some progress this past year. The distribution base was widening again. He didn't know yet if it was pure luck or skill that had caused the turnaround. With Howard severely ill, he hadn't been much assistance.

It was after eleven when Evelyn came back downstairs. He glanced up as she carefully made her way into the living room. "Did you take a nap?"

Evelyn, her face still pale, just shook her head. Sleep

wouldn't be possible for a while. She'd been upstairs trying to do the breathing exercises the therapist had taught her; then she'd read for a while. She needed to control the fear, not let it control her. She knew there was nothing to fear, but her subconscious refused to believe it. The therapist told her that if she didn't get over her fears, they would always haunt her. The thought of spending the rest of her life with a crippling fear was incentive enough to try to get over it. Being physically handicapped was one thing. To be emotionally handicapped was a totally different thing. Feeling helpless was much worse than her time bedridden had been.

Evelyn took a seat. She wanted to pull out the book she had hidden under the chair but didn't dare. She'd kept the novel tucked away since Sebastian had moved in. When she'd been reading upstairs, she'd wanted to sneak down for her other book. "Working again?"

"Someone has to." Sebastian angrily flipped the page. He needed her cooperation, and he had a nasty feeling he wasn't going to get it. And after this morning's emotional trouble, he felt like he was kicking a puppy by pushing her. But perhaps hitting her with it while she was vulnerable would get him further.

Evelyn saw the suppressed anger. This type of fight she could handle. "You wanted to run the company. The meeting is tomorrow. You'll be the president. The company's associates will trust you to have the position back."

"You're not going to fight?"

"Fight what? You, Leslie, and David will outvote

Kimberly and me. I told Kimberly to stay home with Patrick. There's no reason for either of us to attend."

Sebastian flipped another page. "You sound so sure."

"Shouldn't I be?"

Sebastian tossed the papers down. "You're right. I will take over. David and Leslie will vote my way. That doesn't mean you should stay home and sulk like a child. It also doesn't mean you have no position within the company. There's enough work for both of us."

Evelyn folded her arms under her breasts and glared at him. "I ran it alone. You can do the same."

"It doesn't have to be this way." Sebastian could tell she wanted to argue more, but she had a pained look on her face. He thought, just for a second, that she might be manipulating him, but then dismissed it. "What's wrong?"

Evelyn ignored the small spasm caused by the tension from her panic attack. It wasn't anything to get worked up over. "It's nothing. Just a twinge."

The room was quiet, and Evelyn didn't want to break the silence. Though the argument helped keep her mind off her troubles, the past few days she and Sebastian had gotten along fairly well. Whether it was because of Anne's presence or because they weren't at work, she didn't know. Sebastian picked up and continued reading the papers in front of him. It was difficult to pretend she didn't care about the company. She'd devoted herself to it at eighteen, even when she'd been going to school full time. In the past seven years, things had been rocky, but she'd managed to tough it out. Sebastian would do a much better job with the company, and she knew it. Still, it was hard to relinquish control. She had nothing without Brown. It was painful for her to admit it. And more painful to admit it was her fault.

"I'll help you," Evelyn said softly from where she sat.

"Why?" Sebastian hated the suspicions he had, but he wanted to know why she was willing to help him. If she thought he'd allow her to keep her position and give him orders in return for her help, she could forget it.

Evelyn got to her feet. "So suspicious of my motives. It's simple, Sebastian. I don't have much of a choice. I can either cooperate with you or find another job. Since I have no other skills, and no one else will hire a cripple in a position of power, I don't have many options. Without my job at Brown, I might as well finish the job the cliff started five years ago. I've nothing else."

Sebastian rose and rounded the table to tower over her. "You don't believe that. Don't think for a second that I'll allow you to manipulate me by making me feel sorry for you."

Evelyn wanted to hit him in the shin with her cane but refrained. "Think about it, Sebastian. What else do I have? I don't have my own home. I don't have friends anymore. I can barely take care of myself. I have stupid panic attacks in the middle of the night. I freak out over little things. I can't even clean up a mess when I make one."

Sebastian listened while her voice rose. "You have friends and family. You have people who love you. If you have this last surgery, you can take care of yourself."

Evelyn looked as if he'd hit her. "You've spent too much time with my family. Let me guess, you've been elected to try to talk sense into stubborn, pigheaded me. Forget it. If my grandfather's threats didn't work, your stupid arguments won't either."

"I could fire you." Sebastian saw her hand clench into a fist. "Don't even try. I'm a lot bigger than you."

Evelyn watched as Sebastian's fierce features filled with anger. She wouldn't let him intimidate her like this. "You can't fire me. You need me. You just said so."

"Yes, I did. But I can get by without you. I want your help. I don't necessarily have to have it. I ran Brown five years ago. I can do it again."

Evelyn dropped back into the chair. She wasn't up for this. "I said I'd help you. Why do you have to question me? Why do you have to argue even when you get your way?"

"I don't trust you. I'd think the reason would be obvious." Sebastian watched as several emotions passed through Evelyn. Then her face settled on what looked like dejection.

"Forget it, then. If you can't trust me to do as I say, then there's no point in my coming back."

"I know you'll do what's best for the company. It's your motives I don't trust." He sat on the coffee table in front of her. He pushed a few papers out of his way and then leaned forward to see Evelyn's face close up. "I can't let you keep running the company now that I own part of it. I've told you I won't take orders from you."

"No, you won't. We can't be partners in this either. So, you win. Just don't expect me to grovel or suck up. It's not in me any more than it's in you."

"I don't want supplication. And, no, I don't suppose we can be business partners, either." It was the other kind of partnership that he was unsure about. She looked vulnerable sitting hunched over in the overstuffed chair. This feeling of wanting to protect her was unsettling.

"What do you want? You probably don't even know." Evelyn asked him when she saw his features relax. When he wasn't scowling at her, he was almost handsome.

Sebastian agreed. "I'm not sure. For now, I'll settle for you assisting me as John assists you. John has been a big help. You were smart to give him the job."

Evelyn found she could find some humor in the situation. "John figures I did it so I could keep an eye on him. He thinks I don't approve of his marrying my sister. His being your nephew was probably another black mark as far as he's concerned. He figures I wouldn't hire your nephew unless I had ulterior motives. To be honest, he's done a wonderful job. I gave him the job because I knew he would. And since he was dead set on marrying Kimberly, I figured it was a good way to make sure they could support themselves. Kimberly was still in college when they married, and John had been working at Brown."

"Do you approve?" He wanted to know.

"Well, sure, once I knew he wasn't dating Leslie. He loves her, and Kimberly loves him. They're lucky things worked out so well between them. He's a wonderful husband, and he's a wonderful father. Kimberly is very happy. What more could an older sister ask for?"

"What about you? Anne and Kimberly think you've been hiding out here. They say you don't do anything but work." He remembered Kimberly and Anne telling him at the party yesterday that Evelyn hadn't been out on a date since

Andrew.   Five years was a long time.   He'd been uncomfortable discussing Evelyn's personal life but not enough to ask them not to tell him. He knew the relief he felt at her not being involved with anyone was completely misplaced.

Evelyn refused to answer the question. "My personal life is my affair."

"No affairs, as far as I can tell."

"Why do you care, Sebastian? Would you want to date a woman like me? I can't have children because I can't take care of them. I can't be a good wife. I can't even be a decent girlfriend. Would you want to take on the task?"

Sebastian heard the suppressed anger. He understood, but she was wrong. "If I cared enough, yes, I would. Any man would if he cared enough."

Shock caused her jaw to drop. Then she closed it with a snap. "This argument is stupid and irrelevant. Do you want my help with the company or not?"

"Yes, I do. You can start by attending the meeting tomorrow."

"What will that accomplish, other than making me look like the loser?"

"It will show that you care more about the company and its interests than your pride." Sebastian gathered up the papers and left Evelyn to think about it on her own.

It probably wasn't the wisest decision, but he was frustrated with her and himself. He'd only been living here a week. If he was this wound up after eight days, then he was going to be in trouble if he kept hanging around. But he'd promised Anne he'd stay with Evelyn while she took her trip. Anne was just as wound up as everyone else. She'd buried her husband only a month before, and she wasn't even close to accepting it. He'd heard her quiet weeping more than once since he'd arrived. He'd let her be, hoping that he was doing the right thing by letting her be alone with her grief.

But he couldn't leave Evelyn alone as he had Anne. Anne was a lot stronger than Evelyn. Five years ago he wouldn't have believed it, but he did now. Knowing now that Evelyn wasn't as hard and cold as he'd thought, he figured she'd be at the meeting tomorrow. She'd vote her and Kimberly's shares in her favor, then accept defeat. Or so he hoped.

* * *

The meeting was already in progress when Evelyn arrived. She'd heard Sebastian getting ready to leave early that morning. She'd remained in bed, listening. She'd not slept much, but it wasn't the earlier panic of the day that had kept her awake. She'd spent the night thinking about what she was going to do. She hadn't known if she could put aside her pride and do what was best for Brown. She'd come to a decision when she'd heard Sebastian rev his car engine in anger and tear out of the driveway. He'd told her to be up and ready, and he'd drive her into the office. She'd hidden in her room, half afraid he might come and fetch her, regardless of her decision. He hadn't.

Perhaps that was why she'd come to the decision she'd come to. He didn't try to force her into doing as he wanted. He let her make her own choice. No one in the family let her do that anymore. They all interfered; all gave her their opinions on what was best. Sebastian had put them on equal footing, so to speak, and she was grateful to him.

So, she'd gotten out of bed and put on her best summer suit. The white sheath dress fell well past her knees. The fitted jacket with the black embroidery on the hem was a favorite. The straps on her flat sandals were a bright pink that garnered attention. She pulled her hair up into a twist, letting a few tendrils escape to tease her cheeks. She felt good today. Her hip and back weren't bothering her too much, and she felt more in control than she had in a long time. Sebastian had given her this. For the first time, in a very long time, she felt like she had a choice. Now standing outside the conference room, she knew she'd made the right one.

Lenora Whitenstall rose from her desk. "Ms. Bennett. The meeting began a few minutes ago."

Evelyn flashed her secretary a friendly smile. "I know. I was running a little late. Could you get the door for me?"

Lenora smiled back and did as requested. She announced Evelyn. "Ms. Bennett has just arrived."

Everyone in the room turned to her. Department heads were gathered around the table. Sebastian was at the head of it. He rose as she entered the room. David rose as well, and John came around to pull out a chair for her.

"Thank you, John." Evelyn sat carefully in the seat and was grateful when John pushed it in for her. Scooting in chairs was never graceful when she did it, even when the chair was on wheels.

David sat while he spoke. "We weren't expecting you to

show."

"I know. But as I'm still officially in charge, I feel it is the prudent thing to do."

Sebastian remained standing. "We were discussing some changes that I think need to be implemented. We were going to vote at the end of the meeting."

"That's fine." She accepted the copy of the new proposals and ran through them. She hid a smile. There were a few things in the proposal that she had suggested before. Howard had vetoed her ideas and sided with David on them. Howard had been old-fashioned when it came to his business, and he hadn't always been willing to make radical changes. Evelyn had understood when he'd sided with David. Business was business, after all, and Howard had told her and David more than once it wasn't personal.

Not every idea in the proposal was one she'd thought of, and his ideas were very good, although she did have a few doubts here and there. She'd tried her best to do what was right, but she'd been wrong on several occasions. David, despite his unwillingness to run the company, had many good ideas on how things should be done. He just didn't want to be responsible for implementing them.

"Are we voting on the proposal?" Evelyn knew the answer but looked over at Sebastian anyway.

"If I take over the seat, there will be a discussion but no vote. I'm open to suggestions and changes if someone disagrees with my ideas."

Unlike me, she thought, but didn't speak it out loud. She was well aware that her stubbornness had caused more than one problem over the years. But it had been just as useful as well. She remained silent during the rest of the meeting, listening carefully to the ideas and explanations that Sebastian was making. David and John put their thoughts into the conversation but didn't add much. The few department heads were nodding or shaking their heads as Sebastian spoke, but few interrupted. Sebastian was clear and concise. There were few questions to be asked that he hadn't already covered.

Sebastian watched as Evelyn took out a pen and made notes on her copy of his proposal. He didn't know what she was thinking, or why she'd opted to come. She'd not been ready when he'd left the house that morning. He thought he'd been unsuccessful in getting her cooperation. Now that she was here, he expected her to be sullen or argumentative. This silence on her part was unsettling. He'd never considered himself to be susceptible to nerves, but he was having a bout right now. Her face was composed, and she looked as if she were listening.

"Are there any other questions?" No one had any, and they shook their heads. Sebastian watched as Evelyn made a few markings and set the proposal to the side. "In that case, there's only one thing left. As all of you are aware, I now own a fifth of the company. Howard Bennett left the rest of the company to his four grandchildren."

There was a bit of murmuring from the department heads, but nothing Sebastian said was a surprise. Everyone knew that Evelyn and Sebastian were going for the same position, and there was no question of how things would turn out. The dissension between Evelyn and David was not a secret.

Evelyn picked up the proposal and folded it. When she put it in her bag and got to her feet, the room was silent. She looked over at Sebastian. "As I'm still in charge, I'll handle the vote."

Evelyn looked at David. "David votes Leslie's shares. I vote Kimberly's." She looked over at Sebastian. "All those in favor of Sebastian, raise your hand."

The group looked up as Evelyn raised her hand along with Sebastian and David. Evelyn smiled. "Congratulations, Sebastian. The meeting is adjourned."

Conversation flowed freely as Evelyn slipped from the room. She headed for her office after she nodded at Lenora.

The click of her sandals was met with John's heavier footsteps. "What are you doing, Evelyn?"

Evelyn looked over at John. "I'm uniting the company. What does it look like I'm doing? I realize all of you think I'm unreasonable and unable to see the big picture. You think that I can't set my pride aside long enough to do what's right for everyone, instead of what's right just for me."

"No one said—" John stopped when Evelyn turned on him.

"I know what you haven't said. I also know what you have said. And I know how you feel about me and the way I run this company. I was in charge, and as such, I had an obligation to do what was right for the entire company. As far as I'm concerned, Sebastian O'Connor is the best man for the job. The company needs new direction. And since he has previous experience with the company, he not only brings fresh ideas but also the experience to implement them. What more can Brown ask for?"

Evelyn entered her office. Sebastian's suit coat hung on the hook. His coffee cup was sitting on her desk. She shouldn't have been surprised to see them, but she was. She'd known he'd been here all week, but she hadn't known he'd taken over her office in her absence. "I see he made himself at home."

Some of her confidence started to drop. She turned to see Sebastian opening her office door. David was behind him. "I see you've moved right in. Should I clear out my desk?"

Sebastian ignored her sarcasm. "What are you doing?"

"I was going to catch up on what I'd missed this past week only to find I've been booted out of my office. So, I suppose I'll go home if I'm not needed here after all."

David interrupted as he came into the office. "Evelyn, I don't know what to say. Why did you vote for Sebastian? I mean, you knew it was useless to fight him, but I thought you would, anyway."

"Maybe that's why I did it. Maybe I'm tired of being predictable."

"Bullshit. I know you better than that. Why didn't you fight?"

David's response had briefly shocked her into silence. Evelyn squared her shoulders. "It would have been a mistake to keep me in charge."

She sounded so sure, Sebastian thought. He didn't know what was going on in her pretty little head, but he'd give anything for even a small glimpse. "Would all of you leave Evelyn and me alone for a few minutes?"

David and John left the room without argument. Evelyn wasn't surprised. Sebastian was in charge now, but it was odd. When she'd been in charge, they never gave in without an argument first. Evelyn sat in the chair that was in front of the desk, not behind it. It made her position clear, even if it was not the one she wanted. She'd agreed to submit and let Sebastian run the show. If her office made his victory complete, well, she decided she could concede it as well. She still owned a fifth of the company, and she would find a niche for herself.

Instead of getting behind the desk, Sebastian took the chair beside Evelyn. She looked surprised by the move, but he was more shocked by hers. "Why did you back me?"

Evelyn didn't need to think of her answer but took a moment to gather her thoughts. "You know I haven't done a great job. I like to pretend that if I just worked harder, I could control it and make the business a success. But some things are better left to others. I gave it a lot of thought. I don't want you to think I gave up without thinking through what I wanted to do. But you were right. I needed to set my pride aside and do what was best for everyone else. It's best if I back you instead of fighting you. The battle would have been a loss for me no matter what. It seemed as if I should make my own decisions about my future. I could back you one hundred percent, or I could resign completely. I can't resign for several reasons."

Sebastian relaxed. She meant it. "You have several good reasons to remain. I suppose I'm the only negative."

Evelyn shrugged. "I've taken orders from you before. I vowed never to do so again since you couldn't do the same, but some vows are best broken. I've decided it won't be so bad. Ultimately, I wasn't in charge anyway. Grandfather was in charge. I was here in the office, but he had the final say. I hope you know your proposal for some of those changes would have horrified him."

"But they don't horrify you." It was a statement, not a question. Now that she'd accepted defeat, and quite gracefully, she was being reasonable.

"No. Not to sound completely conceited, but there were one or two ideas in that proposal I'd put forth before. Grandfather and David shot me down."

"Did that happen often?" Sebastian couldn't tell from the paperwork how often Evelyn had been allowed to accept actual control. It seemed she'd never really run it on her own.

"Fifty-fifty, I guess. Grandfather didn't always side with David. David has good ideas, but they're not always practical."

Sebastian thought it out and then grinned at her. "David would probably drop dead if he heard you say that."

"David stood by me when he had to. He wasn't always happy about it. David and I don't hate each other. We're not feuding or anything so dramatic. We just don't always agree, and we have conflicting personalities. Grandfather said we keep each other on our toes. But just so you know, we'll do the same to you."

Evelyn rose and grabbed her purse. "See that my things are moved into another office. I'm going to take the rest of this week off. There are some things I'd like to do this week at home, and with the new transition of control, now is a good time for me to let you take over without my interference. And believe me, I'd interfere no matter what my intentions are. I'll be back next week, and then we can decide what it is exactly that you want me to do."

"I'll get my own office. I was only using yours to make things easier for John."

Evelyn disagreed. "Keep it. John is the assistant to the president. Now that's you, so I guess that makes it your office now. Just make sure my paintings are hung in a new room. They belonged to my grandfather, and I want them."

Sebastian looked over to the oil paintings that hung on the wall. He knew they'd belonged to Howard. He had always liked dark, ugly oil paintings of rough seas. If Evelyn wanted them, she was welcome to them. He had thought she'd prefer some watercolors of flowers or something, but he was getting used to misjudging her. She'd surprised him again today. He watched as she left the office. He leaned back in his chair and contemplated the future: the company's and his own.

* * *

Evelyn sat under the awning and watched the rain drain off the sides. The old wrought iron and glass patio set was still holding up. The set was a gift to her grandfather from Anne. The garden in the back of the house had always been the pride and joy of her grandmother, Bernice. When she died, her grandfather had kept it up. Anne had taken over the task when she'd married Howard. Evelyn loved the changes Anne had made. Her grandmother had loved the garden and had obsessed over every inch of it. Anne simply enjoyed it.

The garden, like so much else around the house, had simply fallen into disrepair. There wasn't enough money to waste on flowers when two people in the house required extensive medical care. Sebastian had meant what he'd said. He had already started clearing out some of the overgrowth this past week. Surprisingly, just clearing the garden paths made a huge difference.

Evelyn was still watching the rain when she felt a presence behind her. Anne looked like she had just come in from being out. Her long hair was in a twist, and she was wearing one of her best dresses. "Just get back?"

Anne smoothed her skirt and took a seat. She was quiet for a moment while she contemplated Evelyn. She had on a loose pair of cotton pants. It was rare that she bothered with anything but dresses. "I'm worried about you."

That surprised her. Since the showdown at Brown earlier this morning, Evelyn had been surprisingly cheerful. Perhaps Anne didn't know what to do with her when she wasn't in a dour mood. "How come? I'm outside getting some fresh air. I didn't have a repeat episode last night, and I haven't touched a drop of alcohol, nor have I taken a pill. You should enjoy the reprieve."

"It's not your health I'm concerned about at the moment. Why did you back Sebastian today?"

"John told Kimberly, and then she called you, I take it." Gossip ran fast in this family, Evelyn mused. It had only taken three hours for Anne to confront her about what she'd done today. But then she shouldn't be surprised;

Kimberly took an avid interest in all aspects of the family's daily life now that she was a stay-at-home mom.

"She can't figure out why you did it. John came home for lunch and told her. He said you voted for Sebastian to take over the company. I thought you would never give up control."

Evelyn watched the rain while she tried to answer honestly about something she wasn't completely sure of. "For one, I didn't have much choice. I would have been outvoted. Second, it seemed like the right thing to do at about six o'clock this morning. If Brown is going to completely recover, it needs a strong leader. One who knows the company, one who has the respect of the employees and other local businessmen. Having a healthy, not a disabled, leader is probably for the best."

"Does this mean you'll have the surgery? If you have someone else to run the company, you can take the time." Anne knew she was pushing her luck.

"Can't pass up the opportunity, can you? No, this does not mean I'm getting the surgery. It just means that now maybe I have other options I can pursue." Evelyn looked at Anne. "I'm not always happy at Brown. I know you know that. But most of the time I'm satisfied with it, and I think that despite the troubles, I've done a good job."

"You've done an excellent job. And, of course, I know you didn't want to run Brown. You did it for Howard. He knew it, too. He was as grateful as he was guilty of pushing you." Anne took Evelyn's hand. She was surprised to find it trembling.

"I don't know what I want. Ever since Grandfather died

and the will was read, I've been confused. I probably argued with Sebastian more out of habit than genuine anger. I just wish Leslie, David, or Kimberly would take more interest in the daily work at Brown. I wouldn't feel so much pressure."

Anne released Evelyn's hand. "Evie, you know everyone in the family is grateful to you for taking over, even David. You did it out of family pressure and a sense of responsibility. It might be time to move on. Maybe you should sell your share."

Evelyn heard another set of footsteps as her temper flared. She didn't care if she had an audience. "Why don't you just ask me to cut off my good leg? How in the world am I going to take care of myself if I don't keep my share of Brown?"

Anne tried for a soothing tone, startled by the vehemence. She couldn't understand Evelyn's outburst, especially since she'd just said she would have the chance to find other opportunities. "You just admitted you weren't happy there. You just said you wanted to find something else."

"Being happy and being content are not the same thing. I'm quite content to work at Brown. I just said I could see about other things. I meant in addition to working. Who do you suppose is going to pay all my medical bills if I give up my share? Grandfather is dead. My mother is dead. Brown is the only source of income I have. And I'm not a child anymore. My happiness or lack thereof shouldn't be an issue for anyone but me."

Sebastian hovered in the doorway. Both Evelyn and Anne knew he was there. Evelyn was pretending she didn't care if he overheard, and Anne was looking embarrassed.

Sebastian was the one who responded. "There's no reason to quit or sell out, Evelyn, if you don't want to."

"No, there isn't." The words were an agreement, but they sounded like an argument.

Anne tried to calm her. "Evie, I'm sorry. I just thought that when you said you wanted to make some changes, getting away from Brown would be good for you. You could buy the horses you want."

Evelyn got to her feet. "Don't ever mention horses in my presence again."

Sebastian moved to the side as Evelyn brushed past him. He watched Evelyn take the stairs faster than she should. He was beginning to wonder if she was afraid of the horses she had once loved so much. "Her temper flares pretty fast."

Anne sighed. "I know. She looked happy today. I guess I couldn't take it at face value. She's rarely happy these days. She finds little joy in life."

"She leads too insular a life. From all I've seen, she only associates with her family, and only if it's you or Kimberly. She has no friends, no outside interests. She didn't use to be so isolated." Sebastian remembered Evelyn five years ago. She'd had no shortage of friends or interests. She played tennis and she had her horse. She attended charity and business functions. She might have led a rich girl's existence, but she at least had a lifestyle to maintain. He couldn't figure out her self-imposed prison.

"There were a few friends who hung around after the fiasco of her wedding. There were fewer who hung around after the accident, but the ones who did, Evelyn sent away.

She wanted nothing to do with them. She claimed they were stupid, and they never shut up. She insulted most of them, and they gave up. She was always closer to Kimberly than her friends. Even Kimberly avoided her most of the first two years. Then when Evelyn was working and finally not so angry all the time, Kimberly started hanging around more. As far as the rest of her friends, Evie has never bothered trying to reconcile with them."

"Did she tell you she backed me today?"

"No. Kimberly called me. Evie knew right away Kimberly was the one. I suppose the family is predictable."

Sebastian took Evelyn's seat. "She caused quite a stir when she voted for me. Claims it was the right thing to do."

"Let me tell you something, Sebastian. I'm not sure Evie does anything because it's the right thing to do. You should feel honored she did this time. One thing I learned from Evie's therapist is that she has become extremely self-centered. She worries about herself and not much else. Quite frankly, I think it's time she was jarred. She needs to expand her horizons and get back into normal life. I just wish she weren't so stubborn about getting the surgery. She could be almost normal if she had it. She wouldn't be able to take back up tennis, but she could perhaps get back in the saddle if she took it easy."

Sebastian thought about that. "You know, I think I have an idea."

"What?" Anne placed both hands on the table and leaned closer.

Sebastian couldn't help himself. He laughed. "I'm not going to tell you. I don't know if I can get her to go along with it. In case you haven't noticed, Evelyn and I aren't exactly the best of friends."

"No, you're not. But despite what Evelyn thinks, she could use a good friend. And a little male companionship wouldn't hurt either. The ugly situation with Andrew took second place to the accident, but I know Evelyn dwells on it. She hasn't shown any interest in any of the men Howard and Kimberly introduced her to. She likes to say she doesn't want to be a burden, but it's just an excuse. If she wanted to, she could change that."

"The surgery? You know, maybe everyone should lay off the surgery thing. She might make the decision all on her own if her family stopped treating her like an invalid. I've been here a little over a week and all of you treat her as if she were a child."

Anne gasped. "We do not. She just needs someone to take care of her. We're her family."

Sebastian tried to soften his words, but soothing females wasn't always easy for him. "Look, she might need help with daily stuff, but her brain works just fine. She's an intelligent woman. If you leave her to make her own decisions, she'll eventually make the right one. But the one that's right for her, not her family."

Anne relented and leaned back in her chair. "I know you're right. It's frustrating. She's so stubborn, and she doesn't always ask for help when she needs it."

"Maybe because she doesn't need help. She has a bad hip and some damage to her back. I imagine it's a bit more extensive than that, but her arms and other leg work just fine. Everyone has babied her so much she's never going to learn to take care of herself if everyone does it for her. Evelyn was an independent person when she was younger. She could be again if all of you would let her. She'd probably be more willing to ask for assistance when she needs it if she isn't always being crowded."

"You'll be able to test your theory while I'm gone. Kimberly is too busy with Patrick to pay as much attention to Evie as she usually would. I won't be here to interfere." Anne was silent for a moment and then had to ask. "Do you think she'll decide to have the surgery if we leave her alone?"

"She is capable of changing her mind about a decision she's made. She made her own decision today. I let her be, and she backed me without any prompting. She'd probably be mad if she thought she was being manipulated, but as I said, she's intelligent. She may feel that surgery isn't right for her. But with proper motivation, she might have it done."

Anne rose. "I hope you're right. I'm going to start on dinner."

Sebastian headed into the garden. He needed to work off some of this restless energy.

Chapter Eight

It took about an hour before he started settling into the task. Sebastian ripped out several more branches of the rose bush that had overgrown. He had dozens of small scratches on his forearms, but he hardly noticed them. It had been too long since he'd done manual labor. During his travels throughout Europe, he'd lived in an assortment of hotels and furnished flats. It had been a long time since he'd lived in a house. The last house he'd lived in had been with his wife and children. He missed it.

Some things were meant to be, and he believed that. His ex-wife was happy, and so were his children. Summer vacation was coming up soon, and he was looking forward to spending time with them. He hadn't seen them since last Thanksgiving. He'd visited them, and they had enjoyed the large luxury hotel. As soon as he had some free time, he was going to find himself a house. He wanted to be able to have his children visit, and he didn't want it to be in a hotel again, although his children wouldn't mind.

Daniel was eleven, and he was growing so much. Sebastian was always amazed. He'd bet that Daniel would grow taller than his own five-eleven. Nine-year-old Lucy was still small. Becky was almost as tall as he was, but Lucy wouldn't reach her mother's height unless she had a huge growth spurt during her teens. The thought of having a teenage daughter made him shudder. But he had time before he had to worry.

Sebastian's gaze wandered toward the pasture that ran alongside the house. Lucy had been too little to appreciate it, but Sebastian remembered how much Daniel had been in awe of Evelyn's horse. It was a shame the horse was gone. But Sebastian's friend was raising horses, and he'd have to see if he wouldn't mind if he brought the kids out. They'd get a kick out of Rick's horses. His wife, Angie, would love to see them, too. She had a baby of her own now. Rick had called and told him about the birth of his daughter, Mary. Time seemed to be getting away from him. She had to be close to two now.

Sebastian took hold of another branch and yanked. He really wouldn't mind finding another wife and settling down. Domesticity was starting to look pretty darn good the closer he got to forty. He was only two years from that. If he was going to have more kids, he needed to get a move on. But he had to work. He knew from his relationship with Becky that wives weren't likely to tolerate a man's obsession with his job in the long term. She'd demand equal or greater attention. Sebastian wondered if he'd be able to devote more time to his family than his job if given a second chance. His track record in that department was sadly lacking.

"Sebastian?" Evelyn hovered in the doorway.

Sebastian was startled from his thoughts. Evelyn was standing silhouetted in the doorway. She was wearing a pair of white cotton pants and a pale blue t-shirt. It was the most relaxed he'd seen her. He glanced at his watch and realized he'd been out here for an hour. "Yeah?"

Evelyn cleared her throat. "Look, I just wanted to apologize. I have a hard time controlling my temper."

"It's Anne you should be apologizing to." Sebastian leaned back on his heels and watched her.

Evelyn shifted uncomfortably. "I did already. She likes to accept the blame when I have my outbursts, and it makes her uncomfortable when I apologize. Grandfather had no such problem."

"Come out and have a seat. You can pot some of these flowers as punishment."

Evelyn warily took a seat at the table when Sebastian motioned her over. "I don't know much about plants."

Sebastian dumped a pot in front of her and a bag of soil. "Then it's time you learned."

Evelyn sat patiently while Sebastian showed her the proper way to handle the plants. Her fingers were muddy, and she had gobs of dirt under her nails by the time she was finished. But the activity soothed her nerves, and she was comfortable and cheerful again. It felt as if a huge weight had been lifted off her shoulders. She had Sebastian to thank.

"I'm glad you're taking over the company," Evelyn said absently as she patted more soil around the base of a small bundle of roses.

Sebastian rose and brushed the dirt from his knees. He watched her face carefully, looking for any sign of how she felt. She had a small smile on her lips, much to his surprise. She looked happy playing in the dirt. He'd expected her to argue with him about it, but she hadn't. "You mean that, don't you?"

Evelyn pushed the pot back and swiped at the dirt on her hands. "I never thought I'd say it, but yes. I just wanted you to know that whatever your reasons are, I'm grateful. You know, after I made my decision this morning, I felt good about it. I haven't felt that way in a long time. My therapist kept telling me I need to relieve some of my stress. Brown and my grandfather's wishes caused a lot of my tension. I'm not completely sure what I'm going to do, but at least I don't have to worry about screwing up all the time. I tried to run the company, but I had no experience. You were probably right to refuse to take orders from me. I had no idea what I was doing. But it gave me a goal; a reason to get up every day when I thought I had no reason to. Maybe I've realized that I don't need Brown to give my life purpose anymore."

Sebastian came over and sat down across from her. "There are all sorts of things you can do at Brown that don't involve you making all the difficult decisions. You're smart and you've learned a lot in the four years you were in charge. Maybe if you're left to your own devices, instead of having to answer to Howard and David, you'll figure out what it is you want. Professionally, anyway. I can't guarantee personal satisfaction. Work is a poor substitute for friends and family. I should know."

"But you have it all. You have your job and your friends and your family. You found balance."

Sebastian could only sit and stare. She was right. Somewhere along the line, he had found balance in his life. He was ready now to fill it with other things besides work.

Once the situation at Brown was stabilized, he'd have plenty of time to pursue other interests.

They sat companionably outside and finished potting the plants Sebastian had uprooted. They would be transferred to either the flower boxes on the back porch or to the ones on the front of the house. It looked barren without all the growth he had gotten used to seeing years before. Evelyn might not be able to get down on her hands and knees, but she could wield a hose and take care of the watering. Gardening was a nice, soothing hobby, and Evelyn needed some balance in her life. Sebastian was grinning to himself. It seemed he had appointed himself her keeper, too.

"You seem quite pleased." Evelyn gave him a quizzical look but didn't question him. He had been carrying the pots she'd filled back out onto the patio and arranged them neatly. "You'll probably have to hire someone to take care of the lawn, though. We don't have a lawnmower, and there is too much grass for a push one."

"I'll call around. You could use a landscaper, but since you can't afford it, you'll have to live with my amateurish work."

Evelyn found herself leaping to his defense. "You have done an amazing job. Poor Anne can't get to it. You've brought it back to life again."

High praise indeed, Sebastian mused. Evelyn was actually blushing. He didn't think he'd ever seen her blush. He walked over to her. "Thanks."

Evelyn looked up. He was looming over her. It was making her heart beat faster. Her lips parted as if she were going to say something, but nothing came to her.

"Dinner's ready." Anne came back out to the patio. She stopped in her tracks. Evelyn and Sebastian were staring at each other like they'd never seen one another before. She was backtracking when Sebastian broke the contact and looked directly at her.

"Thanks, Anne. We're both starved." He saw the way Anne was glancing back and forth between the two of them. He knew exactly how she felt. Something very intimate had passed between him and Evelyn. It had been like nothing he'd known before. He'd had a sudden urge to kiss Evelyn in the garden, with the scent of dirt and flowers clinging to her. But Anne had interrupted them. He would have kissed her, he told himself. It might have been a mistake, but he would have done it. Instead, he gave Evelyn one last look before he went inside to wash up. She was still staring at him, a look of confusion on her face. Unable to help himself, he leaned down and placed a light kiss on her forehead.

Evelyn rubbed the spot his lips had touched as she watched Sebastian head inside. She wasn't sure what had just happened. She did know that at that moment she would have given anything for him to have taken her in his arms and kissed her. She wanted to feel those long, muscular arms wrapped around her. She wanted to feel her body pressed close to his, her breasts crushed flat against his chest, his body supporting hers. Her body was throbbing lightly in response to the fantasy.

"Are you all right?" Anne realized that Evelyn hadn't moved.

Her voice sounded hoarse when she spoke. "Fine."

"Go on and get cleaned up for dinner. It's in fifteen minutes." Anne retreated, leaving Evelyn alone on the patio.

It took five minutes before Evelyn was steady enough to go inside. Dinner would be a strained affair, she was sure. Especially if she didn't get a grip on her out-of-control emotions.

So much for a strained affair, Evelyn thought twenty minutes later. Sebastian and Anne were having an extended conversation on pretty much anything that came up. Their shared past was more evident at this moment than it ever had been before. Evelyn had known they were friends, but Anne seemed more relaxed today and open.

Evelyn knew how very sad Anne had been feeling. The weight of her grief was hard to bear sometimes. She missed her husband so very much. Evelyn could only imagine what it would feel like to bury one's husband. But Anne's soft weeping in the night told its own story. But Evelyn couldn't seem to cry. Despite the pain she was feeling about her grandfather's death, she hadn't shed one tear. Evelyn couldn't remember the last time she'd cried. As uncomfortable as he was with tears, her grandfather had told her it wasn't natural for a female not to cry. Evelyn, knowing how he'd react, kept her feelings on the subject to herself. Evelyn hadn't felt like a woman in a long time. Sometimes, she didn't even feel like a person. It was hard to describe the empty, hollow feeling inside to other people. Her therapist seemed to understand how empty she felt. But in the end, she hadn't been able to alleviate it. He had told her that she needed to find something to fill the voids in her life if she wanted to be happy.

Funny how even work couldn't fill the void. But it had filled a need in her: to feel useful and productive.

Evelyn suddenly realized what a spoiled brat she had been since Sebastian arrived.

Evelyn smiled down into her pasta. It was okay to be a spoiled brat at twenty. One was just shaking off childhood completely at that age. But she was twenty-five now, and to be perfectly honest, she'd aged more than five years in that time. Her body certainly felt much older. Wouldn't Anne and Kimberly be shocked if they knew that deep down, she wondered if she should have the surgery? They would probably die from the shock. But on most days, Evelyn didn't want it done. At this moment, sitting beside two very healthy people, Sebastian mostly, she desperately wanted to be normal again.

Evelyn was unaware of the scrutiny. Sebastian saw the small smile on her lips and wished to know what it was she was thinking about. It was rare she smiled. He might have only been with her a little over a week, but he'd figured that out fast. Now that she seemed to have pretty much given up arguing with him, she'd shrunk back into herself.

He didn't like it one bit. But like so many other things, he didn't know what to do about it. They weren't exactly friends. But at least they weren't enemies either.

"You look like you're plotting." Anne interrupted Sebastian's runaway thoughts.

Sebastian gave her a cheeky grin. "I was."

Anne smiled back. Then it faded. "I wanted to ask you if you could go through Howard's desk."

The room was silent for a second. Sebastian gave Anne

an understanding look. "No problem. I wanted to ask you if I could go through some of his papers anyway. There are a few things at the office that have me asking questions. There's mentions of two rival companies but not much actual paperwork."

Evelyn set her fork down. "Which two companies?"

Sebastian forked up another bite. Finally, he spoke. "There was this company called Global Chem-Lab. They were in the paperwork for only three years. Then came a company that popped up called Crown."

Evelyn spoke up. "Global Chem-Lab went under two years ago and filed for bankruptcy. Crown came into existence about that time. Eventually, Crown bought out most of Global's remaining assets. And the name isn't coincidental. The 'b' in Brown was switched to a 'c' and Crown came about. Many of the employees at Global went to Crown when the troubles were first made known to the public."

Sebastian digested that tidbit for a second. Evelyn would know everything that went on. "According to the paperwork at the office, many of our clients went to Global after I left. That can't have been a coincidence."

Evelyn pushed her plate back. She couldn't eat and talk about this. "It wasn't. A large portion of the troubles began after you left. But it wasn't just you. Andrew worked for Global. He knew a lot about Brown's operations because of me and knew who many of our clients were."

Sebastian pushed back his plate, too. "Are you saying he used you to get information about Brown so he could sell it"

"No. It was just a bonus, as far as I can tell. He used the

information about Brown's operations to get a promotion at Global. Put him in a higher position of power. Then while the company was struggling, he created Crown. He set up his new headquarters not that far from Global's headquarters. Then earlier this year, he moved his business headquarters here to California, and the offices are now fully up and running."

Anne spoke up. "Evelyn, let's not discuss Andrew anymore. You only get upset." Anne shot a look at Sebastian that pleaded with him to drop it.

Sebastian got the message. He didn't want to upset Anne. There would be time enough later to get the rest of the information he wanted when Anne was no longer around. There was more to the story. If Evelyn needed comforting after the conversation, he would give it to her. But something wasn't adding up here, and he needed to know. For the business and for himself. His curiosity about Evelyn and what she had gone through these last five years was becoming an obsession.

"Is there anything in particular that you're looking for in Howard's desk, or do you just want it cleaned out?" Sebastian pulled back his plate. He was still hungry. He noticed Evelyn seemed to be finished. She hadn't eaten much.

Anne spooned up another bite, worried that Evelyn wasn't doing the same. "There isn't anything in particular. I have all the bills and things. Howard couldn't take care of the finances anymore. I took over that job, so I have everything."

"I'll put anything aside that I think you should see.

Everything else I'll organize and either take to the office or box it up. How does that sound?"

Anne nodded. "That would be fine."

Evelyn folded her arms around her waist. "If you need help, I can help you. I have spent a few hours at Grandfather's desk over the last few years."

Sebastian was surprised by the offer and wasn't going to turn it down. "That would help. You should know what is what."

Evelyn excused herself and went back into the living room. She was tired again. She decided to lie down on the couch for a few minutes and close her eyes.

It was dark when she woke. There was a blanket across her body and a pillow behind her head. She hadn't meant to fall asleep.

Evelyn turned blindly and tried to see a clock. It was midnight. She'd been asleep for hours. Not surprising since it had been two days since she'd had a good night's sleep. Evelyn struggled out from underneath the covers. She looked around but didn't see her cane.

"Great," Evelyn muttered to herself. Usually, Anne made sure it was nearby. Evelyn remembered walking into the living room. She must have left the cane in the dining room. The thought of stumbling through the darkened house made her mutter louder.

"Problem?" Sebastian opened the study door.

Evelyn let out a little surprised shriek. "What are you doing awake?" She certainly hadn't expected him to be awake at midnight.

"I lost track of time." Sebastian ran a hand over his face.

He was tired now that he wasn't going through the desk. He'd been so intent on reading the papers in Howard's desk that he didn't realize it was so late.

Evelyn began heading toward the dining room. With the light from the office, it was easier to see her way. "It's late. Sorry for falling asleep on you. I didn't mean to."

"Where are you going?" Sebastian left the light burning and followed Evelyn.

"I must have left my cane by the table. I don't like to climb the stairs without it." Evelyn hated to admit it, especially to him, but she wasn't stupid enough to tackle the stairs without added balance. She had an unreasonable fear of stairs. She had unreasonable fears about a lot of things. Her therapist said it was her fear of the future that caused most of her phobias. Evelyn wasn't going to discount that diagnosis. Her therapist was probably right.

"I'll get it for you." Sebastian put a hand on her shoulder to stop her. The flesh on her shoulders was firm. He'd bet that her upper body was a lot stronger than it used to be.

"Thanks. Anne usually leaves it within reach." Evelyn shivered a bit under his warm palm but didn't continue on her way. That hand was as good as a wall at halting her.

"She went to bed shortly after dinner. I think she wanted to be alone. I told her I'd take care of you. I forgot about the cane."

Evelyn snorted derisively. "Hard to forget it."

Sebastian turned. "It's not a bad thing, Evelyn. I don't know why it upsets you so much."

Evelyn took a step back as he came toward her. "It's hard to explain. I hate relying on it, but the alternative is worse than the cane."

Evelyn remembered well the time she couldn't walk. When she'd progressed to the walker, it had seemed like a miracle. But the feeling of accomplishment of walking with the walker had faded quickly. She'd felt like an old woman and an immobile one at that. By the time she was ready to get rid of the walker, she'd not felt any sense of accomplishment. The cane might be more attractive than the ugly metal contraption she'd been using, but it still made her feel helpless. Helplessness was a horrible feeling. Knowing she had to rely on something as fragile as a stick of wood didn't make her feel better.

The only alternative was surgery. She shuddered at the thought and blanked it out.

Sebastian halted an arm's length away. Evelyn was staring at the buttons on his shirt. He knew she didn't want to face him. She'd walked into that lawyer's office on her own power because she was ashamed of the cane. He supposed he could understand it. The family kept saying it was her pride that stood in her way. He understood pride and how important it could be to a person. He couldn't condemn her for it.

"How long have you used the cane?" Sebastian went ahead and decided to appease his curiosity about at least one thing.

"Three and half years." Evelyn remained looking at his shirt. It wasn't any easier. He had nice broad shoulders with a chest that tapered slightly to his waist. He wasn't a big, muscular man, but he was solid. This was a man you could rely on.

He had expected that it would have been longer. But then again, he supposed that after multiple surgeries, the recovery time would have been quite long. But that meant she'd gone back to work while still mostly immobile. Her will was a formidable force. "You really are amazing."

Her eyes shot to his. She couldn't see them well in the faint light, but she could see a sparkle in them. His eyes looked almost black in this light, she thought idly. "Hardly."

"You are." He moved closer. He towered over her. He forgot how slight she was. Her personality was bigger than her stature. "You came through a lot over the last five years. It made you stronger. Some people would have broken."

"I came close. Just ask Anne or Kimberly. They all were worried about me. I had a lot of support. They're the reason I came out of this at all. Had I been my mother, I probably would have found another cliff to toss myself over. As it is, they half think I did it on purpose the first time."

"Did you?" Looking at her now, he already knew the answer.

"Of course not. I was hurt and upset, but I wasn't crazy. I wasn't going to end my life over Andrew. He certainly wouldn't be worth it." She wondered why he was asking her this. And she wondered why he was standing so close. She knew if she didn't back off, she might try to start the kiss she had wanted earlier in the day.

"No, you're not crazy." Sebastian came a step closer. A slight shift and their bodies would brush.

Evelyn felt her legs turning to jelly. "I should go to bed. Are you going to get my cane for me or not?"

Sebastian heard the huskiness of her voice that she tried

to mask with a bit of anger. But buried in it was fear. He shook off his growing desire to sample her mouth and took a step back. "Yeah, I'll get it."

Evelyn took a steadying breath. She was going to have to keep her distance. She would make a fool of herself if she went through with the kiss she wanted. But how she wanted it.

Sebastian saw the glow in her eyes but ignored the invitation. He handed her the cane he was gripping fiercely in his fist.

She thanked him and headed for the stairs. She definitely wouldn't have made it without the cane. There was no strength left in her legs.

Sebastian watched to make sure she made it. He was half tempted to follow her but figured that he wouldn't follow her just up the stairs. His body was sending him another message. He wanted to follow her into her bedroom.

Because that was a stupid idea, Sebastian went back into the office. He had papers he could read. He needed to find a way to burn off this restlessness. Since it was midnight, he settled for reading. It might look silly if he were to try to garden in the dark.

An hour later, he gave up on reading and settled for a cold shower.

Chapter Nine

Sebastian was still chuckling when he hung up the phone. Daniel was quite the storyteller these days. He had heard Lucy in the background begging Daniel to hand her the phone, but Daniel was determined to relate all of his school tales of the week to his father. When Daniel informed him it was seven o'clock and it was Wednesday, he passed the phone off to his sister. Sebastian wasn't sure what was significant about it being Wednesday or why seven was an important time but figured Daniel had his reasons. Lucy then informed him that he was going to watch television. Apparently, television was more pressing than talking to his father.

Lucy spent the next half hour telling him about her Girl Scout meetings and about how her teacher fell off her chair and hit her head. His daughter was a softy. She was making a card for the teacher to tell her that she was sorry she hit her head. Lucy loved to draw flowers, and she gave them away to everybody. He had several cards she'd made for him tucked away. He heard Daniel making gagging noises in the background, ridiculing his sister for making sissy pictures. His voice could be heard saying airplanes were much cooler than flowers. Sebastian silently agreed.

But the conversation had ended, and Becky had gotten

on the phone. The conversations between the two of them were usually brief. Sebastian was beginning to realize he and his ex-wife never really talked much. The fact that their conversations were always about the children made him figure she didn't have anything she wanted to share with him. His lack of communication was just another one of her reasons for having divorced him.

Sebastian glanced into the back garden. Evelyn was reading a gardening book. It was odd to realize he never found it difficult to talk to her. Maybe it was his age; at thirty-eight, he was appreciating women more for their minds. Sebastian chuckled again. He admitted that it wasn't only Evelyn's mind he was appreciating at the moment. She was wearing a sundress again. The wind was blowing this evening, and it plastered the thin fabric to her body. He could see how much her body had filled in over the last five years. Despite the accident, she wasn't wasting away. She had firm thighs and a flat stomach. Her breasts were small but the right size for her body. Her neck was still slender, but it was softened by the hair she let hang down her back.

He bet that in ten years she'd look even better.

"Are you off the phone?" Anne came up behind Sebastian. He still had the phone in his hand but wasn't talking into it. She glanced over his shoulder. She could see Evelyn sitting on the patio. She'd been spending a lot more time outdoors since Sebastian arrived.

"Yes. Becky and I talked for a few minutes. It seems the kids are on spring break next week. Becky, her husband, and the kids were supposed to go on a trip, but something came up at work and now they can't go. Becky offered to let me take the kids next week. I know it's short notice, but I'd like to see them. I know you wanted me to keep an eye on Evelyn."

Evelyn heard her name. She turned to face them and shouted through the patio screen door. "What about Evelyn?"

"I was just telling Anne that Becky offered to let me have the kids next week, but Anne will be on her cruise."

Evelyn put two and two together. "And you promised to babysit me."

Anne frowned. "You know, Kimberly could watch the kids during the day, and they could stay here with you at night. I'm sure she wouldn't mind. Kimberly has the pool, and the kids would love the water. There's plenty of room here for them to stay."

Sebastian remembered Evelyn falling asleep on the sofa. Two rambunctious kids might be more than she could tolerate. "I'm not sure that's a good idea. I usually have my own place, and I hire a professional to watch them when I can't take time from work. Either that or I take them to a hotel."

Evelyn spoke without moving from her seat. She deliberately kept the book in front of her face as if she didn't care what they were talking about, ignoring the vague hurt she felt at his trying to keep his kids from her. She was sure she was the reason he didn't want them here. What did he think she was going to do to them?

"There's no reason they can't stay here. But I don't need a keeper. Take the kids to a hotel if you want."

"Then it's settled," Anne said briskly. "I'll call Kimberly."

Sebastian kept his eyes on Evelyn. "I have some friends nearby. They'll get a kick out of the kids. They're raising horses these days. Kids love horses as much as they love water."

Evelyn flinched at the mention of horses but kept the book stubbornly in her face. "Do whatever you want. As I said, I don't need a keeper. I'm hardly a child."

Anne grumbled. "You sure act like one sometimes. Heaven knows I have to lecture you like you were. I might not have had kids of my own, but I've been around enough of them, including Sebastian's, to know how it's done."

"If I remember correctly, Sebastian's children were well-behaved at your wedding. Having them around for a week might be a bit more of a strain than just an evening, but I don't see it as being a problem." Evelyn turned the page without having read it.

"They are good kids. But they're kids. They get into things. They cause trouble and can be very loud." Sebastian felt the need to clarify.

"So?" Evelyn answered.

"So, they'll probably disturb you." Sebastian felt like an idiot for pointing out the obvious.

"So?" Evelyn couldn't help tossing the one-word question out again.

"So, when you're trying to nap or rest, you won't get much sleep. You seem to keep yourself pretty well-rested. The house is always quiet. You don't even watch television or turn on the radio. Kids thrive on noise and chaos."

Evelyn set the book in her lap, keeping her fingers on the

page. She felt some of her earlier hurt fade. "I prefer to listen to the birds. And I enjoy reading, so I don't usually have any other distractions. Besides, the office is hardly relaxing. Next week I'll be back at work. So long as they pick up their messes and you feed them, I don't see how they'd be in the way."

Sebastian looked dubious, but he wanted to bring the kids. "Fine. I'll call Becky back and tell her I'll fly up on Friday to get them."

Anne smiled. "Wonderful. I'll get to see them before I leave. I don't leave until Sunday evening."

Sebastian had a sudden urge to ask Evelyn to fly up with him, but he knew that wasn't possible. The flight from northern California to southern Washington wasn't a long trip, but he thought it might be uncomfortable being cooped up on a plane for even a short time. But he was pleased she genuinely didn't seem to mind the idea of bringing his kids. He was curious what her reaction would be to them. From what he'd heard, she doted on Patrick. He'd seen her playing with the baby in the pool last weekend. He'd watched her the entire time she'd been in the water, laughing and splashing with her nephew. It was no wonder she'd had to take a nap. After spending the afternoon with his kids, he usually needed a nap, too.

Evelyn remained silent. She wasn't sure how Sebastian's children would react to staying here, but between Kimberly and Sebastian's friends, the children shouldn't be too bored. But Evelyn knew Kimberly would have to watch them. Evelyn grimaced. She certainly couldn't chase after two young children.

She glanced over to the empty stables. She remembered Sebastian taking the children out to see Isabel. Lucy would be too young to remember. Daniel, too, most likely. Both children had been fascinated with the animal. Evelyn knew exactly how they'd felt. She'd been dazed when she'd sat on her first horse. Isabel had been the best present she'd ever received.

Evelyn let the wistful feeling she felt run its course. Like the envy she felt when she saw how happy her sister was, she let the feeling take hold. Fighting feelings usually didn't help much. She missed the feel of a horse under her hands and body. She missed the time she spent in the stable.

Her next words were completely unexpected. "Ever think about getting a dog or a cat?"

Sebastian and Anne turned to stare at her dumbfounded. Anne was the first to speak. "You want a dog or a cat?"

Evelyn shrugged. It was a stupid idea. She turned her back on them. "No. I guess not. An animal in the house would probably just get under the cane and knock me over. You know, like all those old women who have cats that trip up their walkers and cause them to fall."

"Evelyn." Anne gave an exasperated sigh. "You're hardly an old woman. I don't see you tripping over an animal. If you want one, we could think about getting one."

"No. My mind was just wandering."

"Pretty off topic, too." Anne stood undecided. She didn't know if she should argue with Evelyn or let the subject go. Usually she argued with her, but she wasn't sure if this time she should. Anne didn't know if a pet was a good idea. But if Evelyn wanted one, she supposed she could get her one, though she wasn't thrilled with the idea.

"You could borrow one. See if you like it." Sebastian said matter-of-factly.

Evelyn picked her book back up. "It was just an idle thought. We've never had pets. Kids like pets."

"They do. Becky bought all her kids a dog last year." Sebastian followed her train of thought. Or at least he thought he did.

"I don't know if Anne would want a dog. She'd have to take it out for walks and clean up after it."

Sebastian argued. "You could take a dog for a walk. And you could clean up after it. They have contraptions for that kind of thing. But if you got a cat, it would pretty much take care of itself."

Anne spoke up. "Then I'd have to clean a litter box. I'm not sure I want to take on that task. I never had pets myself. The closest I got was a fish tank. I didn't have it long."

Evelyn interrupted, angry that she had started this. "Forget it. We've gone this long without a pet; I think we can live a little longer without one. I was just thinking the kids would like to play with an animal, but it's a bit much for only a week's visit."

Sebastian watched Evelyn's back for a few minutes. He decided he'd see if Becky would like to lend him her dog for the week.

Sebastian also decided something else. "I'm sure Kimberly won't mind watching the kids a few times, but if you don't mind, Evelyn, you could keep them here a couple of days during the week. Nothing is pressing at the office that has to be taken care of next week. We could rotate days while the kids are here."

Evelyn slammed her book down. "And just how do you suppose I keep an eye on them? Kids don't just sit still."

Anne started at the flash of temper. "They're not babies. They can play by themselves outside. And I'm sure that fixing them sandwiches for lunch won't be too hard for you. And they can help you; they can probably do most of it without help. I'm sure they can keep themselves out of trouble until Sebastian gets back."

"We'll see." Evelyn wasn't about to commit herself to babysitting.

Sebastian smiled to himself. They would see. And he would be the winner of this little skirmish, too.

Added to that, the kids would be the perfect buffer between him and Evelyn while Anne was gone.

* * *

It was too much. Evelyn dropped into her chair. Her whole office had been taken over by Sebastian, and he hadn't bothered to have her things moved. He'd left little notes to himself and had tabbed pages of several reports lying around. He'd been busy the week he'd been here. There was a lot for him to familiarize himself with. She just wished he'd done it in someone else's office.

The room even smelled like him.

"Hey, didn't expect to see you here." David lounged in her open doorway, his eyes friendly.

Evelyn, a bit thrown by the friendliness, took the comment literally. "I know. But Sebastian is picking up his children. I wanted to see what he got into while I took a break. I was going to wait until Monday, but figured I'd sneak in and out."

David didn't bother to wait for an invitation. He strolled in the rest of the way and shut the door behind him. He ignored Evelyn's brow raised in question. "I'd begun to wonder if you were going to come back at all. Then when you showed up for the meeting on Monday, I really thought you weren't coming back."

Evelyn felt just a tad guilty. "I needed a break. So much happened so fast. Sebastian was on my case. It's easy for him to bother me at home if he has questions since he's living with Anne for now. Things have been weird. I guess I've been feeling a little stressed."

David sat down and folded his hands, draping them across his knees, leaning in. "I can understand that. Are you all right? You're not sick or something, are you?"

Evelyn sat up straighter, confused. "What do you mean, am I sick? Would I be here if I were?"

"I don't mean physically. I meant mentally. Are you feeling all right? Anne's worried. Kimberly's made similar comments. Then when you didn't show up at work, I began to wonder. Then you turned control of the company over to Sebastian, and then I began to worry."

Evelyn laughed. "You think I'm having a nervous breakdown because I turned the company over? It's really sweet of you, in a convoluted sort of way. You really look worried."

"It's not funny. You said that day you didn't have much of a choice. Anne says you went straight home. She said you almost seemed happy about your decision. Be honest, Evie. It's been a long time since you were really happy about anything. Can you blame us for wondering if you were okay?"

"No, I guess not. I hadn't realized until recently that I wasn't happy. It's funny, but I felt relieved when I told Sebastian the control was his." Evelyn dropped silent. What else could she say?

David wasn't sure what to do with her when she wasn't in full sail. "If you're not sick, how about temporary insanity? Leslie about fell out of her chair when I told her what you'd done. She made a similar comment about your mental health."

"It's nice to know the family is on my side. Just don't fill out the admission papers yet." Evelyn gave him a tiny, wry smile, taking the sting out of her words. She wasn't sure what to do with David in this mood. "You know, you're acting pretty strange yourself."

"Yeah, I know. Too many late nights. I've been busy, and it's been odd not having you around. Besides, I hate being in charge; you know that. I'm more relieved than you are that Sebastian is here. At first, I was kind of panicked, but I trust his judgment. He can argue with you over how things should be run, and I can concentrate on my lab work."

"You're going to have to do without Sebastian for part of next week. He wants to play swing shift with babysitting his kids. He thinks it will be great if he and I take turns. Anne volunteered me for the job."

David chuckled and leaned back, stretching out his legs. "You're going to babysit Sebastian's kids? That I'd like to see."

Evelyn wasn't amused. "It's not funny. I don't know anything about kids. And to be frank, I don't want to learn this coming week. I can't chase after them. I can't take them out to do fun stuff. They're going to be bored with nothing to do all day. Anne said Kimberly would be willing to watch them if we asked her, but for some reason or another, Sebastian seems to have vetoed that idea. It would be much better if they went over there; they'd at least have a pool to play in."

"Keep fighting it." David rose.

"Keep fighting what?" Evelyn stayed where she was.

"You keep finding excuses to close yourself off. You'd be a lot happier if you went out and had some fun once in a while. Kids are a good start."

Evelyn clenched her jaw, ignoring the crack about the kids. "And what do you suppose I do for fun? Run the Boston Marathon?"

David shook his head at her. "Don't be sarcastic. You could go out for lunch once in a while, meet with friends once you find some. You could go shopping. Those granny dresses you wear don't do much for your figure. You could go to a spa and get a massage."

Evelyn shook her head back at him, hurt by his words. "I'll consider that. Get to work."

David saluted her, knowing he'd hurt her feelings but knowing she needed to be prodded once in a while. "Sure thing, boss."

Evelyn felt a childish urge to stick her tongue out at him. She lifted the reports instead. She was here to work. She felt like she had some sort of reprieve. She didn't have to deal with Sebastian for two whole days. He had left early to fly up to Washington. He was going to stay the night up there and come back early Sunday. Then Sunday would be spent, at least until the evening, with Anne. Evelyn hoped to peruse what was here, so she'd know what Sebastian had already gone through.

Evelyn finished going through the reports on her desk and tidied up the office. She liked to keep things in their place, and Sebastian had rearranged her desk. Her pens were in the wrong drawer, and her folders were no longer organized. She had to see about moving her things.

Fortunately, that didn't take long. Evelyn decided to go ahead and move out of the office while Sebastian was gone. When he came in next week, he could rearrange all he wanted. They'd discussed his taking a different office, but she hadn't changed her mind about moving hers. He was in charge now, and it made no sense to move John's and Lenora's offices around for Sebastian. It took Evelyn only an hour to settle into her new space. She wrote an office memo notifying everyone of the office change. If anyone came looking for her, they'd find her down the hall.

Evelyn was hanging her grandfather's paintings when Leslie came in. She almost dropped one in her surprise. "Hello, Leslie."

Leslie looked around the room. "You sure do move fast. David said you were in the other office just over an hour ago."

"You know me, ever efficient. But I had help. What can I do for you?" Evelyn wasn't sure what to do with Leslie.

They were never close, and ever since her brief affair with Sebastian, she had a hard time being around her cousin. The resentment, and yes, jealousy, she felt was hard to deal with. David was hard enough, but Leslie was something else altogether.

"Actually, I'm doing my family duty and checking up on you. David is worried. If David is worried, I figure I'd better be, too." Leslie patted her hair and smoothed her skirt. It was nerves more than concern about her appearance.

Evelyn's back was hurting after so much physical activity. She took a seat and gestured for Leslie to do the same. "I'm fine. I guess I shocked everyone."

"Intentionally, too, I bet."

Leslie didn't sound upset or as if she were being rude. Evelyn wasn't used to Leslie being concerned about anyone; she was never one to fuss. Even when she'd been in the hospital, Leslie hadn't been around much. Evelyn was speechless.

Leslie shifted uncomfortably. "Are you all right? I mean, Anne is worried, but she always is. Kimberly has the baby to worry about, but she and John are concerned. I know David is very levelheaded; he wouldn't be worried without a reason."

"As I said, I'm fine. David thinks I've lost my marbles. But I did give my decision a lot of thought. Sebastian will do a wonderful job. Since he owns part of Brown now, he has a vested interest. He can't walk away. I think my decision is the best one for everybody."

"You know Kimberly and I don't care. David could work

anywhere, but he likes being in control. I don't know why you work here, other than for money. Sebastian loves a challenge. Between you and the company, he'll have plenty."

"Leslie!" Evelyn couldn't believe she had said that.

Leslie was unrepentant. "Oh, please. Everyone knows you two don't get along. He'll have his hands full keeping you and the company in line."

Evelyn stared. "What's your sudden interest in the company? Is it Sebastian?"

Everyone was aware of the relationship between Leslie and Sebastian, and Leslie knew it. Leslie never bothered to hide her true feelings. "He was a part of it, I have to admit. I wouldn't have minded picking up where we left off. Even half-drunk, he was an amazing lover. But after that one time, Sebastian called it off. I doubt he's interested in renewing our affair."

Evelyn tried to hide the ache she felt whenever Sebastian and Leslie's affair was mentioned. "You want him back."

It wasn't a question, but Leslie answered. "I might if it weren't for Philip."

"I heard it mentioned you were seeing someone," Evelyn said, keeping her voice even.

Leslie looked a bit panicked, but her voice was clear. "We're getting married."

Evelyn's shock wasn't faked. "You're what?"

"You're the first to know. Philip and I have been seeing each other a lot lately. I had no idea he was so serious. But last week he asked me to marry him. I said yes."

"I haven't heard much about him. We usually know

more about your boyfriends." Evelyn felt embarrassment flush her cheeks.

"He wanted to keep it low-key. He didn't want everyone to know. He said I had a bad habit of flaunting my lovers. He said if I cared about him, I'd keep the relationship between just the two of us for a while."

Evelyn understood the sentiment. Leslie had had so many different men over the years; Philip probably just wanted to be sure that he was special to her. "It can't be easy for him, either. If he loves you, he probably wants everyone to know."

Leslie laughed. "Oh, he does all right. He can't hide it. And as crazy as it sounds, I love him, too. I do have to say that I'm glad he doesn't want a long engagement. He wants us to get married soon. I told him we should probably wait for Anne to get back, but I'm already getting nervous. He said we could have a small wedding planned by the time she returns. I think we should just elope and have a party when she gets back, but he's pushing for a wedding."

Evelyn couldn't believe she and Leslie were discussing marriage. But it wasn't as odd as she'd imagined it would be. And Evelyn had to admit she liked the idea of Leslie being married and not being around to try to seduce Sebastian again. "I'm very happy for you. I mean it."

"Thanks. I plan on letting everyone know. I don't want the stress of trying to arrange a wedding in such a short time. I don't want the stress at all. Philip is arranging a civil ceremony, and everyone can come. We'll arrange for something afterward."

"That sounds just fine." Evelyn was a tad surprised Leslie

was opposed to planning a wedding, but she let it go. "Your brother will be shocked. Your mother, too."

"Mom will be the worst. David is used to my outrageous behavior." Leslie rose. "I'd better be on my way. I think I'll go make David's day."

"Good luck." Evelyn shook her head at Leslie's departure. She certainly hadn't been expecting that. And Leslie's mother will be shocked, Evelyn acknowledged. Leslie's mother and her mother were sisters. But Leslie's mother, Susan, had a strained relationship with the family, and it had only gotten worse over the years. She'd married a man her father hadn't approved of. When the marriage failed, Susan remained estranged. She had wanted no part of the family, so she hadn't even bothered to attend her father's funeral, and she hadn't inherited anything but a small amount of money. It saddened Evelyn that her aunt didn't want anything to do with the family, and it was even sadder that she'd never reconciled with her father. Now that Howard was gone, they would never have the chance.

But she was happy for Leslie, and it wasn't just because of Sebastian. Leslie tended to go through jobs as fast as men. She couldn't seem to find whatever it was that would make her happy. It seemed the family was rooting for this relationship with Philip to work. Though not friends, Leslie had supported her in her own way when she had been in the hospital and in therapy. Evelyn would support her cousin right back.

After Leslie left, Evelyn finished up the rest of the reports. There were always law changes being made by local and federal agencies. Environmental groups were always accusing the company of illegal disposal of waste. Evelyn shook her head at the latest batch of threats and complaints. The same people who complained about what the chemical companies were doing to the environment still bought the products. They still bought soap, makeup, and various toiletries. They still painted their houses and stained their decks and porches. They still bought bug repellent and suntan lotion.

It seemed that Sebastian made it a point to check out the newer threats and legislative changes. Sebastian had always kept an eye out for law changes, which most companies did. But he also liked to keep track of who was complaining and looked for any groups that might cause trouble. Security was a big issue. Picketing the company didn't do much good, and there were always a few brave souls who would try to break into the company offices and cause a major disturbance.

Among the papers were security changes the company had made. It looked as if Sebastian didn't approve of some of the changes if the yellow highlighted areas meant anything. Evelyn set the papers down, a bit leery of what she'd read. As soon as he settled into his office, or rather her former office, he was going to start making major changes. Some of them that she could see in the papers from his desk would be welcomed. What bothered her was the number of highlighted sections. At the rate of his marker, he would be spending the next year aggravating the staff, making necessary, as well as what she thought were unnecessary, changes to company policies.

Since Sebastian wasn't here, there was no point in

worrying about it today. Evelyn glanced at her watch. It was already after six. Somehow, she'd lost four hours. Evelyn tucked the papers under her arm and closed up her new office. She put the papers back in Sebastian's desk drawer and locked it up. She'd already informed her new secretary she wouldn't be in on Monday. John was the last person she needed to see, but he'd left an hour ago. She left a brief message on his desk and left.

She knew Anne was going to be upset with her. Anne kept making her promise to be home at a reasonable time. Anne didn't consider anything after six to be reasonable. If Evelyn weren't back by five-thirty, she could expect a lecture. It was seven by the time she arrived home.

"I'm home." Evelyn took off her light linen jacket and hung it in the hall closet. She found Anne on the phone.

Anne waved at Evelyn to come closer. Evelyn slipped off her flat sandals, put on her slippers, and took a seat not far from Anne. It didn't take but a minute to figure out whom she was talking to. Sounded like Leslie decided to tell everyone about her engagement. Anne was smiling and laughing. The wedding would keep Anne busy when she got back from her cruise, assuming they waited that long.

Anne set the phone down. "I can't believe it. I thought that of all the grandchildren, Leslie would be the one who didn't get married. This guy must be crazy about her."

"I think it's the other way around. I think Leslie is crazy about him; crazy enough to get married." Evelyn stifled a yawn and leaned back in her chair.

"Leslie said she told you earlier today."

"Everyone is checking up on me. Like you, they all think

I've lost my mind, turning the company over without a fight." Evelyn hoped another discussion about her decision wasn't forthcoming.

"That's because we all care about you and want you well. Why do you have such a hard time understanding that?" Anne pinned Evelyn to her seat with a look.

Evelyn sighed and yawned again. "Maybe because it's overdone. I don't need a babysitter anymore. I'm a grown woman, and I can make my own decisions. Everyone is smothering me. Why can't you understand that?"

"I don't want to fight with you. We should celebrate Leslie's engagement." Anne rose. "Dinner is ready. You're late again."

Evelyn watched Anne's receding back. She knew Anne would remark on her tardiness. Evelyn managed to get back to her feet and headed to the dining room. "Sorry about that. Between David and Leslie, I didn't get much work done this afternoon. I also rearranged offices today to accommodate Sebastian."

Anne's reply was stiff. "You certainly don't have to explain to me. It's your business."

Evelyn stifled a curse. "The guilt trip is unnecessary."

Dinner was a bit strained. Evelyn knew Anne was upset with her. Most of Anne's emotions these days were tough to deal with. Anne was still grieving, and she took a lot of her anger out on others. Evelyn understood. She certainly took her anger and frustrations out on Anne, mostly because Anne was an available target. Having Sebastian around provided her with a new one. And he would fight back.

Anne cleared the table when the meal was over, and Evelyn remained seated. She was tired from the physical work at the office that day. She'd insisted she could carry some of the lighter items. Her files had been boxed and transported for her, but she'd filled her new cabinets. Her body was telling her how much she'd overtaxed herself.

"Are you still hungry?" Anne came in with a tray. On it were two bowls of ice cream. It was a peace offering both were accustomed to.

"I could eat a few bites," Evelyn assured her. "Rough day?"

"I've been packing. It doesn't seem right to leave like this. My husband just died, and here I am taking a cruise." Anne scooped up a bite but didn't eat it.

"Anne, we've been over this. Getting away will be good for you. All this will still be here when you get back. Taking a cruise doesn't make you love Grandfather any less."

Anne dabbed her eyes with her napkin. "I know that. It's just hard to deal with this sometimes. I knew we wouldn't have much time together, but when we met, it didn't seem to matter. We were happy."

"I know. You have many wonderful memories now. They won't disappear while you're away."

"I know." Anne dabbed her eyes again and then went back to her ice cream. "Do you think Leslie will have any children?"

Evelyn almost choked on a bite. "The mind boggles. I hadn't thought it through that far. I don't know."

"Leslie will make a good mother once she calms down

and settles into married life." Anne looked up into Evelyn's horrified face. "Don't worry, dear, I won't ask her right away. I'll give it a few months before I start hounding her."

"Good." Evelyn cleared her throat. "I think Leslie is going to have a hard enough time adjusting to being married. Adding pressure about having a baby might put her over the edge. She looked happy but nervous in my office today."

"I'm glad the two of you talked."

Evelyn considered that. "You know, I think this is one of the few conversations we've had in five years. We aren't adversaries, but after that fiasco with Leslie and John, she avoids me. I still haven't managed to get John to forgive me for it. Something tells me he won't ever. We work well together, but work is all we discuss."

"Kimberly works on him. Having a child will mellow him out."

Evelyn finished her ice cream and rose. "I think I'll go take a bath."

Anne immediately turned on Evelyn. "Are you sure you're okay?"

Evelyn figured lying was useless. "My back hurts. I helped move some things at the office today, and I'm paying the price. A bath will do wonders." And a shot of whiskey, she told herself silently.

"Go on up then and I'll see you tomorrow. I'm going to go read for a while, then go to bed." Anne left Evelyn to her own devices.

Evelyn fixed a drink and took it with her upstairs. The whirlpool tub had been a birthday gift from her family a few years back. It was probably the best gift she'd received, except for her horse. This gift was more practical.

As she sank into the steaming, bubbling water, she let her mind drift. Things were changing. Evelyn knew she'd been living in a strange limbo since her accident. She felt as if things had gone stagnant. With Sebastian's reappearance, things were stirring. Her family was changing. Her job was changing. It would be interesting to see what would come next.

Chapter Ten

A loud commotion woke Evelyn from her position on the couch. At some point last night, she'd fallen asleep. She turned bleary eyes to the coffee table. The mostly empty bottle of brandy was a testament to a night of heavy drinking. Evelyn would have loved to roll over onto her stomach, but her leg forbade it. It was the leg that forced her into this position in the first place. She should have known it would do no good to try to drown the pain.

Saturday was nothing but an unpleasant blur now, and it was mid-Sunday morning. She realized who it was at the front door. The loud squeals of children's voices and Anne's equally excited voice blended into a cacophony that was causing her head to pound.

Evelyn tried to sit up as her memory came back. It had rained early Saturday morning, and she had opted to stay home. She'd had the bright idea that she could finish potting the bulbs Sebastian had purchased. She'd managed to get one pot done. But she'd been eager to finish, and when she'd gone to get the other pot, she had somehow managed to slip on the brick patio. She'd left her cane by the table, and she'd gone down. Hard.

Her leg had twisted under her, and an agony like she hadn't known in a long time had sent lightning streaks of pain down her leg, through her hip, and up her back. Anne had come running to her aid, but she was too late. Evelyn had allowed Anne to help her back into the house, but from there, things had deteriorated. An ugly argument had ensued. She'd yelled that she was not having the stupid operation, and that was final. This would have happened with or without it, and at least this way, she wasn't undoing what good the doctors had done.

Anne had left her alone with her misery. Feeling guilt-ridden, she'd picked up the brandy decanter and managed to drink herself to sleep. Now in the light of the morning, she wished she'd allowed Anne to get her a pill and help her to bed. Pills were not her preference, but right now she felt as if she'd seriously hurt herself. A trip to the tub was in her near future. For now, she had to greet Sebastian's children, gritting her teeth against the pain in her head that echoed the throbbing pain in her hip and back.

Evelyn found her cane beside the table. Next to it was her hated walker. It was folded up beside the table, mocking her. She grabbed her cane, and on wobbly legs that felt like jelly, she put the decanter in the cabinet. She made her way to the hall, gritting her teeth.

The sound of a barking dog almost made Evelyn jump. The medium-sized dog was barking at her. The golden fur and soulful brown eyes were a big contrast to the big, lolling tongue and excited swing of its tail. The dog was on a leash, thank goodness, and calmed down at a stern word from Sebastian.

"I see you made good time." Evelyn leaned with both hands on the cane. The two children were staring at it.

"How come you have that?" Lucy stared up at Evelyn, a sadness filling her eyes as she looked at her.

Evelyn's gaze softened, and she smiled at the girl. This one definitely was soft-hearted, just as Sebastian said. Her dark curly hair was almost the same shade as her father's. Her eyes were the same deep green shade, but the compassion in them was vastly different from the cold, assessing look Sebastian was sending her.

Evelyn would have liked to kneel down to speak to her, but that, of course, was impossible. "I had an accident a long time ago, and I need it to walk."

"That cane looks cool." Daniel stepped closer to look at it. "What are those carvings on it?"

Evelyn glanced at the cane. It had been a long time since she had paid attention to the details on it. She looked over at Daniel. He had blond hair and brown eyes, but his face was his father's. He was standing upright, his face showing a determination she was very familiar with.

"The cane was my great-grandfather's. He loved animals, and the carvings are of various animals." She held it out for inspection.

"That is so cool." Daniel fingered a carving of a bird.

"I suppose it is." She figured there was no point in explaining to the boy that she didn't find it "cool," as he'd put it. It was an aggravating encumbrance, and she would never view it any other way.

"Let's get inside." Anne shut the front door behind them. "The bedrooms are all made up. Sebastian, why don't you take them up and show them which rooms?"

Evelyn shot a wary look at Anne. Sebastian sent a

questioning look her way but followed orders. The two children bounded up the stairs, and Sebastian followed at a more leisurely pace. The dog went with them. Evelyn shook her head at the group. She never should have mentioned a pet.

"Are you feeling better?" Anne's sharp tone caused Evelyn to tear her gaze from the stairs.

"No. But you know that already." Evelyn stood her ground. Anne could bully her all she wanted.

"I had hoped you'd stop acting like this. You seemed to finally come to terms with everything. You haven't drank like this in weeks. One accident and you're back to old behaviors." Anne kept her voice low so as not to be overheard.

"I am an adult, not a child. If I want to drink myself into oblivion, then I will. You have no idea what this feels like. You don't know how bad it hurts, or how much I sometimes wish I didn't survive that fall. You can't possibly know. I'm not an alcoholic, and I'm not addicted to pain pills. I'm walking a very thin line, and you should be happy I'm not totally dependent on substances."

Anne's eyes filled. These arguments between them never had a winner. "I know. You're doing very well. I know how easy it is to become dependent, and the doctors gave us all the warnings about it. Work has been good for you. It has given you something to think about besides your body. I just don't like seeing you this way. You have to stop doing this."

Evelyn put her arm out and Anne took it. Evelyn hugged her and allowed Anne to lead her into the living room.

"Look. I shouldn't have, and I know it. I think I'm going to make an appointment today to see what kind of damage I did last night. It's been a long time since I've hurt myself this badly."

Anne instantly became more concerned. "What do you think you did?"

Evelyn looked at the floor and shrugged her shoulders, knowing that she wasn't going to tell Anne the complete truth. "I don't know. It hurts. I probably just pulled something, and I'm sure it will be fine."

Thudding footsteps were heard on the stairs. The two children, towed by the dog, came into the living room.

"This is better than a hotel." Lucy came and climbed onto the couch beside Anne.

"Maybe. Does Kimberly really have a swimming pool?" Daniel remained standing. "Dad said she does."

Anne laughed at his eager face. "I've already called Kimberly, and everyone is going over there tomorrow."

"My sister loves having company." Evelyn leaned back and rested her head against the back of the sofa. Her clothes were sadly wrinkled, and she needed to wash up.

The children chatted endlessly and introduced the energetic dog as Walter. Walter sniffed his new surroundings while the children practically bounced up and down trying to get Anne's attention. Anne and Sebastian chatted between interruptions. Evelyn felt weak, and she wanted nothing more than to climb back into bed. As punishment for her drinking, she stayed on the sofa and sat quietly.

"Why don't you go take a bath?" Anne interrupted her

light doze.

Evelyn blinked and her eyes refocused. She had almost fallen asleep, despite the noise. She looked over at Anne. "I need help with the stairs."

Sebastian rose. He wanted to know what was going on. He'd felt the tension as soon as he set foot in the house. "I'll help you up. I can carry you if you want."

Evelyn looked horrified. "I can walk."

Sebastian gripped her arm. When they hit the stairs, he spoke up. "What happened?"

Evelyn gritted her teeth as she took the first two steps. "I fell on the patio yesterday."

Evelyn was quiet for a second. Then she decided it might be best to be upfront with him. If he were going to stay here, it would be in her best interests if he knew she might have seriously hurt herself. She sighed resignedly. "I don't want to worry Anne, but I think I might have done some damage. She'll call off her trip if she thinks it's bad."

"Maybe she should. You need a doctor." Sebastian took a firmer grip on her.

"She doesn't need to be here for that. I can still drive. Anne needs to take a vacation. She's been stressed these last few weeks. She needs to get away, and this is the only way the family can see to get her to take it."

"I'll take you if you can't drive." He heard the offer and was mildly surprised by it. He had been lecturing himself not to take a personal interest in her. After having almost kissed her twice, he needed to put things into perspective. This was Evelyn. She was all wrong for him. She was too young and too stubborn. Seeing her now, vulnerable and hurting, his intentions fled.

Sebastian mentally kissed his objectivity goodbye. "Is there anything else I can do for you?"

Evelyn, too, was surprised by his offer. For the moment, pride was set aside. "Yeah, you can get the bath going. I hate leaning over the tub."

Sebastian followed where Evelyn pointed. The bathroom was new. He remembered well the layout of the house, and he remembered Anne telling him about the new bath for Evelyn. The tub was huge. He was sure both of them could fit in it. The gleaming white surface was surrounded by pale blue and green tiles. There were soothing watercolors on the wall. The flooring matched the tile around the tub. As he got closer, he could see jets inside. "Nice tub."

"Thanks. This room was a birthday present. I was having a hard time with the smaller bathroom. I couldn't maneuver around with the walker. Grandfather decided a nice spa tub would be good for me. He hired a contractor to come in and remodel the next-door bedroom."

The room was beautiful, but it was obvious it had been designed for someone with difficult mobility. There were handrails on the tub. The large shower stall in the corner had them as well. The sink had a stool underneath, and if he guessed correctly, she could reach the sink from a sitting position. "Your grandfather loved you very much."

"I know." Her answer was said solemnly, with a large hint of sadness. "Anne is jealous. She sneaks in here now and again. Kimberly wants John to remodel their bath."

Sebastian twisted the taps. He looked over at Evelyn,

who was resting against the wall. Being alone with her in the bathroom was testing his willpower. He turned back to the water. He could easily imagine her naked, immersed in bubbles. He cursed silently and adjusted the water temperature. Sebastian switched topics. "Why is Anne angry with you?"

Evelyn rubbed her brow. "I drank myself to sleep."

Sebastian sat on the edge of the tub. "Kimberly said Anne is worried about you drinking too much."

"Anne is worried about everything. She thinks I can't manage my drinking habits. Quite frankly, it's not the alcohol that worries me. It's all the pain medication. The doctors warn you about becoming dependent. I remember a brief time when I was finally not sedated. I had been on a morphine drip. When I came to and was awake for more than a few minutes at a time, I wanted more. I hurt so bad. I remember popping quite a few pills when they finally unhooked me. It scared me. Anne doesn't understand."

"Anne's father was an alcoholic. She worries about you because she saw what it did to her father."

Evelyn was quiet for a moment. "I didn't know. I suppose polishing off almost half of a bottle of brandy doesn't sit well with her."

"No, it doesn't. Have you told her about the pills?"

She gave him a self-deprecating smile, then rubbed her eyes wearily. "Yeah. I tell her constantly. She doesn't listen to me. She thinks I'm worried over nothing. She says I don't take enough of them to become addicted to them. She thinks the alcohol dependency works faster."

"You just need balance."

Evelyn shook her head. She watched as Sebastian turned off the water. "Anne will tell you I just need surgery. She thinks that's the ultimate solution."

"What do you think?" Sebastian watched as she mulled over his question.

"I honestly don't know what to think. The doctor tells me that it might not be successful but that the odds are good it will be. He makes no guarantees. I won't go through surgery again just to end up where I am right now. Anne's an optimist. But it's my body and I don't know what to do about it."

"No one says you have to make a decision now." Sebastian started heading for the door.

Evelyn blocked his way. "That's where you're wrong. Everyone says I need to make a decision. One of those decisions caused you to own a part of my grandfather's business. He said to get the surgery or else. Well, I got the 'or else.' I got you."

Sebastian felt a flicker of humor. "I'm not such a bad deal."

Evelyn's mouth fell open in shock. She snapped her jaw shut and stepped out of his way. No, he wasn't such a bad deal. Problem was, she was a problem for him. They both knew it. She watched him shut the door on his way out. She carefully stripped once she heard her bedroom door close.

She didn't want to think about surgery. She didn't want to think about Sebastian either. It was hard not to think about either of them.

Evelyn sank into the water and felt her body relax. She

thought about her grandfather instead. Evelyn felt tears sting her eyes, but they didn't fall. Evelyn closed them. She didn't think she'd ever cry again. She missed him terribly. Perhaps as much as Anne, just in a different way. Despite the deaths of her mother and grandfather, she had a supportive family. They might not always agree, and they might not always get along, but they loved each other.

Evelyn dunked her head and came back up. She kept her eyes closed and let her mind drift. The teasing thought that caused her the most turmoil was thinking about what it would be like if Sebastian were family. He was a loving father. He was a good friend. If you asked Leslie, when she was in a good mood, he was a good companion and lover. Evelyn sat up and grabbed her soap and shampoo. Sebastian wasn't for her. She knew that when she met him when he'd still been married. She knew it when he'd been dating her cousin. She knew it now.

But the brief moments of peace between them were tantalizing. She enjoyed the flashes of humor. She liked the way he talked. He was intelligent, and he didn't talk down to people. He was fair and demanding at the same time. The dark, brooding appearance in no way detracted from his looks. His dark hair and skin, and his dark, piercing eyes, were complementary to his forceful nature.

Evelyn finished washing up and lay back down. She pushed the button to turn on the jets and let them soothe her muscles. She stirred when the door opened.

Anne came in with a bottle of water. "I brought you something for your headache. I can tell you have one."

Evelyn took the bottle and eyed the pills. They were

only Tylenol. She swallowed them without argument. "Still mad?"

Anne nodded. "Of course, I am, but I'll get over it. You're an adult. Sometimes I can't help but treat you like an invalid. I suppose you know your limits. I just hate to see you passed out with a bottle of liquor on the table."

"Why didn't you tell me about your dad?" Evelyn set the water bottle aside.

Anne folded her arms across her chest. "I guess I have to have a chat with Sebastian. It isn't any of your business, that's why. I don't like to dwell on the past or on things that I can't change. I can change you, or at least I can try. Maybe I should just let you be, but I love you too much to watch you suffer needlessly."

"I know. I can't promise it won't ever happen again. But I'll compromise. No more talk of surgery, and I'll quit drinking anything more than a small glass in the evenings when it's particularly bad."

"You want to make a deal? All right, no more drinking half a bottle when you're hurt and limit what you do drink in the evenings. Take a pill when it's really bad. No one will think less of you for it. I'll stop harping on the surgery, but I can't promise it will never come up; I'll make an effort not to harass you like your grandfather did. Deal?"

"Deal." Evelyn shifted, then sighed. "One more thing?"

"What?"

"Can you help me out of the tub?"

Anne pinched her lips together to bite off her comment about having surgery and helped haul Evelyn out of the water. Between the two, Evelyn was dressed in her favorite pink and yellow dress, and her hair was braided.

"Are you all packed?" Evelyn settled back on the bed and rested.

"I am. I'm still not sure I should be leaving, but according to the family, I don't have a choice. I know I can't keep dwelling on Howard the way I've been. I just miss him terribly, and it hurts more than I thought it would."

"You can dwell all you want. You're entitled. But you can dwell while getting some fresh air and a bit of sunshine. We just want you to relax. You can cry or not. You can be merry or not. You just need to get away for a little while. You have Sebastian to play babysitter, so you have no excuse not to go."

Anne gave her a watery smile. "I suppose it will at least relax me a bit. I'll admit to being a bit tense."

"When you married him, you didn't know you'd have to take care of two invalids." Evelyn tried to lighten the moment. She failed.

"I would have married him anyway. If you love someone, you take them as they are. I've never believed in trying to change people. Oh, you can change little things, like bad habits. But people are who they are, and you can't change them. The only time people change is when something big happens to them to alter the way they think and live. You've had a life-altering experience. In some ways, it was good for you. You were very cold when I met you. You were introverted. You were not unkind or hurtful, but you were very isolated despite your social life. It was superficial at best. You've changed a lot since then. You've learned to lean on others when you need to; to not be afraid of asking for help. I believe things happen for a reason. I married your grandfather for a reason. You were hurt the way you were for a reason. You just need to figure out what that reason is."

Evelyn remained quiet. She never really thought about it before, but Anne had a point. Five years ago she'd been isolated. She'd gotten engaged to Andrew because she was lonely; a loneliness that had been of her own making. Andrew hadn't seemed to care that she didn't love him. He didn't seem to care that their relationship was a bit superficial. Of course, now she knew why he didn't care that she didn't have anything more than affection for him.

Evelyn watched Anne leave. She hated thinking about Andrew and the time they'd been together.   The engagement had been brief. They had not dated very long before the engagement, either. At the time, Evelyn hadn't noticed. She hadn't responded much to his kisses or his lovemaking. She had felt as if she were someone else. She had felt detached. The few times they were alone together, Andrew had never mentioned her lack of response. For him, sex had been just another act of revenge. For her, it was just something that she accepted as part of marriage, and since they were engaged, she'd allowed it. Her virginity was not something she cared much about, and Andrew had been angry with her because of it. She knew now that he'd figured she was as promiscuous as her mother. When he'd found out that wasn't the case, he'd been upset. She should have known then and there she was making a mistake, but she had chosen to ignore the signs.

Evelyn pushed her thoughts away from Andrew. He'd

never stirred her stronger emotions, not even during the most intimate of acts. Of course, the only man who ever stirred her emotions was Sebastian. And they weren't necessarily sexual emotions that he stirred in her. Anger was her primary emotion. Underneath the anger, there had been passion. One form of passion could stir others. That was when she became highly aware of the fact that he was male. She'd been attracted to him when she met him. During the time they knew each other, she began to see him more as an enemy. Eventually, that circled right back around. The surge of jealousy she'd felt when she found out Sebastian and Leslie were seeing each other had thrown her off balance. She'd not felt such strong emotions about Sebastian before, but they were off the charts then. Her engagement was announced shortly after, and the wedding was to take place in only a few short weeks. Sebastian had left the United States the day after she'd been left at the altar.

Things had come back around. Sebastian was back. Andrew was back. She was back to her old job, and Sebastian was once again in charge. Five years, and she was back where she started. Evelyn carefully rolled onto her stomach. The thought was slightly depressing.

* * *

It was after seven when Sebastian arrived back at the house. He'd taken Anne to the airport late Sunday night and had spent all day Monday at Brown reacquainting himself with the business. The last five years had been hard on the company. Things were starting to look up, though, and he wondered if Howard had been aware of the shift that had started. It was obvious to him that neither David nor Evelyn was aware things had started to turn around if their comments that first day at the attorney's office were any indication. It was a slow start, but it gave him something to build on.

"I hope you brought home dinner." Evelyn's voice floated into the hall from the other room.

It was then that Sebastian noticed that the house was in an uproar. Walter was barking, and his children were laughing very loudly. It made him smile, even while he wondered how Evelyn had fared.

Sebastian found Evelyn sitting comfortably in an armchair instead of lounging on the couch. The dog appeared to be watching the board game that his children were playing.

"No. I didn't come bearing food. Why?"

Evelyn set aside the book she had been reading and gave Sebastian a level look. "I was informed this afternoon that the food selection here in the house 'sucks.' It's the first time I've heard that term used to describe Anne's excellent cooking. Apparently, your children are used to a different type of fare."

Sebastian winced. "Sorry about that. Anne isn't used to cooking for kids. To be fair, I'm not either."

"I'm sure there is something edible in that kitchen, and since you're back, I'm going to let you find it."

Sebastian grinned at her, dispelling her sour mood. "Rough day?"

Evelyn wasn't sure she wanted to be charmed by him, but his sideways grin caused her to sigh and drop the attitude. "All in all, it was fine. We watched some television, the kids played outside with their soccer ball for a while, and then I decided to pull out Anne's old board games." Evelyn looked over at the kids who were now playing tug-of-war with the dog, who looked tired of being ignored.

Sebastian sat on the arm of the chair beside Evelyn and watched his kids wrestle with the dog. "All right, kids, let's go raid the kitchen." Sebastian squeezed Evelyn's hand and rose.

Evelyn watched the kids follow their father. She rested her head on the cushion and took a deep breath. Spending the day with Sebastian's kids was pretty fun. When they weren't bickering, they were quite entertaining. Lucy had regaled her with tales of her friends from school. Daniel told her all about his favorite television shows and comic book heroes. They had then gone outside and run around, laughing and shrieking, and occasionally arguing, for a good part of the afternoon. Evelyn had been worried about entertaining them, but they didn't seem to need her to keep them busy. Listening to the noises from the kitchen, Evelyn grabbed her cane and followed the sounds of laughter.

Evelyn entered the kitchen, and it looked like Sebastian had decided on spaghetti and garlic bread for dinner. Anne had tons of food in the freezer ready to go. Evelyn often wouldn't eat if there wasn't food on hand, so Anne often cooked big pots of food and froze it. Evelyn watched as Sebastian tossed the bread in the oven, put water on to boil, and began heating the frozen bowl of sauce.

Sebastian turned to see her standing in the doorway. "Joining us?"

Evelyn shrugged. "Seemed like a good idea."

She looked at Lucy and Daniel. Sebastian handed them plates and silverware to set the table. The scene in the kitchen was homey and normal. Anne and Evelyn generally ate together. Anne didn't grow up in a traditional home, but when she married Howard, she insisted on family meals. It was nice. Evelyn made her way to the table and took a seat. The kids were talking about things she didn't know much about, but it was nice to sit and absorb. When Evelyn was younger, she never pictured herself as a mother, not even when she was going to marry Andrew. He hadn't struck her as the fatherly type, and at the time, she would not have described herself as the motherly type, though she had planned on having children in the future. It was only since Patrick was born that she found herself thinking about children and what she was missing out on. Watching the children finish setting the table and laughing and arguing at the same time, Evelyn found herself envious of Sebastian and his relationship with his kids. He claimed he didn't spend a lot of time with them, but the kids were comfortable around him, not the way kids who are neglected act.

Evelyn knew how kids who grow up with absent parents acted. After Evelyn's mother had dropped her off with her father, Evelyn had grown very distant from her mother. On the rare occasions that she saw her mother, the relationship was strained. As Evelyn had grew up, the relationship became even more distant. Jeannette didn't know what to do with a grown daughter, and Evelyn didn't know what to do with an absentee mother.

But none of that awkwardness was present in the kitchen as Sebastian finished fixing dinner.

Dinner was served, and the kids found something they liked. Evelyn savored not only the food but also the company. The conversation was lively, and she found herself laughing at some of the more outrageous stories the children told.

Sebastian watched as Evelyn laughed aloud at his children's antics. When was the last time he'd heard her laugh, he wondered? He'd seen her smile a few times, he'd heard her yell, and he'd heard her muttering under her breath. But this was the first time he'd heard her really laugh. He was glad his children had brought some laughter into her life. From what he'd seen during his short stay here, laughter and fun were in short supply.

In short order, the dishes were washed, the table wiped off, and the children were off again to go play. He sent them upstairs to get washed up and start getting ready for bed, but the laughter and loud thumps and bangs coming from the second story told him they were playing more than they were washing up.

Evelyn had settled on the sofa, a book on her lap, but she wasn't reading it. She was surprised when Walter curled up beside her and dozed off. She scratched his ears, and he snuggled closer. "You know, your kids are great."

Sebastian dropped into a side chair, not ready yet to end his children's fun. He spent so little time with them; he hated having to reprimand them, though if they didn't get motivated, he'd have to go up there and supervise bedtime. "It doesn't sound like it was too bad. They seemed to be in a good mood when I got back."

"They mostly entertained themselves. I guess it's easier when you have a couple of kids so they can keep each other occupied." Evelyn stretched out her leg, wincing a bit at the now-constant ache in her back.

"Did you make an appointment to see your doctor?" Sebastian got up and poured both of them a small drink. He handed one to Evelyn. She took it but didn't drink it. He sipped his and waited.

Evelyn looked into the glass, wondering if she should drink it or not. After the other night, she was not quite as eager to use alcohol to relax. "I made one, for all the good it will do me. I'll be taking off a little early from work on Thursday to go."

"I told you I would take you."

Evelyn set the glass down on the table without taking a sip. "I know. I appreciate the offer, but I can take myself. I feel better today. I'll be going into the office tomorrow. Kimberly is going to swing by in the morning to pick up the kids. It's time we both went to work. The transition is going to be uncertain for everyone, and I can't keep sitting at home. And given the amount of work you've already generated, you can't afford to sit at home either."

Sebastian finished his drink and picked up hers. "I suppose you're right. I've been going through reports and some of the papers Howard had stashed in his desk. We need to talk about them and about what happened after I left."

"What did you find in Grandfather's desk?"

Sebastian listened to the increased noise levels upstairs and decided to intervene. He knew he was using his kids as an excuse to postpone the conversation. The conversation he needed to have with her should be held in private. And he had no doubt Evelyn would be upset. Rallying his kids to bed was as good an excuse as any to put it off.

"Tell you what. Why don't you go up to bed? After the day you've had, I'm sure you're looking forward to a little peace and quiet. We do need to talk, but right now isn't the time."

Evelyn wondered at his odd mood but wasn't going to worry about it. He was right. Right now she wanted a hot bath, wanted to grab her newest romance novel, and just relax. She watched Sebastian climb the stairs, calling to his kids as he went up. He wasn't going anywhere anytime soon, and Evelyn wasn't eager to tell him what a fool she had made of herself five years ago.

Chapter Eleven

Evelyn found her way into the office first thing Tuesday morning. She had left Sebastian behind as he finished getting the kids ready to spend the day with Kimberly. Breakfast had been cereal and fruit. The kids had finished their breakfast in short order and ran up the stairs to finish getting ready. Evelyn had barely avoided being run over as she heard Sebastian yelling at the kids not to forget their bathing suits.

Evelyn flipped the report over and tried to concentrate. Now that she wasn't in charge, it was hard to know what exactly her role was going to be. She knew too much and got paid too much to simply be Sebastian's assistant. Had she thought of it sooner, she would have reorganized the company and created a vice president spot that she could have filled. Not being president was hard enough. Not knowing what to do was harder.

"All settled in?" Sebastian lounged in the doorway, watching as Evelyn concentrated on the latest batch of reports he had requested from the staff. He had data coming out of his ears, but without it, he couldn't even begin to assess the company's current financial status and what he should do to start fixing the problems.

The office Evelyn had chosen was already decorated

with her grandfather's paintings and a good number of files and books. She had left very little in her old office. The only things left had been the big desk, a pencil holder, and the files that he had been accumulating in her absence. Already her office looked settled and lived in. She looked at home behind the desk, papers in hand, her hair up. He had an urge to go pull it out of its perfect twist. He'd gotten used to seeing her hair loose around her shoulders, and despite all the lectures he'd been giving himself to stay away from her, he found that tumbled hair extremely sexy.

Evelyn set the papers down. Sebastian didn't seem to be in a hurry to get to the point of his visit. "Did you need something?"

"There are several things I need, but I think it would be better to discuss them back at home. I know we put off the conversation last night, and I was content to let it lie then. But your grandfather was paying a private investigator to follow your ex around. And it seemed like he was not just following his business activities. He was following his personal affairs as well. I'm guessing you know why."

Evelyn pursed her lips. "I knew he was following Andrew, but I thought it was just business. After Andrew ended our engagement five years ago, Grandfather was certain he'd taken some proprietary information with him, not just money. Even with all the security around here, it wouldn't be hard for someone committed to defrauding the company to walk out with a few trade secrets. Andrew was around the office a lot while we were engaged. And as much as you don't want to hear it, when you left, several of our clients left, too. Andrew was always charismatic, and he probably looked like a much better bet than I did to our clients."

"I can buy some of that. It certainly wasn't my intention to cause harm. When I left the country and took a position different from what I did at Brown, there was no risk of clients coming with me. With or without me, the company was still solid and had a good reputation."

Evelyn motioned for Sebastian to have a seat. He closed the door behind him and did as she asked.

"I don't know how much you know about what went on with Andrew. As I said, he worked for Brown fifteen years ago, but the one time I introduced Andrew to Grandfather when we started dating, Grandfather didn't remember him. I don't know if deceit was in Andrew's mind when he first started at Brown all those years ago. I don't know if he targeted me when I met him ten years later, or if he simply saw an opportunity and took it. No matter how you look at it, he succeeded. Brown is not bankrupt, but our reputation suffered, and our financial outlook isn't what it used to be. We've lost some good employees because they were afraid Brown wasn't going to make it for many more years. I'm hoping your presence is going to undo some of the damage Andrew and I did. And as I've said before, I did my best, but I was not the best person to take over the company. I was just the best choice out of the family."

Sebastian remembered Andrew. He had charisma, but something lurked under the surface of his superficial charm, and Sebastian hadn't trusted him. He'd had no proof to back up those feelings, but something about the man didn't ring true. Given that he left Evelyn standing at the altar, used her accounts to embezzle from Brown, and took Brown's secrets with him, he'd been right.

"I think I should at least be honest and tell you that though things are bad, they don't seem as bad as you've been making them out to be. The company has lost some clients, and I agree our reputation is somewhat tattered, but in the financial reports I've been going through, things are starting to get better. You did that."

Evelyn's eyes narrowed as she considered what he said. She liked to think that things were on the upswing, but every time someone quit, or an order was canceled, or a supplier bailed, it was hard to see improvement. "I've been going over the data, and I do see improvements over the last two quarters. But they are not significant, and they could be a fluke."

Sebastian rose. "Anything is possible. But the situation isn't as bleak as you and David make it out to be. You two are too close to the business to see the bigger picture. So it's a good thing I came in when I did."

Sebastian was smiling at her, his tone a little facetious. It warmed her that he didn't think she was a total failure. And truthfully, she needed some reassurance that all her hard work was starting to pay off. There was more to the story about Andrew, but he was right; the office was not the place to talk about it.

Sebastian's next words made her think he could read her mind. "Tell you what; we'll finish this discussion tonight. I need to finish up some work, then I'm going to head over to Kimberly's and get the kids. I have a feeling they're going to be wound up after a day of playing in the pool."

Evelyn thought perhaps the opposite would be true, but they were his kids, and Sebastian seemed to have an unending fountain of energy. A day in the pool and she slept like a baby.

* * *

It was getting late by the time Sebastian got the kids in bed. Evelyn had gotten home before they had arrived. Sebastian and the kids had dinner with Kimberly and John, but Evelyn was feeling tired and had opted to come home instead. The kids had come running into the house and had found Evelyn just finishing up her dinner. They'd told her all about the pool and the fun games Kimberly had taught them. Lucy, still a little shy with her, had told her how she had gotten to hold the baby. Daniel rolled his eyes but managed to keep his opinions about babies to himself. Sebastian had mentioned to Anne that Daniel had still not quite adjusted to his mom getting remarried and having more kids.

An hour after the trio had headed upstairs, Sebastian came back to the living room.

"What can you tell me about Global Chem-Lab and Crown Chemicals?" Sebastian took a seat and opened the file he'd brought with him, flipping through what little information he had on the company.   The private investigator had not gathered much information on the company itself, only Andrew's role in them. There were copies of old news articles about the other company and the contracts it had won in the past couple of years. None of the information was secret; Sebastian would have been able to get all the information contained here without hiring someone. What bothered him was that Howard had the papers at home and there were no copies at the office. He'd looked. He'd had John see what he could find and then they'd sent Lenora Whitenstall to search. She was the most efficient secretary in the company, and if she couldn't find the information, then it wasn't there.

Evelyn looked up from the book she was reading. Since Anne had left for her cruise, Evelyn was aware of feeling isolated with Sebastian. She was becoming more and more aware of his presence in her home. No matter where he was in the house, she knew where he was. But Sebastian was more interested in the paperwork he'd found in Howard's desk than in her, and when he wasn't working on that, he was entertaining his children. In reality, they spent very little time alone in the same room.

Evelyn didn't need to look over at the stack of papers Sebastian held. She knew what they were. She knew why they were there. She still wasn't sure what to tell Sebastian about them, but at this point, full disclosure was her best bet. He would be witness to yet another one of her debacles. But she supposed after the fact was better than a front-row seat.

"Well?" Sebastian impatiently waited while Evelyn stared at the papers. Obviously, she knew something important, or she wouldn't be hesitating. She'd made up for the time she'd taken from the office with the amount of information she supplied him through John. She often seemed distant, and it had started after the night he'd almost kissed her in the garden.

Evelyn took a moment. Then she shrugged. "Andrew was working for Global Chem-Lab while he was dating me, although I didn't know it. He told me he was a stockbroker. Grandfather found out the truth when he got back from his second honeymoon with Anne. With me in the hospital, he was feeling helpless, so he went to work. I guess you could say Grandfather tried a little personal justice. He tried everything he could to sabotage Andrew's career at Global. Grandfather was telling anyone who would listen that he had stolen trade secrets, that he was unreliable, and that he was involved with hostile overseas companies and governments. To be honest, I don't know how many of those rumors were true, and Grandfather wasn't one to make things up, but he wouldn't have hesitated to use those rumors to his advantage. Andrew moved to another division at Global across the country when he realized what Grandfather was trying to do. Unfortunately for Grandfather, his influence didn't stretch that far, and the executives and board of directors at Global weren't interested in what he had to say. I found out about what Grandfather was doing shortly after Andrew moved. While I was in the hospital, there was no shortage of people who made it a point to tell me what was going on outside those four hospital walls. I'm surprised how much I do remember, given what I was going through at the time. Grandfather wasn't aware I knew what he was doing and what Andrew had done. I never told him."

"I see." And he did. He would have wanted revenge against anyone who harmed his children. But Evelyn was a grown woman, not a child. "Did you have a hand in those rumors? Or did it come as a surprise?"

"I didn't care much about anything while I was in the hospital, so no, I didn't fuel the rumors. I can't say I was surprised, though. Grandfather felt he had a good reason to go after Andrew. To be fair, Andrew had his reasons for doing what he did. In his mind, we were even. You'd have to know Andrew; he has a very strict code on things like revenge. When Grandfather tried to ruin his reputation, Andrew felt the scales tipped back out of his favor. Two years ago he amassed enough power and money, bought Global's assets when Global filed for bankruptcy, and merged with a small firm he had started the year before. He called the merged companies Crown. He's in charge of their daily operations. According to gossip, he moved his headquarters here and bought himself a rather large house. My guess is he's working on a plan to sabotage Brown. Just because Grandfather is dead doesn't mean he'll simply stop."

Sebastian tossed the papers on the table. He sat for a moment and absorbed what she'd said. She was leaving big chunks out, but he couldn't be sure they were important or not. "Why move his headquarters here? And why would he try to sabotage Brown? Why did Andrew want revenge in the first place?"

Evelyn rose and leaned on her cane. She was tensing up again. "When Grandfather hired Andrew fifteen years ago, it was when Brown was struggling."

Sebastian swore. "I take it together they turned Brown around."

"No. I don't know how well Grandfather even knew

him. Andrew had been hired on and was a lower-level executive, but Andrew was responsible for hiring new chemists; chemists my grandfather would never have hired. Things went well for a time, and Grandfather only saw dollar signs on their way up. He wasn't paying attention to who was creating those new chemicals. It didn't come out until much later that some of the chemicals the company was making were a lot more dangerous than anyone on the board knew."

Evelyn's eyes darkened as she continued her story. "Less than a year later, Andrew disappeared, taking the more lucrative formulations with him, along with a boatload of cash he'd embezzled. He left without notice, and no one seemed to know where he went. Suddenly, Brown was back on the list of companies that were being targeted by the media and environmental groups. Grandfather was infuriated; the company's reputation was in shreds. It was a few years before Grandfather was able to get things back on track. You came in at a time when things were looking up. It was why Grandfather thought of retiring when he hired you. He had faith that you could finish turning the business around."

"Then, ten years later, Andrew showed up and started dating you?" He wasn't sure yet where this was going.

"Yes. Grandfather didn't remember a man named Andrew Shepherd who had worked at Brown. As I said, Grandfather wasn't paying attention to who was doing what at his company so long as he was seeing results. After Andrew left, Grandfather hired all new people and formed a new management team to rebuild the company's reputation.

There were three people before you in your role after Andrew left. Each one made small strides, but none like the ones you made. You didn't work in the labs, but you did more for the company than those three men combined and reversed the damage Andrew did. I imagine that also is part of his current motivation. He hates you."

"Why was he dating you if he was trying to exact revenge? He left the company voluntarily, and he got what he wanted."

"He left but it wasn't exactly voluntarily. His wife was divorcing him and taking his children with her. It seems there was no money left. His accounts had been wiped out and his wife found out about the affair he was having. He had no choice but to leave and find another job. He was worried the gossipers would find out why his wife was leaving him and with whom he was having an affair. And the fact that his mistress wiped him out."

"Okay, I'll bite." Sebastian started pacing. "Who was he having an affair with?"

"Jeannette."

Sebastian whirled at the one-word answer. "Your mother?"

"She'd been having an affair with him for quite some time. When she tired of him, instead of breaking it off, she went the vindictive route. She emptied his bank account and told his wife. She was the catalyst for his leaving, along with the formulations, but without the cash he'd stolen."

Sebastian swore out loud this time. "So he came back and tried to marry you to get revenge on Jeannette?"

"He didn't want revenge, or not just revenge. First and

foremost, he wanted his money back. The harmful chemicals the lab was using under his direction were his ticket to not only embezzling but also a way of creating the formulas he used to get hired at Global. On paper, he was buying high-quality chemicals, but in reality, he was swapping out cheaper chemicals and pocketing the extra money. It wasn't until an audit was done after he disappeared that Grandfather realized a lot of money was missing. A glance at the finances seemed as if all of the expenses were legitimate. You can't create a new line of products without spending some serious money. But the products were inferior, and no one realized until they hit the market. One part of the lab didn't know what the other part was doing. Added to that, Andrew was using a third-party distributor who wasn't opposed to shipping products they knew very little about. Brown was hit with huge fines for improperly shipping hazardous materials."

Sebastian tossed the papers on the coffee table. "And no one knew? I can't believe Jeannette didn't tell anyone else."

"Jeannette wasn't going to risk jail by bragging, and I'm guessing Andrew didn't want Global to know he'd been having an affair with and was cheated by the daughter of their biggest competitor. Jeannette had stolen all his money, not just the funds he'd embezzled. She may or may not have known the money she stole from him he'd stolen from Brown. I inherited half of what was left when Jeannette died, and I controlled Kimberly's share until she turned twenty. I had just turned twenty, so I had control of my portion. He used me to get into Brown's confidential files, stole my money, and then left. Andrew also emptied a couple of Brown's expense accounts right after he emptied my personal bank account. He used his relationship with me as a way to find out the information he needed to steal back what Jeannette had stolen from him. My work laptop was usually lying around my apartment, and he knew my passwords because I had them written down at home. He knew my bank account numbers, my social security number, and he knew where I kept my records. I was at my grandfather's house getting ready for the wedding while he finished cleaning out my apartment and the accounts."

Sebastian swore loudly. He then took her hand and pulled her gently back onto the couch. He sat beside her, keeping her hand in his. "You told your grandfather?"

"Not exactly. You have to understand, I had my accident not a week later and Grandfather and Anne were away. Andrew had left a horrible letter in my empty apartment telling me why he had left. I don't know why I didn't toss it out, but when I was in the hospital, Grandfather found the letter in my kitchen. He hadn't known about Jeannette's affair with him. He didn't know Andrew was the same man who had embezzled from him ten years earlier. He was sickened that the man would do to me what he did in retaliation. Grandfather used every resource he could to hurt Andrew. But he couldn't do much damage to him."

"So Howard figured he'd get revenge on Andrew where it would hurt him the most. His career. But that backfired because Global was benefiting from what Andrew had done," Sebastian concluded. By the way Evelyn was staring at him, he figured he was right on the money.

"That's what Grandfather tried to do. Global was too

big. Andrew was too important. He's an intelligent man. He made some stupid mistakes, but he's not stupid."

Evelyn gripped Sebastian's hand tighter, not even realizing he still had possession of her hand. "As you can imagine, I wasn't interested in what Grandfather was up to. For the first year, I didn't care about anything. By the time I found out what Grandfather had done, Andrew was long gone, his career was on the upswing, and the money he took was untraceable."

Sebastian turned Evelyn in her seat and started massaging the tension in her shoulders. She was wound so tight he was afraid she might hurt herself from the tension alone. "According to the records at work, we lost a lot of accounts to Global after I left. Andrew used you to keep a close eye on the company's clients, and he knew where to strike. Global must have been paying him an awful lot of money for him to have been able to build his own firm and then buy Global out."

Evelyn took a deep, relaxing breath. "He knew exactly where to strike. I look back now, and I wonder how much information I fed him without realizing it. But to be honest, some days I can't really blame him, even though he was stealing from Brown before he met her. Jeannette hurt a lot of people, including his wife and kids. But he was having an affair with her. He's at fault for cheating, and the consequences are his. He didn't see it that way. He blamed Jeannette for losing his wife and kids, and more importantly, his money. He had a pretty cushy setup. He liked having a wife at home who took care of him."

Sebastian smiled behind her back. "I can't see you in that

role."

Evelyn further relaxed. "No, and he knew it, too. I'm not sure if he had ever intended to go through with the wedding or not. After it was all over, I began to wonder if he originally planned to marry me and use my shares to hurt the company from within. But I suppose he didn't blame Brown; he blamed Jeannette. With my mother gone, I was his only target. Hurting Brown was a bonus."

Sebastian tensed. He knew he should keep his mouth shut but couldn't. "Did you sleep with him?"

Evelyn went rigid under his hands. She pulled away but didn't stand up. "Yes, I did. I know this sounds stupid, but I felt like I had to. I was twenty, we were engaged, and quite frankly, I was curious. I almost chickened out, but I went through with it. It's one of the few things I still feel ashamed of."

Sebastian tried to get her to face him, but she used the cane to hit him. She rose before he could get a hold of her. He rubbed his stomach where the cane handle had struck him. "Why feel ashamed because you slept with him? You're right about being engaged."

Evelyn turned in a fury. "Can you imagine how I feel knowing I slept with a man who'd been with my mother? My mother!" Her voice rose as she let the violent flood of emotions out. "It sickens me every time I think about the intimacies we shared after he'd shared them with my mother!"

"Evelyn." Sebastian kept his voice soft. She was shaking like a leaf. "I know how you feel about your mother."

"I hate her!" She practically screamed it. "The men she

had and the people she hurt were nothing compared to what she did to me and Kimberly. We had to witness all of the things she did. And I mean all of them. She was never discreet, and she didn't bother to hide things from us. Not her men, not her drugs. The only thing Kimberly and I could do was try to ignore it."

Sebastian tried to get a hold of her, but she held the cane like a weapon. "Evelyn, you need to calm down."

"Don't tell me to calm down. You wanted to know." Despite her arguments, she took a deep breath. When it was all said and done, there was nothing she could do to change what happened between her and Andrew. "It's just that I didn't know how I was going to live with myself, knowing what I did about Andrew and my mother. Knowing it was an affair that happened long before I met him doesn't help. Knowing there were other women between her and me didn't help. I went wandering the cliff that day, sick to my stomach that I had ever let Andrew lay a finger on me. I'd been obsessing over what I'd learned; unable to grasp the ramifications of the money he stole. I could only concentrate on the affair he'd had with Jeannette. I couldn't seem to straighten it all out in my head. You know, the accident seemed like punishment for my monumental stupidity. For a long time, I felt like I deserved it for what had happened."

"You aren't responsible. Andrew and your mother are." Sebastian was relieved that she was calming down, even if her words were nonsensical.

"I do know that. But in less rational moments, it's hard for me."

Sebastian remembered Jeannette. He wasn't surprised to find out she'd had affairs with the employees at Brown. What bothered him was the money she'd stolen. At least he knew now, and apparently, Howard eventually found out where Jeannette had gotten her money. Sebastian had wondered if she'd gotten the money from the company. He supposed, in a way, she had.

"Is that everything?" Sebastian was ready to let it go for now.

"I suppose so. It's enough for now, anyway." Evelyn sat down again. "Sorry for hitting you."

"You don't sound terribly apologetic." Sebastian kept an eye on the cane as she set it alongside the couch.

"You deserved it for pushing me." Evelyn closed her eyes and leaned back. "Some days it seems so long ago. Other times, it seems like yesterday. She was interested in you."

It took him a second to put together what she meant. "I know. Your mother had a thing for married men. And she wasn't subtle."

"She's the reason I have such a hard time with Leslie. She's a lot like Jeannette. But Leslie isn't malicious. And she doesn't date married men." Evelyn looked him in the eye. "I have a hard time knowing you were with Leslie."

Sebastian didn't pretend ignorance. Something was happening between them, though it surprised him that she would admit it in even a roundabout way. It would be stupid to pretend otherwise. "After what you went through with Andrew, I can see why. I can't change it, Evie. But you don't have to let it bother you."

Evelyn's eyes widen. "You just called me Evie."

Sebastian sat down beside her but didn't touch her. "Get used to it."

Evelyn let it go. They sat quietly side by side, neither speaking. Evelyn knew he had a lot to think through. So did she.

Chapter Twelve

After such an emotional evening the night before, Evelyn thought she would be feeling some embarrassment, but oddly enough she was in good spirits the next morning. She joined the children for breakfast again, enjoying the routine Sebastian kept to every morning. He was going to drop the kids off with Kimberly again, but for only half a day. After that, she knew he was taking the kids to visit some friends of his. Sebastian had mentioned in passing that his buddy Rick from college had a winery and horse farm not too far from here. He was married, and he and his wife had their first child. Sebastian had offered to take Evelyn with them, but she put him off, claiming she had work to do. Even if that weren't true, she had no intention of setting foot on a horse farm. She still mourned the loss of Isabel and the dreams she had of breeding her. Thankfully Sebastian hadn't pressed.

Later that evening, when Sebastian and the children returned, Lucy was talking about how she was going to own horses one day and how she was going to ride them across the country. Despite the ache deep inside at the mention of horses, Evelyn couldn't help but smile at the child's enthusiasm. She'd been horse-crazy at Lucy's age. Her mother thought it was a phase. Her grandfather had realized it wasn't, and that was why he bought her Isabel. Her grandfather had an uncanny way of understanding how people felt even when they weren't open about their feelings.

But instead of dwelling on it, Evelyn settled into her favorite spot on the couch in the living room to read.

"Evelyn?" Lucy came over to the couch and climbed up beside her. She had a book in her hands.

"Yes, Lucy?" She looked around for Sebastian, but she didn't see him. Despite the fact that it was getting late, she was fairly certain he was out on the back patio with Daniel. The transformation there was amazing. She had seen Daniel outside with Sebastian a couple of times helping to fill pots and water flowers.

"Can you read this to me?" She handed Evelyn the book and waited expectantly.

Evelyn hadn't spent much time around kids. None of her old friends had them. When she stopped and thought about it, Sebastian's kids were the only ones she could remember spending time with. But they were so much younger then. Lucy started to look crestfallen as Evelyn hesitated, and Evelyn didn't have the heart to say no.

"Don't you read?" The child was nine, after all.

"I don't read so good. I have to go to school extra at night to get help with my reading. I'm supposed to read by myself, but I like it when my mom reads to me. I want you to read to me. Please?"

Evelyn's heart turned over in her chest as Lucy cuddled up next to her and laid her head on her arm. Evelyn adjusted the child so she could read the book and keep Lucy next to her. The book was about two twins, a boy and a girl, who solved mysteries. Despite the book being for children, she found herself enjoying reading the tale to Lucy. The girl was listening intently while twisting a lock of Evelyn's hair.

Sebastian found them on the couch together half an hour later, Walter curled up at their feet. Evelyn's foot absently stroked the dog as she read. Daniel had gone upstairs to wash the dirt off. It did funny things to his heart to see his daughter snuggled up against Evelyn as they read together. Sometimes he forgot how much he missed out on being away from his children. He imagined Lucy cuddled up against Becky just like this, while her husband looked on. The thought left a bitter taste in his mouth, but what was past was past. He didn't wish he was still married to Becky. He just wished things had turned out differently.

"Hey Lucy, it's time to get washed up."

"Can't we finish the chapter, Daddy? It's only got a couple more pages." She batted her big green eyes up at him.

He always had a hard time resisting his little girl. "Finish the chapter, then head on up."

Evelyn felt a little self-conscious as she finished reading the chapter, but Sebastian had headed into the other room and let them be. Less than half an hour later, she sent Lucy upstairs, and when she heard the child in the bathroom above, she put the book on the coffee table and relaxed for a moment. Then she had a terrible thought. Where had Sebastian gone? Before he had returned, Evelyn had been in the back den reading her favorite romance novel. The den was hardly used anymore. It was the space her grandfather had called his own, that and his office. Anne and Evelyn spent most of their time in the formal front living room, but Howard had usually been found in the den watching the news or sports. After her long talk with Sebastian last night, Evelyn had been missing her grandfather's presence, and when she got home from the office she had spent a good hour there.

Evelyn picked up her cane and headed toward the back of the house.

Evelyn stepped carefully into the room, the room poorly lit from the back porch light shining through the back windows, and a small table lamp on low. Sebastian was where she feared he was. He sat stretched out on her grandfather's favorite lounger, her romance novel open. It looked like he'd gotten through a good chunk of it.

"I never pegged you as the type." Sebastian closed the book and looked at Evelyn as if he'd never seen her before.

Evelyn shrugged, trying to look nonchalant. "Just something Anne gave me."

Sebastian chuckled at that. "You forget I know Anne better than that. If you'd said Kimberly, I'd have believed you. Anne only reads nonfiction. The biographies you read are most likely hers."

Evelyn started to back out of the room, but the look on Sebastian's face stopped her. He was looking at her, but she could not decipher the look. It kept her frozen in place.

"What do you think of this book?" Sebastian rose and crossed to her.

Evelyn couldn't speak. The book he held was one of her favorites. The characters were so very different from one another, yet they fell in love. The hero was independent, not needing anyone. The heroine was giving, even to those who did not want to accept her help. Through many emotional trials, the pair found a way to bend enough to give and take to make their relationship succeed. It was by far one of the more emotional books she owned, one she pulled out whenever she needed an emotional pick-me-up.

Sebastian set the book down and took Evelyn's hands. "That book says a lot about you."

Evelyn had enough sense left to smirk at that. "Not likely. It's a sentimental, sappy book. It's hardly worth reading. But I find books like it distracting. I'm certainly not the sentimental type."

"Five years ago I'd have agreed with you. But you're not the same woman you were before your accident."

"I am the same person."

"I disagree."

"It doesn't matter what you think." Evelyn tried to pull her hands away, but he refused to let them go.

"You hid it well back then, the softness and sentiment. You don't hide it so well anymore. Your feelings and emotions are very much on the surface these days. As a teenager, you hid them behind that cold wall of yours. Your attitude used to drive me crazy. But they were there; I just wasn't smart enough to see them. I like to think I'm smarter than I was before."

"I don't want you to see anything. I want you to leave me alone."

Sebastian tugged her closer, his thighs brushing hers. "I can't do that. I tried. Since last night I've done nothing but think about you. And if you're honest, you've spent a lot of today thinking about me."

Evelyn almost panicked as he pulled her against him. He settled her hands on his chest, covering them with his own. She could feel his heart beating quickly under her palms. Despite all common sense, she felt her heart rate jump to match his.

There were no more words. Sebastian took Evelyn's lips with his. This was their first kiss, and his head swam with it. She was so far removed from being cold. Her lips were warm and moist against his, though at first, she didn't kiss him back. Her fingertips curled involuntarily into his chest. He could feel her breath as it hitched, and she trembled when she finally kissed him back. Nothing could have prepared him for the impact she had on his senses.

Evelyn stopped thinking the moment his lips met hers. She wasn't sure what she had expected from him, but it wasn't this soft savoring. She'd seen him kiss Leslie before he broke up with her, and it had been rough, almost impatient. This slow sampling seemed like it could go on forever.

Sebastian released her lips for a moment to catch his breath. He inhaled the soft scent of her. She always smelled a little flowery, the scent so light he sometimes thought he was imagining it. She tipped her head for him, allowing him access to her neck and shoulder when he sought the fragrant skin there. He couldn't find any words to tell her what he was feeling at that moment. He could only show her. His hands no longer needed to hold hers to him. He slid his hands up her arms, then down her body to her hips and held her close.

For Evelyn, time seemed to have stopped. She could feel his breath and the soft kisses he placed on her neck and shoulder. One arm slid up and around his neck to get better balance; the other stayed pressed against his chest between their bodies, her palm over his heart. If it weren't for the firm clasp of his arms on her waist, she would have melted into a heap at his feet. Nothing could have prepared her for the devastation of his kiss.

She knew nothing would be the same between them now. She doubted he knew how deep her feelings ran or how much she wanted his soft kisses. She had been pushing her feelings for him aside for so many years that she hadn't realized how much she cared for him. She had imagined him coming to her like this in the past, but this was so much better than anything she had ever imagined. If he had come to her in anger, she would have been able to fight him. She knew how to handle his hostility. But this quiet, silent devouring she had no defense against.

Sebastian brought his lips back to hers, and this time she kissed him back without hesitation. He sank deeper into the kiss, unable to let her go.

Loud giggling from the hall doused the couple in cold water. Sebastian released Evelyn's lips but not his hold on her. He turned to give Lucy a stern look. He saw her eyes widen right before she bolted back up the stairs. She was yelling Daniel's name over and over while still giggling as she took the stairs. Sebastian knew the story of his kissing Evelyn was being shared with his son at that moment.

Evelyn tried to pull away, but he didn't let her go at first.

She tried to find some way of breaking the sudden tension, though she was pretty sure she was the only one feeling tense. Sebastian looked relaxed and satisfied. Evelyn wanted to find some way to explain that the kiss was a mistake. She couldn't have uttered a single word just then.

"I don't want to let you go. If I had my way, we'd finish this upstairs in my bed." Sebastian slowly let Evelyn go, making sure she was steady on her feet. She looked incredibly beautiful with the lamp shining on her hair, her lips flushed pink and swollen from his.

Evelyn mentally shook herself. He was talking about sex. Talking about finishing their kiss in bed. She wrapped her arms around her waist, trying to control the shaking inside. "That would be a mistake."

"Most likely, but at the moment, it's hard to see how."

"We're too different for any kind of relationship to work, no matter how brief."

Sebastian nodded toward the book. "The couple in that book are very different, and I'm guessing they work it out. Being different isn't always a bad thing."

Evelyn just wrapped her arms tighter around herself and ignored the book. She watched Sebastian as he turned to leave.

Sebastian turned back when he reached the doorway. "Any relationship we have could be many things, Evie. But one thing it would not be is brief. I'll see you in the morning."

Evelyn stood in the center of the room, scared with the knowledge that he was right, knowing that if he took her in his arms again, she wouldn't be able to resist him. And she was scared of the knowledge that she didn't want to.

* * *

Sebastian was feeling a little shaky himself as he headed up the stairs to put the kids to bed. He figured he should try to explain what Lucy saw, but wasn't sure how to go about it. He might be free to date whoever he wanted, but his children weren't used to him having a woman around. When he had his children, he devoted what time he had to them. He wanted them to always know how much he loved and cared about them even when he wasn't around.

Lucy was already in bed, her favorite stuffed bunny tucked under her arm. It made him sad to realize she wouldn't be sleeping with stuffed animals much longer. Walter was lying at the foot of the bed, staring at him. The dog was closest to Lucy when it came to bedtime. During the day, the dog was more likely to be at Daniel's side as they played. It was as if the dog knew that Lucy needed the added comfort of his presence when she slept.

"Daddy, how come you were kissing Evie?"

Sebastian smiled at his daughter's mimicking of Evelyn's nickname. He was unsure what to say to that. Daniel chose that moment to come in.

"Are you going to marry her?" Daniel watched his father closely while he waited for an answer.

"Okay, guys, it was just a kiss. I like Evelyn, and sometimes when you like someone, you want to kiss them." That sounded like a reasonable answer.

"Mom was always kissing Dwight, and they got married."

That came from Lucy.

"Kissing doesn't mean you're getting married. I can't say what the future holds for me and Evelyn, but you guys know that you would be the first ones to know." Sebastian pulled the covers up and Lucy snuggled down. He turned and put his arm around Daniel's shoulders. His son might only be eleven, but sometimes he seemed so grown-up.

"So, what do you guys think of her?"

Daniels shrugged and didn't respond. Lucy piped up. "I like her. She's nice and she plays with us. She's pretty and has pretty hair. Walter likes her, too. She didn't even get mad when she caught him trying to chew on her cane. And she read my book, and she didn't make fun of me for not reading good."

"Well." The correction was automatic. His daughter was sensitive about her reading, and he had no doubt some of the kids made fun of her. She had been diagnosed with dyslexia early on in school. Sebastian was paying a very good tutor to make sure she got the help she needed.

Sebastian realized Evelyn really was nice. Like he told her, she hid it well when she was younger. She had grown thick skin because of her mother. He imagined the kids made fun of her because of her mom when she was Lucy's age. He didn't even want to think of what she had endured at the hands of her drug-addicted mother.

Sebastian flipped off the light but left the door open. He kept his arm around Daniel and walked with him back to his son's room.

"Do you like her, Dad?" Daniel crossed to the bed and sat down. He was too old to be tucked in.

"Yeah, I do. I've known her for a long time. You probably don't remember her much, but you knew her when you were little."

"I sort of remember. You didn't like her then."

"Sometimes people change. She changed a lot after her accident, and I like the person she is now."

"Mom says that people change and that's how come you two got divorced."

"I think your mom changed some. But it was because I didn't change that we got divorced. I worked too much, and your mom wanted me around. After a while, she got tired of waiting for me to change."

"Is it your fault you guys split?" Daniel climbed into bed and pulled the covers up.

"Mostly, yes." Sebastian took a seat on the end of the bed. "I wasn't the type of person your mom wanted to be married to. We tried our best because we both love you guys so much. It's why we're still friends. Sometimes marriage doesn't work out. Your mom is much happier married to Dwight."

"I know, but I wish we could see you more." For a moment, Daniel looked like the young boy that he was, vulnerable and unsure.

Sebastian patted his leg through the covers. "I miss you guys so much. We haven't talked about it, but I took over Brown, the company Howard owned. You remember Howard, right?" His son nodded, so he went on. "I'll be staying in California now. I'll have to buy a nice house so you can stay with me sometimes, and I'll be able to visit you guys more often, too."

"Really? How come you didn't say so before?"

"I had to think about what I wanted first. But it's been good to be home. I missed you guys, and I missed Anne and my other friends. I liked living in England, but it's time I came back."

"Are you going to stay this time?"

The question was one he'd heard Becky ask him time and again. This time he had the right answer. "Yes, this time I'm going to stay."

* * *

Evelyn could hear Sebastian talking to his son but couldn't make out the words. She didn't need to hear what they were saying to know that they were probably talking about her. And the kiss Lucy had witnessed.

Evelyn closed her bedroom door behind her, her legs still trembling in the aftermath of Sebastian's kiss. And what a kiss it had been. She stripped her clothes off and tossed them on the floor as she headed to the bath. She was feeling pretty good right now, the usual aches buried beneath the pleasure that still hummed in her blood. She might not need the bath to loosen her muscles right now, but maybe it would help her relax. Sebastian's parting words not only confused her but also pleased her at the same time. Perhaps it was possible that Sebastian was attracted to her. Five years ago she would have laughed had anyone even suggested it. Now she wasn't so sure.

She could toss it up to propinquity. Here they were, a man and a woman alone together night after night. She was and had been attracted to him since the day she met him. A good part of her animosity toward him had to do with self-protection. She would have been mortified had she thought he had guessed at even a fraction of her feelings toward him. The idea that he knew she cared about him no longer seemed like such a bad thing. Telling him the other night that she didn't like the fact he'd been with Leslie had been close to a confession of interest. She had a feeling her response to his kisses confessed her attraction.

Evelyn finished filling up the tub and relaxed up to her neck in the frothing water. She supposed attraction was a mild term for what she was feeling at the moment. Her heart was still racing in remembrance of the feel of his body against hers and that wonderful mouth of his. She would have collapsed at his feet when his mouth trailed kisses down her neck had he not been holding her up. His warm breath against her sensitive skin had sent tiny shivers down her spine. She imagined he had that effect on any woman he chose to kiss.

But why her and why now? He said he thought she had changed. And perhaps in some ways she had. She was more sensitive to other people and their moods. She found herself wanting to befriend her family instead of pushing them away. She and Kimberly were closer now than they had been before her accident. In the years before, they had spent very little time together once Evelyn had gone to college. Evelyn had spent almost every free moment out in the stables or out riding Isabel.

But what was it really that was attracting Sebastian now? Was it her more feminine appearance? Was it just because they were alone together? Or was he attracted to vulnerable women? That last thought grated a bit. She wasn't looking for a white knight to come and rescue her. She certainly didn't want him to care for her out of pity or some weird sense of duty.

Since the bath was not relaxing her as she had hoped, she washed and conditioned her hair, scrubbed down, and got out. The warm water was not cooling her blood, and neither was lying there thinking about Sebastian and his possible reasons for kissing her. If he was attracted to her, she wasn't sure what she should do about it. They were very different. To start with, he was thirteen years her senior. And though she didn't feel young, in reality, she was much younger than he was. Perhaps she lacked the maturity needed to hold his interest for long. He said any relationship between them wouldn't be brief, but it was hard to imagine anything else. And to top it off, she was working for him again. She didn't think they could be lovers at night and business associates during the day. At least she didn't think she could. She guessed Sebastian would be good at compartmentalizing his business and personal life.

And maybe she was just blowing the whole thing out of proportion. She'd known him for ten years, and this was the first time he'd ever kissed her. Perhaps it was just a fluke or something that happened to him a lot. He might not be the most handsome of men, but there was a sense of strength and security in him that was incredibly attractive. His personality alone would attract any number of women. Maybe kissing a woman like that was second nature to him.

Of course, that didn't make her feel any better, but it did slow her heart rate and help her put the kiss into perspective. She supposed the best thing to do was pretend it didn't happen. They both had to work tomorrow, and then she had an appointment with her doctor. At the moment, she was feeling good, and she supposed she had her hormones and endorphins to thank for that. She doubted she'd feel so good in the morning. Although it was amusing to think that perhaps all she needed was Sebastian's kisses to cure her ills.

Chapter Thirteen

"Are these numbers right?" Sebastian tossed the papers over to John.

John looked them over while Sebastian's gaze drifted to Evelyn. They'd locked themselves in the boardroom early that morning and had been going over the various department budgets and reporting. Sebastian had been struggling all morning to keep his mind on work. Evelyn had chosen a soft pink dress today, belted with a green sash. She looked soft and feminine in that dress; it was a struggle not to kick John out of the room and pick up where they'd left off the night before.

"These numbers seem high." John highlighted different sections, and Sebastian could see he didn't like what he was reading.

"We are spending entirely too much money on research. It's almost double what it was two years ago."

Evelyn furrowed her brows as she looked at what Sebastian was talking about. "We've not been working on anything new. The past year we've been working on some reformulations, but mostly we've been focused on distribution and new markets for our top products. David agreed to reduce some of the money his department was spending to focus on rebranding. That's not to say he hasn't been working on development at all, but you're right, this is high. His biggest project has been reformulating some of our cleaning solutions. He's obsessed with finding ways to improve our green products without losing their efficacy."

"We'll need to talk to David. And I want to see the cost breakdown of his current project." Sebastian made a few notations and set the file aside. "I would also say we're spending too much on this rebranding project. I agree on a larger distribution, but why all the fuss about changing the appearance?"

Evelyn felt she needed to defend this decision. "Our packaging is old and outdated. It doesn't appeal to the consumer. I had the marketing department go into the field, and the dark packaging isn't doing us any favors, especially in our beauty line."

Sebastian grunted at that. "I can buy into that somewhat. Sales have been down in our bath and toiletry lines. But again, this is a lot of money."

Evelyn dug through her pile and pulled up the same report. This time her frown was more pronounced. "This isn't the budget I authorized. This is almost a third higher." She grabbed another report. One after another, the budgets were beyond what they should have been.

"I don't understand." John rolled over to where Evelyn sat and watched as she marked up the pages. "When we went over last quarter's numbers, they weren't this high."

Evelyn was almost amused as she watched John scoot back to where Sebastian sat. John had chosen sides, and he'd chosen Sebastian over his boss of the last four years. She never thought he was dumb.

But besides John's defection, she apparently had bigger problems. These numbers were high. And there was no way to account for them. She approved every budget for every department. Money didn't flow out unless she knew about it. Since they'd been struggling financially for so long, she was never lax when it came to money.

"Could it be a glitch?" John looked over at Sebastian for confirmation.

"No. The only reason I have these numbers is that I pulled expenses line by line and tallied them up. I didn't pull the basic reports. This looks deliberate."

Evelyn's stomach clenched at not only his words but his demeanor. "You mean someone is embezzling."

"We don't have proof, but it sure looks like it. I know what theft looks like."

"But who?" John found his voice first.

"Given the history of this company and the fact that Howard had hired a private investigator to follow Andrew Shepherd around, I'd say he's a good candidate. The problem is he'd have to have help from the inside."

Evelyn could only feel hurt when John looked at her in response to Sebastian's theory. But she supposed she couldn't blame him either, since it was her fault last time. On the flip side, it did her heart good that Sebastian was not looking her way, but only flipping through the files. His clenched jaw was the only thing that was giving away the fact that he was angry. Very angry.

Evelyn figured she'd be better off being the one to say it first. "I'm the only person left at this company that Andrew had any ties to. A few people quit when Andrew left five years ago, but none of them tied back to Andrew. That's not to say he couldn't have found someone to bribe."

Sebastian grunted in response. "He's slick, I'll give him that. He could have bribed almost anyone. But it would have to be someone higher up to have access to our accounts."

John stood and started pacing. "That's still a whole lot of people. And anyone with decent hacking skills could probably get into our system. We've not spent a lot of money updating our computer security systems."

Evelyn felt his glance come back her way again. She sighed. "We have decent computer security, but no, it hasn't been updated in a while. That is a huge expense, and since we're not working on any big development projects, I felt it could wait a little longer."

"We'll have to bring someone in." Sebastian tossed the papers and rubbed his tired eyes. "First thing we have to do is find where the leak is. Then we need to find out who is responsible for the missing funds. And I'll need to find the investigator Howard hired and see if he knows anything else."

John stopped pacing. "What investigator?"

Evelyn answered before Sebastian could. "Grandfather hired an investigator to follow Andrew. When he popped up back in town and bought out Global, he thought Andrew might be up to something. Given the bad press we've gotten lately, and now this, perhaps Grandfather was right. Maybe Andrew is trying to sabotage us."

"But why?" John's confusion was genuine. "I know your relationship with him ended badly, but really, embezzling is a serious charge. Not to mention your grandfather couldn't prove he was responsible for the missing money five years ago. When Howard realized the man you were engaged to was the same man who embezzled from him fifteen years ago, he was convinced Andrew was behind the missing funds and lost accounts. It always seemed a bit of a stretch to me. He wasn't working for Brown five years ago, even though he was engaged to you; what was his motive the second time? He's the one who left you, not the other way around."

Evelyn understood John's frustration, but she wasn't going to enlighten him about Andrew's history with her mother. Grandfather had kept that secret, and she was grateful. Knowing you were engaged to and had slept with the man your mother had an affair with was hard enough. She would be humiliated if the family knew. Funny, but she trusted Sebastian to keep her secrets. His next words proved her right.

"It doesn't matter why. People do crazy things for lesser reasons than a broken engagement. He could be mad that he got caught and came back to prove himself. Andrew's career survived the gossip, but there are still those out there who don't trust him. Howard did damage to his career, even if it was minimal. He could simply want revenge."

John dropped into his chair, his frustration clear. "I suppose. Obviously, Howard was keeping tabs on him for a reason. Hopefully, the investigator will be able to tell us why."

Evelyn just hoped that the investigator didn't dig up too much of the past. She would rather her mother's relationship with him stay dead and buried.

Evelyn's phone beeped, breaking the silence. "Sorry, that's my alarm. I've got to head out."

Sebastian glanced at the clock. "Same here. I promised the kids I'd go swimming with them this afternoon. Plus, I'm sure Kimberly is ready for a break."

John flashed Sebastian a smile. "Kimberly has taken to motherhood like she was born for it. She's probably having as much fun as the kids are."

"Maybe, but I'd still better head out. Lock these papers up and don't say a word to anyone."

John started gathering the papers. "Not even David?"

"No, not even David. He'll just get upset and probably try to confront Andrew. That's the last thing we want right now."

Evelyn could only agree. "David has a temper. And if he thought for even a moment Andrew is involved in shady dealings against Brown, he'll drive over to Crown and call him out on it, with or without proof."

"Agreed." Sebastian walked over to Evelyn and took her arm, taking the cane with him. He left John to clean up the papers and walked Evelyn to the elevator. They both missed John's questioning look.

Evelyn let herself lean on Sebastian as they made their way down the hall. "Do you think Andrew is behind this?"

He shrugged. "Of all the possibilities, that's the easiest one to believe. This is a small company, and it would be hard to pull something like this off and not have someone notice. And it's a bit of a stretch to think that a company could be a victim to two different embezzlers in five years.

He got away with it before; he probably thought he could again. Then again, maybe it is someone else. Anything is possible. With Howard's illness and death, it might have seemed like an opportune time. Your and David's focus has been divided lately."

"I suppose I vote it was Andrew, as well. But he has to know we would suspect him."

"He got away with it twice. Perhaps he thinks if he covers his tracks, he'll get away with it again."

Evelyn supposed he had the right of it. It was just a bitter pill to swallow. She knew that she wasn't the cause of Andrew's crimes, but it had felt like it was her fault when it happened five years ago. If she hadn't let him get so close to her, he would never have gotten access to Brown. And though she certainly wasn't his way inside this time, it still felt like it was her fault. Had she died five years ago, she had a feeling he wouldn't be doing this. Of course, she didn't have proof that her accident was intentional, and she couldn't bring herself to voice her beliefs to Sebastian. No one would have believed her five years ago, and she doubted anyone would now.

Sebastian put his arm around her and squeezed her shoulder. "Don't look so glum. This time we know what he's up to and can be ready for him. Last time, it all came as a surprise."

Evelyn tried not to enjoy his arm around her, but of course, she failed. She looked up at him and was surprised to see desire there. She stepped away from him, knowing how out of place it was for him to be looking at her like that in the office.

"You'll tell me how your appointment with the doctor goes, won't you?" Sebastian let her go since the elevator doors opened. He might have otherwise kept her in his embrace.

Evelyn sighed, knowing she wouldn't have a choice. "I will after the kids are in bed."

"I'll meet you in the living room."

Evelyn just nodded. She doubted the living room would be any safer than the den had been last night once the kids were in bed. Part of her wanted to just let herself go and let their relationship go where it would inevitably lead. Another part of her was terrified and unsure. And the last part of her was embarrassed about her body and the visible signs of the trauma she had endured. Her body wasn't pretty. He had seen the scars on her calves, but those were nothing compared to the scars on the rest of her.

* * *

Surgery. No matter how many times the doctor told her that it was her only option, she refused to accept it. Her body had already been through so much. She didn't want to contemplate being sliced open again, or enduring another recovery. This time it wasn't Anne who was going to question her about her appointment; this time it would be Sebastian. This afternoon he had seemed genuinely concerned for her well-being. And though she was still reeling a bit from the incredible kiss they had shared, she wasn't sure how committed she wanted to be. And Sebastian was making her feel more and more committed to him without even trying.

Evelyn parked the van and got out. She grabbed the ever-present cane and went inside. She could hear the kids playing and Walter barking behind the house, so she knew Sebastian wasn't too far away. His presence was soothing. It was beginning to frighten her how much she enjoyed his company and that of his children. She had even gotten used to Walter, who seemed to have boundless energy. She couldn't help but feel Anne knew what she was doing when she left Sebastian alone with her.

The day concluded with what Evelyn was beginning to think of as the family routine. Dinner was eaten, and Sebastian and Daniel went outside to work in the garden. Lucy had curled up against her again, this time without asking, and Evelyn continued reading to her the book they had begun the night before. Sebastian had come in after sending Daniel upstairs and fetched Lucy to do the same. Lucy had given Evelyn a hug and a kiss this time, and Evelyn was glad Sebastian followed Lucy up because she didn't want him to see her very emotional reaction to the affection Lucy so easily gave her. The hug and kiss left a little ache in Evelyn's heart. It had been so long since she had received affection without strings. Anne loved her, but Anne's love was just as complicated as that of the rest of her family. They loved her, but they didn't understand her: her needs, her wants, or her desires. Lucy just gave affection to those she cared about, and it was as simple as that. Funny that a child should be the one to remind her of how love should be.

Her biggest complication came down the stairs forty-five

minutes later. Sebastian poured himself a drink, refraining from getting her one this time since the last time he fixed her one, she didn't drink it.

"So how did it go?"

Evelyn smiled slightly at his jumping into the conversation. He usually was one to get to the point. "The good news is I didn't do any major damage when I fell. I pulled and strained the tendons in my back and bruised my hip, but that's about it."

"That is good news." Sebastian took a sip and watched Evelyn as her hands fidgeted in her lap. "You never did tell me what happened."

"I was wondering how long it was going to take you to ask. You didn't used to beat around the bush."

Sebastian just shrugged at that. "It didn't seem like the right time to ask before."

"Meaning that you feel like it is now." Evelyn leaned back, resting her head on the back of the couch cushions, closing her eyes. "I don't remember a whole lot about the fall or how long I was there. I'm told it wasn't very long. I would have been dead if someone hadn't found me. I didn't fall too far really. It was more of the rocks and the hard surface that did the damage. I was in and out of consciousness. I remember the thunder and great flashes of light across the dark sky. I had tethered Isabel to a tree and had been sitting on the ledge, just staring at the horizon. I was hurting from the letter Andrew had left me, still reeling from the fact that he had done what he did because of Jeannette."

"The family wonders if you jumped." Sebastian watched

her closely to see her reaction. They'd touched on this before, but he wanted to hear it again.

Her reaction wasn't much of one. "Yeah, I know what everyone thinks. I can honestly say I never contemplated suicide. I did contemplate running away. Kimberly's and my relationship was strained. Leslie was mad at me. Grandfather and Anne didn't deserve what I was responsible for putting them through. You left, and I was in charge at Brown. Everything was spiraling out of control, and I didn't know what to do. The next thing I knew, I was falling. I passed out, and sometime later I woke. There was a couple on the trail who didn't realize a storm was coming and got caught in it. They were walking on the path when they happened to see Isabel wandering. She was no longer tethered to the tree, which was why Grandfather was convinced she had tossed me. That's just not how I remember it, not that my memory is all that reliable."

Evelyn paused and opened her eyes to look at Sebastian. He looked like he could wait patiently all night for her to finish her story. "So the couple called for help. One of them, not sure which, climbed down and covered me up with a blanket they had used for a picnic. The rain hadn't come yet, but lightning was rippling across the sky. The person had climbed back up and they waited for help." She couldn't share with him the terror she had felt when the rescue team had come to help her. Their dark clothes and shadowed faces still gave her nightmares.

"I was rushed to the hospital and the trauma team did all they could to help me. I had fallen straight down. The impact broke several bones. My weight fell mostly on the left. The femur broke in my left leg. I still have a rod in there. Both the tibia and fibula were broken in both legs. My pelvic bone broke, as did the left hip joint. The impact went up my back, breaking several discs and vertebra. Thankfully it didn't go all the way up to my neck and my spinal cord wasn't severed. I was wearing my riding helmet so the impact to my head when I hit the ground wasn't as bad as it could have been. I had a small brain bleed, but it didn't require surgery. I'm told it was a miracle I don't have permanent brain damage from the fall. And my internal organs were all intact. I had some open wounds and contusions, but overall, I was lucky."

Evelyn paused and was startled when Sebastian swiftly rose from where he had been sitting, sat beside her, and drew her into his arms. He didn't offer sympathy or platitudes. And since he wasn't offering her pity, she rested against him and let him absorb the sorrow she felt anytime she told the story. She was blessed to be alive, and it still shamed her that there were times when she wished she were dead. And she still felt shame when she had an outburst, some of which Sebastian had now been an audience member to. Her eyes burned a bit, but no tears fell.

"You went through hell, Evelyn, and no one should have to go through what you did."

Evelyn wrapped her arms around his waist and simply enjoyed the comfort of his arms. "I barely remember the surgery on my femur. I do remember all the pins and screws. And I remember when some of them had to be removed. I don't want to have my hip replaced, and I don't want to have surgery on my back again. The doctor says it would be a matter of replacing a few discs and probably a spinal fusion. And of course, the hip is shot. It hurts so bad sometimes. But then I remember the surgery and physical therapy, and I don't want to go through it all again. And there is no guarantee my back will be better. I'm told that my back will always hurt because of the impact of the fall. Some, but not all, of the damage can be undone. I can live with the ugly scars; I just don't know how much longer I want to live with this level of pain."

"You're thinking of having the surgery, then?"

Because it was a question and not a command, Evelyn lifted her head and kissed him lightly. It was the only way she could think of to thank him for asking and not demanding. "I don't know. Sometimes. Times like right now I think it's time to bite the bullet and do it. Other times, when I stop and think about what surgery will mean, I refuse to even consider it."

Sebastian set her away from him and looked into her eyes. "You were never so indecisive. You used to get an idea, and that was that."

Unsure what else to say when he looked at her so intently, she gave him a shrug and scooted away from him. "I guess maybe I have changed some."

"I'm glad you'll admit it."

They were both quiet for a time. Evelyn didn't feel like interrupting the peace of the moment.

"It must be the domesticity of the situation." Sebastian turned to face her on the sofa, grasping her hands and drawing her back to him.

"What are you talking about?"

"That's going to make me kiss you again."

Evelyn stared at him for a moment. That was the last thing she expected him to say after her story about the fall. Then it dawned on her what he meant. The children were tucked in bed. Walter was asleep by the hearth. The sun had set, and only the softest light filtered into the living room from the other rooms. The lights were low, and the house was quiet.

Evelyn tried to think of something to say, but nothing came to mind. Then her mind went blank just as it had the first time he'd kissed her. Sebastian lightly cupped her cheek and placed a couple of light kisses on her lips.

"I think I need to try that again." Instead of simply kissing her again, Sebastian carefully pulled Evelyn to her feet. He hoped the unsteadiness in her legs was because of him and not aftereffects of telling him what had happened.

Evelyn felt the strength leave her, and she leaned against Sebastian. His kisses were so much nicer, so much sweeter than any she'd received before. The first time he kissed her, she was so dazed she couldn't think. This time was the same, but she somewhat managed to keep her wits about her.

Sebastian pulled her closer, and Evelyn's arms wound around his neck, just as he needed them to. He gave in to the inevitability of the moment. His kiss deepened, and Evelyn responded beautifully.

"I've missed this." Sebastian pulled slightly back and pressed Evelyn's cheek to his shoulder.

"Missed what? You only kissed me once."

Sebastian chuckled at that. "That's not quite what I

meant. I mean times like this. It's getting late. The kids are in bed. I can steal a moment."

Evelyn pulled back, but Sebastian's arms stayed around her. "You mean you miss your wife."

Sebastian tightened his arms around her, pressing her closer to his body. "I don't mean my ex-wife. I mean a woman. A soft woman. One who responds to me without hesitation. One who is just as involved as I am. Right now you're that woman. It's a little strange, but it also feels right."

Evelyn wasn't sure how to take that comment. It didn't make her feel good that any responsive woman would do. But she was the woman at the moment, and she wanted more. Evelyn pulled Sebastian's mouth back to hers. She might regret it in the morning, but right now it was what she wanted.

Sebastian had no idea how long they stood there. He kept his hands on her waist to keep them from straying. He could feel the trembling in Evelyn's body, and he knew, for now, this couldn't go beyond kissing. But the kissing was good. Very good. And if he didn't stop, his internal promise to keep his hands to himself would be broken.

Sebastian set Evelyn away from him gently and watched her closely as her lashes fluttered open. "We should go to bed."

Evelyn wasn't sure she had heard him right. Then the temper she couldn't quite get under control sprang free once again. "Is that what you think? A couple of kisses and I'd hop into bed with you?" For some reason, his assumption hurt as much as it aroused.

Sebastian shook his head and took her hand. "No. I mean separately."

Evelyn let Sebastian lead her up the stairs and left her at her door, her brief burst of temper forgotten. The soft kiss he gave her before ushering her into her room reassured her that he had enjoyed it as much as she had.

Sebastian walked to his door and turned back to face her. "There may come a time when we don't go to separate beds. I know you need more time. And if I'm honest, I do too."

Evelyn knew what he meant. He could barely stand her most of the time. And although kissing her was something she had wanted him to do again every moment since he had kissed her the first time, it was more the circumstances of the night than any true desire on his part. It was a sobering thought for her. Sebastian didn't like her. She had to keep that in mind, or she just might find herself in his bed, mangled body and all.

Chapter Fourteen

Evelyn rubbed her brow and tried to get the numbers to stay in focus. She and Sebastian were locked in the boardroom again, trying to sort out the financial reports. The original reports Evelyn had didn't match the ones Sebastian had put together himself. She relied on the computer to give her final tallies and to balance the budget. Sebastian, for whatever reason, had pulled the numbers and tallied them up himself. Had Evelyn done the same, she would have noticed months ago that money was missing. The amounts started small, but now the embezzler was getting bolder.

John was helping to go through the numbers again, and this time they brought in David. David was scowling at the documents in front of him. She could tell he was extremely angry but was reining in his temper. At least for the moment. She hoped she wasn't around when he let it loose.

"How can this possibly be? Since Andrew, we've been careful about the books. How could this be happening right under your nose? Again?" David addressed his anger at Evelyn, and rightly so. She was the reason Andrew was able to steal last time, and she was charged with the company's finances.

Sebastian came to her defense. "I would have missed

this. So would you and John. This is subtle, or at least it was at first. Someone in this organization is stealing money or is helping someone on the outside do it. The reports that Lenora brought in are the same ones I ran when I first arrived. Those reports and the ones Evelyn had are identical. It wasn't until I did some comparisons to the actual bank accounts that something looked off. It's taken me all week to get these numbers together."

David shoved the papers away. "All I know is that Evelyn is in charge of the finances, and I run research. I file my budget and enter my expenses weekly. Your numbers are not what I entered. What I entered is not on Evelyn's reports."

His next angry retort was directed at Evelyn. "If you had been around lately instead of hiding out at home, we could have met like we should have been. I would have noticed your numbers weren't right."

She didn't have a counterargument. Up until a couple of months ago, they had been meeting regularly. After their grandfather had died, though she'd been physically in the office more than before his death, she had been putting David off. His defensive attitude got on her nerves. With Howard's death, she hadn't been up to sparring with him.

John spoke up and asked the question he had asked yesterday. "Who do you think did this?"

Evelyn shrugged, and David just crossed his arms.

Sebastian looked over at Evelyn. "I'm guessing it's an insider. And I'd bet money he or she is working with Andrew. I think it may be time to pay him a visit."

"I don't know what good that will do. He'll just deny

everything.   I think we should hire the investigator Grandfather hired to look into it."

"What investigator?" This came from David.

Sebastian answered.   "Howard was not happy that Andrew was back. After what happened with Evelyn, he was trying to protect her. As far as the investigator could tell, Andrew and his company are completely legitimate. There wasn't anything the investigator found that could implicate Andrew in any wrongdoing. That's not to say he's not guilty, but the investigator couldn't find proof."

"Then why bother now?" David got to his feet. "I can't deal with this. This is your problem, and you had better fix it."

Evelyn, Sebastian, and John watched him storm out. John followed him.

The room was quiet for a moment before Evelyn spoke. "Do you think I have something to do with this?"

Sebastian's response was immediate. "No, I don't. And neither do David or John."

Evelyn folded her hands on the table, unable to look at him. "It was my fault the last time. I trusted Andrew, and he used me to steal from the company. It was bad enough he stole from me, but when I found out what he did, that was harder to live with than anything else that happened. I may not have stolen the money myself, but it was my fault. You can't deny that."

"You're not responsible for what he did." Sebastian slid his chair next to hers. He took her chin in his hand to force her to look at him. "You were his victim. There was no way for you to know what he was planning. No one suspected that he was going to steal from the organization, and your grandfather was still in charge at the time. Given that it had happened before, Howard should have had precautions in place that would have caught him in the act."

Evelyn sniffled a bit but refused to let the tears fall. "I felt like such a fool. My first day back after my injury was the worst day. Some people were trying to comfort me and tell me that what happened was not my fault. Others looked at me with accusatory eyes but refused to call me out on it. I didn't know how in the world I was going to run the company if no one trusted me. I know I blamed the company's problems on you for leaving, but so many of the problems were simply that no one trusted me. David certainly doesn't, but he doesn't know how to step into my shoes. It's why he's happy you're here. John doesn't trust me, though I don't think he blames me for the money. His lack of trust is personal."

Sebastian stroked her cheek with the back of his hand. "I trust you. Right now, that's all that matters."

Evelyn had to choke back more tears. She couldn't get her words past the lump in her throat. Instead, she placed her hand over his.

"David just needs to cool off." John entered the room, shocked to find the pair of them, knees touching, and Sebastian stroking Evelyn's cheek.

Evelyn practically jumped out of her chair, her eyes wide as she realized John had caught them in an intimate moment.

"Am I interrupting something?" John closed the door behind him, his eyes wary as he watched the pair.

Evelyn knew she looked guilty, but Sebastian looked as if nothing had happened.

"Yes, you are.   But we've got more work to do." Sebastian gestured to the chair for John to take a seat.

Evelyn watched John's gaze swing back and forth between the two of them. She had no doubt he would be telling Kimberly he had caught them touching. Evelyn knew that even though they had not been caught in a compromising position, there was no doubt something was going on between them. Evelyn still wasn't sure what that something was, but there was something.

The rest of the afternoon was uneventful. After four more hours of poring over the papers, the trio was pretty sure they had a fairly accurate account of what was missing. Sebastian had suggested hiring a forensic accountant to go over the books, and Evelyn agreed. If their numbers were right, over the last six months, over a quarter of a million dollars had gone missing. The company spent double that just on marketing every year, so with money being siphoned off in different departments, it had not been easy to find. An outside accountant was their best option.

"So do we call the cops?" John rubbed his eyes and rose to pace the room.

"We'll need to inform them of what's going on, though there isn't much they can do until we have more facts. White collar crimes are investigated by the FBI. I'll make that call tomorrow."

Evelyn shook her head at that. "You're going to be taking your children home in a couple of days. Maybe we should wait until you get back. A few more days won't hurt.

I can get the accounting department to start a full audit in the meantime."

"Yeah, unless someone from accounting is behind this." John stopped his pacing and looked out the window.

Sebastian looked at Evelyn. "Perhaps you're right. Tomorrow we'll all be at John's house. Then I fly back with the kids first thing Sunday morning. I won't be around to talk to the Feds, and I really should be here and give them my full attention. Go ahead and talk to the head of accounting first thing Monday. I'll put a freeze on the accounts in the meantime. I want everyone on board to go through the numbers and check for discrepancies. I'm sure the FBI will have their people go through the records, but I'd like to have full cooperation from our team. And hiring an outside firm to investigate can't hurt either. Let me think about it."

"And if the person responsible is in the accounting department?" John headed for the door.

"It's a risk we'll have to take for now. There are any number of people in the accounting and finance departments who could be responsible. But honestly, anyone with good computer skills and knowledge of the company could probably get away with it. And if Andrew is involved, he would know exactly what he is doing, and his partner could simply be following orders."

"I'm heading out then. I promised Kimberly I'd be home at a reasonable hour for a change. It's already after six, and she's been texting me for the last hour. I'll see you two tomorrow."

Evelyn looked up at the clock. "I think we should also

call it a day. There is nothing else we can do until you get back."

Sebastian nodded. The kids were spending the night at Kimberly's house, so he didn't have to worry about them. "Go on home. I'll be there later. There are a couple more things I want to take care of before I go."

"I could stay and help."

Sebastian shook his head. "I think it's best if you go. I can't concentrate with you in the room. Not when we're alone."

Evelyn would have been insulted, but she knew what he meant. It was getting harder and harder to concentrate when he was in the next room, much less the same one. And she had no doubt that had John not interrupted them, Sebastian would have kissed her again. And after he told her that he trusted her, she would have willingly gone into his arms regardless of where they were. She would have wanted to stay there. Perhaps a bit of breathing room was what they both needed. Her feelings toward Sebastian were spiraling out of her control. She didn't know what she would have said to him had tears not been threatening, but she was afraid she would have embarrassed herself by telling him how much she wanted him. And by telling him how much she feared she was in love with him.

* * *

"Are you going to tell me what is going on between the two of you?" Kimberly handed Patrick to Evelyn and took a seat beside her sister.

"I hadn't planned to." The man in question was in the pool playing with the kids. She'd been watching him for the last half hour or so. It was hard to look away when he was only wearing a pair of swim trunks and was covered in droplets of water all over his incredible chest and back. Evelyn was just grateful her dark glasses hid the fact that she was admiring him.

"Come on, Evelyn. John said he caught you two in an embrace in the boardroom."

"It wasn't an embrace. He was touching my face. That was it. Don't make more out of it."

"Please. I know better. John said he looked like he was going to kiss you."

"I guess we'll never know." Evelyn picked up her lemonade, letting Patrick play with the glass. Patrick squealed a bit as the condensation dripped on his legs, but he didn't seem to mind.

"So is he? I bet he is."

"Is what?"

"A great kisser. You can tell just by looking at him."

Evelyn didn't want to answer that question. Didn't want to admit the answer was yes. "You're not supposed to speculate. You're married."

"Yes, I'm married. But come on. Look at him. No woman on this earth could help herself from wondering what it would be like. Acting on it maybe, but not wondering. So is he?"

"What makes you think I know the answer to that question?" Evelyn bounced Patrick on her right knee and feigned innocence.

"I can tell. There's something about you lately that's different, and it all started with Sebastian's arrival. I could just go ask Leslie."

Evelyn growled a bit at that. Right now, Leslie was chatting with John and her fiancé, but Leslie was still throwing a look at Sebastian once in a while. She supposed none of them could help themselves. John was attractive and easy on the eyes, but he wasn't half-naked in the pool. But Evelyn thought of John as she did David; they were both attractive but family, so she never wondered if they were good kissers.

"All right, yes, he is." He was an amazing kisser, but she didn't say that part out loud.

"Ha, I knew it. You did kiss him." Kimberly's voice rose a bit. She saw a few heads turn their way, and Evelyn immediately turned red. It didn't help that Sebastian was grinning at her from the water. She didn't know how he had heard that over the children's laughter. The children seemed oblivious.

Evelyn lowered her voice and played with Patrick to cover her embarrassment. Leslie was glaring at her, and John looked bemused. "I didn't need the family to know about it."

Kimberly just grinned at her. "Is it serious?"

Evelyn set the lemonade down and turned Patrick on her lap. She bounced him up and down, and his giggles were almost as loud as the kids in the pool. She then held him to her for a moment and just savored his sweet baby smell.

"Come on, I need details." Kimberly took Patrick from Evelyn and set him in his bouncer.

"There's not much to say. He kissed me. It was nice. I don't know how serious he is, and I haven't asked."

Kimberly snorted unladylike at that. "Nice, my fanny. The first time John kissed me, I completely forgot who and where I was. It was amazing. I bet Sebastian's kisses are like that, and nice is not even close to how I would describe them."

It was odd to hear that Kimberly's first kiss with John was not all that different from hers with Sebastian. Of course, Kimberly's kiss led to marriage and a baby. Though Evelyn hoped marriage and family were in her future, she wasn't sure she should be hoping Sebastian would be the man. But how could she not?

"Okay, it was better than nice. But don't put too much thought into it. We were alone, it was late, and it just happened."

"According to John, it looked like it was going to happen again. Why fight it? You're both single, he's gorgeous, and you obviously like him."

Evelyn's shoulders drooped. "Yes, but does he like me? You forget who we're talking about. Sebastian is the man who left the country so he wouldn't have to take orders from me."

"That was different. Not wanting to have you boss him around and him wanting to kiss you are two very different things. John would be horrified if I were his boss."

"I doubt that. I've been John's boss for years, and he's pretty laid back."

"Yes, but he doesn't want to kiss you." Kimberly eyed her husband, a soft look coming into her eyes.

Evelyn saw the look returned. She still wasn't sure how she could have missed the electricity between those two. She still felt like a fool when she thought about her accusations all those years ago. "Do you think he'll ever forgive me?"

"Sebastian? Sure. He's not as tough as he looks. Any man who plays with his kids like that has a pretty big soft spot."

Evelyn gave a sad laugh. "I didn't mean Sebastian. We've called a truce for now. I meant John. He was embarrassingly happy when Sebastian took over."

Kimberly was quiet for a moment, and her tone was serious when she spoke. "I think he has, though he still has some resentment toward you. He was more surprised than I was when he told me he caught the two of you together. He thinks Sebastian is making a mistake getting close to you. John has a big heart, but I'm not sure he trusts you. Sebastian is his uncle, and he doesn't want to see him hurt."

Evelyn supposed that was the crux of the matter. John didn't trust her. Neither did David or Leslie. Anne and Kimberly did, but Evelyn was sure they had some doubts. Sebastian's words that he trusted her had meant the world to her.

"All I can say is that Sebastian can take care of himself. He doesn't need John to protect him. And he certainly doesn't need to protect Sebastian from me. We've said some harsh words to each other over the years. Sometimes when I look at him, I can't associate him with the man I used to know. I can't seem to dig up the animosity I used to feel."

Kimberly's tone was still serious. "How do you feel

about him?"

Evelyn shook her head at her sister. "I don't know. But I do know I'm the one who needs to be careful. I don't think I can take any more heartache. With Grandfather gone, Andrew back, and my career hanging in the balance, I'm not sure I can take any more disappointments right now. I couldn't handle it if Sebastian broke my heart, assuming I let him close enough to do so."

Kimberly patted her hand. "Sometimes we don't have a choice in who we fall in love with. And I'm not sure you could keep Sebastian at arm's length if you tried. He's a determined man when he wants something."

Evelyn's heart raced at that. Kimberly was right. If Sebastian decided he wanted her, her resistance would be nil. Of course, that didn't mean they'd live happily ever after. Evelyn wasn't sure she believed in happy endings anymore. She wasn't sure she ever had.

* * *

The house was entirely too quiet with Sebastian and the kids gone. Even Walter had been good company. She was seriously considering getting a dog. Maybe a small, cute, fuzzy lap dog she could cuddle. Walter played hard during the day with the children and crashed at night. She was sure she needed a dog that was a little less rambunctious. But he was a sweet dog, and a couple of times he'd climbed on the couch with her, much as Lucy had.

Evelyn was going to miss reading to Lucy at night. She was going to miss Daniel and Sebastian playing in the garden together. She was going to miss their noise, their laughter, and even their arguments. The kids fought as much as they played, especially at the dinner table. Evelyn could remember when she and Kimberly had been that way, arguing one minute and playing together the next. It made her smile.

At loose ends and unsure what to do with her time, Evelyn settled into the den and relaxed in her grandfather's chair. There were a couple of her books still tucked away back there. Sebastian still teased her about the romance novels, but she had gotten over her embarrassment. It was nice not to have to hide them. She didn't like people thinking she was the sentimental type, but deep down she was. What she wouldn't give to have someone love her the way the heroes in her books loved the heroines.

Evelyn was just starting to doze off when the house phone rang. Confused by the ringing, she got up to check the caller ID. No one ever called the house phone. Her grandfather had insisted on keeping the landline in case of emergency, but since his death, no one had called it. She didn't recognize the number and let it go to voicemail. The caller hung up without leaving a message. An hour later, it rang again. Once again startled by the ring, Evelyn got up and checked the caller ID again. It was the same number.

Curious, Evelyn answered. "Hello?"

"Hello, Evelyn." The voice was faint over the line as if the caller were speaking softly.

Her heart raced, her stomach ill at the voice she recognized on the line. It had been five years since she'd heard that voice, but she doubted she'd ever forget it. "What do you want, Andrew?"

"I need to talk to you."

"I don't think so." Evelyn went to hang up the phone, but his urgent voice stopped her.

"If you care at all about your company, you'll listen to me."

Evelyn's heart rate sped up and her stomach clenched. "What can you possibly have to say to me?"

His voice was still low on the line. "I need you to meet me before your boyfriend returns. Meet me at our old restaurant."

Andrew's remark about her boyfriend stopped her for a second, but then she realized he meant Sebastian. But that meant Andrew knew Sebastian was out of town. The knowledge gave her the creeps. Was he keeping tabs on her? "I most certainly am not. If what you have to say is so important, you can tell me over the phone."

"Too bad, darling. I want to see you. Meet me tomorrow for dinner. Your boyfriend's flight isn't until late. You can pop in to see me before he gets back. See you at six."

The line went dead, and Evelyn simply stood there clutching the receiver until it started beeping at her. She didn't want to talk to Andrew, much less meet with him. What could he possibly want? She would have bet money he would avoid her at all costs. What does a man say to the woman he promised to marry out of revenge? What does a man say to the woman he stole from and cheated?

Evelyn thought she was going to throw up but managed to get her stomach under control. Dozens of scenarios came to mind, none of them comforting. She supposed she should be grateful he hadn't asked to meet her someplace private. There was no way she was going to be alone with him ever again. She supposed she could refuse to meet him, but she knew he could be persistent. And she wasn't sure she would be able to sleep until she confronted him. The part that scared her the most was the fact that he knew Sebastian was gone and when he was coming back. She could understand Andrew not wanting to confront Sebastian, although it might be inevitable if Sebastian has his way.

Evelyn slept poorly that night. She was tempted to take a pill but had a feeling the drug wouldn't do her much good. With as wound up as she was, she doubted the pill would be effective. Andrew was up to something; she had no doubt. Her grandfather hadn't found any proof, but the call was all the proof she needed. She had two choices: meet with Andrew or wait until he came to her. Since the idea of Andrew hunting her down made her feel trapped, she figured it was best to meet him on his terms and do her best to keep control of the situation. She just hoped that she could get through the confrontation without breaking down.

Chapter Fifteen

Evelyn had stood outside her closet the next morning, unsure of what to wear. It was almost funny that she was taking so much time to decide. One of her flowy dresses was out. They were much too feminine. The pantsuits she used to wear might look like she was trying to look aggressive. Evelyn had opted for a pair of gray slacks, a long-sleeve blouse, and a pair of nude flats. She had wished she could grab a pair of heels, but that was out of the question. She'd grabbed a sweater on her way downstairs. Though it was warm outside, she was freezing.

Evelyn spent the morning with John. David was avoiding her, which was nothing new. He hadn't even spoken to her at Kimberly's on Saturday, though he'd tossed a few curious glances her way after Kimberly's announcement that she'd kissed Sebastian. Of course, it was even sadder proof that her social life was non-existent. Everyone assumed Kimberly was talking about Sebastian, which she was. But no one even thought for a second it could be some other man she had kissed.

Lenora set another cup of coffee in front of her before heading out to lunch. Evelyn smiled, grateful to her. Evelyn's new secretary was still in training and trying to figure out the computer systems. Rose was a sweet girl and was trying her best, but Lenora had been with the company for so many years that she was indispensable.

Evelyn took a sip and smiled. It was perfect. John had been her assistant for a long time, but he refused to fetch and carry, not that Evelyn expected him to. Often people around her took extra pains to make sure she had everything she needed before they left the room. She supposed a little sucking up to the boss never hurt, though it was not a belief John embraced. She imagined it had more to do with who she was than any unwillingness on John's part.

"How is the transition going?" Evelyn broke the silence, unable to bear her own thoughts anymore. She was dwelling on her upcoming confrontation with Andrew. The distraction of the coffee was welcome but short-lived. She thought about telling John about her phone call last night but figured he'd just try to talk her out of going. On top of that, he'd probably call Sebastian.

"It's going well. Sebastian understands the organization and what it needs." John didn't bother to look up when he spoke. Oftentimes their meetings went like this. She'd talk and he'd answer with one or two sentences, depending on what she asked. He rarely discussed anything other than business. When she'd picked him to be her assistant, she had tried to get him to relax. She'd ask how Kimberly was doing and how things were. He'd say fine and drop it.

They were both quiet for a while, going over the plan of how to audit the books. John had been researching private accounting firms that specialized in fraud. She had been outlining what needed to be done. Sebastian would be back in the office tomorrow, and they needed a strategy.

"So how long have you been sleeping with Sebastian?" John's angry voice broke the silence.

Evelyn almost choked on her coffee. "What?" She was certain she'd heard him wrong.

"You heard me. How long? He doesn't strike me as your type, but if you're desperate enough to hold on to your power, I imagine you'll do anything."

His words hurt. Not only was he insulting her, but he was insulting Sebastian as well, though she doubted he saw it that way. "Not that it's any of your business, but we're not sleeping together. Who do you think you are to even ask me that?"

John rose, not bothering to hide his feelings. "Sucks, doesn't it? It doesn't feel good to be accused of sleeping with someone for the wrong reasons. To have someone question your motives."

Evelyn slowly got to her feet. "Is that what that question was about? Revenge? What are you going to do, spread rumors around the company that I'm sleeping with the new boss? That's hardly in your best interests. Sebastian is your uncle, but don't think for a moment he wouldn't fire you. Don't think for a moment I won't."

"Keep your threats to yourself. You know full well I won't spread rumors, nor am I going to be fired. I just find it convenient that all of a sudden you two are all cozy. The company is being defrauded; you're the most likely suspect, by the way, and you, who five years ago couldn't stand to be in the same room as Sebastian, are all of a sudden acting all warm and fuzzy toward him."

"Sometimes, John, people change." It was the only response she had.

"And sometimes people just get better at manipulating others."

"Is that what you think? You think I'm manipulating Sebastian? I've nothing to gain and everything to lose, in case you haven't noticed. Not to mention Sebastian can't be manipulated. If he thought for a second I was trying to seduce him to regain control, he'd have fired me himself."

John started to speak but stopped when he saw the tears in her eyes. "Look, Evelyn…"

She lifted a hand to stop him. "I think we both need to get back to work. I'll take these back to my office. Finish your research on the accounting firms and go home. We've been spending too much time at the office and too much time together."

Evelyn headed to her office, her eyes dry once again. She needed to get a grip. That was twice now she'd almost been reduced to tears; three if you counted how emotional she had gotten when Lucy asked her to read to her. Sebastian's arrival had been having a profound effect on her. If she didn't get herself under control, she'd find herself crying like a baby.

Ten minutes later, John was in her office doorway. "Evelyn?"

He waited until she looked up at him from behind her desk. "Look, I'm sorry. I shouldn't have attacked you like that. It threw me for a loop when I saw you two together the other day. Kimberly thinks it's great, but I think it's a disaster waiting to happen. The last thing this company needs is its two top executives having an affair. If things go sour, it could get extremely awkward. I know I give you a hard time, but you've done a good job. Sebastian can take the company to a new level, but you've been the one holding it together. It's why I agreed to be your assistant when you offered it to me."

Evelyn gave him a cautious smile. "I thought it was because I offered you a big salary and a nice bonus."

John didn't smile back, but there was humor in his eyes. "It didn't hurt."

"That's what I figured. You were the best man for the job."

John took a seat. "Look, Kimberly told me you asked her if I could forgive you. It kind of ticked me off. Kimberly thinks it's sweet you care about her, but I saw it as a personal attack. You acted as if I were some kind of gigolo or something. You insulted my integrity. But what really ticked me off was that you insulted your sister."

Evelyn's mouth hung open for a second. "Insulted my sister?"

"Yes, your sister. Did you think she was so naïve as to be taken in by a con man? You were accusing me of sleeping with Leslie and using your sister. If she thought for a second I was sleeping with Leslie, she'd have kicked me to the curb. Right after she kicked my ass. She's a lot stronger than you give her credit for."

It was slightly humorous to hear John swear, even mildly, but she was smart enough not to let it show. "John, I don't know if I ever actually apologized, but I am sorry. I've been caught up in my own problems lately."

"Just remember one thing. You're not alone. You've got family. I may not be your best friend or anything, but you're still my sister-in-law, and if you need help, all you have to do is ask."

"Thanks, John. It means a lot. And I know." She watched him leave, her heart feeling a little lighter, though he hadn't actually accepted her apology. They may not be best friends, probably never would be, but she knew she could count on him and that's all that mattered.

Of course, if he knew what she was going to do after work today, he might not be so understanding. It was a sure bet Sebastian was going to be furious with her when she told him. A glance up at the clock on the wall told her she had another two hours before she was to meet Andrew. She did a few breathing exercises to calm her nerves, finished up her work for the day, freshened her lipstick, and left.

* * *

Evelyn entered the restaurant and saw Andrew sitting in a corner booth. She'd lost count of the number of times she'd eaten here with him. He didn't bother to stand up as she made her way toward him. She hated that she had the cane, that he could see even that amount of weakness in her, but her legs were shaking so badly there was no way she could have walked in without it.

"Hello, Evelyn. You're looking good."

She ignored his comment. He wasn't looking so good. He'd gained some weight in the last five years. That alone wouldn't have been so bad, but he wasn't clean-shaven, his hair needed a serious cut, and he smelled of alcohol. She glanced at the table, and he had a scotch clutched in his fist. There was a salad on her side of the table and what looked like the remnants of a steak on his.

"Thought you might be hungry. You always loved that salad."

There was no way she was eating or drinking anything. Even if her stomach allowed her, she wasn't touching anything that had been sitting out in the open. Who knows what he might have done to it. Given her history with him, she wouldn't be surprised if he'd drugged it.

"What do you want?"

"What, no pleasantries? You used to have better manners."

He was baiting her, and she knew it. It didn't help that the moment she had walked in the door, she'd felt fury take over. This was the man who not only stole her money but also the man she had let sleep with her. Somewhere after disgust with herself ended, fury with him for being such a heartless bastard took over.

Anger had her speaking. "You want to chitchat? Catch up on old times? I've got a question for you. Why did you want revenge on my mom?"

"She left me because she was blackmailing your father, and she didn't want me in the way."

"My father?" That stopped the beginnings of her tirade. She didn't even know who her father was, and she didn't particularly care.

He seemed to take pleasure in the telling of his story. "Yes, your father. She hadn't told him about you. I guess she was saving you for a rainy day."

None of that made sense, and she told him so. "Why should I believe anything you're saying? What type of person would pay blackmail to my mom?"

"A man who didn't want anyone to find out about him." He stopped then looked as if he'd come to a decision. "Your mom told me the whole thing. He was a banker. The two of them had plotted to embezzle from one of her boyfriend's businesses. Your mom had a lot of boyfriends back then. When their relationship went sour, he took the money and ran. Needless to say, your mother was mad. A couple of years later, she hooked up with me. I didn't know what she was then. She took great pleasure in ruining my marriage. She had a plan hatched to blackmail your dad. He was up to his old schemes, only this time she figured he'd be a bit more cooperative because of you. The money was found missing, but they couldn't pin it on your father. Your mother threatened to go to the press and tell them that she knew he had stolen the money because they had been having an affair. You were proof of that affair. And since he was up to his old schemes again, your mother figured it was only fair she got a piece of the pie since she had been denied her share all those years ago."

Evelyn interrupted his story. "And since my mother had stolen all your money and told your wife about your affair anyway, you came up with a similar scheme. You were going to blackmail my mother because you found out what she was up to. Instead, she died, and you couldn't. So you came after me and Brown instead. Am I close?"

"Look, Evelyn, I'm not exactly proud of what I did. But

I'm in a fix, and this time I'm innocent."

"You can look at it as payback for what you did to me. For what you got away with. Twice."

A look of intense hatred flashed on his face before he masked it. "You're so much like your mother sometimes. She was always acting like she was better than everyone else. You think you are, too. You think because you're running a big corporation that you're better than the rest of the world. But we're even now."

"What do you want, Andrew?" Her fury was lessening, but in no way was she letting her guard down for a second. His story was pathetic, and she wasn't buying a word he was saying. If Jeannette knew who her father was, she would have sued him for child support.

"To get you to call off your boyfriend. I'm not the one embezzling from your firm. I've got my own business to run, and I can't afford to have your boyfriend running around spreading rumors."

"Don't think for a moment I'm buying your story. You know I can't prove you're the one behind the thefts five years ago or fifteen years ago. Right now, I think you should concentrate on being grateful I can't prove you're the one behind the missing money. Yet. And if you have half the brains I've always credited you with, you'll keep away from Sebastian. He won't be as polite. And when he finds proof you're behind the latest thefts, you'll end up in prison."

"He's the reason I'm here. He won't believe I'm not behind this. You need to prove otherwise."

"I don't have to do anything. You're a fraud. An

embezzler and an attempted murderer. If you think I'll help you, you're out of your mind. And you can bet I'll tell Sebastian about our little chat."

He ignored the last part. "You're crazy! I've never tried to kill anyone. And you can't prove I did."

She thought she saw real panic on his face but couldn't be sure. She never realized before what a good actor he was. "I'm proof. What you did to me. I didn't fall off that cliff. I was pushed. And you are the only person who had a motive."

"You can't be serious." His voice rose, then he realized that they weren't alone. The waitress was watching them from across the room, as was half the restaurant at his outburst.

"If you think you can trick me into confessing to taking that money, you can forget it. I didn't push you. I had already left the state. I wasn't going to hang around. I'd accomplished what I came to do."

"You expect me to believe that? You should have quit when my mother died. It should have been enough for you. She paid for her crimes with her life."

"Death was too good for her. It's too good for you. I wanted her to suffer for what she did."

She watched him as he tried to get a rein on his temper. "If you admit you stole from me and Brown to the FBI, I'll believe you."

"Do I look crazy to you? The only reason I'm here is to get your boyfriend off my back."

That brought up the one question she wanted to ask. "How did you know Sebastian was out of town? For that matter, how do you know he was looking into your affairs?"

"You should be more careful about who you hire. That private investigator your grandfather hired told me. Since your granddad is dead, that stupid investigator was willing to spill his guts for the right price. His ethics only stretch so far. He didn't feel any loyalty to your boyfriend, and he didn't care who bought the information he'd acquired while working for your granddad, not even the guy he was spying on. Imagine my surprise when I found out someone was embezzling from Brown and that your boyfriend was sniffing around me. I'm legit these days, and you can't prove otherwise."

Evelyn struggled to remain calm. "And how did you know Sebastian was out of town?"

Andrew laughed at that. "I've had that investigator spying on Sebastian. I needed to know what he was up to. I recently found out he'd taken over at Brown. Looks like the queen was overthrown."

She ignored that. "So why tell me this? You're a lot of things, Andrew, but you're not stupid."

"I fired him. I don't need an investigator poking around who can be bought off. Besides, all I needed was one opportunity to get you alone."

Evelyn's stomach clenched at his leer, but she tried to keep him talking. "So this is the grand plan? I tell Sebastian you're innocent and he goes looking elsewhere for my embezzler? I don't think so."

"But what if I'm telling you the truth? What if you do have someone besides me embezzling from you? Maybe he won't stop at just the money."

This time Andrew was staring at her breasts. She automatically crossed her arms over her chest. As much as she would rather storm out, she knew she had to see this through. He seemed sickly satisfied by her move, but his eyes went back to her face, and that was all that mattered to her.

"Are you threatening me?" Her voice shook despite herself. Andrew was dangerous, and she would be a fool to ignore it.

"Not me. But someone is." He pulled out a folded piece of paper and handed it to her. He dropped it in front of her when she refused to take it from him.

Seemingly satisfied with the encounter, Andrew abruptly got up and left.

Evelyn got a grip on her raging emotions. Being this close to him made her ill, and the smell of the salad dressing was curdling her stomach. She looked down at the salad Andrew had ordered and pushed it away. It was disturbing that he remembered what she used to order. And she couldn't say she wasn't worried about him or what he would do. If she knew one thing, it was that Sebastian would keep her safe. When she told him about this meeting, Sebastian wouldn't knowingly let her get within a mile of Andrew again.

Taking a deep breath, she unfolded the paper. It was a typed message on generic paper. It was addressed to Andrew. The letter was very short and very clear. It suggested that if he knew what was good for him, he'd confess to the missing money at Brown. It went on to say that the author had proof of his guilt and wouldn't stop until he was exposed. What scared her was the reference to Sebastian and herself. The unknown author said jail was too good for Andrew and that he, Evelyn supposed it could be a she, wouldn't allow Sebastian or Evelyn to interfere. The letter demanded that Andrew tell them to back off or they'd be sorry.

Andrew had any number of enemies, male and female. Evelyn doubted she was the only person he'd cheated and swindled over the years. Men like him made a career out of it. It was odd, though, that this began after Andrew bought his own business. Crown Chemicals was doing well, and it looked as if the author wanted revenge. But why involve Brown? The person who wrote the letter had to know about Andrew's personal history with Evelyn and the company. Of course, her accident right after their non-wedding had made the papers. Her grandfather had been very vocal in the local and regional communities that Andrew was a thief. It would probably be easier to compile a list of people who didn't know about their relationship.

Of course, Andrew could have written the note himself. But something about his appearance today spoke of desperation. What if he was telling the truth and someone else was embezzling from Brown and trying to frame Andrew? Every part of Evelyn said that Andrew was guilty and that he was playing games. But that was emotional.

Evelyn tucked the note in her purse. She looked up in surprise as the waitress handed her the bill. Disgusted with herself for letting Andrew get the better of her again, she paid the bill, tipped the waitress, and bolted from the restaurant as quickly as she could. She never wanted to see

Andrew or the restaurant ever again.

Evelyn drove home slowly, being extra careful. She was feeling highly emotional at the moment. She wanted to get home to the comfort and safety of her bedroom. She wanted to strip off the clothes she was wearing and throw them in the trash. Burning them would be better. Just Andrew's gaze on her breasts made her feel dirty. He hadn't touched her, but she knew he was remembering the few times he had seen her naked.

Evelyn made it to her driveway and out of the car before she threw up. She hadn't eaten anything today, so there wasn't much in her stomach other than the coffee and water she'd drank. She heaved a few more times but managed to get her stomach under control. Her legs were shaking, and she badly wanted a drink. She grabbed the cane from the van, cursing it and herself, as she made her way to the door. Her legs managed to stay under her until she stripped and climbed into the tub. She didn't even bother to wait until it was filled before she scrubbed her body down. She spent over an hour in the tub until her skin was so shriveled she had to get out. She pulled on her favorite house dress but didn't bother with anything else. She blow-dried her hair and stretched out on her bed.

It was after nine when she heard Sebastian enter the house. She didn't need to get up and check; her instincts told her it was him. But instead of staying in bed where she could avoid him, she tugged on her robe over her dress and went down to meet him.

She found him in the kitchen, raiding the fridge. His black hair was a bit mussed. She imagined he'd been combing it back with his fingers again. When he was thinking hard or frustrated, he ran his hands through his hair. Her fingers itched to touch, but she clasped her hands behind her back instead.

"Welcome home." Evelyn gave him a smile that hid the turmoil she was feeling.

"Thanks. I'm starving." Sebastian rummaged around and pulled out the leftovers from the last meal with the kids.

Evelyn stayed in the doorway and just absorbed his presence. "Are the kids happy to be home?"

Sebastian took a bite and swallowed before answering. "Yeah. They're so excited when I come to get them, but they miss their mom. They were glad to be back. Walter was especially happy to have his nice fenced-in yard back."

That won a small laugh from Evelyn.

He gazed at her and realized something wasn't quite right. "Are you okay?"

Evelyn nodded. "I'm fine. I had a bit of a stomachache today. I'm feeling better." And she was, now that he was back.

"Did you eat? Anne warned me you skip meals a lot." He waited to see if she was going to tell the truth. He could see it in her eyes when she lied.

"No. I forgot. And I suppose I drank too much caffeine. I gave up alcohol, so I figure I'm entitled to at least one of my vices."

"Why don't you sit down and have a bite." Sebastian kicked out a chair for her.

Evelyn crossed the room and took a seat. She wasn't sure she could eat, but perhaps a bite or two wouldn't hurt.

She took a piece of cucumber off his salad and chased it with a bite of his chicken. When that didn't threaten to come back up, she snagged another bite of the chicken. She watched as Sebastian rose and poured her a glass of milk. Though she wasn't fond of milk, she thought it might help settle her stomach.

"Is everything set at the office?" Sebastian finished his salad before digging into his chicken. It looked like Evelyn was done. But since she drank the milk, he figured that was good enough.

"I don't want to talk about work right now. It will keep until tomorrow."

"So what do you want to talk about?" Sebastian finished his meal and took his dishes, including Evelyn's glass, to the sink. When he finished washing up, he turned to face her.

"Well?" Sebastian smiled at her, but it faded quickly as she stared at him.

"I was thinking we could talk about you and me. And how badly I want to go to bed with you."

Chapter Sixteen

Had any other woman asked him that question, he might have laughed and carried her straight up the stairs. She was dead serious, but something in her eyes told him that something was wrong.

"I suppose we could talk about it." He crossed over to her and held out his hand. She hesitated for a second, then took it.

"We're not really going to talk about it, are we? You're just supposed to get naked and have your way with me." Evelyn let him lead her to the living room.

"If you didn't look ready to slug me, I might have. You need to tell me what's wrong." Sebastian didn't turn on the lights when he tugged her down on the couch to sit beside him.

"I'm not ready to tell you yet. But I promise I will." Evelyn took his hands, silently examining them. He had nice, strong hands. Hands that would never hurt her, deceive her, or lie to her. It was those hands she wanted on her body. She wanted those hands to erase the memory of Andrew's hands. She'd been lying in her bed, waiting for him. Common sense told her to stay put. But five-year-old memories of Andrew's touch and today's wandering eyes had her making her way downstairs. She might not be able to erase Andrew from her life, but tonight she could erase his touch. Sebastian was the only man who could do that for her.

When she looked up at him again, a plea was there in her eyes. Whatever had happened today, she wasn't ready to talk about it. He could respect that, knowing she would keep her promise to him. She had kept her promise to tell him about her accident and about Andrew, so he trusted her to keep her promise this time. Something in her eyes was sad yet angry. The anger he could deal with; the sadness he struggled with.

"Evelyn, do you really want to go to bed with me?" It was the only question he could think to ask. Since she'd asked him in the kitchen, his body was raring to go. But she was distant right now, not at all soft and wanting.

"I said I did. We can't have sex on the couch or on the floor. My back wouldn't allow it." Evelyn rose and headed for the stairs. When he remained on the couch, she asked over her shoulder. "Are you coming?"

Not sure if he was making a mistake or not, he followed her up the stairs. He wasn't sure what he expected when he reached her room, but he didn't expect her to practically throw herself at him. She hit his chest hard enough to knock him back a step. She quickly wrapped her arms around his neck and kissed him. Her mouth was a little too hard and a little too demanding. She seemed desperate, but that made no sense.

He grabbed her arms and pulled her from him. "Evelyn, you're starting to worry me."

She shrugged at that, pulling away from him and

stripping off her robe. "I'm fine."

She reached for the buttons of his shirt, but he held her hands still. Her breathing was too fast, and he thought he saw tears in her eyes. Not knowing what else to do, he kissed away the tears. He kissed her left eye, then her right. Her hands tensed on his forearms where she'd grabbed him, but otherwise didn't move. His mouth drifted down her cheek, pressing soft kisses against her incredibly soft skin until he reached her mouth. He kept the kiss soft and let her take a moment to relax. When her body went lax against his and her hands loosened, he pulled her closer and deepened the kiss. This time she joined in, but not with the same force as the last time. She was enjoying the kiss as much as he was, and that was what he wanted.

Evelyn stood docilely in his arms, her anger subsiding. Sebastian's kisses took her out of herself. In her anger, she had forgotten how much his kisses moved her. This time, when her hands went to the buttons of his shirt, he let her undo them.

"Evelyn, are you sure you want to do this?" Sebastian asked her again, this time cupping her face when he asked it. Desire was in her eyes this time, not the anger and sadness he had seen there earlier.

Her voice was breathless when she answered him. "Yes."

Sebastian carefully lifted her and carried her over to the bed. He stood her on her feet and kissed her again. Her hands fumbled on his shoulders as she removed the garment. The trembling in her hands was highly arousing. He had no doubt this time she did mean yes when she said it. For a few moments, he was content to continue kissing her, letting her hands roam his chest and back. When her nails raked across his nipples, he decided it was time to return the favor.

Sebastian stroked her body from shoulders to thighs, and it quickly became apparent that she was not wearing anything under the dress. He shuddered and reached for the hem. Evelyn was watching him, her eyes a little unsure.

"It's not pretty under there." Her voice was soft when she said it but allowed him to remove the dress.

"I'm not worried about your scars, Evelyn. Every part of you is beautiful." His hands climbed higher and stroked her thighs and backside as he slowly removed the dress.

She knew he was giving her a chance to stop him, but she no longer was worried about what he'd see when he pulled off her dress. His rough fingers on the backs of her thighs and the kneading caresses on her backside felt wonderful and removed her reservations. No one had ever touched her so thoroughly, and he'd only touched half her body. She watched as he finished removing her dress, her eyes not leaving his. She had her knees locked to keep her from falling. She couldn't stop the soft moan when the base of his palms caressed her breasts as he finished stripping off the dress.

The light was faint in the room, but it was enough that Sebastian could see. Now was not the time to talk about her scars, though they made his heart ache at what she'd been through. Now was the time to show her how desirable she was, how much he wanted her. When he got home tonight, he certainly hadn't expected her to ask him to bed. He wasn't even sure it was a good idea. But with her standing nude in front of him, he didn't want to turn back.

Evelyn was feeling uncertain under his gaze, but it was quickly dispelled when he reached for the snap of his jeans. He kicked them off and quickly stripped off his boxers. She tried not to stare, but it was hard not to. His aroused body was magnificent. She'd seen him in nothing but his bathing suit, but this was something else entirely. As she looked him over, his body swelled even more.

"Now we're even." Sebastian couldn't hide what her approval of him was doing to his body.

Evelyn actually giggled.

His voice was serious when he spoke, but his eyes held humor. "You're not supposed to laugh when you see a man naked."

Evelyn blushed at that. "Sorry, it was the idea that we're even. We're not even close."

Sebastian pulled her close, his hands hungry to explore what he'd uncovered. Her breasts weren't large, but they were firm and flushed. He watched her as he dipped his head to explore her body. He started with her neck, pushing her hair back from her shoulders in a soft caress, suckling and kissing her as he went. Her collarbone was next, and her entire body swayed when he reached her breasts. Up until that moment, she had seemed frozen in place, but now she moved her hands to his hair, her grip slightly painful as her hands clenched while he sucked and then lightly bit her.

Evelyn realized she was gripping his hair too hard when she saw him wince. She released his hair and gripped his shoulders. What he was doing to her felt too good to accidentally stop him. Her nails dug into his shoulders instead.

Sebastian released her breast and looked up at her. Her eyes were closed, her breath coming quickly between her lips. Unable to resist, he kissed her again.

Evelyn wrapped her arms around him, crushing him to her as much as she could. His mouth tasted wonderful. The feel of the crisp hair on his chest against her bare breasts was equally wonderful. Unable to decide which she wanted more of, she just clung to him.

This time, Sebastian laughed, but there was no humor in it. She had pressed herself against him, but she seemed focused on kissing him back. He broke off the kiss, grabbed her hips as firmly as he dared, lifted her, and pressed his erection firmly against her. She stood still for a moment, and he was afraid that maybe he had hurt her. But she sighed and opened her legs a bit so he could nestle closer.

"I think it's time I got you into bed." Sebastian stumbled a bit because Evelyn refused to release her grip on his neck. He followed her down onto the bed and settled his body next to hers.

Evelyn's eyes opened in disappointment. "Sebastian, I want you."

Sebastian quieted her with another soft kiss. "I know. Just give me a minute. I want to savor this."

Evelyn was still as she watched him as he set about savoring the moment, savoring her. She wanted to touch him the way he was touching her, but she couldn't seem to move. Her muscles had turned to mush, and she didn't want to distract him from what he was doing.

She never realized how sensitive her body was. She'd

become so accustomed to pain that the pleasure he was giving her was almost unbearable. His fingers trailed up and down her body, finding and lingering on incredibly sensitive spots. She was too distracted to care that he was touching the scars on her body she had been embarrassed for him to see. He kissed his way down her body, following the trail of his fingers. She didn't know a kiss on her belly would have her entire insides quivering. She didn't know that her body would arch and lift into those kisses. She did now.

Sebastian was breathing heavily and reaching the point where he needed to feel her hands on him. Since she seemed immobile at the moment, he lifted her arms to his chest. He paused for a moment to grab an extra pillow to prop her up so she wouldn't have to strain to reach him. She cooperated with him as he lifted her and began to follow the same pattern down his body with her hands that he had on hers.

Evelyn realized what she had been missing. The textures of his body, so different from hers, felt wonderful under her hands. He arched just as she had, pressing his body against her hands, his eyes closing, a low groan emanating from his throat. Unable to resist, she let her hands drift down his stomach. She'd never touched a man so boldly in her life, but she needed to feel him, to touch what would soon be inside her body.

Sebastian's groan was louder this time, and he guided her hands to show her how to touch him. Then he stilled those soft, wonderful hands. "Enough."

Evelyn couldn't help but giggle again. She wasn't sure

what prompted it, but out it came anyway. Sebastian looked in pain, though she knew he wasn't. Her body was throbbing, the ache inside reaching its peak.

"Enough for me, too." Evelyn grabbed his shoulders, pulling him back to her. This time he very carefully parted her legs and settled between them. There was some pain in her hip, but she didn't want him to stop, so she simply shifted her body to accommodate his weight better. She'd had enough physical therapy that the pain was nothing compared to what she had experienced then.

"Okay?" Sebastian was trying not to put all of his weight on her, but he desperately wanted to be inside her. When she nodded, he settled a little more firmly between her legs.

Sanity asserted itself for a second. Sebastian wanted nothing more than to finish what they'd started, but he had to ask. "Are you on the pill?"

Evelyn nodded. "The doctor put me on it. After the fall, my periods were incredibly irregular."

Sebastian, relief in every line of his body, guided himself back to the entrance of her body.

It was Evelyn's turn to groan when Sebastian, instead of pushing inside her, pressed his fingers against her instead. He stroked her and slid a finger inside, as if making sure she was ready for him. She wished she had a voice to tell him she was, but she couldn't find the words. She instead reared off the bed, this time grabbing his butt to pull him closer.

The time for playing was over, but Sebastian wanted to be certain he didn't hurt her. He was already worried enough about his weight, and the last thing he wanted to do was hurt her in any way. He probed her body one last time and replaced his hand with the flesh that was throbbing in tune with his heartbeat. Slowly he sank into her, watching her face to make sure she was still okay. Once he was completely inside, she let out a satisfied sigh and released her grip on him. She slid her hands up his back instead, her eyes on his as he slowly moved inside her.

Evelyn gripped his body with her legs, wanting desperately to please him as much as he was pleasing her. His slow movements picked up pace as she moved with him, his body now driving both of them toward the release that was waiting for them. Evelyn closed her eyes, unable to keep her eyes open as the pleasure he was giving her drove her higher. The friction of him inside her body was unlike anything she had experienced before. He angled his body to bring her fully against him, knowing he wasn't hurting her. He pushed a little further inside than he had before, and her body began to pulse around him.

Evelyn's breath froze as her climax hit her. She was first surprised by the pleasure he had given her, then helpless because she could do nothing but let the sensation take over. She squeezed him with all her strength and felt his climax only moments after hers ended. Utterly satisfied, she completely relaxed under his body.

His breathing was harsh in her ear, his body now lying heavily on hers, and she never, ever wanted him to move. She stroked his back, running her fingers from the top of his neck to the base of his spine. She couldn't help the grin on her face any more than she could have gotten up and run a marathon.

Evelyn wasn't sure how long they stayed like that, but

eventually, Sebastian lifted his chest and propped himself up on his arms so he could see her. He returned her grin for a moment, then lifted himself completely off her. He didn't get up but settled himself beside her. Evelyn had a hard time getting her left leg back where it belonged but managed. What she wanted was to curl herself around him, but her hip was already protesting the movement.

"Are you okay?" Sebastian turned on his side so he could face her. He had seen her wince.

"I'm fine." She didn't want to spoil the moment by telling him her hip hurt. She'd endure a little ache in her leg to have him climb back on top of her again. Of course, what she really wanted was to be able to climb on top of him, but since she couldn't do that, she'd settle for doing what they just did again. Maybe tomorrow when she could breathe and her heart rate slowed to normal.

Sebastian leaned down and kissed her again. Evelyn felt a slight stir in her belly, but it felt nice. This feeling was soft and feminine, and she wanted it to linger for a while.

Sebastian broke off the kiss and gathered her as best he could to him. She was still lying flat on her back; at some point, she had tossed the extra pillow he'd used to prop her up. He assumed that was usually how she slept, though he did recall the time he'd seen the scars on her legs for the first time and she'd been lying on her stomach. Not wanting to spoil her relaxed mood, he simply sifted her auburn locks between his fingers, enjoying the feel of her warm flesh against his.

Evelyn sighed and relaxed a little more. "I feel like I should thank you or something."

Sebastian's eyes opened, and saw her facetious grin. "I can think of ways you could thank me."

"Mmm." Evelyn lifted her hand to his cheek. "Maybe when I can move again."

Sebastian's laughter made her feel happy. A little while later, Sebastian helped her up so she could go to the bathroom and wash up. When she came back, she lay back down, one arm pressed alongside him, and the other draped across her belly. She closed her eyes and went to sleep. Shortly after, Sebastian did the same.

* * *

The alarm clock woke them the next morning. Evelyn glared blurry-eyed at the clock. She couldn't remember the last time she'd slept so deeply, nor the last time the alarm had actually woken her up. She felt the weight next to her shift and lie over her to shut the clock off. Memories from the night before came flooding back.

"It can't possibly be time to get up." Sebastian buried his head in the pillow next to hers.

For some reason, his remark amused her. "Not a morning person?"

A grunt was his only response. He buried his head deeper in the pillow.

Evelyn, feeling incredibly happy, carefully rolled over and kissed the back of his neck. Though he stirred, he didn't lift his head. She kissed his neck again, and this time let her hand trail down his back. She couldn't reach all of him from her position, but she could reach enough. He unburied his head, but otherwise didn't move.

"Feeling frisky this morning?" Sebastian brought himself closer so he could reach her mouth. By the time he pulled back, they were both breathing heavily.

"Maybe, but I think we need to brush our teeth before this goes any further."

Sebastian rolled her onto her back and settled between her legs. Evelyn smiled up at him, realizing how careful he was not to move her too fast. For that alone, she loved him. Despite the erection pressing against the inside of her leg, he was more worried about her and made no assumptions.

Trying to lighten his mood a bit, she ran her hands up his chest and wrapped her arms around his neck. Using the strength in her arms to lift herself, she pressed wet kisses everywhere she could reach on his chest. "I hope you like the missionary position."

In response to her teasing, he bit her shoulder. "I like any position I can get you into."

Knowing now what awaited her, Evelyn pulled her legs up higher and urged Sebastian closer so she could really kiss him. Her body was already aching for him, and he seemed to know it. This time he didn't hesitate but slowly pushed his way inside her body. She responded to the invasion. "Sebastian."

It was all she said and all the permission he needed. A short while later, they were both spent and panting.

Evelyn pinched his butt. "Ready to get up now?"

The look he gave her was incredulous, but he didn't respond in kind. Instead, he climbed out of her bed and helped her up. "I need a shower, along with the teeth brushing."

She thought he would leave her there, but instead, he pulled her with him. He pulled the shower door open and turned the faucets on. Steam was pouring out of the shower in a matter of moments. When he pulled her inside with him, she only hesitated for a moment, not that she had a choice. He was stronger than she was, and he wanted her in the shower with him. But it was one thing to be naked with him when it was dark and the lights were off, even if he could see her somewhat because of the porch lights that came through her window at night. It was another thing entirely when the sun was pouring through the windows.

"You're going to have to get used to it. We won't be going back to the way things were before." Sebastian pulled her under the spray with him. Her grandfather had gone all out, not only in the tub but also in the shower. Multiple jets and a large rain showerhead were able to accommodate both of them.

"They look bad." Evelyn hated the scars on her thighs most of all.

Sebastian kissed her and let his fingers drift down her legs across the scars. His forefinger drew a line over a surgical scar. "This simply means you're alive, and you should be grateful for them. I know I am."

That made her smile as he knew it would. He turned her around and washed her hair. She returned the favor and washed his back. Though thoroughly aroused again, she wasn't sure she could go another round. It had been five years since she'd let a man touch her. And though this was nothing like her unsatisfying bouts with Andrew, Sebastian was physically much bigger than Andrew, and she was sure she would be sore.

Sebastian knew the moment she withdrew from him. The anger he had seen in her eyes flared there once more. Sebastian finished washing up and Evelyn finished conditioning her hair. Once done, he towel-dried both of them. She smiled at him once again, but the shadow was still there.

"We're going to be late for work." Evelyn went in search of the robe left on the floor of her bedroom. Sebastian picked it up for her so she could pull it on. She headed straight for the closet and pulled out some clothes, then headed back to the bathroom to comb her hair.

Sebastian watched her as her agitation grew, his concern growing with it. "Are you going to tell me what's wrong this time?"

Evelyn shook her head and finished combing out her hair. "I'm not ready to fight with you yet."

"You sound pretty sure we're going to fight. Not to be crass, but after last night and this morning, I'm not feeling up to sparring right now. I'd rather be back in bed."

That garnered him another smile, but it quickly faded.

"Really, you should go get dressed. We have a meeting with John in an hour."

He took a step closer to her. "I'm not worried about John. I'm worried about you."

That warmed her heart. She set her comb down and walked over to him. She kissed him lightly and laid her head on his chest. His arms came around her and just held her. She turned her head so she could see his face. "I promise to tell you, but I think it would be better if I told you, John, and David at the same time. It will be easier that way."

Sebastian was not feeling accommodating at the moment. "I think we should talk first. I'd rather have a plan when we meet with them since it's obvious you're upset about something at Brown."

"Please?" Evelyn pulled away.

He didn't like it, but he let it drop. The plea in her eyes stopped him, just as her plea last night had. She was upset, but he knew how stubborn she could be. Unless he wanted to start the fight she said they were going to have, he had no choice but to let her be for now.

"I'll go get dressed and start breakfast. I'll also send John a text to let him know we're running a little late."

Evelyn looked at him through the mirror. "Just don't get upset if he figures out why we're late. After Kimberly blurted out that I kissed you, he's a bit bent out of shape."

"Why? It's not like he wants to take you to bed."

That was almost humorous but not quite. "His words were something to the effect that nothing good could come from an affair between two top executives. He didn't come right out and say it, but I think he's afraid that we're going to have an affair, and if it ends, ruin the company. Or at the very least, make work for everyone else extremely uncomfortable."

He was happy she said if, not when. "What do you think?"

"I think last night was inevitable since the first time you kissed me. Kimberly thinks you'd be a great kisser. I can only agree."

"You talked to Kimberly about you and me?"

Evelyn turned, surprised by the delight in his voice. "She's my sister. She wanted details. I didn't have many to give her, but she wasn't going to drop the subject."

Sebastian crossed back to her and dropped a light kiss on her lips. "You'll have details now. Finish getting ready. I have a feeling today is going to be a long day. Come down when you're done, and I'll make sure you get fed."

Evelyn surprised herself by humming while she finished getting ready for work. She took a few extra moments to add a little makeup. She put back the original outfit she'd chosen and instead pulled out her favorite work dress, one she was sure Sebastian would like. She stopped for a moment when she realized she was dressing and primping for Sebastian. But it made her happy, and she needed to feel this way for a few more minutes. She dried her hair, kept it down because she knew Sebastian preferred it that way, grabbed the cane he'd left for her in the doorway, and headed downstairs to be fed.

Chapter Seventeen

"You what?" The voices of three very angry men assaulted her ears. Evelyn had hoped having the three of them in a room together when she told them what she'd done would control their anger, not intensify it.

"Have you lost your mind?" That was John.

"Only an idiot would confront a criminal." That was David.

Sebastian was suspiciously quiet, and that worried her most of all.

When she turned to face the men, John looked worried, and David looked outraged. She couldn't tell from Sebastian's face what he was thinking, but she'd seen that look before. He was furious and struggling to keep his temper under wraps. She had hoped never to see that face again, but it was only wishful thinking. Five years ago, she could push his buttons. It looked like she hadn't lost the knack. When she told Sebastian she didn't want to fight, it was that look she hadn't wanted to see. Especially not after what they had done in her bed.

Evelyn did what she did best. She stood her ground. "It wasn't that big a deal. We met in a public place."

This time, Sebastian spoke. "And that makes it okay?"

Unable to formulate a response in the face of his anger,

she shrugged as if she didn't care.

"What did he want?" John spoke when it became obvious that neither of them was going to.

"He said he wanted me to call Sebastian off." She kept her eyes on John, unable to continue facing Sebastian.

"Yeah, right. Like that's going to happen." David pulled out a chair and sat.

"He called the house and said to meet him. He didn't give me a chance to say no. And I know him well enough to know he would just have kept on pestering me until I agreed. I figured the best option was to meet on his terms the first time he asked instead of dragging it out."

"Of course you know him; you were engaged to him." David's retort didn't do anything to calm the tempers flaring in the room. And the last thing she wanted was a reminder of her stupidity.

Evelyn glared at him.

"So that was the big meeting? He just wanted you to tell Sebastian to take a hike?" David spun from side to side in his chair, his agitation growing.

"Yes, that is what he wanted. He came in, ate lunch, ordered me a salad, then waited. I wasn't there more than fifteen minutes." Sarcastically, she added, "I ended up paying for lunch if that makes you feel better, David."

Sebastian held up a hand. "This is getting us nowhere. What else did he say?"

Evelyn pulled out a folded piece of paper from her purse. "He said he was being threatened. He said the person who was stealing from Brown was planning on framing him if he didn't come clean and confess."

"And you believed him?" Sebastian's voice was barely audible, but everyone in the room heard him.

"Why not? She believed him before. I guess some lessons have to be relearned." David practically spat the words at her.

Evelyn shuddered and wished she had never started this. If she could have dropped through the floor, she would have. Instead, she stood her ground, pushing down the hurt he was purposefully causing her. This was not the first time she and David had a go-round. It wouldn't be the last.

"I did believe him. He was unshaven, probably hadn't showered in a couple of days, and stank of booze. He was trying to frighten me. Five years ago, Andrew was all charm and charisma. This Andrew was scared and didn't bother to hide his disdain for me."

"But why would he warn you?" John was ever the peacemaker.

"Because he is scared. I told him Sebastian would only help him if he went to the Feds and confessed what he'd done. He mocked me and told me what he thought of that idea. But honestly, I can't think of any reason why he'd tell me."

Sebastian walked over to her and took the note from her hand. It took only a moment to read it. "He told you because the writer of the letter told him to. I think you're right. He's scared. But this doesn't threaten Andrew. It threatens you."

"And you." Evelyn could tell he was still furious with her, but his mind was focused on the letter.

"And me. Whoever wrote this knows a heck of a lot

about what happened here five years ago."

Evelyn nodded. "Yes, but when I stopped and thought about it, that could be any number of people. Grandfather didn't hide the embezzlement from the press. He used it to try to ruin Andrew. But he had no proof. Andrew covered his tracks well, and the money he took was never found. Local businessmen knew. Anyone who read the newspapers knew."

John pulled up a seat. "Even your wedding, or rather non-wedding, made the papers. Andrew used that to counter your grandfather's accusations. He claimed it was just an old man's attempt at revenge for not marrying his granddaughter. I was inclined to believe Andrew. It seemed far-fetched, and your grandfather had completely lost all perspective after you were hurt."

Evelyn and Sebastian stood across from each other, her eyes wary as she met his gaze, but it was Sebastian who responded to John. "I suppose you have a point. We need to find out who wrote this. Assuming Andrew didn't write it, and that's a big if, then we've got another embezzler on our hands. This one could be dangerous."

Sebastian tossed the note on the table. They could have it dusted for prints, but he doubted any prints besides Andrew's, Evelyn's, and his own would be found on it. Still, he set it down instead of crumpling it into a ball and tossing it out the window.

Evelyn found her voice again. "Don't go back to the private investigator. Andrew bought him off. That's how he knew you were looking into his affairs, and that's how he knew you were out of town."

Evelyn flinched when Sebastian swore, but she remained where she was.

"So what now?" David stopped fidgeting in his seat and looked over at Sebastian. "I take it you have a plan."

"My plans haven't changed. I will head to my office and call the FBI. John will head down to accounting and start organizing the department for a full audit."

David headed for the door. "I'm going back to the lab. If we don't get our product reformulations done on time, it won't matter who is embezzling. We won't have a business to worry about."

John nodded and rose as well. "I've got an appointment with the department heads in twenty minutes. It won't hurt if we start a little early."

Evelyn was left facing Sebastian alone. Without speaking, he grabbed her cane, took her hand, and led her out of the room and down the hall. He was quiet the entire time, dragging her behind him. When he reached his office, he told Lenora to hold his calls and not to disturb them.

The moment the door closed and he had locked it behind him, Sebastian turned on her. "What in the world were you thinking, confronting him alone? He could have hurt you, grabbed you in the parking lot. He could have attacked you, and you wouldn't have been able to defend yourself."

"I didn't think he'd hurt me. I thought he was going to rub what he did in my face, maybe gloat. But I couldn't not go."

"I swear, Evie, I could take a paddle to your backside. It was a stupid, reckless stunt. This is the man who lied to you, cheated on you, stole from you. What makes you think he wouldn't have attacked you? He could have grabbed you, dragged your body into an alley, and no one would have been the wiser."

Evelyn wrapped her arms around her midsection, her stomach aching at the anger he was unleashing on her. What upset her was that he was right. Though he denied it, Andrew was probably the one who pushed her off that cliff. But of course, she hadn't told Sebastian of her suspicions. If she told him now, he would probably go nuclear.

"Look, you're right. I shouldn't have gone alone. I should have at least taken John with me."

"Wrong, Evelyn. You should have waited for me. You should have come to me the minute I walked in the door and told me what happened."

Her voice was a whisper. "I couldn't tell you, not then."

"Why, because you were so eager to go to bed with me? I should have known something was up last night."

Evelyn's stomach clenched, and she had to struggle not to double over. "How can you say that? How can you think that?"

But she knew why, because before he'd come home, she had been thinking about Andrew, not Sebastian. She had been thinking how she wished she'd never met Andrew. She had used Sebastian to try to chase the demon that was Andrew from her mind.

Evelyn wasn't sure when the tears began to fall. "That wasn't all he said. He told me that my mother had been blackmailing my father. He said my father had been embezzling from one of her other boyfriend's businesses and that my mother was helping him. Andrew said my father double-crossed my mother and ran off with the money. A few years later, she hooked up with Andrew. Andrew found out she was blackmailing her old boyfriend, threatening to go public with their affair. He said I was my mother's proof that the affair took place."

Sebastian took a step toward her, but she took a step back. She couldn't seem to stem the tears, but she knew if he touched her, the dam would break. "I don't even know who my father was, so I don't believe Andrew knows. Everything he was saying was all twisted, and he seemed to get sadistic pleasure in telling me. Unfortunately for him, my mother ran off with all of the money Andrew stole. That part I believe. For revenge, Andrew ran away with all of my money and found a way to steal from Brown again. It should have been enough, but it's never enough, not with Andrew. I had to go. I had to meet him. All of this is my fault. I should be the one to fix it."

Sebastian took another step toward her and glared when she took another step back. "Evelyn, if you want to blame someone, blame Andrew. If you have to, blame your mother. He only wanted to hurt you and scare you. There's no proof that anything he said is true."

"But what if it is? Or parts of it? How many men did she hurt? How many of them are going to come out of the woodwork looking for revenge? If the embezzler isn't Andrew, then who is it? Another old boyfriend? My own father? Who?" Evelyn bent over, her arms around her stomach. She was afraid she was going to be sick again.

"Evelyn." This time Evelyn didn't pull away from him. Her tears were washing away the fury he'd been feeling since she'd walked into the boardroom and told them she'd confronted her ex-fiancé. Never in all the years he'd known her had he ever seen her cry. He held her to him, pressing her face into his chest. These were not just tears; this was a terrible weeping she couldn't seem to stem. Knowing there was nothing to say, he simply held her.

Evelyn was hardly aware of the stream of tears pouring down her face. Her breathing hitched, and her nose was running, but the ache deep inside her wouldn't go away. She cried for the five years of pain she'd been enduring; she cried for the grandfather she'd lost, and she cried for the man who was holding her. She hadn't meant to hurt him. It seemed she couldn't stop hurting the people she cared about.

"Sebastian, I am so sorry." She wrapped her arms around his neck, and the tears fell even harder. She felt Sebastian lift and carry her. They ended up on the couch. She was on his lap, and he was pressing tissues into her hands and mopping her face with another one. That one was quickly soaked, so he simply held her against him and let her cry it out.

Sebastian held her tighter, half afraid the horrible weeping wasn't going to stop. But slowly, the tears lessened and Evelyn's grip on his neck loosened.

Evelyn lifted her head and looked at Sebastian's tear-stained shirt. Her mascara had run all over his blue dress shirt. She was pretty sure her tears had washed her eye shadow off as well. The pale pink stain of her gloss was also smeared on his shirt. She pressed her fingers to the spots, unable to look at him.

"Feel better?" Sebastian's gaze followed her fingers. His lips kicked up in a small smile.

"Maybe." Evelyn's nose was completely stuffed up, and her head was pounding. She was afraid to get up and look in the mirror. She must look like a mess.

Sebastian tipped her chin up. "I have a burning desire to kiss you right now, Evie."

Evelyn straightened but didn't slide off his lap. "That's twice today, you know."

"Twice what?" Sebastian wiped away the last of her tears. Her eyes were bright red, and it would take a cold compress to get the swelling down.

"That you called me Evie."

"I told you, I like it." Sebastian carefully lifted her to her feet and led her to his, formerly hers, private bathroom. He turned on the warm water and wet a rag. He washed off the rest of the makeup she was wearing and wiped away the last of her tears. He then set the water to cold and soaked the rag. He handed her the rag and led her back to the couch.

"You need to lie down. Put this over your eyes. It will help. I can't have the office saying I made you cry."

She smiled at him and did what she was told. The cool rag felt wonderful on her overheated face. "No, I guess we can't have that."

They were both quiet for a while, lost in their thoughts.

"Are you still mad at me?" A few minutes later, Evelyn sat up. The rag was no longer cool, and she knew she needed to face him. The tears might have stopped him for a moment, but no way did he forget. Sebastian's words surprised her.

"No, I'm not mad anymore. I guess I understand why you did it. After what you've gone through, you were looking for answers. But sometimes the answers don't make you feel better. There is nothing Andrew can ever say or do to change what happened. And you know as well as I do that he doesn't care about you. Everything he does is about self-preservation."

"So you think he was telling me the truth." It wasn't a question.

"I wouldn't take it that far. I'd say he told you most of the truth. If someone is trying to get him to confess he stole the money, then that person knows for a fact that he did. How many people know him that well?"

"I don't know." Evelyn thought about it but didn't have any answers. "I guess when you get right down to it, I don't really know him that well. I only know what he wanted me to see. He wasn't even trying to hide his true colors yesterday. He tried to charm me at first, but it lasted less than a minute. I wasn't following the plan he had set in his mind, and I think I made him mad. It's why he told me what he did about my mom."

"He knew your mother well for having had just a brief affair with her."

Evelyn had an answer to that. "She was always chatty when she drank. And she drank a lot. I can see her spilling her guts to him after a bender. The things she used to tell me shocked me when I was a little girl. It's the reason my grandfather sued for custody."

"I thought she dropped you and Kimberly off." Sebastian grabbed her hand to still it. She was pulling at the skirt of her dress, twisting the fabric in her hands.

"She did. But she came back for us. Grandfather refused to let us go with her. I still remember Kimberly and me clinging to him, begging him not to let her take us. There was no way he was letting us out of that house again. Kimberly used to tell him stories about our mom, but she was young and didn't remember as much as I did. I kept most of it to myself, but he knew without asking that he couldn't let us go with her. She left with a wad of cash instead of her children. He called his attorney the next day."

She was an amazingly resilient woman, though she would deny it if he told her. Deep down she thought she was weak, but she was anything but. The tears she cried were proof of how hard she fought against the trials that had come her way in the last five years. Anne had told him that Evelyn hadn't even cried at her grandfather's funeral, as if all the tears in her had dried up after the accident. But they hadn't dried up; she bottled them up. He was glad that he was the one there for her when she needed to let them out. He was grateful he could be strong for her when she couldn't be strong for herself. In that moment, Sebastian knew he was in love with her.

* * *

An hour later, Sebastian got off the phone with the FBI. An Agent Trainor was going to lead the investigation of the theft. John had called from the accounting department and work was underway to start gathering data. Earlier they had agreed on an agency to do a private audit, so that was one more task lined up. David had sent someone from the lab up with his handwritten budget notes for Evelyn to go over. David hated computers and avoided them when he could.

Sebastian watched Evelyn as she went over the papers David sent. She had combed out her hair and tried to fix her makeup. She almost looked back to the way she had when she left the house that morning. It was getting harder and harder to remember what she looked like five years ago. Long gone were the severely tailored suits and the boyish haircut. She looked feminine in her dress, with her hair tumbled around her shoulders; she almost took his breath away.

He wasn't sure what it was about her that he admired most. She was intelligent and did her best to run a company she didn't want to run. She survived life-threatening injuries and was a stronger person for it. She confronted her ex-fiancé because she felt it was her responsibility to right past wrongs. She was sweet to his children, giving little Lucy the love she had been missing while away from her mom. She didn't yell at the dog that had knocked over a table and broken a vase. She had given up her horse because it pained her grandfather to keep it around. She convinced Anne to take a break, knowing that Anne needed to get away to come to terms with the loss of her husband.

"You really are amazing, Evie." When her eyes shot up to his, he realized he had spoken aloud.

Frown lines formed between her eyebrows as she denied his words. "Hardly."

Because he knew she would deny it, he didn't respond.

Instead, he sat next to her on the couch and pulled her close to him. She sighed and dropped her head on his shoulder.

Evelyn turned a little so she could rest against his side when his arm came around her. "It's been a rough day. Once the Feds get here, it's going to get worse. All of the old rumors are going to be resurrected, the embezzlement and the wedding. Probably my accident, too. Of course, if Grandfather were here, he'd be applauding your efforts. Five years ago, he couldn't get enough evidence to take to the Feds."

She hit on the head what he was worried most about. Even the strongest people had their breaking point. Evelyn's tears were proof she was reaching hers. "It's not going to be easy for you. A lot of people didn't believe your grandfather's accusations. The Feds are going to hear about that, too. There are plenty of people who think he fabricated the entire tale to get even with Andrew. They aren't going to have a lot of evidence to use to investigate him and his company."

Evelyn simply wrapped her arm around Sebastian's waist, needing his presence close to her while they discussed a past she wished she could bury and forget about once and for all. "Some people think he was guilty. If he had gone through with the wedding, he would have looked less guilty. Of course, then he would have been saddled with a wife he'd just cleaned out financially. Then not only did he leave town, but he also left the state. Running made him look guilty, too."

Sebastian was stroking her hair, trying to keep her calm. It seemed to be working. Plus, he enjoyed holding her like this. He hoped there would be more moments like this one, many more days and nights close to her. Once this mess was behind them, they needed to talk about their future.

"We have proof money is missing. We have what little the investigator was able to dig up on him, though it isn't anything incriminating. Of course, the investigator's track record isn't exactly reliable. We have the fact that Andrew tried to warn us off. And we have the note he gave you. It's not much, but it's more than your grandfather had five years ago. But what we need is to track that money if we're going to find out who is behind this."

"Hopefully the Feds can take care of that. At the rate we're going, it will take us a while to get an accurate amount and trace where it went."

Sebastian thought about that. "It could have gone multiple places, too. Hopefully, Agent Trainor knows what he's doing."

A knock on the door interrupted them. Sebastian got up and unlocked the door. John was at the door with a strange man.

"I was at the front desk when Agent Trainor arrived." John waved the agent in.

Sebastian held out his hand. "I'm Sebastian O'Connor." He glanced over at Evelyn, who was having a bit of a hard time getting off the couch.

Evelyn grabbed her cane and managed to get to her feet. "I'm Evelyn Bennett. We're glad you could come so quickly."

Agent Trainor looked typical of a television FBI agent. He wore a black suit and tie and what looked to be rubber-soled black dress shoes. His badge was visible on his breast pocket. Evelyn was pretty sure there was a gun discreetly hidden under his jacket. His hair was a sandy blond cut very short. He walked with authority, completely comfortable in his surroundings.

"Given that you waited a few days to contact us, I figured enough time was wasted." Trainor entered the room, his eyes taking in everything.

Sebastian gestured to the chair in front of the desk, and the agent took a seat. Evelyn took the chair beside him, while Sebastian took his place behind the desk. John stood behind them, looking unsure of what he should do next.

Sebastian was not easily intimidated. "I had some personal matters to take care of first. Given that this has been going on for some time now, a few more days weren't going to hurt one way or the other."

The next couple of hours were extremely uncomfortable for Evelyn. They all decided the boardroom was the best place to discuss what was going on. David was called in, and John accompanied them. She was right when she said the past was going to get dredged up. The agent asked dozens of extremely uncomfortable questions about her and Andrew's relationship, Andrew's history with the company, and with her grandfather, and because full disclosure was the best thing for everyone, he asked uncomfortable questions about Andrew's relationship with her mother when she mentioned it to him. She saw the shock on both David's and John's faces as the agent asked Evelyn questions about the affair, but thankfully neither said anything about it. Evelyn was mortified that they now knew.

David didn't have a whole lot to add. He spent most of his time in the lab and didn't know much about the organization outside of research and development. He also didn't know Andrew well, so after answering a few questions, he excused himself and went back to the lab.

John answered what he could. Given his role as Evelyn's assistant, he knew almost as much about the company's financial status as she did. Occasionally he would add his opinion.

Agent Trainor looked over his notes. "What is your history with the company, Mr. O'Connor? I have here that you were recently elected president and have taken over the business."

"I used to work for Howard Bennett, Evelyn's grandfather. He passed away recently, and he left a fifth of the company to me."

"You used to work for him? When did you quit?"

"I quit five years ago and took a job overseas."

Agent Trainor made another note. "Why?"

He smiled at Evelyn. "Miss Bennett took over the company when her grandfather retired. We had some differences of opinion, so I took a job that had been offered to me."

"Looks to me like the two of you are getting along now. No more differences of opinion?"

Evelyn smirked at Sebastian but answered Agent Trainor's question. "We've called a truce. I relinquished control of the company, not that I had much choice. My skills at running the company are not on par with Mr. O'Connor's. And given his job skills and previous experience here at Brown, my grandfather chose him as his successor upon his death."

"Just to be clear, your relationship with Andrew Shepherd ended five years ago, and you hadn't seen him again until yesterday?"

Evelyn hid a shudder. "That's right. I hadn't seen or heard from him since he left me standing at the altar while he was wiping out my bank account."

"But you have no proof."

Evelyn's head shot up and swiftly looked at Sebastian. "There is the letter he left for me at my apartment. It doesn't come right out and say what he did, but it's implied. My grandfather took it. Was it in his papers?"

Sebastian shook his head. "I didn't see it."

Agent Trainor flipped his notebook closed. "Unless he confessed, it probably won't do much good. But it could be used in court if it comes to that. That letter, taken with whatever other evidence is gathered, could be useful. But to be honest, you have very little to go on other than you think he did it. Given what you've told me, I'm inclined to believe you could be right."

Evelyn breathed a sigh of relief as Agent Trainor stood. "Is that all?"

The agent nodded. "For now. You've answered all my questions. I've got all of your numbers if I think of anything else. The most important thing is to find out where that money went."

Sebastian shook his hand, and John walked him out.

"Do you think he believed what we told him? He sounded a bit skeptical." Evelyn wrapped her arms around her waist and walked to the window.

"It's his job to be skeptical. First, he has to rule us out. We've as much motive as anyone else to embezzle the funds. I've been gone for five years and suddenly show back up. You are in a financial bind because of your accident and could use the money. David and John both have means and opportunity. Once he rules all of us out, he'll run background checks on key staff members. And I have no doubt he'll start digging into Andrew's past."

Evelyn considered what he said. "I guess I hadn't thought of that. I guess it's a good thing you're in charge."

Sebastian came up behind her and massaged her shoulders. "Still happy you're not in charge anymore? I'd understand if you were still feeling resentful."

Evelyn dropped her neck and let his hands ease the tension that had been building there as Agent Trainor asked his questions. "I don't resent you. Over the last couple of weeks, I've proven I can still be useful. I guess that's really what I need. To know I can do my job and do it well."

Sebastian found a particularly tense muscle, and she moaned. He kissed the top of her head while working the knots out. "Think you'll stick around? I know you said you couldn't quit because you had nowhere else to go, but that's not true."

Evelyn leaned back and trusted Sebastian to keep her upright. "I can't imagine working anywhere else. So, yes, I plan to stick around."

"I was hoping you'd say that." Sebastian eased his body in front of hers, so she faced him. He bent down to kiss her. Things might get complicated around here in the next couple of weeks, but Evelyn wasn't a quitter. And neither was he.

Chapter Eighteen

The rest of the week fell into a pattern of sorts. The audit was underway, and Agent Trainor had come back to ask more questions. Sebastian, Evelyn, and John spent part of the workday going over reports from the previous day while trying to fulfill the dozens of daily obligations they had with running a company the size of Brown.

Friday afternoon, Evelyn sat in her office, staring at the latest batch of reports. Sebastian and John had pretty much taken over all aspects of the investigation. That was fine with her. She was handling the daily problems so Sebastian could focus. She knew what his immediate plans were for Brown, and she knew how to go about implementing them. She spent most of her days with department heads going over Sebastian's updated strategy for the company as a whole and the departments as individual groups.

Outside of work, Evelyn couldn't remember being happier. She and Sebastian had fallen into a routine at home, as well. She had taken over most of the cooking, and Sebastian did the cleanup. They were now driving into work together, so they were arriving home at the same time now. After dinner, they would spend part of the evening much as they had when the children were there. Evelyn read while Sebastian was outside.

For her, the best part was when they went to bed. Since their first night together, he had spent every night in her bed. He hadn't asked if he could, and she didn't expect him to sleep anywhere else. And since her room had a private bath, and her bed was specially purchased for her back, he had moved into her room. A good amount of his clothes was in her closet, and his shaving supplies and assorted toiletries had made their way to her bathroom as well.

Anne had called her last night, reminding her that this interlude wasn't going to last forever. Evelyn couldn't imagine Sebastian sleeping in her bed once Anne was home. She doubted they could hide the change in their relationship, even if they wanted to, but when Anne returned, they would go back to separate beds. It would still be a couple of weeks before she returned, but it just didn't seem like enough time.

If anyone else noticed the change in their relationship, they didn't say. David was mostly oblivious to what was going on around him. John already suspected they were having an affair, and since he'd already told her what he thought about that, he hadn't mentioned it again. Evelyn was just grateful she hadn't seen Kimberly. She wasn't sure she wanted to discuss her relationship with Sebastian with her sister, but she was pretty sure she'd blurt it out if pressed. Evelyn was incredibly happy, and she wasn't sure she could contain it. On the other hand, she would see Kimberly tonight, and she didn't want a repeat of the last time they'd talked about Sebastian.

The week had brought a few surprises as well. Leslie had come by and personally delivered invitations to her engagement party late Tuesday afternoon. The party was tonight at a local restaurant. Part of Evelyn wondered if Leslie would make it down the aisle, but Leslie seemed happy, so Evelyn hoped she did. Her haste in organizing the engagement party boded well.

Evelyn's alarm chirped to tell her it was five. She had a dress hanging on the back of her door so she could change for the party. Evelyn couldn't remember the last time she had been to a party of any kind, and she was looking forward to the evening. She was hoping she could convince Sebastian to dance with her. Leslie hadn't invited him, which wasn't surprising given their history, but Evelyn had asked him if he would attend with her. They'd never gone on a date, so she had been a little nervous when she'd asked him. But he had seemed pleased by her invitation and had agreed to go. Since it was pointless to hide the change in their relationship, Evelyn figured the party would also be a good way to subtly announce it to her family. Most everyone would be focused on Leslie and Philip, and she hoped she and Sebastian just sort of slipped in under the radar.

Again, Evelyn had chosen her dress with Sebastian in mind. Her clothing choices the past few days had all been with him in mind. In the morning, he would watch her dress almost as intensely as he watched her undress. It was sometimes disconcerting to be the center of all that masculine attention, but since she enjoyed returning the favor, she didn't complain.

Sebastian arrived at her office at six. He didn't bother to knock when he entered. "Are you ready to go?"

Evelyn was sitting at her desk, touching up the last of her makeup. She smiled at him, signaling that she was ready.

The drive was a short one and mostly a quiet one. Now that they were on the way to the restaurant, Evelyn was feeling a little uncertain. She was uncertain about her relationship with Sebastian, and now she wasn't so sure they should be telling her family, even indirectly.

"I'm getting good at reading your mind, Evie." Sebastian found a parking space near the restaurant and shut off the car. He didn't immediately open the door. "Your family is going to find out about us. It might as well be now when everyone is relaxed and happy."

She knew he was right. "But maybe Leslie's engagement party isn't the best time. She didn't invite you. Maybe she doesn't want you here."

Sebastian shrugged at that. "Our relationship was a long time ago, and it wasn't much of one. It didn't last long enough for either of us to have become attached."

It had been long enough, Evelyn thought. Stupidly she voiced it. "It was long enough for you to sleep with her."

"I can't change the past, Evie. You have to accept that it happened, it was a long time ago, and that she wasn't important to me. It only happened because I was recently divorced and still a bit raw from it. I admit she wasn't one of my better ideas."

"She's still attracted to you."

"Maybe. But she's engaged, and even if she wasn't, she and I wouldn't happen again." Sebastian wanted to snap her out of it and knew just how to do it. "You know, you're cute when you're jealous."

Evelyn knew it was stupid, but she'd been jealous when it happened, and it still bugged her. She might be the woman currently sharing a bed with him, but it still irked her that Leslie had been there first. Of course, Sebastian said it was only one time. Evelyn certainly had spent more than one night in bed with him. Oddly, it made her feel better.

"I'll forgive you if you promise to dance with me. I've been fantasizing about it all day." Evelyn gave him a sultry look, or what she hoped was one.

Sebastian felt a quick surge of lust that he had to quickly tamp down. "Don't look at me like that, or we won't make it to the party."

Evelyn watched, amused, as he opened his car door and came around to help her out. His movements were a little stiff. She took the hand he offered her and let him lead her to the restaurant.

It looked as if everyone had already arrived. John had left work early to get Kimberly. The pair was in conversation with some old family friends. David was there, but Evelyn didn't recognize the woman he was with. His girlfriends were usually short-lived. The women he dated tended to get impatient with him when he spent more time at work than he did with them. Evelyn wasn't sure he'd ever settle down, nor was she sure he wanted to.

She looked around and spotted Leslie. She and Philip were sipping what looked like champagne and accepting congratulations from the various party guests. Evelyn didn't recognize everyone but assumed half of the guests were Philip's friends and colleagues. Bruce, her grandfather's lawyer, was also there since he was Philip's boss. He was with a woman Evelyn assumed was his wife. When Bruce spotted them, he came over.

"I wasn't expecting to see you here." Bruce addressed his comment to Sebastian and shook his hand.

"Evelyn invited me." Sebastian accepted two glasses of champagne from a waiter who offered them and handed one to Evelyn.

Bruce gave the pair an odd look. "How are things going? I've heard rumors there has been some trouble. If there is anything I can do, I'd be more than happy to help. I've been the family's lawyer for years, and Howard was a good friend."

"What kind of rumors have you heard?" As far as Sebastian knew, they had kept the theft under wraps. Of course, with the audit going on, it wouldn't be hard for information to get out with all the employees who were involved.

"I heard there was some money trouble. Something about theft, but the details weren't specific. A client of mine who knew Howard mentioned it to me. He'd heard about it at the country club."

As far as Evelyn knew, her grandfather wasn't a member of a country club. But it was a good bet he had friends who were. "Anyone I know?"

Bruce shook his head. "I don't think so. He recently moved to town and he's a new client. I think he was just looking to gossip."

Sebastian and Evelyn chatted with Bruce for a few more minutes before Bruce excused himself to go back to his wife.

"I can't help but wonder who is spreading the rumors." Sebastian took Evelyn's hand as they mingled in the crowd, making their way over to give their congratulations to Leslie and Philip.

"This whole situation is strange. Brown is not a publicly traded company, so it doesn't make the papers, except for when we get an environmental group on our tail. But that never lasts long. We strive to make sure we adhere to all of the EPA regulations, and even some that are not legally enforced. I suppose Andrew could be spreading rumors, but if he's not behind the theft, then he'd want to keep the theft as low profile as possible. He certainly wouldn't want to attract attention to himself or Crown."

"I don't like this. Something about this entire situation is strange. This doesn't seem like it's just about money. If the embezzler wanted money, they would have taken what they could and disappeared. If it's not Andrew, then the embezzler is still hanging around, stirring up trouble. It worries me. If stealing money is part one of a bigger scam, I can't help but wonder what part two is, or when it will take place."

That gave Evelyn pause. Sebastian might have a point. What if the embezzler was dangerous? He or she had already threatened her and Sebastian if they didn't back off. They had no intention of doing that. Evelyn's hand tightened around Sebastian's.

"Don't worry. We'll figure this out and who's behind it." He gave her hand a gentle squeeze.

Evelyn wasn't given a chance to respond. Sebastian was shaking Philip's hand and congratulating him on his engagement to Leslie. Evelyn hugged Leslie.

"Congratulations, Leslie. We're all very happy for you."

"Thanks.   I never thought I'd be celebrating an engagement."

"You just needed to find the right man." Evelyn let Sebastian's hand go while he chatted with Philip.

"Isn't that the truth? I didn't think there was a man on this planet who could convince me to get married. My parents' marriage only lasted a few years. David and I were so young when they split. Both of them remarried, but neither of those weddings stuck either. I guess I figured I'd be a bad bet."

"To be fair, your mother and my mother had too much in common. Neither of us is like our mother. They both liked their freedom." Evelyn didn't like talking about her mother but hadn't been able to think of anything else to say.

Leslie took Evelyn's wrist and pulled her a short distance from the crowd. "Philip and I figured it was best to tell the family tonight instead of waiting. It's not like we can hide it much longer. But you can't tell anyone outside the family yet. Philip and I are having a baby."

Evelyn had taken a small sip of her champagne and almost choked on it. She stared for a moment. When she saw the happy look on Leslie's face, she snapped out of it. "Leslie, that's wonderful."

"I think so, too. I wasn't so sure at first. I hadn't told Philip yet when he proposed to me. I was so shocked he asked me to marry him that I blurted it out at him. He was stunned but then he kind of whooped out loud in excitement. He had told me he wanted to get married and have kids when I first met him, but at the time it wasn't in connection with me. But the reality is we're both old enough to know what we want, and if we're going to get hitched and have kids, we might as well have gotten started early. I'm not as young as I used to be."

Evelyn couldn't help the big grin on her face. She hugged Leslie and was surprised by the strength of the hug that Leslie returned.

Leslie looked past Evelyn, and Evelyn realized she was looking at Sebastian. She was going to say something when Leslie spoke again.

"I see you brought Sebastian. Kimberly says she thinks you two are an item."

Evelyn looked over her shoulder at Sebastian. "We are, I guess. We haven't talked about it or made it official or anything. This is sort of our first date."

"I'm happy for the two of you. Maybe it's because I'm in love myself, but I have this urge to see everyone else I know get married." Leslie giggled at that. "Well, maybe not David. The woman he brought tonight isn't terribly bright. David needs to find himself a smart woman. Maybe one that's smarter than he is."

Since Evelyn could only agree, she just nodded. Both women watched as Sebastian made his way over.

"I think I owe you a dance." The music had faded to a slow song, one he knew Evelyn could dance to.

Evelyn looked over at Leslie, who waved her away. Evelyn took the hand Sebastian was holding out to her. The dance floor was crowded, so there wasn't much room to do more than sway to the music. Since that was all she could do, she eagerly went into Sebastian's arms.

She had hoped he would dance with her. All afternoon she had imagined him taking her in his arms, her breasts brushing against his chest, their thighs touching in rhythm with the music. She had imagined laying her head on his shoulder while his hands rested on her waist. He had made love to her every night since that first night, but when they were in bed she was usually lying on her back. It was hard to cuddle up to him from that position. A physical closeness outside of making love had been a growing desire all day. And since the night would end with him in her bed, she let herself relax as he took her in his arms and guided her into the slow dance.

Sebastian was enjoying the dance as much as she was. She had wrapped her arms around his neck and pressed her body lightly against his. The rhythm of the music was slow, and the lyrics were about lovers. He hadn't given any thought to dancing with Evelyn but was glad she had. Her eyes were closed, her hair loose and flowing over her shoulders. The pink dress she wore brought out the flush in her skin and enhanced the color of her eyes, though at the moment he couldn't see them. He couldn't help but run a hand over her hair and down her bare arms.

"You are incredibly beautiful, Evelyn." He whispered the words softly in her ear.

Evelyn trembled in his arms, and her throat choked up. She pressed herself closer to him, her fingers stroking the back of his neck under his hair.

They danced a couple of dances before the music changed to something with a little more tempo. Sebastian had to disentangle Evelyn's hands from his hair. She didn't seem inclined to let go. He led her to a nearby table so they could have dinner.

Evelyn sat at the table while Sebastian fixed both of them a plate from the magnificent buffet that had been put together for the evening. When he returned, she gratefully accepted the plate. He had piled on enough food for two. "I see you're making sure I'm well fed again."

Sebastian dug into his meal. He'd been guilty of skipping a few meals himself the past few days. There was so much to do that meals took a low priority. "Someone needs to. I hope you like what I picked. You seem to favor things with lots of veggies."

"It's all part of the new and improved Evelyn. My doctors tell me nutrition is important for my body and mind. Anne is the one responsible. She knows I'll just eat whatever is at hand, so she keeps the fridge stocked with leftovers."

Sebastian took a stab at some shrimp on her plate. "So how come you're cooking now?"

Evelyn blushed. "It's different when you cook for someone else. When it was just me, I didn't care much. But I can't feed you what I would have eaten, and since you're cleaning up after me, it seems like a fair trade to at least make you something semi-nutritious."

"Anne babies you too much, but it's in her nature. She's a born nurturer. It's a shame she never had children of her own."

Evelyn tasted the shrimp he had just tried. "Speaking of children, I got a surprise a few minutes ago. Leslie and

Philip are having a baby. She asked me not to tell anyone outside the family, but I figure you're close enough."

"Huh. I guess you never can tell. I'd have bet good money Leslie wouldn't have kids. I'm guessing Kimberly will have half a dozen if she has her way."

He was right about that. "I expect Kimberly to announce that she and John are having another one within the next six months. Patrick is six months old now, and Kimberly said she wants to have her kids close together."

"What about you?" Sebastian couldn't help but ask now that they were talking about children.

Stunned by the question, Evelyn couldn't answer at first. When she found her voice, her words were soft. "I do want them. Every time I'm around Patrick I can't help but want. But I can't take care of a child unless I have the surgery, and perhaps even after I won't be able to. The surgery isn't a guarantee that I'll be all fixed. And I suppose I'm old-fashioned. I think I should have a husband first, and men haven't exactly been swarming around me since the accident. My social life was pretty pathetic five years ago, and it's non-existent these days. And five years ago I chose Andrew, which was a huge mistake."

Sebastian didn't want to drop the subject. "So if you met the right man, you'd have the surgery, and in a perfect world, have babies?"

"We both know the world isn't a perfect place. But I'm still young, so I suppose anything is possible."

Sebastian pressed her, his need to know suddenly urgent. "What about me?"

"What about you?" Evelyn's heart beat faster at what he

was asking.

"Being the father of those kids. I know we haven't talked about the future, but what we've got going on is pretty spectacular. I know your first affair ended sour, but marriage can be wonderful when both people want the same things."

"Then why did you get divorced if marriage is so wonderful?"

Sebastian figured he'd set himself up for that question. "When I married Becky, we were happy. We wanted, or I thought we wanted, the same things. Becky and I got divorced because I couldn't give her the security she wanted. Money was never a problem, but Becky wanted to move into a home and spend the rest of her life there. She wanted to raise her kids in that house and grow old and die in that house. I moved her one too many times."

Evelyn thought about that. She knew he'd moved a lot over the years, and part of her couldn't help but wonder how long he'd be content at Brown. And how long he'd be content with her. "So why didn't you stay put for her sake?"

"I just couldn't. When I was growing up, my dad had spent thirty years working for the same company, living in the same house, married to the same woman. For the most part, my mom and dad were happy. My sister was born when they were in their twenties and thirties. I was born when my mom was almost forty and my dad was almost fifty. I was a young kid when he got let go from his job. The company was on the verge of bankruptcy. My dad had spent all his life at that job, and at almost sixty he had nothing to show for it. He lost his pension and his benefits.

He had to get another job, and the new one didn't pay nearly as well. My mom ended up having to work. They sold the house they'd lived in since they had been married and had to move into an apartment in a rough neighborhood. My mom hated that apartment, but she loved my dad, so she didn't complain much."

"That is sad. Did they stay together?"

Sebastian could smile at that. "They did. Once I finished school and was making good money, they were able to buy a new house. It's a small one, but my mom is happy with it. I gave them the money for a down payment. My dad was too proud to take the money, but my mom wasn't. They're both retired now, but they still live in that little house. But my father losing his job taught me a lesson. Don't stay at a job too long, especially if there are better opportunities. I guess I was always looking for a better job, better benefits, better pay. I got what I wanted, but I lost Becky in the process. Her husband now is the type to lay deep roots. She's happy."

Evelyn set her fork down, no longer hungry. "What about you? Are you happy now? You've tied yourself to Brown, at least for the near future. You could let someone else run the company and move on to a new job, but you're not the type to let others control what's yours."

Sebastian supposed she was right about that. "When I read the letter from your grandfather, he made a convincing argument. He knew me well enough to know that what I needed was a challenge. And Brown is nothing if not a challenge. What's different this time is that I own a piece of it. He knew ownership was what I'd been missing in my other jobs. It wasn't just you I didn't want to take orders from. Every position I've held in the last ten years has been one where I gave orders more than I took. Brown puts me in charge, and that's the key."

"That's what the letter said? That's it?" Evelyn took a hasty sip of her champagne. "I've been trying to figure out what in the world he could have said that would make you take those shares. All he did was appeal to your ego."

Sebastian couldn't help but laugh at her incredulous expression. "What did you think he said? Did you think he threatened me or something? And just as a fair warning, I do have a big ego. Your grandfather knew I was always on the lookout for a new challenge. What could be more challenging than owning and running your own company?"

"I suppose so, but you smiled when you read that letter, and you didn't even hesitate to accept your new role. You have to admit that for a man with wandering feet, you've recently planted some roots of your own."

"You're right. And you've also successfully distracted me from what we were talking about."

Evelyn turned her head and gazed into the crowd. She feigned innocence. "What topic was that?"

"Babies, Evie. We were talking about babies. And marriage."

"Given how recent the change in our relationship is, maybe we should wait a while before we talk about those subjects." She hoped she was coming off as nonchalant, but the idea of marrying Sebastian and having his babies was having a profound effect on her. She didn't want to embarrass either of them by taking what was probably a hypothetical conversation and turning it into something more. She wasn't sure her battered heart could handle it.

Sebastian took a sip of his champagne and watched Evelyn as she tried to ignore him. He smiled to himself. She might not be ready yet to consider marriage and children, but he had no doubt he could change her mind. After all, they worked together, they were currently sharing a bed, and he had no plans on leaving. He'd been thinking about roots recently. He missed his children, and Brown would provide him with enough of a challenge that he wouldn't need to find a new job. And maybe Evelyn could help fill some of the holes in his heart that were left when Becky divorced him and separated him from his children.

Chapter Nineteen

Evelyn should have known her perfect evening wouldn't end in a perfect night. And the evening had been perfect. Despite the short-lived discussion about marriage and babies, Evelyn had learned things about Sebastian she hadn't known. She didn't know anything about his parents or why he had been so driven to succeed over the years. Becky probably had known but hadn't understood. Evelyn, who had been fighting her own demons for the last five years, and truthfully before that, understood how he had been driven to work hard to the exclusion of his and his wife's happiness.

After their talk of family, and after he had emptied his plate, he took her back to the dance floor. They danced a few more dances, and Evelyn had enthusiastically gone back into his arms. The champagne and delicious food relaxed her so much that she fell asleep in the car. When they arrived home, Sebastian had woken her and gotten her undressed and in bed in record time. She was no longer sleepy by the time he'd finished undressing her. She felt a little wobbly on her feet but had fully participated in the lovemaking that followed.

It was around three o'clock when the nightmare started. Evelyn fitfully slept while visions of black figures in a black storm chased her over the California hills that were only a few short miles from her home. One particular figure reached her, and with arms stretched out, pushed her over the edge.

Evelyn woke up with a scream.

Sebastian jerked upright, unsure at first what had woken him, but he quickly realized Evelyn was awake with her arms braced on her thighs, her breathing heavy, and she was trying not to cry.

"Evie." Sebastian flipped on the bedside lamp and gathered Evelyn into his arms. She pressed her face into his chest, her breath heaving as she fought for air. Her body was trembling wildly, and her hands were fisted. He could see her nails were digging into her palms hard enough to leave marks.

He just held her and rubbed her naked back. Because she was trembling so hard, he leaned over and grabbed the robe she kept nearby.

Evelyn wasn't sure how long it took for the panic attack to subside. The nightmares were bad enough, but she hated the panic that sometimes took over. Oftentimes her mind had a hard time distinguishing her dreams from reality. The sensation of falling while sleeping was usually the cause. Sometimes the figures didn't reach her. But sometimes they did, and it was those times that panic took over.

"Feeling better?" Sebastian continued to stroke her hair and back in long, slow sweeping motions he hoped were calming. He remembered the night of the thunderstorm before Anne had left. Evelyn had come downstairs with dark circles under her eyes and tension in her body. How many nights did she wake alone in terror?

Evelyn murmured her response against his chest. She doubted he understood what she said, but it must have been enough to satisfy him because he didn't ask again.

"Want to talk about it?"

Evelyn rubbed her cheek against his chest, his skin warming her. She lifted a hand so she could place it over his heart. The steady rhythm was soothing. "Not really. It's just a stupid dream. I've been having them since my accident."

"Sometimes talking about it helps."

"I talked about them with my therapist. That didn't stop them." She flexed her fingers, enjoying the feel of his skin under her hands. As she lightly stroked his chest, his heart rate increased. She smiled.

"Okay then, no talking." Sebastian lifted her chin and kissed her instead.

There was no hesitation in the kiss. Evelyn moaned into his mouth as he immediately deepened the kiss. She tried to turn herself in his arms so that she could press her breasts against him. She felt the robe slide off her back as Sebastian helped her. She was no longer cold.

Evelyn gave herself over to him. She playfully bit his lip when he tried to withdraw his mouth. She smiled, then moaned again when he returned the favor. His hands found their way between their bodies, his hands unerringly finding her breasts and caressing them until she was begging for him.

Sebastian wanted to erase all memories of the nightmare. He laid her down on her back and found her breasts with his mouth. When she arched herself fully to him, he sucked her flesh harder, knowing the lighter caresses were no longer enough.

Evelyn's hands grasped at his back, desperate now to have him inside her. She rubbed the muscles of his back and arms, but he still held himself back from her. His mouth drifted down her belly, his tongue then going lower to trace the scars that she hated so much. Her body quivered under his ministrations, but she didn't complain.

Evelyn would have begged had she had the breath. His hands were now caressing her legs and inner thighs as he slid his body back up the length of hers. She couldn't help but respond to every touch of his hands. At some point, she had wound her arms around his neck, but her weight wasn't hampering him from finding all the places he liked to touch on her body. When his fingers worked their way from her thighs to her body's core, rubbing and caressing her where she wanted him most, all she could do was hang on to him.

Sebastian stopped for a moment and unwound her arms from around his neck, much as he had done when they had been dancing. He grabbed her hands and entwined their fingers. Evelyn spread her thighs as he settled between them. Ever so slowly, he entered her, watching the pleasure on her face. Evelyn's thighs closed around his hips, wanting to pull him fully inside her. He resisted her and took his time, not wanting to rush them.

Evelyn went limp when he finally found his way completely inside her body. She was acutely aware of his stomach pressed against hers, his chest crushing her breasts, his breath on her neck. He had her body fully anchored to the bed, her arms spread to the side of her body, and his hands pressed against hers. When he finally moved, it was ever so slowly, his entire body caressing hers from neck to loin. He slowly rocked both of them to the peak. When her climax finally came, she shrieked his name, unable to keep silent with the exquisite pleasure he'd brought her. She felt him thrust a few more times, this time quickly. His climax was as powerful as hers had been, his impassioned cry muffled when he buried his head against her pillow.

* * *

It was morning when she woke. The nightmare was nothing but a vague memory. Sebastian's thorough lovemaking had wiped away all the residual fear from the dream. Evelyn stretched a bit, her hip protesting the movement. She winced, but thankfully it was just a twinge. She looked over at Sebastian's side of the bed, but he had already gotten up. He had left her robe lying where he had slept.

Though it was Saturday, they had planned to spend a good part of their day working. She imagined he was in her grandfather's study. When he worked from home, that was usually where he liked to go. She imagined her grandfather would be pleased that Sebastian had moved into his study. She wondered if he would be happy that Sebastian had moved into her bed. She imagined he would be, though he would have demanded marriage before he would have allowed him to share a bed with her.

Evelyn rolled onto her stomach, using Sebastian's pillow

to rest her head. On mornings when she woke and thought of him, she would miss her grandfather terribly. But this morning the ache was not as acute as it usually was. As hard as it was to accept sometimes, life went on. Life with Sebastian was making the pain a little more bearable.

Evelyn lay there a few minutes longer before getting up. Her back and leg were hurting this morning, so she ran a bath instead of getting in the shower. If Sebastian were up here, they would have showered together. But since he was already up for the day, he probably had taken his shower already. But this morning she needed the bath and was glad he had already gotten up. Though she had been sharing a bed with Sebastian for almost a week, her body had not gotten accustomed to the workout it got when he made love to her. As she lay in the tub, visions of what it would be like if her body were healed danced through her head. Her mind had them making love in the shower, on the couch, against a wall, and in a hammock. Because the fantasies were making her ache, she turned her thoughts to the day ahead.

Not much progress had been made with the investigation. She supposed that was to be expected since Sebastian had already found where most of the money had gone missing from. Andrew was still coming up clean as a whistle, and that bothered her. She wanted him to be guilty, not only because he had been guilty before, but because that would mean the investigation would be over and she wouldn't have to worry anymore. The letter that had threatened her and Sebastian had her scared, and she knew that Sebastian took the threat seriously. He'd been making sure the alarm was set every night when they returned home. He also made sure that if she left the building for any reason, he was with her. They were sharing the commute now, and though it was partially because they were now sleeping together, she had no doubt that if they were sleeping separately, he still would have insisted they drive to and from work together.

After her body had been sufficiently massaged by the jets, she washed her hair and body and got out of the tub. She quickly dressed and made her way downstairs. Sebastian was sure to have made coffee and possibly even breakfast since she'd slept in.

Evelyn headed for the kitchen first. She found sliced fruit and yogurt in the fridge waiting for her. She smiled as she pulled the bowl out. Taking it and a fresh cup of coffee with her, she went in search of Sebastian. She didn't find him in the study as she had imagined. Instead, she found him in the garden. He was sitting quietly, drinking a cup of coffee at the patio table.

Evelyn set her cup down and took the seat across from him. She scooped up a bite of the yogurt. "You're spoiling me, you know."

"I just can't seem to help myself. How do you feel?"

Evelyn shrugged and took another bite. "Okay, I guess. Your therapy works a lot better than the therapy I paid boatloads of money for."

That got a laugh out of him. "And it's free." He took a sip of his coffee before asking the question he knew he had to ask. "What was it about?"

Evelyn closed her eyes for a moment and took a breath.

Just thinking about it made her heart start racing. "As I'm sure you've guessed, it's about the accident. My memories of the fall are hazy. I remember walking on the cliffs. I remember the sun was starting to set. When I would go riding on the cliff paths, I would always make sure to give Isabel plenty of time to get back before it got dark. Isabel didn't like the dark. She would get antsy and get startled by every shadow. She wasn't usually so timid, but something about the shadows made her jumpy. I figured I had a good twenty minutes or so before I had to start back. But as you know, I ended up over the edge instead."

She took another deep breath and continued. "The thunderstorm was on its way by the time I came to. The shadows had deepened, and I couldn't see much beyond the ledge above. I think it was the man who found me, and I think he's the one who climbed down while his girlfriend called for help. But the storm was coming, and he didn't stay with me. He climbed back up the ledge and they got to safety. Isabel had torn free from the tree I had her roped to. She was wandering the cliff, but she was just a dark shadow. I don't know when I started to cry, but the tears came, and I could hardly breathe. Everything hurt so much it was hard to know where the pain was coming from. I was panicked and hysterical by the time the rescue team found me. At some point, it had begun to rain. The rescue team was wearing black raincoats and hats to keep the rain off. I was in shock and hypothermia was starting to set in. The rain came down in a downpour as the team brought the gurney down. They looked like demons coming for me. Flashlights were directed to where I was, and I couldn't see much because they were blinding me. I was screaming when they reached me. They were talking to me, trying to get me to calm down. They stabilized my body and strapped me down to a board. I couldn't move, and I still was having difficulty breathing."

"No wonder you have nightmares." Sebastian took her hand, rubbing his fingers over the knuckles that were clenched.

"In my dreams, shadowed figures are coming after me. I'm running from them, but I'm just not fast enough to evade them. Usually I wake up when they reach me. But sometimes the figures reach me, and one of them reaches out and pushes me over the ledge I'm standing on. I can feel myself falling, but there isn't any ground beneath me. The shadow just watches me as I'm falling."

Evelyn looked across the garden. Sebastian was waiting patiently, as if he knew her tale wasn't over. "That afternoon on the cliffs, I was sitting down near the ledge. There's a particular spot on the ledge that has a little seat. I was sitting there looking out over the horizon. Sometimes my mind would drift and shut out everything around me. I didn't hear the birds chirping; I didn't hear voices from other people on the trail. I was oblivious to everything around me. Then while I had my arms wrapped around my knees, I felt someone push me right in the middle of my back."

Evelyn looked up at Sebastian, her eyes clouded with memories. "Someone pushed me."

It had to be shock; that was the first thing Sebastian thought. No one would have a reason to push her. Then he looked in her eyes and knew she believed she was pushed. Then he realized someone did have a reason.

"I'll kill him." Sebastian's voice was low, but the look on his face was frightening.

Evelyn pulled her hand from his and crossed her arms protectively across her chest. "Andrew didn't do it."

"How can you be so sure?" Sebastian paced, his rage preventing him from sitting still.

Evelyn didn't know how to calm him, so she didn't try. "The day I met Andrew, I told him he was a liar and murderer. Attempted murderer, anyway. His face was shocked, really shocked. At first, I didn't believe him, but he lost his cool after that. He had been confident and smug up until then."

Sebastian closed the distance between them and pulled her to her feet. He felt completely impotent. If it wasn't Andrew, then he had no one to direct this rage at. He wanted to tear apart whoever had hurt her.

Evelyn wrapped her arms around Sebastian's waist when he simply stood there before her. She knew how he felt. When she had finally recovered enough to remember what had happened, she had felt a terrible fury. She had directed it at Andrew, but he was gone, and she couldn't vent it on him.

Then Evelyn realized Sebastian believed her. That, more than anything, was what she needed. "My therapist said it was just the trauma and shock. She said that my mind was trying to come up with a valid reason why I fell. She said it was easier to blame someone else than to blame myself. When I told her about my nightmares, she said it was just my mind twisting the events of that night. She said I have post-traumatic stress and that's what induces the nightmares. Storms usually trigger dreams because of the storm I was rescued in. I couldn't tell my grandfather I thought someone pushed me because I knew he would hunt Andrew down. I feared what he would have done. I was also pretty sure no one else in the family would believe me, so I didn't tell them either. And sometimes even I believed I had made it all up."

Sebastian buried his face in her hair, letting the clean floral smell of her hair soothe his temper. This put a whole new spin on the theft and threats. Andrew had an enemy, and that enemy had tried to kill Evelyn. The question was why? And why go dormant for five years? Why hadn't he tried again?

Evelyn was tired, and she let Sebastian hold her up for a few moments. When she pulled away, his jaw was tense, and she could tell he was thinking about what she'd told him.

"What is it?" Evelyn laid her palm on his jaw.

"I'm wondering who hates Andrew so much that they would go after you. Whoever pushed you five years ago never came back to finish the job. Andrew was gone, so maybe that accounts for it. He left you at the altar, so you were no longer important to him. Maybe the person didn't know that your wedding hadn't taken place."

Evelyn followed his train of thought. "You think it's a woman."

"Yes, I do. She wanted you out of the way. Now she is bent on getting revenge and setting Andrew up to take the fall for embezzlement. We both know he's guilty of the crime, just not this time. She would know about what he'd done. And if she's the one who pushed you, then she knew a lot about you. Andrew would know you spent a lot of time on the cliffs. Maybe he told her."

"Lots of people knew I spent time out on the cliffs. Even you knew that. I had a truck and horse trailer, and I used to drive Isabel out to the cliffs to go riding on the trails all the time. Practically everyone in the office knew how much time I spent riding. I even drove the truck to work once in a while when the roads were too slick to take out the sports car. She might have been able to recognize it."

"That means the woman worked for Brown and still does."

Evelyn shuddered at that. It was disconcerting to think that the person who shoved her off the cliff could be someone she saw every day.

Sebastian rubbed his palm on his jaw, massaging the tension. "I think we need to take a break. We've been looking at those reports and trying to come up with a suspect. It's there somewhere; we just aren't seeing it."

"I'm all for a break. Any suggestions?"

He thought about taking a drive along the coast but didn't think she could handle being in the car that long. He thought of something else. "My friend Rick invited me out, but I've been busy, so I told him I couldn't make it today. How do you feel about having lunch with a couple of my old friends?"

Evelyn remembered his friend Rick from the tales Lucy had come home with about horses and babies. "Isn't he the guy who has a farm nearby?"

"Rick and his wife own a small winery. They also raise horses. His wife's family has raised horses for the last couple of generations. Rick had his heart set on a vineyard. They compromised and are doing both."

Perhaps it was time to exorcise a few more ghosts. "I think that would be lovely."

Sebastian excused himself and went inside. Evelyn took a few more bites of her fruit and yogurt. She wasn't feeling hungry but knew she had to eat. She walked past her grandfather's study on her way back to the kitchen. She heard Sebastian ask for Agent Trainor, so she knew he was relaying her story and their theory to him. She didn't want to hear the conversation, so she continued to the kitchen and cleaned up their breakfast dishes. She went back upstairs and changed her clothes to something more appropriate for a winery and horse ranch. She'd vowed never to get near horses again; it was just too painful to be close to something she wanted so badly. But she'd gotten used to being around Sebastian when she wanted him, more than she ever had horses, so she figured after him the horses would be a breeze. Besides, just because they had horses didn't mean she had to go see them.

She came back down a few minutes later. She waited inside the doorway of the study while Sebastian finished his call.

"We'll be there in a couple of hours." Sebastian ended the call and looked Evelyn over. "It's been ages since I've seen you in a pair of jeans."

Evelyn looked down at the denim. She used to wear

jeans all the time when she was riding. They seemed appropriate under the circumstances.

Sebastian walked over to her and put his arms around her waist. She had to bite back a moan when his hands settled over her bottom.

"You look incredibly sexy in those jeans." He backed her up against the doorway. It was his turn to moan when he settled his hips against hers and began nibbling on her neck.

Evelyn was breathless when she responded. "Had I known they would have this effect on you, I'd have worn them weeks ago."

"We can't do this right now. We need to go." Instead of pulling away, he settled firmly against her.

Evelyn hated, really hated, to stop him, but she had to. "Sebastian, we do need to go. I don't think my hip can handle another round right now."

Sebastian groaned and eased away from her, a bit disgusted with himself. Of course, she couldn't. It was only a few hours ago that he'd had her. His unruly body had gotten out of control when he'd seen those slim legs of hers encased in a pair of jeans. "You should have said something earlier. Did I hurt you?"

She hated to have put that look on his face. She'd been trying not to tell him that her body was aching. She hated that her body wasn't strong enough to keep up with his, but the reality was it wasn't. She kissed him, not knowing any other way to reassure him. "I'll be fine. I had a nice hot bath this morning."

Evelyn watched him for a moment. She could tell he was extremely aroused and fighting to get himself under control.

He hadn't been kidding when he said he liked the jeans. She watched him for another moment, an idea coming to her. She brazenly approached him and gently pushed him against the wall. "I can't, but that doesn't mean that you can't."

Sebastian wasn't sure what she meant until he felt her unsnap his jeans. She eased her hand inside, carefully measuring and stroking his flesh. She pressed herself against him, her breasts rubbing against his chest as she moved her hand. His knees buckled, but he managed to stay upright.

Evelyn couldn't help but watch his face as she caressed him. She used her other hand to peel down his jeans so she had better access but left his boxers in place. It didn't take long before his body was straining closer to her, his breathing ragged and choppy. All the times they had made love in the past six days, she had been focused more on herself and what she felt. It was exciting to have all of her focus on him this time. When he climaxed, she pressed the full weight of her body against his so he wouldn't collapse on the floor.

It took a minute before Sebastian's breath returned to normal, and he regained control of his legs. "Evie." His voice was gruff when he finally spoke, and all he said was her name.

She smiled and kissed him lightly, her tongue tracing his bottom lip. "You should go get changed so we can get out of here."

Sebastian didn't think he could blush, but he had a feeling he might have turned a little pink. She was right; he needed to change. She released him, and he quickly went upstairs. When he came back down, Evelyn was waiting at the door. He frowned when he saw her leaning heavily on the cane.

"Are you sure you're up to this? We can stay home so you can rest."

Evelyn shook her head. "We both need to get away for a little while. We've been cooped up either at the office or here at home. As you said, we could use a break, and I'd like to meet your friends."

Sebastian took her hand and helped her down the front steps and into his car. The route he took was scenic, and both he and Evelyn couldn't help but relax and forget about the problems at Brown. Evelyn pointed now and again at something that caught her attention, but for the most part, the drive was a quiet one. Neither of them was particularly chatty, and today was no exception.

It took an hour to get to his friend's vineyard. The house was set apart from the fields that looked like they stretched for miles behind the house. The stables were also a bit of a distance from the house, set to the right with a huge fenced-in area so the horses could roam outside. Evelyn felt a little wistfulness, along with a little envy, as she saw one of the horses grazing outside. It was a beautiful mare from what she could see from a distance.

The front door opened, and a rather large man appeared in the doorway. He looked much taller than Sebastian, and he was not small by any means. Sebastian waved at his friend while he helped Evelyn from the car. He grabbed her cane but took her arm in his for support instead of handing it to her.

A tall woman holding a toddler appeared behind him. The couple met them halfway. Sebastian quickly introduced them. "Evelyn, this is Rick and his wife Angie." Sebastian tickled the little girl Angie was holding. "And this is Mary."

Rick shook Evelyn's free hand. "It's great to meet you. I was surprised when Sebastian said he was bringing a lady over."

Angie shifted the toddler and gave Evelyn a hug instead of a handshake. "Any friend of Sebastian's, and all that. Come on in. We'll get you comfortable."

"Thank you. You have a beautiful home. And that mare is gorgeous." Evelyn couldn't help but glance over at the stables again.

"You like horses?" Angie opened the front door and set Mary down. The toddler took off at full speed after a small, white and brown, spotted dog that was now barking at the new arrivals. "Ignore Sophia. We got her a few months ago, and she hasn't quite learned her manners."

Evelyn took a seat on the couch Sebastian had led her to and leaned back. Sophia took it as an invitation to jump in her lap. Evelyn adjusted her on her lap and scratched her ears.

"See, no manners. Would you like something to drink? It's a little early in the day for a glass of wine, but I can get you some water, tea, or lemonade if you'd like."

"Lemonade would be nice."

"I'll get it." Rick headed out of the room, and Angie sat at the other end of the couch.

"Sorry if we're overwhelming. We don't have much company. My parents are getting too old to make the drive up here, and my old friends live a couple of hours away. We just moved here this year, and I haven't met a lot of the locals yet. We've been too busy building the winery and settling in."

Evelyn thanked Rick when he handed her the lemonade. Sebastian had taken a seat in the chair opposite her.

"If you ladies don't mind, I'm going to take Sebastian out to the fields."

Everyone looked at Evelyn. She smiled at them. "Go on. We'll be fine."

The men headed out and Angie gave her a big grin. "Rick loves to show off. He's already shown Sebastian the winery buildings, but he's so proud. Plus it gives us a chance to get to know each other. I was happy when Rick said Sebastian was bringing a friend. I'm sure you've noticed, but Sebastian doesn't have a lot of them. There's you, of course, and I know he was friends with your grandfather. And I've met Anne a couple of times. But that's it besides me and Rick."

"He's friends with my sister Kimberly. She married his nephew, John. But you're right. Sebastian and I have known each other for years, but I guess you'd say our friendship is new."

Angie picked up Mary, who was grabbing at her legs. "Sebastian had mentioned an Evelyn before, but he didn't have a lot of nice things to say. That's you?"

"Guilty. We used to get on each other's nerves. But things changed. I had my accident, and when my grandfather died, and Sebastian came back, I'd changed. We somehow managed to start getting along."

"I'd say by the way he looks at you that you're more than getting along." Angie set Mary down, and the girl toddled off. "I'd like to see Sebastian settled down and married again. He's great with kids."

Evelyn took a sip of her lemonade to unblock the lump in her throat. "I know. He spent as much time with his kids as he could while they visited. He's a wonderful father."

"Do you feel up for a walk? I could take you out to see the horses, and we can gossip without worrying about the men coming back."

Evelyn nodded and rose. Angie seemed eager to show her the horses, and since she'd glimpsed the mare when they arrived, she wanted to get a closer look.

They slowly made their way to the fence, little Mary holding her mother's hand as they walked. Angie turned Mary's hand over to Evelyn and vaulted over the fence. Mary was shouting what sounded like "horsie," but it was hard for Evelyn to tell. Angie grabbed hold of the bridle and walked the mare closer.

"This is Trixie Bell. She's one of two mares I have. The other is in the stable; she's breeding and has been a little fractious lately. I don't want Mary to get too close to her. I have a stallion as well, but he's with a breeder friend of mine right now." Angie handed Evelyn the reins and picked up Mary so she could pet the horse.

Evelyn tightened her grip on the reins and leaned on the fence for balance. She rubbed the mare's head. "She's beautiful. I had an Appaloosa five years ago. I had wanted to breed her, but I didn't get the chance. I toyed with the idea of raising horses, but my grandfather needed me at his company. After my accident, I had to get rid of her."

Trixie Bell snorted and made Mary giggle. Evelyn couldn't stop the tears that filled her eyes. Angie had everything she wanted for herself. She had a husband who loved her, a child she adored, and was raising the horses she prized.

Angie set Mary down and vaulted back over the fence. "I can't imagine how hard that must have been for you. I'd be devastated if I had to give them up." Angie rubbed her face against the mare, who was now nuzzling her shirt.

Angie fished a carrot out of her back pocket and handed it to Evelyn. Evelyn broke it in half and fed it to Trixie Bell. The mare nipped at her fingers to get the other half but didn't bite. Both women turned as they heard the men's voices.

Sebastian came to her side and wrapped his arm around her shoulders. She knew he was aware of her fragile emotions and let her absorb some of his strength. The two couples headed back to the house, trailing behind Mary, who was skipping back home.

Chapter Twenty

Evelyn enjoyed herself immensely. They had adjourned to the house to have lunch on the back patio. Evelyn liked Angie. She was down-to-earth, funny, and loved to tease. Sebastian and Rick squirmed a bit in their seats when Angie felt the need to share embarrassing stories about Sebastian and Rick, but it was all in good fun, and all four of them laughed.

The wine Rick served with lunch was delicious. She knew he'd only been at it for a year, so his selection was limited. He gave her and Sebastian a couple of bottles to take home.

After they had eaten their fill and chatted, Sebastian interrupted Angie. Angie was talking about anything and everything that came to mind, so interrupting was the only way to get a word in. "Is the surprise ready?"

Angie's eyes lit up. "I almost forgot. It is."

Sebastian and Angie left the patio and went inside. Rick relaxed in his seat. "Sorry about Angie. She's excited to have company. I forget how lonely she gets sometimes for female companionship. I'm hoping you and Sebastian will come to visit often. She likes you."

"Your wife is very nice. I hope we do, too." Evelyn was surprised by how much she meant it. She had Kimberly and

Anne, but they were family, and it wasn't quite the same. Angie didn't ask awkward questions or nag her. It would be nice to have Angie as a friend.

Evelyn's smile turned to shock when Sebastian came back to the patio and handed her a puppy. The puppy was mostly white like her mother, with tiny brown speckles instead of spots. She had short, floppy ears and a short muzzle. The puppy bounced in her arms and licked her face. Sebastian was grinning at her.

Angie followed, holding a second puppy. "That's Libby. I'm holding her brother, Little Rick. When we got Sophia, we didn't know she was pregnant. When we took her in for a checkup, we were in for a surprise. We decided to keep Little Rick because Mary adores him. I've got an extra collar and leash for you. I also have some puppy pads, chew toys, and some puppy food. Sebastian didn't ask, but I also got a carrier and a kennel. You're going to need it."

It took a moment before Evelyn realized Angie was giving her a puppy. She looked over at Sebastian, who was still grinning at her. She realized he had planned this. Evelyn hugged Libby closer and buried her face in the soft baby fur. She was tiny and probably wouldn't grow any bigger than her mother. She couldn't stop the tears. "I don't know what to say."

Angie's eyes teared up in response to Evelyn's. "Sebastian said he wanted to get you a dog, so I suggested Libby. She's weaned and can go home with you tonight. Plus, she's really smart and mostly goes to the bathroom outside. And she loves to cuddle. Little Rick is a bit hyper, but Libby would be perfect for you. Sophia is only twelve pounds, and the vet doesn't think Libby will get any bigger than that. Whoever daddy was, he probably wasn't much bigger."

Evelyn stood with Libby still clutched in her arms. She transferred the puppy to one arm so she could hug Angie. "She's beautiful, and I'd love to take her home."

Evelyn looked at Sebastian, who was no longer smiling. He brushed a tear from her cheek. Evelyn put an arm around his neck and kissed him. She didn't bother to hide her happiness, and the kiss grew a little heated. She broke off the kiss when Rick loudly cleared his throat.

Sebastian winked at her when she flushed bright pink. He took a seat, and Evelyn did the same.

Angie couldn't help but sigh and lean against her husband. "There was something else I wanted to tell you. All the babies around here rubbed off. Rick and I found out we're having another baby. We're two months along."

Sebastian rose, slapped his friend on the back, and kissed Angie's cheek. Evelyn couldn't help but be happy for them. She congratulated them while trying to keep Libby from wriggling out of her arms.

When Sebastian took his seat again and glanced over at Evelyn, his heated gaze made her squirm in her seat. All she could think was that he shouldn't be looking at her like that in front of his friends.

* * *

For the rest of the evening, Libby wasn't far from Evelyn. The puppy played with her brother and mother, and Mary chased all three of them around the yard. But once the play was over, she came back to Evelyn to get picked up.

An hour later, Sebastian and Evelyn got ready to leave. Sebastian loaded the car up with all of the puppy's things. Evelyn didn't want to put Libby in the dog carrier but wanted to hold her on her lap. Evelyn hugged both Angie and Rick goodbye, and Sebastian helped her and Libby into the car.

Evelyn was nuzzling the puppy when something occurred to her. "Did you tell Anne you were giving me a puppy?"

"Nope. But I have no doubt she'll fall in love with her the moment she gets home."

"She might not be so happy about cleaning up Libby's messes."

Sebastian shrugged. "I'll be around while she's being trained. And you can bring her to the office. I'm sure Rose won't mind taking her out. And I had Angie pick up a scooper so you can pick up the messes she makes outside by yourself."

Evelyn felt a moment of sadness when Sebastian said he'd be around while she was being trained. She was sad because she knew he wouldn't be around forever. He'd eventually start looking for a house of his own. She knew he would eventually leave, and she didn't want to dwell on it. She stroked Libby's soft fur while the puppy started to fall asleep in her arms. "You've thought of everything, haven't you?"

"What are you going to call her?"

Evelyn looked down at the sleeping puppy. "I like Libby.

I'm going to keep it." She looked over at his profile illuminated by the dials. "Thank you, Sebastian. I love her."

"You're welcome." He glanced at her and then at the sleeping puppy. He reached over and scratched Libby's ears.

Libby was full of energy when they got home, and Evelyn watched her as she bounced around the yard. Sebastian stayed nearby in case the puppy decided to run. He hadn't put the leash and collar on her yet. But Libby was content to play by Evelyn's feet, eventually attacking the sneakers she was wearing. Once Libby was finished, they brought her inside. Sebastian set the kennel up in the living room. It was too late to give her food and water, and it was time for bed.

Sebastian set the puppy inside the kennel with one of her toys. He stripped off the t-shirt he was wearing and tucked it in the kennel with Libby. The puppy cried a bit when he shut the door, but it didn't take long for her to settle down. Angie told him she had been getting the puppy used to the kennel.

Evelyn's heart broke a bit as Libby started crying again when they left the living room. Sebastian insisted she would be fine alone. Evelyn had never had a dog and wasn't so sure. Thirty minutes later, Sebastian went and grabbed Libby and the kennel and set it up in Evelyn's room. Once assured she wasn't alone, Libby went to sleep in her bed.

Evelyn tucked herself alongside Sebastian. He was lying on his side facing her, his arm wrapped around her waist. When she realized Sebastian had every intention of simply going to sleep, she closed her eyes, took a few deep breaths, and let herself join him.

* * *

Evelyn was sitting in the garden with Libby when Sebastian woke up. He'd been up a couple of times in the night to take Libby outside. She was still too young to go all night without going out. The courtyard was fenced so Libby couldn't get into any trouble. She was sniffing everything her little pink nose could reach.

Sebastian leaned down and kissed Evelyn. "Good morning. Sleep well?"

Evelyn nodded as she watched Sebastian pick up Libby. She watched as he roughed up her fur with his hands and settled her against his chest. "I know she kept you up most of the night."

Sebastian set her down and patted her rump to send her off to play. "I knew when I brought her home I'd be up with her. She's no different than having a baby."

Sebastian grabbed her coffee cup and went back inside. He came back with a fresh cup for her and one for himself. "It's a good thing the garden is finished. She wouldn't have been able to play back here before."

That brought to mind something Evelyn had been thinking about last night. "You like this house, don't you? You seem comfortable here."

Since her question seemed serious, he answered with an honest answer. "Sure. It's a great house. It needs a little refreshing, but it has solid bones."

"Anne would sell it to you if you wanted it." Evelyn took

a sip of coffee before she continued. "Anne and I have been talking about selling. She and Grandfather had been planning to sell it before he got sick. I'd just finished up my last round of physical therapy, and he was upset I hadn't agreed to have back and hip surgery. I think he thought if he weren't around, I'd have no choice."

Knowing Howard as well as he did, he knew the old man had probably thought he could manipulate his granddaughter by selling the house and making her take care of herself. No doubt, with Anne around, Evelyn hadn't been doing much for herself.

"I didn't know that." Sebastian thought about it. "Why does Anne want to sell? With Howard gone, I would think she'd want to keep it."

"Grandfather was never attached to the house, so Anne isn't either. Honestly, he wasn't attached to anything other than his family and Anne. To him, it was just a house. He and Anne talked about moving to the beach. Now with Grandfather gone and all the expenses over the last five years, we've been talking about selling it again. As you said, it needs some work, and neither of us can afford it. I was going to get an apartment before Grandfather got sick. If Anne does sell, then I'll have to move anyway. Kimberly and Anne were talking, and Kimberly offered to have Anne move in with her and John. Kimberly wants to have more children, and Anne could help. Anne said she'd think about it, but I know she'd like to be closer to Patrick, and Kimberly has plenty of room for Anne to move in. Plus, there is the swimming pool, and their house is close to the beach."

"How serious is she?"

"It's one of the things she's supposed to be thinking about while she's on the cruise, but she's serious. Selling it to you would make it easier for her. If I get a small apartment, it won't be much for me to do my own cooking and cleaning. And if I get a washer and dryer on pedestals, I can handle that by myself, too. I have Libby now, but I can get a pet-friendly apartment. You should think about it."

"I will." Sebastian took her hand. "But if I did buy it, you wouldn't have to move."

Evelyn's heart beat faster at his look and tone of voice. "What are you suggesting? You think we should live together?"

"No, Evie, I think we should get married."

Evelyn stared at him, but his face was unreadable. She could tell he was serious. She had put him off at the restaurant when he'd mentioned marriage and children. But something had changed in their relationship yesterday when she'd kissed him in front of his friends. She knew he felt it, too. That change had her frozen in place under his gaze. "Are you asking me?"

Sebastian's gaze darkened. "Yes. Evie, will you marry me?"

Evelyn nodded because she couldn't speak. She squealed a bit when he lifted her out of her seat and kissed her. She molded her body to his, her lips trembling against his. Libby bounced around their feet, eager to play. Sebastian laughed and released Evelyn. Her eyes were wet, but the tears didn't fall. He gave her a quick kiss, this one on the tip of her nose. He bent and picked up Libby. She wiggled in his arms, trying to lick his chin.

"Libby can be a bridesmaid."

That made Evelyn laugh, as he had intended. "She'll be the cutest one there."

Because her sister would kill her if she didn't call her, Evelyn kissed Sebastian again before taking Libby from him. "I'm going to go call Kimberly and tell her. If I delay telling her, she'll be mad."

Sebastian wrapped his arm around her waist. "Want to go over there and tell her? We can bring Libby."

Since that was a better idea, she agreed. "I should go change."

Sebastian halted her. He took Libby back from her and opened the front of her robe. He put one of his arms inside, slowly bringing her closer. "There's something we have to do first."

"What's that?" She tipped her head to the side so he could kiss her neck.

"We need to celebrate our engagement."

Since she seconded that idea, she took the robe off the rest of the way and dropped it on the floor. She was nude under the robe, and Sebastian looked her over from head to toe. She kissed him while he walked her backward toward the stairs. They managed to get Libby into her kennel before Evelyn pulled Sebastian onto the bed.

* * *

"Oh, Evelyn, I'm so happy for you!" Kimberly grabbed her sister and hugged her as hard as she could. She released her and then threw herself at Sebastian and kissed him on the mouth. "It's going to be so much fun planning your wedding. Leslie won't let me help. She insists all she wants is to go to the Justice of the Peace. I'll be surprised if she even invites us to go."

John gave Sebastian a brief hug and turned to Evelyn. He gave her a small smile and a hug as well. Evelyn couldn't remember John ever touching her in any way, so the hug was surprising.

"Guess I was right about the two of you. When are you doing the deed?" John was the first to ask.

"I guess we should wait until Leslie gets married first. And we have to wait for Anne to come home. But I don't want to wait too long." Sebastian took the bottle of water John handed him.

"You have to give Anne and me enough time to plan." Kimberly took it for granted that she would get to help. "We'll need at least a year."

Sebastian told her what he thought of that. "You can have three months."

Evelyn smiled behind her glass of lemonade, holding a wriggling Libby in her lap as she tried to lick the glass. Kimberly looked outraged. "Don't think you can plan a wedding in three months?"

Kimberly turned her outrage on Evelyn. "Don't tell me you agree with him? It can't be done. You can't book a hall, get a dress, a cake, and everything else in three months."

"I think we should be married at home. We're making Libby a bridesmaid, so I'd like to have it there." Evelyn looked over at Sebastian, who nodded. "And I'm sure if

Sebastian coughs up enough money, we can get a dress, flowers, and a cake, no problem. What else do you need?"

"There's catering, and music, and a photographer." Kimberly sat down and pulled Patrick from his bouncer, who was starting to fuss.

Evelyn looked at Sebastian again. "Do you think Angie could help?"

"She'd be ecstatic. I'm sure she and Mary could stay with us for a few days and help." Sebastian took a large swallow of his water and watched Evelyn as she successfully calmed Kimberly down.

"All right, I'll see what we can do in three months." Kimberly bounced Patrick. "What's the hurry anyway? You're not pregnant, are you?"

Evelyn flushed but managed not to stammer. "No, I'm not pregnant. I'll let Leslie do that first, too."

That redirected Kimberly's enthusiasm. "I was shocked when she told me. I can't wait to throw her a baby shower. I already got her permission since she refused to let me throw her a wedding shower."

John piped in. "She seems to be handling impending motherhood better than her wedding. I won't be surprised if she announces she and Philip went off to Vegas. I heard her trying to convince him at the engagement party."

"How did David take it? I didn't talk to him at the party." Evelyn leaned back and enjoyed the sun beating down on her bare legs. She had pulled out a pair of shorts to wear, another first for her in a long time.

John laughed at the question. "Resigned. He stopped being shocked by her behavior years ago. But I think he's excited to be an uncle. Despite his gruff exterior, he plays with Patrick, and if he could find the right woman, he might settle down himself. Looks like he's the last single one among us."

They chatted for a few minutes about David, weddings, babies, and puppies, but it was inevitable that the conversation would turn to work.

"Any word yet from Agent Trainor? He said he'd call if anything came up." John took Patrick from Kimberly, taking comfort in his son as they talked about Brown.

"I talked with him yesterday morning. Evelyn and I were chatting, and we think the person behind this is a woman. And we're sure she works at Brown."

John digested that. "Why a woman?"

Evelyn spoke, hugging Libby to her chest for comfort. "This is about revenge. And it smacks of a woman scorned. Andrew conned Brown. My mom conned Andrew. Andrew conned me. It got me thinking about how many men my mother cheated over the years. That led me to wonder how many women Andrew might have cheated over the years. The woman knows about me and Andrew. She wants revenge. She told Andrew to warn Sebastian and me not to interfere with her plans. She wants to dole out justice, and she doesn't want anyone in the way. The fact that the woman knew both Sebastian and me well enough to feel threatened by our interference tells me she knows us, as well as Andrew. She knows he embezzled five years ago. She demanded that he confess to the theft. She wasn't specific about which one, but she had to know about the last time to have come up with this plan to accuse him this time.

She knows Andrew, and Andrew is scared."

Kimberly took John's hand. "Do you think she's dangerous? Maybe Andrew knows who she is."

Sebastian answered this time. "He probably does, or at least has some idea, but he's not talking. Agent Trainor brought him in for questioning, but he was closed-mouthed and just requested a lawyer. As far as the woman being dangerous, it's hard to say. Five years ago she was, but this time all she did was make threats."

Kimberly looked at Evelyn. "What isn't he saying?"

Evelyn looked at Sebastian, who nodded. "Five years ago, someone pushed me from that cliff. It wasn't Andrew, like I'd always thought."

Kimberly and John sat in shock. Kimberly's voice was a whisper. "Pushed you? Are you telling me someone pushed you off that cliff?"

Patrick started crying when he heard the tension in his mother's voice. She took him from John and rocked him slowly. Her voice was calm when she spoke again. "Why are we just hearing about this now?"

"I couldn't tell Grandfather because he would have gone after Andrew. When I told my therapist, she said my mind was making it up to try to make sense of the fall. It didn't seem worth upsetting everyone over it and risking it getting back to Grandfather. And to be honest, I didn't think anyone would believe me anyway, not after what my therapist said."

"But you're sure, and you think this woman did it?" John looked skeptical.

Sebastian kept his voice down to try to keep everyone

calm. "I believe her, and I think whoever this woman is, she's responsible. It fits in with Andrew's behavior. The problem is there are any number of women at Brown who could fit the description. Agent Trainor is looking into the backgrounds of every female employee who has been with Brown for five or more years. He should be able to narrow it down."

"So now we wait?" John looked between Sebastian and Evelyn.

Sebastian nodded. "Yes. We wait."

Chapter Twenty-One

Monday morning found everyone back in the boardroom. Evelyn did decide to bring Libby with her, feeling guilty about leaving her at home when she knew they would be gone all day. She brought the carrier, Libby's favorite toy, and the puppy pads. Rose was more than happy to take the puppy outside. A few people had teasingly asked her if they could bring their dogs to work. Sebastian vetoed that idea, and everyone took it gracefully.

"The perks of being the boss." John teased Evelyn about the dog as well, but it was good-natured. He had played with her a bit himself. Evelyn knew John was now dodging discussions with Kimberly about getting a dog. John had reminded her last night that they were trying to have another baby, and that the last thing they needed was a dog. Kimberly had sulked a bit, so Evelyn had distracted her with talk of planning her wedding. Once they had thoroughly discussed their problems at Brown, talk had quickly changed back to happier topics. Kimberly had called Leslie to tell her about their engagement, and Leslie had told David. David had popped into the boardroom briefly to congratulate them, then popped back out.

It was after two o'clock when Sebastian took a call from Agent Trainor. He asked if Sebastian could meet him at his office downtown.

"John, why don't you come with me? We'll take your car." Sebastian hung up the phone and grabbed the suit jacket he'd discarded earlier.

"Let me grab my keys, and we can go."

Evelyn watched as John stood and grabbed his briefcase. Once John left the room, Evelyn turned to Sebastian. "What did he want?"

"He thinks he knows who she is. But he doesn't want to discuss it over the phone. He said he wanted to show me the evidence he'd gathered before he said. He wants my unbiased opinion."

"I guess that makes sense. What should I do?"

Sebastian gave her a quick kiss and handed her his car keys before he headed out. "Business as usual. I'll call you when I know. If I'm not back, don't leave the building alone. Make sure someone walks you out. And set the alarm when you get home."

Evelyn nodded and picked up Libby. She headed back to her own office where she could be alone. At four o'clock, Evelyn had Rose take Libby out for one last walk before Rose left for the day. Since Sebastian hadn't called her yet, she figured he was still at the FBI office.

It was well after five when he finally called her. His voice was weary when he spoke. "You're not going to believe this, but it's Lenora."

"What?" Evelyn almost dropped the phone in shock. "She's been with Brown for years. She was my grandfather's secretary. She was my secretary."

"I know. When Agent Trainor started digging into her

past, he found old records that indicated she and Andrew had been having an affair. Lenora had hotel charges on her credit cards, but the person who signed in at the front desk was Andrew Shepherd. That was from before he started seeing you. Their affair began when your mother was still alive. As far as Trainor can tell, Lenora was involved in the original scam. I know you think you're the one who divulged secrets, but I think it was Lenora. The money was never found in Andrew's possession because the funds were transferred through accounts he didn't have access to. We're not sure if he ended up with the money or if Lenora did, but I'm guessing Andrew backstabbed Lenora after she got the money, and that's why he disappeared. He cleaned out your account and your apartment as a security measure."

"But why come after me?" Evelyn tried to digest what he was telling her. It was hard to believe.

"I don't think he had originally intended to leave you at the altar. I think he was going to marry you. He and Lenora had the money she embezzled, but why stop there? I think he was going to marry you and force your grandfather to pay him off to get rid of him. But I think he saw an opportunity to get the money Lenora stole and settled for cleaning you out instead of marrying you. I don't know if Lenora even knew the wedding hadn't taken place. Who knows? The FBI is working on an arrest warrant right now. Do you know where she is?"

Evelyn wasn't sure. "It's getting late. Most of the office is cleared out. Rose left fifteen minutes ago. Since you're not here, I assume she went home. She'd have no reason to stay."

"All right. I want you to have security walk you out and go home. There's nothing else we can do right now. She's probably on her way home."

"I will. And Sebastian?" Evelyn hesitated.

"Yeah?"

"I know this is probably a really bad time to tell you this, but I love you. Please be careful."

The phone was silent for a moment, and Evelyn wondered if he had heard her.

"Yeah, you picked a heck of a time to tell me. I love you too."

Evelyn smiled but realized he couldn't see her. She gave him a slightly giddy, lighthearted laugh. "Good. We'll celebrate when you get home."

"You know I love celebrating with you. You be careful, too. I've got to go."

Evelyn dropped the phone back into the cradle and picked up Libby and hugged her. "Ready to go home, sweetie?" Libby licked her face in response. Evelyn put her in her carrier and fastened the door. She was gathering up the rest of Libby's things when the door opened behind her.

Evelyn stood completely still when Lenora closed the door behind her. She tried to think quickly but couldn't. "What are you still doing here?"

"You know the answer to that. Sebastian should have called your cell phone instead of your office line. Habit, I guess."

"Why did you do it?" Evelyn set Libby's carrier on the floor behind her desk, hoping she would be safe back there.

Lenora didn't answer at first but pulled a small gun from her pocket. "I was in love. Why else? Andrew had charmed me, but you know all about that, don't you?"

"So you wanted revenge against me because I was engaged to Andrew? If you had told me, we both could have ended our relationship with him. Neither of us had to let him hurt us."

Lenora held the gun steady. "I didn't care about his relationship with you. He never intended it to last long; at least that's what he told me when he first started dating you. But then he got engaged to you. He said he had a plan, but I didn't like that plan. We had the money; there was no longer any need to string you along."

"But instead, he allowed me to plan the wedding. Did he break off his relationship with you?"

"Of course not. He wasn't stupid. I was the only one of us who had access to the accounts the money was hidden in. He talked me into his scheme to marry you and blackmail Howard. I wasn't comfortable with that plan. Our plan was never about you. You were just a means to an end. But Andrew got greedy, and you agreed to marry him."

"It certainly seemed like it was about me when you shoved me off a cliff."

Lenora let out an aggrieved sigh. "I wanted you permanently out of the way. I found out he hadn't gone through with the marriage, but he still hadn't focused his attention back on me. He was so obsessed with his revenge that he ignored all the plans we'd made. I didn't know he'd left when I pushed you. When I got back, he was gone, and he'd taken the money with him."

Evelyn turned the rest of the way to face her head-on, but said nothing. The gun was still pointed at her, but now Lenora's hand was shaking.

"I was glad when I found out you weren't dead. I really like you. You've always been kind to me and treated me with respect. With Andrew gone, it didn't matter that you survived. I knew your death would upset your grandfather, so I let you be. There was no way to tie me to your fall, and Howard thought it was an accident. But you knew, didn't you?"

"I knew the fall was not an accident. My memory is vague about that night, but I remember being pushed." Evelyn tried to keep calm, lifting her hands in surrender. "I know you didn't want to hurt me. Andrew made you do it."

Lenora laughed at that. "That man thought he controlled me, but he was wrong. He believed your fall was an accident, though he certainly wasn't going to shed any tears over your demise."

"That wasn't all he did. He stole all my money. He stole most of the contents of my apartment while he was at it. I believed he pushed me, but I had no proof."

Lenora sighed again, lowering the weapon. "You have suffered a lot because of him. Your fall, your money, and if he had his way, your business. I feel a bit sorry for you. You'll never know the man he really is. Had he not become obsessed with using you to get revenge against your mother, we could have stayed together."

"I don't think either of us knows the man he really is. Everything with him is a game, an act. Did you think that if you destroyed the business this time, he'd come back for you?"

Lenora raised the gun again. "He loved me for a time. And I loved him. I've always loved him. I loved him when he was screwing your mother. And I still loved him when he was screwing you. He said we would get married as soon as he had what he wanted from you. But I knew it was a lie. His first wife was weak and didn't understand him. Fool that he is, he was upset when she divorced him and had set his plans for revenge in motion. But while he was jumping from his wife's bed to your mother's, he was also in mine. I knew when his wife divorced him he would never marry me, any more than he would have married your mother. So to answer your question, no, I didn't think ruining Brown was going to get him back. He doesn't know how to be faithful."

Evelyn latched onto that. "But you do. You know how to be faithful. You've been faithful to him all these years, haven't you? He is the one you want revenge against, not me."

Lenora tipped her head to the side, studying Evelyn for a moment. "You could be right. I knew if I had the money I embezzled from the company, I could use it to get back at Andrew for what he'd done. I never imagined he would go running to you, asking you for help. It was funny, really. I thought by telling him to tell you and Sebastian to keep out of my affairs that he would do the exact opposite. Trust him to actually do what he's told when I didn't want him to. I was glad Sebastian was having him investigated, and I certainly didn't want to stop him. I was glad to see you had the sense to tell him to get lost."

"So what are you going to do now?" Evelyn was staring at the gun, unable to look away. Lenora had tried to kill her once. Would she try again? And given how close she was to her, any shot would hit its mark.

Lenora took a step back. "I'm going to end this once and for all. I realize now it wasn't you I should have tried to kill. I should have killed Andrew. With Andrew gone, maybe I can be free."

Evelyn mirrored Lenora and took a step away from her. "Do you think killing Andrew will fix everything? Believe me when I tell you this, it won't. Right now you can still get away. You could run. You haven't killed anyone. You don't want to be a murderer."

Lenora smirked at that. "It's a bit late. I may not have killed you, but I tried to. A court would put me away for attempted murder, extortion, and embezzlement. I don't plan on spending the rest of my life in jail. But you are right. I don't want to be a murderer, but I don't have a choice."

Evelyn panicked and tried to run, but Lenora stopped her with a shout.

"Stop or I really will shoot you. I don't have the patience, and I don't have the time. I know the FBI is looking for me." Lenora gestured with the gun. "Get in the closet."

Evelyn almost collapsed with relief. She watched Lenora as she sidled over to the closet. Lenora was slowly approaching her.

Once inside, Lenora slammed the door. "Just stay where you are."

Evelyn heard a chair being dragged. Lenora was going to

lock her in. As panicked as she was to be trapped in the closet, she was relieved that Lenora hadn't simply shot her where she stood and taken off.

Evelyn tried to force the door, but it didn't budge. Ignoring the pain in her back and hip, she used the wall to scoot down to sit on the floor and concentrate on her breathing. Now that the danger was over, she was hyperventilating. Her cell phone was in her purse lying on her desk. Sebastian thought she had gone home. When Sebastian found her, he was going to be furious. She could almost picture it, familiar as she was with his temper. In the meantime, he was going to be panicked. She prayed he didn't do anything stupid.

Once her panic subsided, Evelyn tried to stretch out in the small closet as best she could. She could hear Libby crying in her carrier, and she could only hope someone heard her whine. If not, she had no doubt Sebastian would find her. His car was still in the parking garage, so he would know she hadn't left.

It was at least an hour before Sebastian found her. She heard him shouting her name as he came barreling into her office. Lenora had locked the door behind her, and it took a couple of good slams from Sebastian's body to open the door. Evelyn heard another voice she didn't recognize, but she focused on the sound of his voice.

The first thing Sebastian saw was a chair lodged against the closet door. Hopeful but terrified, he dragged the chair away from the door.

Evelyn was trying to stand, but her legs were asleep from being crammed into the small space, and her hip was protesting her position.

"Thank God." Sebastian knelt and helped Evelyn to her feet. Once she was upright, he pulled her into his arms, his body shaking in reaction to finding her alive.

Evelyn couldn't stop the tears and didn't care. She buried her face in his neck and let the tears fall. She could feel Sebastian's hands trembling as they stroked her back, and he whispered soothing words in her ear. She didn't understand everything he said, but it was the tone of his voice that mattered.

When she pushed lightly against his chest, he loosened his grip enough to look down into her face. "Are you all right? When you weren't at home, I panicked. I called Agent Trainor, and he said you were here. She could have killed you."

Evelyn gripped his wrist. "I'm not her target. Andrew is. She said she was going to kill him. You have to call Agent Trainor."

The strange man in the room spoke. "Agent Trainor was en route to Andrew's house the moment he heard her say she was going to kill him."

"Evie, meet Agent Jackson. He met me outside. Agent Trainor had all the offices, and the boardroom bugged. We knew someone at Brown was responsible, and we hoped to catch someone either in the act or on the phone. Our computers were also being monitored, as well as our phones. It never occurred to me that Lenora would be listening in on your calls. If anything, I thought whoever was responsible would listen in on mine. I purposefully excluded you from the investigation so you wouldn't be a target."

Evelyn thought about being angry with him for excluding her but figured it was a waste of time. Sebastian did things his way and for his own reasons. Since he was only trying to protect her, she couldn't be mad at him. She was, however, extremely annoyed that he hadn't told her that her office was bugged.

"Did Agent Trainor arrive in time?"

Sebastian looked over at the agent, who took that as his cue to excuse himself to call in. Instead of answering her, he asked, "Where's Libby?"

Evelyn was warmed by the fact that he cared about her dog. "She's under my desk, and she probably needs to go out."

Sebastian knelt and pulled the carrier out. He talked calmly to the dog, who was shaking in her cage. He pulled Libby out and handed her to Evelyn. "She's just scared. We do need to get her outside, though."

Evelyn let Sebastian take her and Libby outside. The lobby was empty. When they got outside, she saw Agent Jackson leaning against his car. Evelyn ignored him and set Libby down. Her leash was attached, so she couldn't wander far.

"We'll need you to come in and make a statement, Miss Bennett." Agent Jackson didn't move from his car but waited for her to finish with Libby.

"As long as I can bring Libby with me." She wasn't ready to let the dog out of her sight.

Agent Jackson smiled at her. "I think that can be arranged."

Sebastian opted to drive Evelyn himself, and they followed Agent Jackson. Though he had already spoken to Agent Trainor, there was no way she was going by herself.

One of the women settled Evelyn into one of the offices and brought Libby a cup of water. She and Sebastian didn't have long to wait before Agent Trainor arrived.

Agent Trainor made her go over everything that happened in the office even though they had the conversation recorded. It was almost an hour before he was satisfied that she'd answered all of his questions.

"What about Andrew? Did you arrive on time?" Evelyn couldn't help but think about how certain Lenora had been that Andrew had to die.

"Almost. We got there right after Ms. Whitenstall did. She was already inside his house. She panicked when we arrived, and she shot him in the back before we could subdue her. Unfortunately for Mr. Shepherd, she was right next to him when she fired. He's in critical condition at the hospital. The doctor thinks he'll live, but she severed his spinal cord. He won't walk again."

Evelyn folded her hands in her lap, unsure of what she should be feeling right now. Andrew was a criminal, but he wasn't the one who tried to kill her.

"Don't waste your sympathy on him. He doesn't deserve it." Sebastian took her hand from her lap and held it in his.

She nodded but kept her head down. "What about Lenora?"

Agent Trainor answered. "She's in custody. She's singing like a bird trying to cut a deal before Mr. Shepherd gets a chance. It won't matter; we have her confession on tape, and after some digging into her accounts, we located the money she stole. She implicated him in the theft five years ago, and I've no doubt a court will find him guilty. He'll spend a few years in a federal penitentiary, but he'll spend the rest of his life in a wheelchair. Ms. Whitenstall will be lucky if she ever sees the sky outside a prison yard again. We have two charges of attempted murder against her, along with the embezzlement charges."

"It's no less than she deserves," Sebastian spoke to Evelyn, who finally looked up at him. He was looking at Evelyn when he spoke. "Can I take her home now? It's been a long day."

"Yeah, you can take her home. I'll be in touch soon to finish going over any missing details for my report, but I can give you a couple of days. You'll also need to testify when it goes to trial, but after what you've been through, it will be a cakewalk in comparison. All you have to do is tell the jury what happened. My team is already gathering the evidence we've collected and turning it over to the D.A.'s office in the morning."

Sebastian gathered up Libby and took Evelyn's hand as he escorted her out of the building. The sky was clear, and the stars were out. He set Libby in the front seat of the car but closed the door before Evelyn could get in. He cupped her face in his palms and looked her in the eyes. Her gray eyes sparkled as the moon shone in them. "I love you, Evie."

She grasped his wrists to hold his hands in place. "I love you, Sebastian."

He bent his head to kiss her. He kept the contact light but increased the pressure as the fear he'd felt earlier overwhelmed him. "I couldn't have borne it if she had hurt you. You mean everything to me."

Evelyn slid her hands from his wrists, up his forearms, around his biceps, and up to his shoulders. The muscles under her fingers lost some of their tension under her caress. "You mean everything to me."

The pair stood embracing under the stars until Libby's cheerful barking forced them apart. Evelyn laughed and hugged Sebastian before he helped her into the car. She clutched Libby in her arms and relaxed as Sebastian took her home.

Chapter Twenty-Two

When Anne arrived home, Sebastian and Evelyn threw a welcome home party. Kimberly was there with John and Patrick. Patrick had discovered what a fun toy Libby was and was giggling as he played on the floor with the puppy. David had come without the date he'd brought to Leslie's engagement party, and no one was surprised.

Leslie was also there, and it came as no surprise when she announced she and Philip had eloped. They had taken a quick flight to Vegas to get married before she could change her mind. What did surprise everyone was the newly formed baby bump that she was proudly displaying for all to see.

Rick and Angie had driven down as well, and Mary joined Patrick on the floor, much to Libby's delight.

When Anne arrived home, she was greeted by all the members of her family. She shed a couple of tears and hugged everyone.

"I'm so grateful to be home. The cruise was great, but I missed everyone." Anne bent down to pick up Patrick so she could nuzzle him.

Evelyn hugged her, squeezing Patrick between them. He squealed in delight at the attention. "We're so glad you're back."

"Did I miss anything?" Anne set Patrick back on the floor to play.

Kimberly giggled. "Boy, did you ever. Tell her, Evie."

Evelyn gestured for Anne to follow, and they took a seat on the couch. "Well, first we got a dog." She gestured to Libby, who was still playing with the kids.

Anne frowned at that. "I know we talked about it before I left, but I didn't think you were going to go out and get one."

"You can blame Sebastian for that. He got her for me. But there's more."

"More? Please tell me you didn't get a cat, too."

Evelyn couldn't help the light-hearted laugh at that. "No, but I did get a fiancé. Sebastian and I are getting married." She held out her hand to show her the diamond ring Sebastian had bought for her. It was a lovely setting with a square-cut diamond in the middle, flanked by smoky diamonds that matched her eyes.

Anne's mouth hung open for a moment. "I had hoped you two would make friends." She glanced over at Sebastian, who gave her a shrug.

"Well, we are friends, so that should make you happy." Evelyn was unsure for a moment when Anne was quiet.

Then Anne looked at her, her eyes filling with tears. "I'm so happy for you. And your grandfather would be happy for you, too." She gave Evelyn a long hug and then went to Sebastian. She kissed his cheek.

"So when's the big day?" Anne asked after she had wiped her cheeks.

Kimberly piped in. "We have two and a half months to

get it planned. Sebastian says he can't wait. All the ladies are going dress shopping tomorrow. We were waiting until you got back, so I hope you're up for it."

Anne looked at Evelyn. "You're not pregnant, are you?"

Evelyn shook her head and smiled. "No, I'm not pregnant. I'm going to have the surgery first before I try to have any children."

Anne whooped at that. "Now that would make your grandfather happy too."

"There's more as well. Sebastian and I would like to buy the house if you're still interested in selling it." Evelyn wanted to get it all out in the open.

Anne was stunned. "Yes, if that is what you want. Your grandfather wasn't sentimental, but I am. I'd love to see another generation of Bennetts grow up here."

"They'll be O'Connor's, too." Sebastian came over and sat beside Evelyn. Libby bounced over and tried to jump in his lap but missed. He picked her up and settled her into his lap. She quickly began to doze.

"I certainly hope you don't have any more surprises for me. I was only gone for a month."

Evelyn, Sebastian, Kimberly, and John had agreed it was best to tell Anne the rest of the story right away. Surrounded by friends and family was best.

Shocked was a mild term for what she knew Anne was feeling. She took it better than Evelyn expected, but Anne held Evelyn's hand during the tale, and her grip tightened painfully as Sebastian told her the story.

"I can't say I'm sorry for what happened to Andrew. He's as much to blame as Lenora.   And God rest your grandfather's soul, he would have been horrified to know it was Lenora who pushed you. She worked for him for years. When I think of the tears she cried at his funeral, I could just spit."

Evelyn squeezed her hand and was relieved when Anne finally let it go. "It's all over now."

"Please tell me there are no other surprises. I don't think my heart can take it."

Evelyn looked at Sebastian, but he shook his head. "We're good."

John cleared his throat. "Actually we have one more surprise. Kimberly's pregnant."

The family cheered, and congratulations were shared. Anne was beaming, Kimberly was glowing, and John was accepting thanks for all his hard work.

Evelyn glanced at Sebastian, who couldn't help but smile.

* * *

Six months later, Evelyn was standing in the front yard watching while Sebastian worked out at the stable. The shutters over the windows had been replaced, and a fresh coat of paint gleamed in the sunlight. It was chilly outside now that winter was here, but she didn't mind. The fresh air felt wonderful after spending so much time indoors.

Their wedding had taken place on time and had all the necessary elements. Evelyn had found a beautiful sheath dress with crystal embellishments that needed little altering. The flowers had been pink roses with carnations dyed gray. The same gray as the stones in her ring. The cake had been an elaborate piece, decorated with edible versions of the roses and gray carnations in her bouquet. Kimberly had found a band, a caterer, and a photographer willing to work with them on short notice. Their wedding portrait hung in her grandfather's, now Sebastian's, study.

Evelyn walked down the steps of the porch, still amazed that she no longer needed the cane. She had the surgery after she and Sebastian had gotten back from their honeymoon. Right after the surgery, she had cursed herself and Sebastian for having gone through it. The physical therapy and rehabilitation had been difficult for her, but now, months after the surgery, she was feeling stronger. Her hip had to be replaced, as did some of the discs in her back, and she had to have a spinal fusion. Parts of her body might now be artificial, but she felt much better than she had before. She didn't need the cane anymore, and that was what mattered most. Her back still ached, and it probably always would, but it was such an improvement that she couldn't complain. A soak in her tub was usually all she needed to ease it.

Evelyn smiled when Libby came bounding out of the house behind her, barking as she ran to the stable. She had become particularly attached to Sebastian, though it was Evelyn's side of the bed she slept on. Now pretty much fully grown, Libby still only weighed ten pounds. Libby had grown into a loving, friendly dog, her white fur and her adorable brown speckles a constant companion for Evelyn.

Evelyn wasn't spending much time at the office these days since her surgery. She was working part-time right now, and that was fine with her. Sebastian had settled into his role, and the company was thriving under his leadership. He told her she could quit working if she wanted, but she wasn't quite ready to quit altogether. It was her grandfather's company, after all, and she felt a part of it.

Evelyn followed the path Libby had taken. She leaned up against the recently repaired fences. "Are you almost done in there?"

Sebastian grunted from somewhere inside, but didn't come out.

She smiled. Her wedding present was finally old enough to come home. Sebastian had purchased a mare who had been sired by Angie's stallion last year. Angie had met with her breeder friend and introduced him to Sebastian and Evelyn. Sebastian had looked the mare over and had purchased her on the spot. Sebastian had hired a crew to come out and fix the stable and fencing while she'd been going through therapy. He also lined up a local kid to muck the stalls out and do the heavy work that Evelyn wouldn't be able to do on her own. She had been waiting all week to see the stable, but Sebastian said he had to just add a few finishing touches before she could see it.

Evelyn smiled, waiting patiently for him to finish. Her doctor had told her there was no reason she couldn't ride horses again. He cautioned her not to get on any animal that was high-strung or likely to throw her. And he did caution her to keep the rides short. He ruined the seriousness of his tone when he cautioned her not to join the rodeo. She had been ecstatic when he told her she could ride again, and she promised not to join the rodeo.

Of course, along with being able to ride horses came her

ability to do a lot of other things as well. Once her doctor cleared her, she had gone home and climbed on top of Sebastian that night. He teased her a bit, but the teasing quickly changed when he realized she was serious. She still blushed a bit when she thought about that night. She was just glad Anne had moved in with Kimberly before their wedding. She would have gotten an earful.

"Penny for your thoughts?" Sebastian finally came out of the stable. He was a little sweaty but greatly pleased with the results.

She blushed, and he raised his eyebrows at her. She knew he had a pretty good idea of what she had been thinking of. "Not right now. I want to see what you've been up to."

Sebastian helped her climb the fence. Libby fit under the fence line and followed them inside. "You've got to close your eyes."

Evelyn obeyed. Sebastian guided her inside. She felt his breath against her ear when he told her to open them.

When she did, she was stunned. He had redone most of the inside, and a fresh coat of paint covered the walls. The stalls had been redone, replacing the old wood that had started to rot from neglect. The windows were new, and the panes sparkled as the sunlight came through. The whole stable was bright, and new lights were hung from the high ceilings. There were fresh bales of hay and buckets of feed ready to be hung. There was even a bed tucked away for Libby, new toys, and bedding ready for her use.

"This is amazing. I can't believe you did all of this." Evelyn walked, turning in circles as she took everything in.

Though the building was not huge, it looked so much bigger than it used to.

"Rick and Angie are going to drive the mare themselves. I think Angie is just looking for an excuse to visit. Rick is worried about her since their baby is due in a few weeks, but Angie is insisting."

"I'm glad. We haven't seen them since the wedding. Once the baby arrives, we'll need to go visit them."

Sebastian pulled her into his arms, her back against his chest. He nibbled at her ear.

Evelyn sighed and wrapped her arms around him from behind. "We still need to go see Leslie today. She's home from the hospital. She and Philip said the family was free to stop in. I'd like to go see the baby."

"We can do that." His hands drifted from her waist then up her sides so that his fingers brushed against the sides of her breasts.

Her hands fisted alongside his thighs as his fingers found their way under her shirt and bra. "You haven't seen Peter yet. Aren't you interested in seeing him?"

"Sure I am. I was just too busy getting the stable ready to get up to the hospital." He lightly bit her neck and continued to rub her breasts against his palms.

"I can tell how interested you are, but it's not with Peter." Her breathing sped up as he removed his hand from her bra and started massaging her belly.

"Noticed, did you?" He was pressed up against her bottom, and he knew she could feel him growing against her. "I made a special place just for us for occasions such as this."

Still holding onto her from behind, he guided her toward the back of the stable. There was a room back there that had been used by the previous owner when a mare was about to give birth, or an animal was sick and needed monitoring. Sebastian opened the door.

Evelyn stilled his hands that were still on her belly. The room had also been redone. A double bed had been added. The pale green walls and pink floral bedspread looked very much like the colors in her bedroom. The double bed had a white antique metal bed frame.

Sebastian wriggled his fingers out from under her hands, and she released them as she spoke. "I have a surprise for you, too."

Sebastian wasn't interested in anything else other than what he was currently doing. He found the button of her jeans and undid it. His fingers found their way inside her underwear.

Evelyn had just enough sense left to remember what she was going to tell him. "I met with my doctor yesterday during lunch. I went off the pill today."

Sebastian's hand stilled for a moment. He tried to see Evelyn's face, but it was hard from their current position. He reluctantly eased his hand out of her underwear and turned her in his embrace. "Are you sure? We could wait a little longer."

Evelyn nodded at him. "I'm sure. It's time. I have to catch up with Leslie, Kimberly, and Angie. Angie and Kimberly are already two ahead."

Sebastian couldn't help but laugh. He picked her up and lightly tossed her on the bed. He followed her down. "Then we'd better get started."

* * *

Bridgette Anne O'Connor was born twelve months later. Evelyn held her newborn daughter, admiring the full head of black hair. Her daughter had her more delicate features, but that hair was definitely Sebastian's. She thought it would look just like Lucy's hair when she was older. She secretly hoped that her daughter had her eyes; though given the hair, she might just end up with her father's green ones.

Sebastian yawned and woke up from the nap he'd taken. The family had been in and out all day. Leslie and Philip had visited briefly, bringing Peter with them, who was now a year old and walking.

Kimberly and John had shown up shortly after with Patrick, who was now two years old, and their daughter Josephine, whose first birthday was next month.

Angie and Rick had driven in and were staying at a hotel for the night. Mary was now three and a half, and their other daughter, Rosalyn, was now a year old as well.

Anne had been there the whole time and had been present for the birth. Anne was going to the airport in the morning to pick up Daniel and Lucy so they could meet their new sister.

Sebastian stretched and winced as the bones in his back popped. "Did Anne leave?"

"Yes, she was exhausted. Almost as much as you were."

"Why don't you look tired?" Sebastian rose from the chair he'd slept in to kiss his wife and admire his daughter.

"I'm still wound up. I can't believe she's finally here."
Evelyn handed the infant to her father.

"It's been a wild ride, hasn't it?"

Not only had it been a wild ride, it had been an amazing
journey. When she stopped and thought about what her life
was like six years ago, she was amazed at how far she'd
come. She was now a wife and a mother. She had a
husband whom she loved more than anything and a career
they now shared. She had her dog and her horse. She had
the surgery she'd been afraid to get, and now she had her
daughter. Life was perfect.

Evelyn scooted over so Sebastian could join her on the
bed. He sat on the edge, holding Bridgette as she slept.

"I love you, Sebastian." Her voice wavered as she leaned
up against him. He stretched out on the bed beside her.
One arm cradled their daughter while the other went
around Evelyn's shoulder.

"I love you, too." He leaned back and brought his wife
closer, kissing her brow. He smiled when she fell asleep in
his arms.

<u>From The Author</u>

This novel holds a special place in my heart as the first book I got the courage to publish. Sebastian is strong but can bend. He can be difficult, but always does what's right. Evelyn has gone through something very traumatic, something that fundamentally changed her personality. When they first met, they were adversaries. The second time around, everything falls neatly into place, and they find a lasting love.

If you enjoyed the book and would like an email on my next release, please sign up for my newsletter @ elizabeth-castle.com/contact. Please be assured that your email will never be sold (I wouldn't want mine sold, so I wouldn't do that to someone else). You can also follow me on Facebook @ facebook.com/elizabethcastle.romanceauthor

Also, if you enjoyed this book, or any of my other titles, please consider leaving a rating at your favorite retailer, Goodreads and/or Bookbub. And if you have the time, a text review would be lovely. Indie authors rely on readers like you to tell others how much you enjoy their books.

Happy reading,

Lizzy Castle

Books by Elizabeth Castle

Single Titles:
  Going Home
  This Kind Of Love
  Chasing Hope
  The Babe & The Librarian (novella)

The Heart's Way Series:
  For Now and Always
  Ask Me To
  Say You Love Me
  Forever Love

Bennett Family Series:
  This Time Love
  A Bride For David
(novella)

All Of Me Series:
  All Of My Days
  All Of My Nights

Cantwell Series:
  Falling Slowly
  Unraveled
  Hidden Away
  Entangled

Contemporary "Retro" Romance Series:
  Loving Jordan

Visit elizabeth-castle.com for newsletter sign up and up-to-date releases.